THE KEEPER OF LOST ART

LELITA BALDOCK

This is a work of fiction. Names, characters, businesses, places, events and incidents are either the products of the author's imagination or used in a fictitious manner. Any resemblance to actual persons, living or dead, or actual events is purely coincidental.

Copyright © Lelita Baldock, 2025

The moral right of the author has been asserted.

All rights reserved. No part of this book may be reproduced or used in any manner without the prior written permission of the copyright owner. This prohibition includes, but is not limited to, any reproduction or use for the purpose of training artificial intelligence technologies or systems.

To request permissions, contact the publisher at rights@stormpublishing.co

Ebook ISBN: 978-1-80508-836-3
Paperback ISBN: 978-1-80508-838-7

Cover design: Eileen Carey
Cover images: Arcangel, iStock, Shutterstock

Published by Storm Publishing.
For further information, visit:
www.stormpublishing.co

ALSO BY LELITA BALDOCK

The Baker's Secret
The Girl Who Crossed Mountains

PART 1
BARI, 1943

ONE
ALESSIA

The ration line was long that day. Alessia stood alone, a worn tea towel gripped in her hands. A gentle breeze rose off the Adriatic, flowing freely between the tight white rows of homes that formed the winding streets of Bari Vecchia, the old town. The air was moist with the sea and carried the cool touch of season change. A northern breeze. Alessia tightened the scarf at her neck, tucking a lock of her blonde hair beneath the cotton. It wouldn't do to get sick. She shifted her weight, working to relieve the pressure on her blistered feet. Her shoes were too small for her, hole-riddled and stretched. They rubbed painfully when she walked.

She needed new ones, but there were none to be had. Not now as Italy crumbled under the weight of a bloody war.

The wind brought the scent of unwashed bodies to her nose and she sniffed in distaste. She was poor, the whole country was poor, but that was no excuse for dirtiness.

The line inched forward and her soft brown eyes tracked to the small shop before her. How much flour would she be able to secure today? Enough for pasta? Or only biscotti? She glanced at the tea towel and sent a prayer to God that it could be filled to bursting this time.

Niccolo was growing. Always tall for his age, her vibrant, energetic brother had stalled. The joy had faded from his laughter, and his shining eyes and hair were going dull. He needed more food.

The sound of laughter and a string of words she could not understand drew her attention. A group of British sailors walked casually past, eyes watching, assessing, but calm. It had been a smooth transfer, from Axis to Allied. At least in Bari. The British came without a single bullet fired through the narrow streets of her city. There had been bombs though.

Alessia knew the north had been far less fortunate. Conflicts, gunfire, death. War across Europe. Yet all Alessia could think of was flour. Food. A way to fill the gnawing hole in her hollow stomach. A way to plump her brother's sunken cheeks.

As the sun neared the peak of the sky she entered the small grocery store. The old storekeeper, Maria, looked up from the counter, eyes hard. "Cloth," she said, voice sharp. Alessia handed over her tea towel, as every woman had before her. Maria portioned out less than a cup of flour.

It was not enough.

Alessia opened her mouth to plead for more. Not for her; she often went without. But for Niccolo. Before the words left her, Maria was already scowling, shaking her head from side to side.

"Next," she called, looking past Alessia as if she wasn't even there.

Alessia understood. There was no more flour.

Choosing to be grateful for what she had, Alessia twisted the edges of the tea towel to secure the bundle and left.

Outside, beneath the midday sun, the cobbled streets lay empty and still. Already people were returning indoors for siesta. As she cut across the Piazza Mercantile, she spied the wealthier grocery stores that fed the soldiers and the rich of Bari Vecchia. Bright fruit and vegetables lay on display, shiny and plump. In the butcher's window, legs of pork hung curing for winter. But not for Alessia, not for her family.

Perhaps that was what turned her feet away from the stairs that led to her city wall home, down instead towards the large harbour that curved along the outcrop of land on which Bari stood. Passing the old sandstone fort of Bari, built long ago to defend her walls against invasion, the docks of Porto di Bari came into view. The port was lined with British and US naval vessels, their large grey hulls rearing up from the water, blocking out the sea beyond. Sailors in uniform teemed on their decks. Above them the sky shone, fluffy white clouds gathering to float slowly by. Calm. Peaceful.

Soon though the seas would change, the azure waters would turn grey with the promise of storms. Bari was a port city after all, lashed by winter winds and driving rain. The time to stay indoors was fast approaching.

A group of sailors looked up from their toil, eyes tracking her unashamedly as she passed. Alessia held her head high. It was always the way with young men, she knew, even though she considered her figure too slim and girlish to attract attention. Young soldiers were the worst of all.

Then she saw him. Tall and lean, his stride loose and calm. James Prior. A smile, small and secret, curved his lips, his head bobbing in a nod of acknowledgement. A flush crept up her neck, sudden and unwelcome and she adjusted her scarf to disguise it. Their eyes met and Alessia turned quickly away, the heat of her skin cooling instantly. She could not face the glint of pity she saw there, the flick of his gaze to the small parcel of flour she clutched in her hands. She would not accept his sympathy. He was an outsider. He had no right to judge her, or her country.

And she had no place enjoying his attention. What would Marco say if he saw the looks that passed between them? What would her nonna say? She shook her head, suppressing the sigh that pressed on her lips. It had been a long war. No letters had arrived from Marco in months, to her or to his mother, Pina, across the street. And none from her papa either... She closed her eyes, forcing down the panic that rose from her belly to clutch her throat.

Her papa only went because of Marco, joining to fight for Italy in the Balkans.

Where were they now? Were they together? Were they safe?

Alessia shook her head sharply and picked up her step, keen to put more distance between herself and the sailor whose eyes she felt sure were burning into her back. She felt her hips shift beneath her skirts, the muscles of her back tighten, self-conscious and uncomfortable under his assumed gaze.

Before her the sandstone cliffs of her city rose steeply from tranquil blue waters, white-painted houses built in haphazard sizes pressing right to the cliff edges. Rounding the corner of a terraced set of homes she began the walk up the small incline to her papa's house. Along the street her neighbours went about their days. Pina and Lucia were tending to the pots of herbs that grew on the cobbled lane. Further down, old Giuseppe sat on his wooden chair, puffing on his pipe, the white smoke framing his greying face. Alessia waved and turned for her home. The simple wooden door, cracked and splintering, sat open, allowing the cooling currents off the seas to air out the house. A white linen sheet, trimmed in delicate embroidery, hung in the doorway curling in the breeze, keeping mosquitos at bay. The paint on the doorframe peeled, the window shutters on the second floor hung at an odd angle and the wood split. It needed a man's touch, but there was only Alessia.

Lifting the sheet aside, she walked into the cool stone interior. "Nicco?" she called, letting the sheet fall behind her. She heard the thump of running feet on the stairs, and then her brother stood before her, already home for lunch, brown curls falling into his eyes, just like their papa. She would need to give it a trim soon.

Smiling at her brother, she pressed a kiss to his brow and led him into the kitchen, where her Nonna Bianca sat, watching the world outside through the small window.

"Hello, Nonna," Alessia said, as she placed her small parcel of flour on the table, then fetched sugar and a bowl. Niccolo unwrapped the tea towel carefully, a frown forming on his wan face.

"So little," he said.

Alessia watched her nonna rise to her feet and shuffle painfully to the boy. "Flour goes much further than you think," she said sagely, her heavy jowls shaking with each word. "I will turn this into biscotti and your belly will be full before you know it."

Niccolo eyed her dubiously but didn't argue. He was too well brought up for that. Alessia's heart cleaved at the hollows beneath his cheekbones, where once a rosy plum had shone.

"Your papa was grown on my biscotti," her nonna was saying, her old, knotted hands smoothing the flop of Niccolo's hair from his eyes. "Your papa has always had a belly." A cheeky grin twisted her mouth as she placed her hands over her stomach. "I will feed up your belly too!"

Niccolo laughed, patting his own slender tummy in mimicry, sharing the light moment with his grandmother.

"Bring me the flour," Alessia said from her side of the table. Nodding, he walked around the table and wrapped an arm around her waist, hugging her close. His arm felt thin and frail. At nearly thirteen years old, he should be starting to fill out. But his cheeks remained flat, his smile fleeting and wary.

Setting her worry aside and focusing on the moment,

Alessia squeezed her brother in a side hug. "Right, now, you can mix..."

Later, as the sun slid behind the buildings of Bari, speckling the white walls of the city in the pale orange of dusk, a knock sounded on the front doorframe. Niccolo looked up from the kitchen table where he sat doing Italian practice for school. It was important that he mastered the national tongue and not just the local Barese dialect. Alessia turned from the kitchen sink. Wiping her hands dry she made her way to the door, gesturing for Niccolo to stay put. It had been many years since a neighbour had dropped in unannounced for supper, or come to beg an egg or cup of sugar. No one had anything to spare. Not for a long time now.

She shifted the curtain aside. Peering out into the dusk she blinked in surprise. A young woman, of an age with Alessia at twenty years, but stronger, broader and better fed, stood on the street. She was well dressed, in a tailored coat of the latest fashion from Rome. A small black hat was perched on her head, and her lips were brightly painted. At her feet sat a large brown suitcase.

Slowly Alessia drew the curtain fully aside, laying it over her shoulder to hold it out of the way. The woman had a pretty face, large brown eyes, full mouth, and perhaps an over-bold nose, but that was being picky. She really was quite beautiful.

Alessia coughed, clearing her throat. "Hello, may I help you?"

"Is this the home of the painter Auri di Bari? Curator at the Pinacoteca metropolitana di Bari? The local art gallery?" The woman asked in perfect school Italian, confirming what her attire suggested; she was not from Puglia.

"It is," Alessia said. "But he is not in residence. The war—"

"Of course," the woman interrupted. "Of course, but this is his home?"

"Si, I am his daughter, Alessia."

The woman stared at her, her throat bobbing nervously. "My name is Siena. I know your father, or at least of him. We have a mutual contact in Rome. I... I didn't know where else to go."

Alessia frowned, cocking her head to the side. "Where else to go?"

"Rome, my home, it is no longer safe. The Nazis took him..." Tears filled her big, beautiful eyes, her chin quavering with emotion. "I was told to come here, to be safe."

"I..." Alessia began, taking a step back, unsure.

"Wait!" Siena opened her purse, fishing around a moment before producing a small, well-worn slip of paper. She handed it to Alessia who took it warily.

Unfolding the page, she saw a sketch of the sea, of waves and boats. Undeniably the harbour in Bari. Undeniably by her father's hand.

"Where did you get this?"

"She gave it to me, told me to come here."

Alessia looked at the young woman at her front door.

"You had better come in."

TWO

ALESSIA

Alessia led Siena through to the kitchen.

"Nicco, time for bed," she said as she gestured for Siena to take a seat.

"But I'm not finished..."

"Come, child," Nonna Bianca said, gathering up Niccolo's workbook and moving for the stairs to their rooms above. "An early night for you." Niccolo rose slowly, eyes flicking between Alessia and Siena.

"Quickly now," Bianca chided and waited until he'd reached the stairs, offering a hand to help her climb. He was a good boy.

Turning her attention to their unexpected guest, Alessia offered a hot drink. "Chicory, not real coffee. Rations are tight."

"Of course, and si, grazie," Siena said. Taking a seat, she set her suitcase close to her on the floor and removed the dainty hat from her head, revealing a stylish set of curls and a clearer view of her face. Her skin was polished and fresh, where Alessia's felt dull. Her eyes were bright, and she had a fullness to her cheeks, not concave like Alessia's family's. Alessia lit the stove and placed a kettle of water on to boil.

Chicory coffee made, she returned to the table. Siena had placed the sketch face up on the tabletop. Alessia stared at the paper, her fingers edging towards it. A picture out of time. By her papa, now so far away at war.

"You came from Rome?" Alessia asked, swallowing the swell of worry for her papa that had gathered in her heart.

"Si, from Rome." A pause, then the woman said, "I don't know how much you have heard of events in the capital?"

"Some. Germany has occupied there. Here, the British forced them out."

"It has been a dangerous time. Rome is... unsettled. There are bombing raids and arrests. It has become unsafe."

"And you know my father?"

Siena shook her head gently. "No, my... employer, Dottore Racah, from the Galleria di Arte in Rome. They were in contact through their work in the gallery archives. And Mila Pettiti. When the soldiers came, she told me to run, to come here. The sketch, it was hers."

She fell silent and Alessia didn't push. They'd all heard the news. It was the talk of the streets. Bombed by both sides of the conflict, homes and lives destroyed, Rome had been conquered.

"I am sorry for your home."

"Grazie," Siena said, eyes shifting nervously.

Alessia frowned. Siena was keeping something back, she was sure. Then a breath of shame puffed from her lungs. This poor woman had just fled here from Rome. Her city blasted apart, her family gone. Alessia knew the heartache of bombs, the devastation and fear. The blasts that had fallen on Bari just months ago still rang in her ears at night. The image of her nonna's terrified eyes, of Niccolo's fear and for Alessia the feeling of complete powerlessness. By God's grace, Bari Vecchia had not been the target. But it was close. Too close.

Siena had not been so lucky in Rome.

What had she seen? What had she been through?

Licking her lips nervously, Alessia said softly, "You are safe now."

"Do you know Mila Pettiti? Or perhaps Dottore Romano?"

Alessia shook her head. "I do not know those names, did they say anything else?"

Siena shrugged. "They met in Florence, at the Accademia—"

"That could be it," Alessia interrupted. "Papa was a tutor there when I was small. But that was nearly twenty years ago..."

"I think connections formed by art are for life. Mila had that sketch. It must have been important to her."

Alessia wasn't sure how she felt about that assertion and moved to steer the conversation down a different track. "Then you must keep it for her, to return it." She watched as Siena ran her finger over the edge of the picture.

"You have a love of art? Have you studied?"

A wistful smile played across Siena's face. "I do love art, so very much. I was always drawn to it." Her hand drifted to her chest, wrapping around a small ornament that hung there. "But I never got to study it. The only paintings I knew were those of saints and Jesus from church. Worthy and beautiful of course. But only one style. I didn't know how magical a painting could be, not until..." She broke off, her attention turning inward.

The rush of sadness caught Alessia off guard. A life with no art, how sad. She had grown up sitting at her papa's feet as he wielded his brush, ladened with paint. Knew the scent of oil and canvas as well as that of the salty Adriatic. She'd loved watching him work, her fingers itching to grip the brush herself and attack the canvas. But she had other duties to attend to, Niccolo to care for. "A woman's first job is her family," as her nonna had always said.

"Do you know what has become of your family?" The words were out before she had considered them. "I am sorry," Alessia stammered. "I should not pry."

Siena gave a dismissive wave of her hand. "No, no, it is all right. I am a stranger arriving at your door in the late evening, asking for help. You are right to ask questions. Truly, I don't know what to tell you. The soldiers came and took Dottore Racah and then Signora Pettiti told me to run."

Alessia sipped her chicory, bitter and oddly sweet. Placing her cup on the table she took a deep breath. "She told you to come here, to escape the Germans. But we are not truly free here in Puglia, the British control things. In the face of the war effort, we have little say," Alessia said. "Life in Puglia is not easy."

Siena's gaze flicked across the room. Alessia saw her eyes fall on every spot of peeling paint, every splintered window seal, every blemish. It lingered on the empty cupboards behind her.

"I have money."

"It matters little, rations are tight." *For us*, she thought angrily, *not for the wealthy*.

"It may help later, as things improve."

"I don't expect your money," Alessia said, standing to gather the cups and rinse them in the sink. Silence fell between the women as Alessia splashed water over the cups. Above she heard the creak of a floorboard and knew her nonna was retiring for the night. Niccolo would be safely in bed.

"I meant no disrespect," Siena said from behind her. "I am weary, it has been a long journey from Rome. But I see that your circumstances are difficult. I don't expect board for me, but if you could host me just a night or two..."

Alessia turned at the sound of paper crackling, watching as Siena folded the sketch and slipped it into her skirts, the movement small and nervous.

Her resistance caved. This woman had a sketch of her papa's, she had come from Rome and was in need. There was a connection there, assuredly. No one was safe in Italy these days. How many families had opened their doors to strangers as they fled the conflict of the north? Or the bombs that still fell over their region? Just last week, Pina's mother and father and three of their neighbours from Taranto had arrived unannounced. As a widow whose son was at war, it was a lot to ask of Pina. Yet she had welcomed them all in without hesitation. Her home now bursting; mouths to feed, and no increase in rations. It was the same across Bari, people harbouring family, even strangers. Offering shelter and hope. How could Alessia turn this young woman away?

"I will move into Nonna's room, you can have mine," Alessia said. She would keep her papa's room closed. To use it was to invite fate. "Of course you may stay. This is a house of God. We are connected, by my papa. And you are in need. That will be honoured, always."

"Grazie," Siena whispered, relief clear on her face. "Thank you."

Curling a stray lock behind her ear, Alessia reached for the biscotti tin. "When did you last eat? I have fresh biscotti."

"I would be most grateful."

That night, as Alessia listened to the soft wheezing of her nonna sleeping beside her, sleep would not come. Bianca had agreed with Alessia's decision to allow the woman to stay. "A child of Rome sent here for safety through seeming coincidence. God does not work this way. She is here for a reason; it is part of God's plan. Granddaughter, of course she must stay. Si, it is what your mamma would have done."

Alessia knew her nonna spoke true. Even though part of her wished the older woman had disagreed and ordered Alessia to send Siena on her way. How she wished her mamma were here to make the decisions, to guide their household, to protect Niccolo. To be her mamma once again. She prayed her mamma watched over her from heaven.

Because Alessia could not shake a sense of doubt that crept

along her limbs; that Siena knew more about the relationship between Signora Pettiti and her papa, about the sketch she'd brought for proof; that there was more to her arrival on their doorstep.

She would have to find out.

THREE

SIENA

Siena hadn't lied to Alessia, not really. It wasn't a lie to only tell part of the story, was it? It was taking control.

Placing her suitcase on the small bed, she slowly sat down. The springs of the bed squeaked as they took her weight but that didn't stop the rush of relief that slacked her shoulders and rounded her belly in a deep, soul-calming breath.

She was here. She was safe.

She closed her eyes, lips moving in a fervent prayer. For him.

Stretching out along the lumpy mattress she lay an arm over the suitcase. She was not done, not yet. But she was tired, so, so tired. She just needed a moment's rest...

The train rocked, the scent of rosemary filled her nose, a soft voice on the edge of her perception.

"Run, Siena, you have to go."

"Come with me."

Siena awoke with a start, her hand clutching her chest. "Run."

She'd fallen asleep, so exhausted from her journey she'd not even changed from her day clothes, and the nightmare had come. Her heart pounded. Her breath came in tight bursts, slowly settling as the dream faded. It was the old dream that had visited Siena since childhood; the rock of a train, the feeling of fear, and now added to it, Mila's command, "run."

Blinking rapidly as her eyes adjusted to the soft dawn light she sat up, and the memories flooded her mind. Streets alive with soldiers, blazing headlights and shouts of fear and terror. Men and women and children all across the suburbs of Rome forced from their homes into trucks, guns pressed to their backs. Soldiers racing from door to door. Terror engulfed her, hot and heavy and as suffocating as the stench that rose from the filthy Tiber, Siena ran and ran and ran.

She hadn't stopped her flight until she reached the door to Signore di Bari's home.

Now, she sat warm and safe in his daughter's bedroom. Down the hallway the family slept. The house was silent around her. Rubbing her cheeks roughly to bring her skin awake she swung her legs over the bed's edge. Kicking off her heels, she collected up the suitcase and crept to the door.

The hallway stood dark and still. Carefully, she padded down the hall to the stairs, her step light and slow. Down she went to the front room that led to the kitchen, and the worn carpet that lay across the floor. A telltale creak as she'd crossed it when she arrived the evening before, a sag in the otherwise rigid stone floor, had told her what she would find here.

Kneeling, she flicked the carpet back revealing the splinted wooden cellar door. She allowed herself a small smirk; she'd been right. With deliberate movements, she pulled on the rusting ring that opened the door, up and back, laying it gently against the folded carpet. With a quick glance behind her to check for prying eyes, Siena inched down the dark stairs. The cellar around her smelt of dust and paint, the soft light of morning catching the dance of dust motes disturbed by her passage. It had been some time since the family had ventured down here to clean. Perfect.

Her stockinged feet hit the rough stone floor and Siena paused, allowing her eyes to adjust to the darkness. Slowly the room came into view. Rows of shelves, an easel, stacked paints and various items of worn wooden furniture.

Moving swiftly now, she placed her suitcase on a desk and opened the clasps with a click. The suitcase whined as she opened the lid. Nestled safe and sound against a few items of clothing was a single book, large, bound in black leather, and beside it a sealed envelope. Slipping the envelope into the waist of her skirt, Siena lifted the book from the case and breathed a heavy sigh of relief. She had made it. The book was safe. She crept across the dusty floor to a large cupboard. The floor around it was covered in an undisturbed layer of dust. The perfect hiding spot. She eased the door open. Rummaging around the cupboard, she found a blanket and wrapped the book snuggly, then moved a few items and secreted the book inside, closing the door with a soft click.

Something at the back of the room caught her eye. Exposed by the fall of light from the open cellar door, a mound covered by a white sheet sat pressed against the far wall. Curiosity piqued, Siena slipped towards the mound and lifted the sheet.

Paintings.

Her breath caught in her throat, a bolt of shock rocketing through her limbs. Hands shaking, she reached out and loosed a canvas from the stack. A bold painting of blues and creams met her stare. The art of Auri di Bari. No, not just his works, but those of the great painters of Puglia: Morandi, Vivarini, Bordon. Hidden in his cellar. Just as Dottore Romano had done in Rome.

She should not have stayed to look. She should have waited until a better time, returned to her room and been patient. But the paint called to her, as it had from her first days in Rome.

The sweeping brush strokes, the detailed lines, the splashes of colour, pale and bright. She pulled a few more paintings back, eyes taking in mountainsides and wild seas, portraits of families and kings. So many classically brilliant depictions. These were no amateur attempts; these were paintings by the great artists of Italy. Stacked in a quiet cellar on the East coast of Italy. She continued looking, fingers walking over the frames, eyes sucking in the canvases.

One of two children, small and sweet. One of an old man, pipe in hand. And one of an older couple and a young man. The painting caught her attention for some reason. She pulled it up, revealing delicate brush strokes, detailed expressions and a large tear along one side of the painting.

Frowning, she studied the faces of the three people depicted, and her throat closed over. Her fingers tightened around the cotton pouch at her neck.

The scuff of footfall, a wash of light. Siena whirled around. There at the base of the stairs stood Alessia.

"What are you doing down here?" she asked.

What indeed?

PART 2

FLORENCE, 1920

FOUR

EVA

Eva tipped back her head. Rising above her to block out the sun was the beautiful curved dome of the Cattedrale di Santa Maria del Fiore. The terracotta tiles of its famous Duomo roof blazed in the morning sun.

"Breathtaking."

Eva turned to her twin brother Elio and smiled.

They had made it. They were in Florence.

Theirs had been a long journey to this dream. Applications to the Accademia di Belle Arti di Firenze begun six years ago had been halted by the shot of a gun in Austria. The world at war, her brother was shipped off to fight. The shadow of those years in the trenches still shaded his deep-brown eyes. But today Elio's gaze was soft, hopeful. Because they were here.

The letter from the Accademia had come two months before. Acceptance. Not just for Elio, but for Eva too. Unprecedented, a brother and sister had both gained admission to the most prestigious art school in the Nation. And for Eva, one of the few places for a woman at all. Women had long been kept to the background of the art world, but war had brought a shift, small but noticeable. Eva was ready to take advantage of the change, for as long as the opportunity shone.

It was good that Elio had got in also. He could watch over her. Old to still be unmarried, at twenty-six, Eva needed her brother's protection. She wasn't unusual, the Great War cast a long shadow on the lives of everyday people. But it didn't stop the judging eyes when Eva corrected them to address her as "signorina". Perhaps attitudes hadn't changed so much after all.

"A stroll to the Arno?" she suggested.

"And then the Uffizi Galleries?"

"Perfect."

The siblings linked arms and began their stroll, framed by the cobbled streets and piazzas of Florence, white-tiled buildings and red roofs that shone around them. Two dark-haired, dark-eyed children of the world, together from birth in all things. Now together in Florence. As the Arno River that cut through the city came into view, brown and churning, Eva took a deep breath into the very depths of her lungs. The haphazard expanse of the Ponte Vecchio, with its windowed shops lining the very edges of the bridge, told a tale of long ago. But for Eva it represented the future. Held back by war and tradition for so long, finally, Eva was here, in Florence.

This was her moment, her time. She could not wait for everything that was to come.

The halls of the Accademia were cold, the click of her heels rang off the shining tiled floor, echoing up and along the high ceilings. Eva paused, eyes flicking to her brother walking beside her. A wave of appreciation for her twin washed over her. It was good to face this moment together.

At the end of the hall, they paused outside a grand double door: the office of Professore Renzetti, the talented painter who would be their tutor.

Bracing her shoulders Eva stared at the door. Sweat gathered on her palms, her knees wobbled.

"Ready?" Elio whispered beside her.

She nodded and reaching out a tentative hand, knocked on the door.

"Enter."

They stepped inside.

Professor Renzetti stood by a ceiling-high window at the far end of the room, framed by sunlight. He was tall, his shoulders broad. As he turned to face them the light played over the slicked-back waves of his pale grey-streaked hair. He was older than Eva had expected, lines of age cutting into his cheeks, but there was something magnetic about him.

"Artists!" he announced. Warmth lit his features as he stepped forward to clasp Elio's hand in a firm shake. Then he looked directly into Eva's eyes and smiled just at her and the world spun.

"Come in, come in. Sit, sit."

The siblings allowed themselves to be ushered into two leather armchairs situated in the centre of the large room. Renzetti moved to his desk, perching on its top, eyeing them. It was a look of scrutiny and assessment, yet something in his face put Eva at ease. Was it the casual way his arms rested on his knees? The small quirk of the corner of his mouth? She wasn't sure, yet the butterflies that had fluttered in her stomach as they made their way to this meeting suddenly stilled.

"It is a great pleasure to meet you both," Renzetti was saying. "Your application was remarkable. Tell me, who taught you to paint?"

Elio glanced to Eva, before clearing his throat to take the lead. "We have not studied formally."

"Extraordinary," Renzetti replied, finger tapping his chin in thought. "There are of course some refinements needed, some stroke habits that must be broken. But the vision in your work, the ability to capture of the essence of the moment. This piece truly spoke to my heart."

Eva's heart began to race. The piece on the canvas before them was her application painting. Her mouth slackened in surprise as she looked up at Professore Renzetti. The professor held a hand to his heart. "Truly," he repeated. And Eva believed him. This man, this master of painting, this scholar of the world she loved, had been moved by her brush strokes, her vision. A simple image of blues and cream, the seaport where her family holidayed in the summers, broken by the loss that war had brought to the nation, the cracks in the stone once patched by fathers, the silence of the streets once loud with the laughter of boys, the still port, boats empty, no sons to pilot them to fish. The losses of war, the raised heart of a nation that now sought to rebuild.

Professore Renzetti felt her sorrow for this city, for all of Italy.

Eva's heart soared. Fingers twitching in mimicry of sweeping a brush stroke over a canvas, Eva found her voice. "I am honoured to hear your positive feedback—"

Renzetti stopped her flood of words with a simple hand in the air, a small smile playing at the edges of his mouth. "Now that I meet you, I am even more impressed."

Eva cocked her head in curiosity. Renzetti continued. "Your likeness, it is remarkable. A perfect centre point for the painting."

His hand drifted over the canvas, fingers almost brushing the raised strokes of paint. The image of Eva standing to the side of the port, her head turned away, the curls of her hair obscuring most of her face, revealing only her plump lips, resting together as she gazed out over the seas.

Pride and something more exciting stuttered to life within her chest. "I never really thought I was the focus," she said. As a girl from a small farming allotment surrounded by the dry, flat plains of Puglia, water was always the focus. Those summers by the sea, the salty air, the lapping waves, they drew Eva's heart.

The professor smiled knowingly. "It is a skill to realise what you have captured."

Eva recoiled, cursing herself for revealing her naivety, her inexperience. She was always too impulsive.

"I have so much more to learn, I know. But I also have further plans, ideas, stories to capture..."

"You will, and you will capture them all," he said. "But first, technique correction. We must have the basics before we can fly."

"Of course, I didn't mean. Of course," she stammered.

Renzetti paused, his elegantly curved brows pinching, then gave a small shake of his head and addressed Elio. "And you, young sir, a tutor in the making I suspect. It was your hand that guided your sister's, was it not?"

Eva blinked in shock, turning to stare at her brother. A muscle twitched in Elio's cheek, red creeping up from his collar. He kept his eyes forward, focused on Professor Renzetti. "I was first drawn to paints," Elio said. "I watched the men in our local Galleria as they covered the walls in frescos, reviving the style. In time they noticed me watching and gifted me paints to use, to try. I did my best to copy their skills. Later, when we both were able to work in our father's olive groves for pay, we saved our money for paint and canvas. We did that together." He faced Eva at last, apology in his eyes.

Her ire softened. This was all true. Elio had brought the love of painting into their home and into her heart, and together they had worked and saved to pursue the passion. He'd stretched the truth to say he had taught her, but perhaps that had secured his place here at the Accademia, his place in Florence with her. And with that place, her passage here also.

A small lie, for a greater purpose. Eva understood. She just wished he had told her first.

Later, as the setting sun cast the white buildings of Florence in a gentle blush of pink, Eva took her brother's hand. "We are here," she said. "We made it to Florence."

Elio nodded, eyes tracking off to watch the waters of the Arno, purple-tipped and churning. "Your portrait got us here though, you see that, don't you? I have work to do."

Eva read the disappointment in her brother's stance. It was an ego blow, to be outshone by his sister. A setback too raw for his still-healing soul. The Great War had stripped that soul bare. Had paused his life, the lives of all the young men and women of Italy. Leaving them all feeling left behind, desperate. Lost time to recapture, a life to rediscover.

Eva stopped her walk, turning her brother to face her, a hand cupping his cheek. "You brought paint into our world," she said. "I paint because of you. There is no age limit on this path. Your greatest work is before you. You will see."

A soft smile touched his lips, but not his eyes. "I am proud of you, Eva," he said. "Please know that."

"And I am proud of you. Together, then?"

"Since day one, Eva. Always. Together."

As they continued crossing the River Arno and passing the Piazza de' Pitti on their way to their rented rooms on the far side of the city, Eva felt his disappointment in each step. Elio spoke true, she knew he was proud of her. But he was also ambitious, he wanted to be the best. She acknowledged that, and supported it, to a degree. But she was here in Florence too. A woman, to be tutored by Professore Renzetti himself. She felt her determination solidify. She was here, and her professore was impressed.

Eva was here.

Eva would soar.

It was up to Elio to see if he could keep up.

FIVE
EVA

Eva's feet hit the cobbles of the street, and she sucked in a deep and steadying breath. It was done. Her first class with Professore Renzetti was done. She'd been so nervous that morning as she made her way to class, torn between fear of failure and an unexpected flutter of anticipation at seeing the professore again. Elio hadn't been much help. Lost in his own thoughts, he'd barely spoken to her over breakfast or on the walk to the studio opposite the Uffizi.

Straightening her posture and rolling her shoulders, Eva allowed her eyes to rest on the view before her. A simple laneway, small balconies jutting from the walls above. The homes of the people of Florence. The observations slowed her heartbeat, reminding her of the world that existed outside of her ambition.

One of her classmates stepped up beside her. Eva looked over at the pretty girl, Emilia. She was shorter than Eva, with a round face and large enquiring eyes.

"We survived," Emilia said, smiling.

"You were nervous?" Eva had taken particular note of Emilia, who was staying at the same boarding house as her and

Elio. The woman seemed utterly serene. Composed and calm, whereas Eva felt a wreck of nerves, completely out of her depth.

Now, Emilia turned to Eva. "Nervous? That doesn't feel a strong enough word. I thought I would pass out from fear!"

"But you looked so calm," Eva protested.

Emilia winked at Eva. Elio and a few of their other classmates walked out to join them.

"We are going for gelato," Elio said. "Come along?" he addressed Emilia. Eva frowned.

One of the other men in the class, Eva thought his name was Oskar, said, "I know a lovely place. This way."

The group filed away down the lane. Elio's head dipped low in conversation with Emilia. Eva watched them go for a moment, feeling oddly displaced, then hurried after them.

The cafe was tiny, with chairs and patrons spilling out onto the street. Elio bought an espresso for himself and a vanilla gelato for Eva but sat next to Emilia, leaving Eva with the only other woman in their class, a Roman named Alessandra. Oskar and Matteo made up their little group.

"The professore is an interesting one," Matteo began, sipping his coffee and leaning back in his chair, one short leg crossed over the other. "Rather confident in himself, isn't he?"

"He is our teacher," Elio said. "Of course he is confident."

"He is inspiring. Truly inspiring," Eva said, a strange bubbling feeling filling her belly as she pictured how Renzetti's eyes shone when he smiled.

"I preferred the history professor, his knowledge is incredible," Emilia said. "You could feel his passion for the development of artistic culture, how the world shaped the canvas and the canvas the world."

"I am excited to learn from them both," Oskar said. "I came here from Germany to meet great artists."

"I am here to become one," Matteo said confidently. "What about you? Why are you here in Florence?" He directed the question at Elio. Eva felt her stomach tighten. She knew how Elio had been struggling to find his confidence in the days since their arrival in Florence; his insecurity mirrored her own. How would he respond to such an indelicate question?

She waited as her brother set his cup down on its saucer with practised precision, then fixed Matteo with a stare. "To craft a talent such that I never have to go to war again."

It was as if they all stopped breathing at once. The sudden silence fell over them as his words hit home.

"You served?" Matteo asked, eyebrows climbing up his face.

"Si, I and many of the men from my region."

"I am sorry," Oskar said, bowing his head with deep shame.

"I blame no one individual," Elio said. "We all suffered on those fields of battle." Still, Oskar looked away, tense and uncomfortable after Elio's revelation.

"It was a bloody thing," Matteo said into the awkward tension that had descended over the group. "But it is past. We won't see its like again in our lifetime."

"Italy lost too much," Elio said, face morose. "There is a long way to go for our nation to recover and rebuild. I know where I want my place to be in that new Italy."

"At the top?" Matteo said, his eyes shining greedily.

"Si, and in control."

"Well I will drink to that," Matteo replied, standing and walking towards the bar. "A round of grappa is in order."

"I'll take my leave," Oskar said, gathering his briefcase and pushing his chair under the table.

No one made a move to stop him. When Matteo returned from the bar with five glasses of liquor, he chuckled. "Oh well, more for me." He raised his glass of grappa in a toast. "To being on top. If that fails, I'll become a priest."

Everyone laughed.

Eva felt heavy on the walk back along the Arno. Beside her Elio kept pace, occasionally casting a worried glance her way.

"It has been a challenging day," he ventured. "I was nervous too; it has been a lot."

Eva's brow creased, and she shook her head slightly. He was right. The day had been framed by stresses and worry, the start of the journey she'd longed for since she was a girl. But that wasn't what sat weighing down her heart.

"It has," she agreed. "But it's more than that."

She stopped moving to rest her forearms on the side of the Ponte Santa Trinita, eyes gazing out over the Arno. The brown river rippled along the stone-lined banks. Lights were coming on in the windows of the Ponte Vecchio, the gentle glow twinkling on the water.

"It all feels so big," she said.

She felt Elio come to stand beside her. "What do you mean?" he asked, leaning back against the bridge.

Eva took a breath, the smell of river mud and grass filling her nose. "Today, when Oskar mentioned the war. It is just such a big thing. You were gone for so many years. Everything stopped. We all waited. Now we are trying to find our path forward but..." She stopped. "I am sorry. You were actually at war. It isn't right that I complain."

Elio stood beside her in silence a moment, his strong jaw clenched tight, the only sound around them the lapping of the water below. "It was a lot for us all," he said. She turned to her brother, eyes shining with tears. "You never talk about it."

Elio released a heavy sigh. "I don't want to remember. I want to move forward."

"Did you mean what you said to Oskar? That you don't hold it against him, as a German."

"Si." Elio nodded, the curls on his head bobbing. "I watched his countrymen die too. There are no winners in war, even if we were technically on the victorious side. I see the scars that are still on the streets of Italy. The war orphans, the widows, the men who will never be able to work again to look after their families. Once we were the centre of the world. Art, science, new thought, philosophy. Now," he shrugged, a deep frown cutting across his forehead. "Our politicians have not done enough for the people of Italy, and the king has allowed their failure. But we can change our fortune. We can shape our future."

"We are here," she said softly. His words mirrored her dreams, the future she had imagined for herself every day that he was away on the front.

"Exactly."

They fell silent. Then suddenly Elio brightened. "Ha!" he cried, racing across the bridge and down the banks.

Eva looked on in startled confusion as he made his way to the long grasses that lined the river. "What on earth are you doing?" she cried. He looked up, face splitting into a broad grin.

Leaning down he plucked something from the riverbank then rushed back up to Eva.

He stood before her, lips quirked in amusement. "For you, signorina," he said and with a dramatic flourish produced a small posy of purple irises from behind his back.

Eva laughed in delight. "Oh, they are beautiful. Were they growing by the river?"

"Si," Elio said. "I know how you love them."

Eva reached out, taking the dainty flowers from her brother. "I do, grazie, Elio."

He sketched a rough bow, and Eva giggled. Turning back towards their rooms, Eva linked her arm with his. "It will be all right, won't it, Elio?" she asked.

"Si, Eva, si. I will make sure of it."

PART 3
BARI, 1943

SIX
ALESSIA

"I said, what are you doing down here? How did you even know we had a cellar?" Alessia had hidden the entrance under the rug, how had Siena found it? What was she looking for?

"Who is this man?" Siena asked, holding up one of Papa's family portraits, painted from memory during his time in Florence. Her hands were shaking.

"My father," Alessia answered, the response automatic. "That is him and Nonna and Nonno. Though her likeness is wanting. He painted it from memory while studying in Florence. I don't believe he was ever happy with it."

"Is that why it's torn? An artist's anger, or something like that?"

Alessia considered, eyes tracking the tear, so brutal, so jagged. Why had she never thought to ask that question? She'd seen the painting all her life. One of many her father had discarded to the pile of "failure". She'd known it was him as a younger man with his parents. Other details hadn't seemed important. Weren't important. She'd always preferred the painting of her mamma.

"I suppose so," she answered. "I really don't know." And

anyway, that wasn't relevant right now. What mattered was why this stranger was in her papa's cellar.

She'd been sleeping fitfully, the soft mass of her nonna squeezing her to the edge of the small bed they'd had to share to accommodate Siena. The worries over feeding Niccolo. The question of who Siena really was.

"Now answer my question," she said, levelling her stare on Siena's face. "Why are you down here in the cellar? The entrance is obscured. You must have been snooping through the house. There is nothing of value here – if your aim is to steal."

"Steal?" Siena's face fell into lines of indignation. Setting the torn painting down she crossed her arms over her belly defensively. "I do not steal."

Alessia skewered her with her eyes.

Siena released a long, heavy sigh, as if her whole essence left her in one swoosh of air from her lungs. "I am sorry, I understand how this must look. I can explain…"

She paused, but Alessia was not yet ready to ease her discomfort, she waited in intentional silence.

Siena's hands fluttered nervously before her. "When Mussolini changed the law to allow Italian art to be sold internationally, I heard of people hiding paintings. The floor creaked when I arrived and I wanted to see if—"

"These are my papa's paintings, mainly. And he is the curator of the Galleria," Alessia said, straightening her posture. "He has not hidden them; they are his responsibility."

"Of course," Siena said.

The corner of her mouth ticked in sorrow as Siena looked down on the stack of paintings against the cellar wall. "My boss, Dottore Romano, has a wonderful collection. Had a wonderful collection…" She paused, eyes bright with tears in the harsh light of the cellar light bulb.

Alessia smiled sadly, a wave of understanding flooding through her. The love this woman bore for her employer was palpable. It reminded her of her own love for her papa. And her fear.

"We've heard the stories. Of the pieces of history stolen to fill the halls of the rich of Germany. I am sorry your dottore has lost his pieces. I am sorry for what you have been through."

Alessia watched as the tears slipped out of the corners of Siena's eyes.

It was a sadness she understood. All of Italy lived under the cloud of the unknown.

Pity tightened in her chest.

"It is all right, I understand. We are all just scared. There has been so much to be scared of…"

"I know I am not the only one to have faced the fear," Siena said.

"Come up out of this cold, dusty place. There is nothing to fear, at least not now."

"If you would give me a moment, just to collect myself. I don't want to worry your brother with my tears."

"Of course." Alessia climbed the stairs, filled the kettle and portioned out the chicory. Breakfast would be chicory dipped biscotti for Niccolo, and chicory for the rest of them. Her stomach grumbled its complaint and she patted it absent-mindedly. *No point fussing*, she thought; they had to go on.

She glanced across the house, eyes landing on the dark space in the floor where the cellar door lay open. An echo of the past chimed through her mind. The recollection of her papa shuffling in the cellar. Of Marco, his deep brown eyes turned up at her as she called into the cellar, streaks of fluffy dust in his dark hair, a glob of paint on his hand as he waved in greeting.

"Papa? Marco? Why are you down there?"

"Come, come," her papa had said, calling her down to them.

Alessia had bunched her skirts tight around her legs, lest they balloon out immodestly, and descended the stairs. At the bottom, Marco waited, offering her a hand down the final step. Her father had disappeared into the deep shadows of the cellar.

Still holding Marco's hand Alessia stepped into the fickle light of the cellar, the smell of paint and rotting wood rising to her nose. She sniffed, eyes flicking to Marco in embarrassment. The cellar really hadn't been well maintained. As the woman of the house, she felt ashamed at her lack of regard for this space. But it simply wasn't important, they never used it. What was her papa doing?

She had her answer soon enough, as her papa shuffled forward, a large canvas gripped between his hands. "Marco, a hand?"

Marco dropped her hand and moved to take some of the weight of the canvas from her papa. Her palm felt cool where his touch had been moments before, and she felt a flush of nerves rush along her arms. She'd forgotten they'd been holding hands, it had felt so natural. Grateful for the dim light that covered her flustered state, Alessia followed.

Slowly, as her eyes adjusted to the gloom, the room came into focus. A layer of dust coated the floor, and old furniture – a broken chair and a wonky shelf – was pushed against the side. And along the very back wall, beyond the fall of the light of the lamp, were her father and Marco. Together they manoeuvred the canvas to the back wall, before leaning it delicately against another large frame, covered in a white sheet.

"Papa? What are you doing?"

"Hiding my art," Auri said as he slid the canvas into place. "Marco here has been a great help. He is staying for dinner. I trust that is all right?"

Her papa gave her the briefest of glances, then returned his attention to the canvas, pulling the sheet up and over to cover its face.

"Your art? Here? Papa, why have you moved your paintings from the Galleria? Are you even allowed to do that?"

"'Allowed', ha! Daughter, they are my paintings... mostly."

"What do you mean *mostly*?"

Her papa didn't answer her, instead clapping Marco on the back and saying, "I think we've time for one more round before dinner. What do you say?"

"I am fresh and ready." Marco grinned.

"Excellent, come then."

"Papa? You didn't answer my question..."

"Later, later, there's no time now. I will explain later," Auri said, mounting the stairs.

Alessia might have pressed him, but Marco stepped past her, his arm brushing hers in the tight space. Their eyes met, and Marco paused. Alessia felt her heartbeat quicken. Marco lifted the corner of his mouth in a shy smile before heading up the stairs after her papa, leaving Alessia standing in the middle of the cool cellar space.

As they'd shared a simple dinner of her nonna's stew, Auri had made them promise. "Never reveal the art. It is mine, and it is Italy's. Keep it hidden."

"Si, my son," Bianca had promised.

Alessia hadn't known it then, but in that moment of her papa deciding to hide his art, the war had really come to Alessia's home.

SEVEN
ALESSIA

After walking Niccolo to school and lining up for the daily flour, Alessia was making her way back along the harbour when he approached. Had she known he would? Is that why she'd lingered, watching the seagulls gliding on the winds that whipped up the cliffs, their wings wide and white, their flight a soaring freedom that called to her heart. Did it matter?

Her mind was so full of confusion. Finding Siena in the cellar, her hands on papa's art... Nonna Bianca had only shrugged when Alessia told her. "Curiosity is natural." But Alessia had seen how the old woman's eyes had studied Siena more closely that morning over breakfast. Her promise to her son narrowing her pupils in suspicion.

She smelt him before she saw him. That mix of ship grease and sea brine that all the sailors smelt of. But she didn't turn to face him; she waited, eyes turned to the horizon, shimmering blue despite the dark clouds that gathered around the coast. There would be a storm tonight, the first of the new season, a reminder that life in Bari could be beautiful and idyllic and dangerous and unpredictable.

"I was hoping I would see you today." His voice was soft, gentle. It warmed something cold inside her.

She turned to him and smiled quickly before studying her feet. James Prior, the English sailor and translator for the navy stationed here in Bari. She'd met him on a washing day as the fresh sea air blew the scent of soap suds through the winding streets of her home. Alessia had been upstairs, hanging tea towels on the twine slung outside the window. Across the street, old Terese had dropped a shirt, the wet garment billowing in the breeze. Alessia had been about to call across to offer to collect the shirt for the sweet old lady when movement down the street had caught her eye. Two men in the uniform of the British navy strolled casually down the street. One looked up. Spying Alessia, his face had split into a wide grin. The sunshine caught his blonde hair and his pale eyes. He gave an easy wave. "Buongiorno, signorina, may we speak with you?" She'd been shocked. This man in his British uniform had spoken to her in perfect school Italian.

They'd come to enquire about her papa's art. Recently hidden in the cellar to protect it from exactly this moment. But it wasn't the fear of discovery that set her heart racing. As James spoke, his eyes, blue and sparkling, made her stomach flip, her skin warming under the glow of his appraisal. She hadn't felt such a rush of excitement since Marco had left for war.

Today as he came to her side he kept a respectful distance; he'd learnt that was one liberty she was unwilling to bend on. He could speak to her in public, two steps away. It was appropriate to be polite to their allies, but she was an unmarried woman. She had to be careful.

"I have something for you."

"No," she said, eyes flashing at him as she stepped back. "We have been through this. I cannot take food from you. Give it to the hospitals. I will not accept your favours."

"Peace, peace," he said, holding up his hands to show her

that they were empty. "I understand you will not accept gifts of food. Though as I watch you wither, I really wish you would reconsider..." He paused, face hopeful. Alessia looked away.

A heavy sigh. "So you will not accept my help directly. But maybe there is something else I can offer?"

Her eyes slid to watch him from the corner of her vision, just as her stomach rumbled once again. She prayed he couldn't hear it. James was handsome, she could not deny it, no matter how she wished she could. He radiated a confidence that was unexpected, and very appealing. He couldn't have been more different from Marco if he tried. Perhaps that was what intrigued her. The way his lips quirked when he looked at her, the shine in his eyes that set her blood on fire. It was thrilling. A moment of excitement amidst the long, hungry days of war.

He was dangerous for her. She was not a fool; she knew no matter how careful she was, people would talk. Yet she still walked by the port on her way home, and likely would again tomorrow.

"We are looking for help. Local workers. Young and strong to help with dock maintenance tasks, ship repairs. Your army is needed for other tasks, but your young men, like your brother..."

"Niccolo has school," Alessia cut in. Education mattered. Her papa would be furious if Niccolo gave up his schooling.

"Of course, of course. But perhaps after school? Weekends. The roles can be flexible. And come with meals provided of course..."

"Meals?"

"Yes. A snack before shift and then supper after. Sailor rations, like I get. And the experience of working would be beneficial too, for a growing lad."

Alessia stared out over the port, watching the sailors as they went about their various tasks, washing the decks, checking cargo. A group sat, shirts off in the gentle sunlight, cigarettes dangling from their fingers, resting before their next shift.

"He would be safe?"

"On my honour," James said, hand over his heart. "I will see to it personally that he is given the safest tasks. But really there is nothing to fear here. Bari port is secure now. The fighting is in the north."

"And you will keep watch over him? Keep him from the likes of them?" She flicked her hand at the smoking group.

James laughed. "Oh, that's just Bill and John and their crew. They're nothing to be scared of."

Alessia eyed him pointedly.

"All right, all right," James said, hands in a gesture of placation. "No Bill and John. So... what do you say?"

"I will think about it."

"Good, good. If Niccolo is interested, have him meet me here on Saturday morning. 0800 sharp. You are welcome to see him here if you wish."

"He is my brother. I can escort him anywhere I wish."

Amusement twinkled in James's eyes. "You are a marvel," he said. Then he straightened, gifting her a loose salute. "Until Saturday," he said and jogged away to join the smoking crew.

Alessia watched him go, an uneasy feeling uncoiling in her stomach. Could she trust him?

Her own people, people like dear Marco, Giovanni, Enzo and her papa were away fighting this stupid war, because of outsiders like James.

She shook her head. It didn't matter. Ultimately none of it did. James had offered Niccolo work. Work that came with food. She closed her eyes, her mind filling with the sight of her brother's gaunt cheeks, his spindly legs. Food would be good. The company of men would be too. Good men at least. Men like James. Niccolo was missing his papa. They all were.

She would suggest this idea to her brother. He might pick up some English too. The way the world was turning, the extra skill may well be advantageous. In this Italy, a nation on its knees, mired in poverty, any advantage was important.

Nodding to herself in a gesture of decision, Alessia turned from the port, heading towards her white terraced home. Looking up, she saw her. Neat black hat tilted over her eye, and skirts shaped to her body, Siena was looking at her. How long had she been standing there? Had she been watching her?

Alessia smiled an acknowledgement, but Siena only sniffed before turning away.

She had definitely seen the interaction between Alessia and James. Alessia heaved a sigh. Something she would have to explain to her nonna that evening no doubt.

Trudging up the cobbled road to their home Alessia chose to let it go. James meant well, and Niccolo needed food. Who cared what anyone else had to say about it? If it meant her brother got some meat on his plate, Alessia could weather the judgement of the nonnas of Bari.

Let them talk.

EIGHT
SIENA

The letter slipped innocently into the postbox, and Siena breathed a heavy sigh of relief. Turning from the post office she felt the weight of expectation sluice from her shoulders. She'd done it.

It had rattled her, seeing that torn painting in the cellar and being confronted by Alessia. With her papa at war, and no evidence of her mamma's presence, it was clear to Siena that Alessia ran the household. She might have thrown Siena out and what would Siena have done then? She'd nearly lost her nerve. But she'd got through it and completed her mission. Siena always completed her missions.

Breathing deeply, the salty brine of the Adriatic filled her nostrils, and she paused. There, glistening beyond the city, were the deep blue waters of the sea. The sight stopped her in her tracks. She'd been so focused on her task, so full of fear from fleeing Rome, that she hadn't taken in her surroundings. Such a vista. A perfect scene, wild and free. After the intensity of the last few months, time seemed to slow down. Siena had never seen open water with her own eyes, only the confined brown murk of the Tiber River in Rome. Or paintings in the Galleria di Roma. She was always drawn to those images, powerful and inspiring. Now, standing here in the coastal city of Bari, Siena realised the real thing was even more magnificent. The Adriatic was beautiful.

Movement caught her eye, and she swivelled.

Siena spied Alessia pacing over the cobbles. Though she moved with grace and dignity, each step the young woman took looked heavy, weighed down. Tired. Siena understood. All of Italy did. Under the shadow of war, every day was a struggle.

Guilt, sharp and tight, gripped her belly in a knot. The truth and her past. Her future.

She knew her presence here was distressing. An extra strain on a family already pushed to the brink by food shortages and war. But she could work to ease the burden, to be a support to this family.

Their eyes met across the street and she turned away. Siena knew what she had to do.

"I have flour," Siena announced.

Alessia looked up sharply from the kitchen sink where she was busily chopping vegetables. Small and shrivelled, but at least some colour.

"What do you mean you have flour?" she asked, eyeing Siena suspiciously. "I already collected our ration today."

"And I collected mine," Siena answered. She heard the swagger in her voice and did nothing to temper her boastful pride.

At the kitchen table, Nonna Bianca remained impassive, focused on her knitting, seemingly ignoring the exchange between Siena and her granddaughter. Though Siena was sure she marked each word. The old woman had barely taken her eyes off Siena all day.

"There is no ration for you," Alessia said. "You aren't from here."

"The old lady didn't mind when I paid her..."

"You have taken from another." Alessia crossed the floor, anger making her lips tremble. Siena sighed heavily. Part of her had known this would be Alessia's reaction. But it was an attitude she would not accept. Life in Rome had taught her well. You took what was yours, without remorse.

Something told her that argument would fall on closed ears with Alessia.

"Listen," she said softly, raising a hand in a calming gesture. "I understand it was not strictly right for me to take this flour. But..." She paused, taking Alessia's hand in hers. "Surely you have seen the wealthy stores in the central Piazza? Your own people take this same advantage." She stepped forward, holding out the parcel of flour to Alessia. "You have taken me in, given me shelter. But your resources are strained, and your cheeks thin. Accept this extra, just this once. We can make penne."

She noted how Alessia's eyes moved over the parcel of flour she held before her. Taking it gingerly, Siena saw the weight of the portion register, the swallow of longing that rolled down her throat.

From the kitchen table, Bianca sniffed loudly and said, "We waste nothing in this kitchen."

Alessia glanced over at her nonna, then back at Siena, her face set in a determined frown.

"We will make orecchiette," Alessia decided. "I will teach you. And we will invite the neighbours to dinner too. This will go further."

"A wonderful plan."

What happened that afternoon was something out of a dream. Niccolo returned home from school, plums bouncing in his bag, pilfered from a local orchard. The farmer was at war, meaning the fruit, left overlong on the trees, was rotting and bruised. And ripe for the taking.

Neighbourhood ladies from three separate houses came, each bringing their flour ration, their eggs and butter, their shrivelled vegetables. They gathered on the street outside, dragging tables and sharing bowls. And the pasta making began. Flour on wooden boards, water in jugs, one nonna's bare hands moving the mixture as another poured water into the flour at intervals known to them by instinct.

Siena watched on in fascination as the flour and water came together in a lump of dough. Then, under skilful, practised hands, the dough was rolled into a long stick. Finally, taking up a fork, each woman sectioned off a small portion of the roll, around the size of a thumb tip, and curved it into a small, textured cup-like shape.

"Your turn."

Siena looked to her side. There Nonna Bianca stood, fresh cup of flour in her hands.

"I've never done this," Siena said, shaking her head.

"Then you learn," Nonna Bianca replied, setting down the flour and stepping aside. She took up a small pitcher of water and waited.

Rolling up her sleeves, Siena moved to the flour.

"Slowly, slowly," Nonna Bianca said as she poured a small amount of water over the flour. Siena pressed her fingers into the flour and water mixture, felt it cling to her fingers, thick and gluggy.

"Slow," Nonna Bianca repeated and Siena kneaded. As she moved her hands, Nonna Bianca poured more water and slowly the flour formed into a dough.

"Perfecto. Now, roll."

Siena rolled, a long snake of dough forming across the table top.

"Now, cut."

She separated off a tip with a fork and curved the dough. A laugh, rich with affection, sounded from one of the neighbours.

"You make orecchiette like a Biscegliese," she said.

Bianca smiled at the lady. "Si, Pina, she is a greedy one."

Siena looked up sharply at Bianca and Pina, expecting to see derision on their faces. She found only indulgent warmth.

Niccolo appeared at her side. "I want your orecchiette," he declared.

Bianca ruffled his hair. "You want all the sauce."

Confused at the banter, and unsure of how to respond, Siena cut another piece of dough, forming the cup, trying to make it smaller, more dainty, like Bianca's.

It was even bigger.

Frowning in consternation, she tried again and felt the frustration bubbling through her. Siena hated to fail.

"Calma," Bianca said, her gnarled hand coming to rest over Siena's dough-covered ones. "You make orecchiette how you make orecchiette. We learn, mamma to mamma. Each region of Puglia makes them slightly differently. You make it like a Biscegliese. It is good. Biscegliese are strong fishermen."

"They also have big ears!" Pina joked, holding one of Siena's cups to her earlobe. "It is what orecchiette means, earlobes!" Laughter rang down the table, but it was warm and happy.

Siena looked at the old woman and saw the sincerity in her eyes. A small nod, a pat of her hand. "Now, continue."

Once the flour was all turned into pasta, it was laid out on mesh trays, left in the air to rest. The women retreated inside to Alessia's kitchen. There Alessia stood before the stove, a large pot of vegetables bubbling steam into the small space. The rich smell of herbs filled the house. Steam poured out of the open window to fill the street with the delicious scent.

Curious, Siena looked into the pot. A swirl of carrots, tomatoes and onions bubbled.

Alessia leaned around her, adding fresh rosemary that grew in her nonna's pots on the street.

"It is better a day later, but this will do," she said.

As the sun slung low over the port below, the women gathered inside. The orecchiette was boiled, the small cups portioned into bowls and ladled over with vegetable and herb-rich sauce. Then the women and children poured outside to sit on chairs dragged from homes, or to perch on old stone steps. Pina settled beside Alessia, smoothing a lock of her hair from her eyes in a gently affectionate gesture. As they ate, an old man from down the street shuffled up. Bianca was on her feet in an instant, calling him in. "Giuseppe, come, come," before filling him a bowl. The street sang with the voices of the nonnas, the children and the women as they laughed and chided and gossiped, and ate the shared meal of vegetables and pasta. Simple, but filling. As the bowls emptied and the sun disappeared beyond the horizon, voices fell silent, a quiet peace settling over the gathered neighbours. Siena sat on the edge, watching in wonder as almost at once, they all stood and stretched, gathering up their bowls and utensils and chairs, then made their way back to their own homes, waving goodbye, a chorus of "Ciao, ciao," filling the air.

Siena followed suit, gathering up her share of dirty plates and heading into Alessia's home. The women gathered at the washing tub, dipping the plates in water and cleaning away the remnants of the shared meal. Niccolo disappeared down the street, football under his arm, Pina's younger son, Luca, by his side.

Siena picked up a tea towel and went to help.

"It was good," Bianca said, hands covered in suds. "It was overdue."

Beside her, Alessia's lips quirked to the side, a gesture of agreement.

Siena realised, this gathering, so natural and impromptu, had happened because of her. A cheeky extra portion of flour, intended to win over the family, had been a catalyst for what was clearly a local tradition, to gather together and share food and eat.

Despite being the outsider, Siena had prompted this to happen.

She picked up a dish and began wiping away the suds. Warmth spread through her belly. From the satisfying food and the joyful voices, from the sense of community standing here in the kitchen of strangers, and from knowing that she had contributed to this moment.

As the rest of the family made their way up to bed, Siena's thoughts turned back to Rome. The people she'd left behind. And her mission, the book she'd fled across Italy with, now secreted in Alessia's cellar.

Would it be enough?

Only time would tell.

PART 4
ROME, 1938

NINE
SIENA

Stepping off the bus onto the busy street in central Rome, Siena was hit by a blast of cold air and a stench that made her eyes water. Wrapping her cloak tightly around her, she sucked in a deep breath and scanned the crowded streets before her, her lips spreading in a wide grin.

Around her a melee of buildings rose, pressed tightly together, fighting for space. A raucous chorus of sounds assaulted her ears: the rattle of a tram, the blast of car horns, the shouts of street vendors, the chatter of women, the laughter of children. As she pressed through the throng, a group of boys came running towards her, arms raised in play, mouths wide with joy as they kicked a worn ball between them. One almost collided with Siena, his lithe body twisting at just the right moment to avoid a crash.

"Watch yourself, urchin!" she cried after the lad, her tone playful and light. The boy glanced back before grinning and saluting Siena and going on his way.

Grey clouds amassed in the sky above her, the scent of a building thunderstorm on the wind. Siena quickened her step. Her destination was the Galleria di Roma, for her first day working for Archivist Dottore Romano Racah. The Galleria was unlike anything Siena had ever seen. Rising from the dust-coated streets into the blazing blue skies, the white marble building shone like a beacon and took her breath away. As her foot hit the first step to the grand entranceway, Siena's heart began to thump in her chest and her empty stomach grumbled. She hadn't had the money for bread that morning; it was hard to make ends meet in Rome. It didn't matter. Her nerves would probably have prevented her from eating anyway. She paused, hand fluttering to the small ornamental pouch that she wore around her neck.

"Remember why you are here," she whispered to herself. Closing her eyes she took a deep, settling breath and stepped inside.

Inside, the Galleria was cool, its high vaulted ceiling stretching up and away, creating a large open space flooded with light. Siena made her way to the reception desk and asked for directions. She was pointed down a long hallway, that snaked away to a series of offices. At the fifth door on the left, she knocked. "Come," a disembodied voice called from within.

The room was full of light, the curtains drawn back to allow the morning to shine its glory through the room. The walls were lined with books, the smell of ageing paper permeating the space. In the centre sat a wide desk, books and papers stacked haphazardly across its top. And behind that mountain of paperwork, hunched, eyes squinting at something in his hands, sat Dottore Racah. His attention was focused on a document before him. Small and bent, white wispy hair fanning out over his head in fine feathers, glasses sliding down his long nose as he squinted at the page. Siena stood still, waiting patiently for him to acknowledge her arrival.

Butterflies fluttered through her stomach and the sheen of sweat from nerves tickled her skin.

Then he looked up. He stood slowly, his small body

unfolding stiffly. He reached for the cane that rested beside him and hobbled unconvincingly around the table towards her.

"Siena Innocente?" he asked, voice raspy with age.

"Si, Dottore Racah," she answered. "I am here to start work as your secretary."

He looked at her closely, his milky eyes scanning her up and down. Siena swallowed, a fresh sweat breaking out across her forehead.

Then he smiled, and the world changed.

"My young protégé!" His arms opened out wide to gather her into an unexpected embrace, startling Siena. "How wonderful to have you here with us." He turned, aiming his voice at a side door that ran off the main office. "Dario, come, come!"

A young man appeared in the doorway, auburn hair neatly greased to his head with pomade.

"Dario, this is Siena, my newest assistant. Siena, this is Dario, he is studying for his Laurea in Fine Art. He is here researching for his thesis, hoping to become a dottore, like me." A small smile. "You will be helping him with his research also."

"Pleased to meet you, signorina," Dario said.

Siena nodded to the young man, her mind barely able to keep up with the rapid and warm reception.

"The pleasure is mine," she managed. "I am honoured to be here to work with you and Dottore Racah."

"No more 'Dottore Racah'," the dottore said. "Call me Romano. Now follow!"

What followed was a flurry of information. Siena was shown to her desk, appraised of her responsibilities in supporting Romano's work at the Galleria, and given a quick tour of the offices and the library of supporting literature the Galleria stored, as well as a mountain of other vital information.

By the time the dottore's list of instructions found its end, Siena's mind was swimming.

She felt herself sway on her feet, her empty stomach threatening to growl its protest at her missed meal, her body manifesting the overwhelm that her brain was experiencing. This would be her first real job, and Siena was fast learning that her days helping the nuns in the orphanage, cooking food and cleaning sheets, had not prepared her for this task.

Not at all.

"Signorina?" Romano enquired. "Are you well?"

Pulling herself together, Siena nodded quickly. This job mattered to her, more than she could acknowledge. She could not show weakness. Weakness would get her fired. She had no family name behind her to pave her way in this world. Siena only had herself, her wits and determination. Breathing in through her nose and focusing on the comforting weight of the necklace against her chest, Siena tried to smile. "Si, si, I am quite well, just excited to start."

The dottore squinted his eyes at her, then pivoted on his heel. "Dario, close up the office. I think it is time for lunch."

Dario appeared again, jacket slung over his arm as he pulled his office door shut.

Romano approached Siena, offering her his arm. She took it instinctively. "There is a lovely little cafe just down the street if you would indulge me?"

A warning blared through Siena's senses. She had just arrived for work, but her employer wanted her out of the office. Was he already so disappointed? Was she about to be fired before her first day was through?

Romano patted her hand where it rested on his arm, a smile full of understanding spreading on his thin lips. "We all need time to find our feet," he said softly. "I find a full stomach helps."

Siena studied his face for one moment, two, and found not a hint of mockery. Something inside her loosened. Romano led her from the Galleria.

They sat on the street on small rickety chairs. Romano ordered three plates of cacio e pepe pasta and a bottle of red wine. When the meal of spaghetti, parmesan and butter topped with pepper arrived, Siena's mouth watered. Hesitant and ravenous at once, she twirled the pasta over her fork. It hit her tongue and melted. Siena chewed slowly, savouring the explosion of taste on her tongue. As her first bite slid down her throat, warmth infused her body, and her limbs finally calmed. She caught Romano watching her from across the table and saw the glint of joy in his eye. A flush of embarrassment heated her face. Despite her best efforts, he'd read her like a book, seen her hunger and her nerves. And taken her to lunch. Ordered a dish that would soothe.

Caution and curiosity danced within her. Unaccustomed to surprise acts of kindness, Siena wasn't ready to trust him. Not yet. But she continued to eat her pasta, nonetheless.

So, together they ate and sipped wine and Siena listened as Romano and Dario chatted amiably about art and study, and their own personal lives. Siena observed, her senses heightened, looking for any sign that this was a trick. None came.

"And what of you, Siena?" Dario asked, his dark eyes meeting hers. "Why did you come to work at the Galleria?"

Playing for time, Siena picked up her glass and sipped her wine, before launching into her pre-prepared answer. She'd known this question would come and had no intention of answering truthfully. So she'd devised a reply, one that drew on the truth, but without revealing it fully. Carefully setting down her glass, Siena focused on her empty pasta bowl and answered as honestly as she would allow.

"I have always been drawn to painting, though I never had the opportunity to try it. I have not had the means to study, but I have a keen mind and can read and write, and speak some French. Working at the Galleria with Dottore Racah, Romano, seemed a wonderful way to connect with the art of painting that I have always longed to learn of."

Her eyes flicked up, nervously appraising the response from the two men before her.

Dario was watching her with open interest, Romano had leaned back in his chair, studying her closely. She smiled, hoping her features looked sincere. It wasn't really a lie, after all.

Romano sniffed once, his eyelids twitching. A question hovered between them. She could tell he was not fully convinced by her answer. Siena braced herself in anticipation. Then the sparkle reignited in his eyes, and he leaned across the table, reached out and patted Siena's hand. "All should have access to art," he said. "Would you like a tour of the Galleria?"

Siena blinked at him in surprise. He hadn't pushed her. He had known she was holding something back, she could tell. But he hadn't pushed her.

"But surely you need me to work this afternoon?"

Romano smiled. "Your education is vital for your work. Art first!"

He stood, leaving a wad of cash on the table for the waiter.

"Come," he said, offering Siena his arm once more.

Again, Siena was unmoored. None of this interaction had gone as she had expected, or planned for. But a tour of the Galleria from the curator himself? She could not stop the beaming grin that split her lips. Linking her arm with Romano's, they ambled back into the cool interior of the Galleria. Dario followed a step behind. Glancing back at him, Siena didn't miss his wry smile of amusement.

They walked the Galleria for hours, listening as Dottore Romano detailed the great works of art on display. Siena was drawn to the brightness of Michelangelo, the reservation of da Vinci, the spirit of Botticelli. Caught up in the moment, Siena gave voice to the conviction that flooded through her veins. "They open the door to the human heart."

Silence fell. Siena blinked, realising that she had spoken aloud. Clenching her teeth tightly together in embarrassment, she glanced at Romano. "Sorry, I didn't mean to speak out of turn."

But no anger showed on the old man's face.

"You have nothing to apologise for. You have the eye. My dear, you are the answer to my prayers."

His hand patted hers once more, his skin paper-dry. "Art is my passion, as you know. But passion withers in solitude. How pleased I am to have you to share it with. Your language skills add so much to the interpretation of the foreign artists."

Pride swelled in Siena's chest. Something deep inside her began to thaw.

That evening when Siena left the Galleria, tired but inspired, Romano was still bent over his books.

"Good evening, Dottore? It is getting dark, I thought I might—"

"Si, si, of course. Dario? Will you walk Siena to her bus?"

"There is no need—"

"Nonsense, I have kept you late. Go now, I look forward to seeing you tomorrow." He nodded once, then returned to his reading.

Dario appeared by her side. "I'll collect your coat."

They walked along the lengthy corridors of the Galleria, the click of Siena's heel echoing around them. At the door, Dario paused, one hand on the doorknob. "Well done today," he said.

Siena gave him a quizzical look. "What do you mean?"

Dario lifted one side of his mouth in a lopsided grin. "The dottore likes you. Which means that I like you. He will look after you, you know. He is a good man."

Siena nodded slowly. "Si, I think I can feel that," she said, honestly.

"But don't take his kindness for granted. Work hard. He deserves that much."

"Of course."

Dario stared at her, sharp eyes narrowed on her face, watching for any flick of emotion that might betray her as false. Siena held his stare.

"All right, let's get you to your bus," Dario said, pushing open the large Galleria door.

She'd passed the test.

Now her search could begin.

TEN
SIENA

Siena settled into her work at the Galleria smoothly, guided by the ever-gentle presence of Romano and the jovial company of Dario. Her role consisted mainly of helping Romano to catalogue and track the great artworks that came to the Galleria for special exhibitions, or for restoration, and those that went out on loan. When Romano did not require her efforts, she was at Dario's disposal to look through the large collection of academic books on the history of art, providing assistance in his research for his thesis. She enjoyed working with Dario. She learned he was from Turin in the north and was newly married. He'd moved with his wife to Rome so Dario could earn his Laurea and become a dottore just like Romano. "Then I can get a well-paying job, and Amara and I can start a family."

A family. It was a beautiful idea. As the weeks wore on, she found herself working longer hours to support Dario's research.

But no matter how much work they had to do on any given day, there was always time for a Galleria tour. Just as she had on that first day, Siena walked arm in arm with Romano, hanging on his every word as they explored gallery after gallery within the grand Galleria. As always, the paintings spoke to her, drawing her in, heart and soul. Her eyes searching each canvas for a clue to her real purpose.

It was only a few weeks before Siena began to wonder if she was not the only one in their office with a secret mission.

Siena worked diligently, recording the distribution of art through the Galleria, Romano's keen eye always reviewing her records. But she noticed that after a collection or delivery, Romano would take out a separate book from his desk drawer and make an entry.

At first, she thought he was keeping a second record, not trusting her to be fully accurate. He was nothing if not meticulous. As she grew more confident in the job, she began to feel somewhat put out by his private notes. Despite how smoothly she'd felt her employment had been progressing, Romano's seeming insult to her work made her begin to fret. So, one evening as Dario walked her to her bus, she plucked up the courage to ask him what he thought.

"A second book?" he asked, head turned to the side in curiosity. "Are you sure?"

"Si, every time I make an official record in the ledger, he makes a separate one in a book in his desk."

"Hmmm," Dario mused, then shrugged. "I wouldn't think too much of it. Romano likes to maintain order. He is probably just keeping a backup to ensure there are no mistakes."

"So, you don't think it is because he doesn't trust my work?"

"Siena," Dario said, amusement lightening his tone. "The dottore adores you. You have nothing to worry about. I promise."

The next day, when a delivery arrived, Siena recorded the details in her ledger as she always did, Dottore Romano watching on. After, when all had been processed accordingly, she sat at her desk, watching Romano, knowing soon his black book of records would appear from his desk drawer. Only this time, it didn't.

Instead of returning to his desk and making his own notes, Romano set about reordering his bookshelves, whistling quietly to himself as he did. Feeling suspicious, Siena tracked Romano's every move for the rest of the afternoon. Not once did he reach for his book. Nor did he the next day, nor the next. Unsettled by the change in routine, on the fourth day, Siena waited until Romano went out to inspect the Galleria. Sneaking across the carpeted floor so as not to alert Dario in the adjacent office, Siena slipped behind Romano's desk and opened his top drawer. Dip pens, ink wells, a case of cigarettes, but no black book. Frowning, she opened the next drawer. Paper, a few pencils and a ratty-looking glasses case. She opened the final drawer. It was empty.

No black book. It had vanished.

Perplexed, Siena asked Dario that evening, "Did you say something to Romano about me and the book of records?"

Dario frowned at her. "No, why?"

Not wanting to admit the truth, that she had been rummaging through their employer's drawers, Siena simply said, "Because I haven't seen him make a note since I mentioned it to you."

Dario gave a nonchalant shrug. "Perhaps he just trusts you now," he said.

"Hmmm," Siena murmured. "Perhaps."

But that didn't sit right. And Siena couldn't help but think that Dario had said something to Romano. Though she couldn't understand why he would.

Whatever the truth, Siena didn't see Romano's black book of notes again. Soon, an announcement captured her attention, making her forget all about the mystery of the black book. Broadcast throughout Italy on radio news, in the newspapers, gossiped about in hushed whispers in every food market, and over every shared coffee or cigarette, the news gripped all of Italy in a vice.

Benito Mussolini, the ruler of Italy, Il Duce himself, was coming to Rome. And he was bringing his most admired friend: Adolf Hitler.

"Siena! Come quickly, come. He is here!"

Siena looked up from her desk in Romano's office. Dario stood in the doorway, eyes wild with excitement. Standing, she gathered up her cardigan and joined her friend as he raced out onto the streets of Rome. The city was in chaos. Women and children hurried along the strada, and groups of young men ran, hand in hand, mouths wide in cheers.

"Siena, watch the cars!" Dario screeched beside her. Siena only looked at him and grinned, stepping out onto the busy strada with brazen confidence and forcing her way across the street. Dario followed on her heel, head shaking rapidly.

"Mio Dio, you really are a local," he said. "I can't get used to this traffic."

"People won't move for you, you have to make them shift," she replied, striding ahead.

Dario and Siena were swept up in the crowd and pushed along the street, around the corner towards the Palazzo Quirenale. There, along the Boulevard that led to the royal palace, stood an honorary guard of Italian soldiers, their uniforms shining in the sun, the tips of the rifles that were slung across their backs glinting dangerously. Along the strada the red flags of Hitler's Nazi party that had been erected for the parade waved in the spring currents that rose off the Tiber. The crowd pressed as close as it dared to the parade of soldiers, fathers swinging children onto their shoulders, lovers lifting their girlfriends high to see.

Dario and Siena were pressed between the bodies of Rome,

a smell of sweat and excitement on the air. She pushed up onto her tippytoes, craning her neck to see above the crowd. A loud cheer rose in the distance, moving towards them in a cascading wave of sound as people raised their arms and cried out in excitement and joy.

He was coming.

Il Duce was coming.

The cheers crescendoed around them, crashing down before rising up in a fever. Then she saw them. Row after row of Italian soldiers marched, dressed in all their finery, medals adorning their chests. Then, led by policemen on motorbikes, a stately car drove into view. Standing in the back seat were two men in military uniform. On the left, Mussolini, Il Duce himself, the ruler of Italy, solid and strong. On the right, his honoured guest, the leader of Germany. He stood taller than Il Duce, his eyes focused forward, unwavering as the crowd around them celebrated. As the car drove past, Hitler raised a single hand in salute, and a few of the people of Rome saluted back. In their wake came a stream of military officials in multiple black cars. As the parade moved on past the palace, the wave of shouts from the crowd with it, Siena felt a dark cloud descend over herself and her city.

As she walked home from her day with Dottore Romano that evening the streets felt unusually quiet, as if the city had exhausted itself in its cries of love for Il Duce. Frantic, intense, desperate cries, born more from despair than genuine joy. The people had not called out to Il Duce in celebration that afternoon but in a plea. A plea for the dream of Mussolini's Italy to come true. For jobs and freedom and food and hope. The grand Italy of the past that Siena saw in the Gallerias of Rome – the regal kings on statuesque horseback, the delicately dressed women, the shining bowls of fruit and grain – was not the reality on the streets where the fruit and vegetable sellers toiled and children with scabbed knees ran errands and begged coin.

Rome was a marvel, a beautiful city steeped in history and glamour. But it only took a glance down the wrong street to see her underbelly. Today in the crowd, pressed against the sweat of the masses, Siena had felt a different energy in this city – an anger, a tension and a question that Il Duce had to answer.

A month later the soldiers came.

They arrived just after opening, three men in grey uniforms, their boots polished to a high shine. Romano was called to reception, Siena went with him. The soldiers were polite and courteous. Siena took notes as they explained their purpose in heavily accented school Italian.

"I am Officer Baca. We are here on behalf of Il Duce to collect art for distribution and protection. Will you show us the collections?"

Sweat beaded on the officer's brow, the heat of Rome clearly oppressive in such a thick and tailored uniform. But he did not display any further signs of discomfort.

Romano was a different story. The old man's step was more unstable than normal, his legs wobbling so badly he nearly tripped twice. Siena took his arm, concern pulsing through her at his sudden physical trouble. The dottore was old and unsteady, but this was much more severe than usual. Still he made it down the stairs into the archives, his breath coming in a heavier and heavier pant. The soldiers wandered down the first row of stored artwork, their eyes scanning hungrily.

"Will you tell me of this one?" Baca asked.

Romano wheezed heavily and shuffled over before giving a halting account of the Botticelli before Baca. Siena watched on, her concern over the dottore rapidly growing into fear.

But she didn't know what to do. The soldiers, with their shiny boots and perfect hair, were intimidating. Moreover, she was just a secretary. What could she ask them to do?

In the end, Officer Baca seemed to realise just how much Dottore Romano was struggling and left after only a short trip, taking with them a single Bellini.

"We will return another time," Officer Baca said. "Hopefully you will be in better health."

"Grazie, Officer," Romano said. "It is the summer, a difficult season for my humours."

"Of course," Baca said.

As soon as the doors to the Galleria shut behind the last soldier, Romano straightened, his step surer as he strode back to his office.

Siena made herself busy at her desk, but she did not miss the change in the dottore's vibrancy and the focus in his stare. She resolved to learn why.

Siena didn't have to wait long.

She arrived at the office early the next day, thinking to take another look in Romano's drawers, to see if there were any correspondence or other clues to his strange behaviour the day before. But Romano and Dario were already there. She opened the office door and stopped dead in shock. The two men stood in the middle of the room, and around them leaning against desks and bookshelves were four framed paintings from the archives.

As the door creaked open their heads snapped around, taking her in.

Dario's eyes narrowed in suspicion, but Romano only smiled calmly. "Ah, Siena, come," he said, gesturing her inside. "Be sure to shut and lock the door behind you."

Siena did as asked before standing warily at the edge of the room.

The two men continued conversing as if she wasn't there.

"So, the Masaccio, and you say the Bellini?" Romano was saying.

"Si, he can take two he said."

"Good, good, and the Michelangelo?"

Then Romano looked up. "Siena, as you are here, please gather the black book from my desk and record this for me."

Siena froze, staring at Romano. So, he did know that she'd noted the black book. But it wasn't in his drawer, was it?

Romano noticed her hesitation and a knowing smirk curled his lips. "Ah, yes of course," he said, seemingly to himself. "Top drawer, at the back there is a groove. Hook your finger in the groove and the false bottom will come up. Then you will see the book."

False bottom. The words crashed into Siena. Why would Romano have a secret compartment in his drawer? More to the point, why would he put a book of backup records in that secret drawer?

Mind whirling, Siena crossed to the drawer. Slipping her hand inside she located the groove to open the false bottom, just as Romano had said. She pulled the extra panel out, revealing the book within.

The book was bound in high-quality black leather, so large and heavy she almost fumbled it as she drew it out from the drawer.

"Right," Romano said. "Now record as follows."

"Me?" she squeaked.

"Si, use my dip pen."

Siena opened the book. Flicking through the pages she saw note, after note, after note – line items of artworks that had been distributed to galleries and private collectors across Italy, and internationally. Many matched with her own records; she remembered several entries from her weeks in the office. But some did not.

She came to the final entry. "Ready?" Romano asked, then proceeded to dictate an entry for each of the four paintings there in the room.

"Now," Romano said. "In your official book..."

Siena gathered her own ledger and pen from her desk.

She was about to begin transcribing the entries from the black book into her official one, when Romano interrupted. "All four to the Galleria Dell'Accademia in Florence." Siena blinked at him in surprise, but Romano ignored her. Hands shaking, Siena did as Romano instructed.

"Good," he said. "Dario?"

Dario took hold of two paintings and started for the door.

"Siena, if you would be so kind?" Siena stepped forward and reopened the door.

"Now, I'll take the Masaccio, Siena please take the Bellini—"

It was too much.

"What are we doing?" Siena blurted, confusion straining her voice, forehead tight with anxiety as she faced Romano.

The old man looked at her, face serene and sure. "Saving the history of Italy," he said. "Take the painting and come."

Siena could only stare at him as he crossed the threshold and headed toward the back of the Galleria. She hurried to follow.

Siena trailed Dario and Romano out a side door to the Galleria, the painting heavy in her hands. There a truck sat, engine still running. The driver leapt from the truck and Siena blinked in surprise. Short and round the man was unremarkable, except for his clothes. He was dressed in the black attire of a priest, a small black hat perched on his head. The priest helped Romano and Dario load the art they had carried from the gallery into the back.

Romano exchanged a few rapid words with the priest, before they shook hands and the man jumped back into the truck. The vehicle jerked from the kerb and disappeared around the corner into the busy streets of the city.

Romano released a heavy sigh. "Four more pieces, safe."

Siena looked at him, mouth agape. What on earth was going on?

Two records of art, but one wildly incorrect.

A secret drawer.

A priest with a van.

Romano smiled kindly at her. "You are confused."

Siena could only stare, the shock rendering her mute.

"You know that Mussolini is stealing our history?" Romano began.

She nodded. Everyone in the art world knew. The year before Il Duce had changed the export laws relating to the great masterpieces of Italy, allowing for them to be sold internationally, and promptly started gifting pieces to Hitler and other powerful men in Germany. "We can't let them take it all," Romano said.

Siena blinked as understanding dawned on her. "You are hiding the art? Sending it away so it cannot be stolen?"

Romano tapped the side of his nose with a finger. "The art is simply being distributed. I have a network from my days in Florence. Father Massimo does the deliveries. No one suspects a priest. It's really quite brilliant."

"That's what is in the book," she said, wonder opening up inside her. "The real locations of the artworks."

It was astonishing and terrifying. Right in the heart of Italy's grand capital, in a brazen stand against Il Duce and the threatening foreign power of Germany, Romano and Dario had been involved in a smuggling network. Defending their history. Hoping for a better future.

"And a list of those taken out of Italy. A record of what we have hidden, and what we have lost. So later, we can recover it," Romano said.

"Will that be possible?" she asked.

"Anything is possible," Romano answered.

"Why? I mean, I know you love art but this..."

"Because of what it stands for. Art is the essence of our nation. Our history, our pride. We were once a powerful nation, a leader in the world. What have we become under Il Duce?"

The weight of that question bore down on her.

"Mussolini is destroying our history and our culture. Only those in his elite thrive. The rest of us live on scraps," Dario said into her silence. "I feel it every day."

Her eyes met his. She knew it was true. She'd felt it as Il Duce's parade drove through the heart of Rome, heard it in the desperate cries of her people, seen it in the thin cheeks, the sunken eyes of the workers, the concave bellies of the street urchins. The everyday citizens of Rome were hungry and scared.

Siena stared at Romano. This was dangerous. What if they were discovered? What would be the penalty for going against Il Duce? Their leader was not known for his soft touch.

"I see your fear," Romano said gently. "Please understand, I never intended to involve you. I wished to keep you ignorant—"

"That would not have helped me," Siena interrupted boldly. "You know it would not have."

Romano's eyes lowered, studying the cracked pavement beneath his shiny black shoes.

"I know," he whispered. His gaze found hers. "I will relieve you of your position. Write you a stunning reference to the Galleria of your choice. I do not wish for you to be in harm's way. Unless..."

"Unless what?" Siena whispered. Her voice had gone low, she knew what she was being asked.

"Unless you would like to join us?"

Siena's eyes flicked between Romano and Dario. She'd thought she had a secret. That was nothing on this. But what Romano had said was true. Italy was flailing. Her people suffering. But what if that could change? No one ruled forever. Could a memory of before, inspired by the great minds of the past, really bring them out from the dark?

Siena didn't know. But she was ready to try.

"I will join you," she said.

Romano smiled.

Less than a fortnight later, he was fired from the Galleria.

ELEVEN
SIENA

Things happened rapidly that summer in 1938. When Signore Gallo, head of the Galleria, first came to the office, Siena had feared the worst: the black book of records, the hidden art, had been discovered.

For better or worse, the real reason for his visit was simple racism.

A suite of antisemitic laws, passed by Mussolini earlier in the year, finally came to knock on the dottore's door. The laws were sweeping. Jewish citizens of Italy could not hold public offices, teach or marry non-Jewish citizens, and if they held a dual nationality, they were rounded up and sent to camps across the country.

As a Jewish man, Dottore Romano was no longer allowed to hold a position of esteem, such as being the head archivist at the Galleria di Roma.

Signore Romano packed up his things and left.

Dario went next. Jewish citizens could not study in Italian institutions, so his leave to study at the Galleria was cancelled.

"I don't know what I am going to do," he'd confessed to

Siena as he walked her to her bus for the final time. "No one will employ a Jew."

Alone, Siena continued her official work at the Galleria, but without Romano and Dario the magic of the place evaporated. The priest with the truck arrived with the browning autumn leaves, but Siena had nothing to give him. Without Romano's guidance, she didn't know what to smuggle, or who to. The priest had left, eyes filled with worry. Standing in the alleyway watching his truck rattle away, the weight of failure had pressed down on Siena. In her months working at the Galleria she had found friendship and connection, passion and purpose. And recently, something to work for that was bigger than herself. Something for Italy.

With the stroke of a pen, Mussolini had destroyed it all.

What had become of Dario and his wife? Of Dottore Romano?

Resolve settled over Siena. She spun on her heel and raced back up into her office to collect her things. It was time to visit the dottore at home.

Gripping her purse tight, Siena made her way through the overheated streets of Rome. The unseasonably warm autumn sun beat down from above, covering Siena in sweat, a layer of street dust plastered across her exposed skin. Mouth parched, thighs tight from exertion, she made it to her destination.

Dottore Romano's house, nestled on the edge of the urban Quartiere San Lorenzo, was unlike anything Siena had ever seen. Stretching across a lush green garden, it rose like a marble statue, white columns reaching from the paved drive up towards the sky. She made her way down the drive, marvelling at the border of flowers in pinks and creams that ushered her along. At the entrance a sweep of stairs led to a grand double door, complete with large brass doorknobs. Patting her skin dry with a handkerchief, Siena took a deep bracing breath and knocked.

The estate took her breath away, but the man who opened the door broke her heart.

In the months since he had left the Galleria he had aged a decade. Always thin, now his clothes hung off of him, his grey hair turning white.

"Dottore," Siena had said. "It is so good to see you."

"Si, si," he answered despondently, not even correcting her on the use of the honorific, as he led her into the dark interior.

She followed him into a small sitting room. Dust was layered over the surfaces of the tables and chairs, a musty scent rising from the carpets beneath their feet.

"Dottore, do you have a maid?"

"No," was all he replied.

"Who cooks for you?"

Romano only shrugged.

"Where is your kitchen?"

Siena followed his instructions and found the large estate-style kitchen in the back of the house. Rummaging through the cupboards she found little produce. Determined not to be thwarted, she managed to prepare a meal of stale bread softened in water, topped with preserved figs. It wasn't much, but it was something.

Back with Romano she watched him eat in silence, her keen eyes not missing how his spoon missed his mouth, the food that slipped from his lips, catching in his unshaven beard.

"Dottore," she said gently. "What has happened? Why have you stopped working for the network? The priest came today."

Romano held up a shaking hand, the bulbous knuckles red and inflamed.

"I cannot help them any more," he said sadly. "My use was my position at the Galleria. And now," he paused, his face mournful. "Now, I am nothing."

That night in her tiny apartment across town, Siena could find no rest.

Her heart bled for Romano. During her months at the Galleria he had taken her under his wing and offered her his trust. Together for two beautiful weeks, they had worked to protect the art of Italy. Then everything had changed, leaving Romano a shell of his former self.

But that could not be the end of it. Siena wouldn't allow it.

All night she tossed and turned and prayed and ground her teeth in frustration. What could she do? What could any of them do?

As the first rays of dawn fell across her bed, welcoming the day, Siena had an idea.

Rising swiftly, she dressed and rushed out onto the streets. The morning air was cool, but the breeze promised warmth as she strode towards the large central food market. Taking the last of her money from her purse Siena bought as much food as she could on her ration, then took a bus to the apartment Dario shared with his wife.

Surprised, Dario let her in and led her to his kitchen at the back of the apartment. A small woman, plain of face but with kind eyes, sat at a table.

"Amara, this is Siena. We worked together with Dottore Romano."

"Pleased to meet you," Amara said.

"Likewise. It is good to see you are well, and together," Siena replied. Amara was not Jewish like Dario. Their union was technically illegal now.

Dario crossed the room, wrapping his arm around his wife's shoulders. "We keep a low profile. The law really only affects new marriages."

Siena nodded. "Have you been to see Romano?"

He shook his head.

"The dottore is not well. He has no help, no cook. He is weak and grey—"

"There is nothing I can do for that," Dario interrupted. "Amara is my responsibility."

"Si, si," Siena said, mind racing, changing tack. She needed Dario for her idea to work. They needed to be in this together. Raising her hand she indicated the four walls that bound the room and asked, "How much longer can you stay here? Have you found work?"

Shame reddened Dario's cheeks and he looked down at the floor. "We are overdue on our rent by three weeks already. It will not be long now..."

Amara gave a small sob.

Pity flooded Siena's heart, but she pushed it down. Now was the time for action, not commiseration.

"What if I told you I had an idea?"

Dario eyed her sceptically.

"An idea for what?"

"An idea to help the dottore and you and Amara?"

Dario sucked a breath in through his nose. "I'm listening."

Romano opened his door to Siena and Dario, hand unsteady on the door.

"Buongiorno, Dottore," Dario said.

"Dario is here to visit," Siena said. "And I am here to cook."

Leaving the men to catch up in Romano's drawing room, Siena took over the kitchen, rolling flour into spaghetti, frying some butter and whipping together a sauce of melted parmesan, all topped with pepper. Home-made cacio e pepe, the same dish Romano had bought for her on their first lunch together.

When it was ready she filled three bowls to the brim and carried them out on a tray to the men.

When Romano spied what she had cooked, his mouth quirked into a small smile, a little of the old light shining in his eyes. He remembered.

"Grazie," he said as the last of his pasta slipped down his throat.

"You are welcome," Siena said, then glanced at Dario. He nodded. It was time.

Leaning forward, Siena took Romano's dry hand and asked, "Dottore, if there were a way continue our work hiding art, would you do it?"

He looked at her sadly, his eyes misty with tears. "I cannot, you know I cannot. There is no way I can return to my role at the Galleria."

It was not fair. *None of this is fair*, Siena thought.

"It was injustices like this that drove us to hide the art in the first place," Dario supplied, echoing Siena's unspoken words. "A path back to reason and higher ideals."

"The art," Romano whispered, wiping the moisture from his cheeks.

Siena squeezed his hand. "You miss the art?"

"Si, and our work to save it. And time with both of you."

The words were sincere, Siena felt them in her heart. She took a deep breath. "You still have your book of records? The black leather one?"

"Si," Romano said, voice wary now, eyes narrowing on Siena.

"Then I think you should employ me as your housekeeper."

Romano cocked his head at her, a confused frown on his brow. "I could, but your work at the Galleria, you love it. It matters to you, I know it does."

"It is a ruse, to save the art of our nation that I love so much."

"As do I," Romano agreed sadly. "But working here can't save it."

"What if I told you it can?"

He turned to her, eyes filled with cautious hope. This

dream had been stripped from him once before; Siena understood his hesitation to believe.

Gripping Romano's hand tighter, and taking Dario's in her other hand, Siena laid out her plan.

Romano was a wealthy man in his own right, and he was still in touch with the network. Before, he was the source of the art, sneaking it across the country to be secreted in cellars and attics and sheds. Now, he could be the hiding place.

Owner of a massive private art collection, it was natural that Romano would procure pieces from all over Italy. He would purchase a lesser piece of art, then when it was delivered, take possession of something more valuable to be hidden in his cellar below. His role of recording and coordinating the deliveries of other artefacts meant he knew the contacts in the network and could easily continue his work.

But he would need help. Strong arms and backs to carry the art and hide it. Young legs to pass messages to contacts.

"Me and Dario," Siena said. "And Dario's wife can help keep us fed."

Romano looked at her, then Dario, in the fading sunlight. Siena could see the desire in his face, how desperately he wanted to believe this could be done.

"There is one challenge." Siena paused, gathering herself. "Dario cannot find work. He and Amara are soon to be removed from their rental apartment. I can't do this alone."

"And what solution have you thought of for that?"

"They could move in here. Take care of your home, support you and help coordinate the network. In exchange, you allow them food and board."

"And you?"

Siena blinked. "Me? I have my job at the Galleria. I will come here out of hours under the guise of supporting your home. But really I will work for the network, and I will remain a contact in the Galleria to secure art."

"No," Romano said. The air went out of the room. Had Siena judged their relationship so poorly? He was so wealthy, clearly. Would he set aside this plan just to save a few coins on food?

"But—"

Romano held up a hand for silence. "I said no," he reiterated. "I refuse to pay Dario and Amara only in food and board. That is not suitable." He turned to Dario. "This is an arrangement to support us all during these unsettled, awful times. I will open my doors and share my table with you willingly. But when this all ends, and it will someday, one way or another, you all need something to move forward with in your life."

Siena frowned. "But Dario can't find work—"

"And you," Romano continued, "cannot work at the Galleria and perform that role for the network. Not without me. It is too risky. You do not have the experience or position to permit art transfers. You would be discovered. You must resign."

Siena gaped. "But—"

"So I must employ you, properly," Romano concluded. "All of you."

"Employ us?"

"Si, employ you. Here, as my house staff. Dario has the look of a gardener to me. And I am sure Amara could use some help in the house."

"Are you saying you want to pay us?"

"No, I am saying I will pay you."

"But food and board—"

"And a salary. Take it or leave it."

Siena chewed her lip in thought. "All right, if you are sure."

"Settled," Romano said, eyes coming alive with passion. "My dear, you never cease to amaze me," he said.

"So you will do it, Dottore?" she asked. "You will hide art here? We can be part of the network again?"

"No 'dottore'," he retorted. "Just Romano. And si. Si, I will do it." The old Romano was back. Pushing up to his feet he took up his cane in a fierce grip. "I must call Father Massimo."

Siena moved in that afternoon. Then Dario and his sweet and gentle wife Amara. Together under Romano's magnificent roof, they got back to work for Italy.

TWELVE
SIENA

1939

"Careful!" Romano admonished as Siena and Dario made their way down the stairs into his labyrinthian cellars. Her hands sweated, slipping dangerously on the solid golden frame of the massive painting in her grip.

They'd been living in Romano's home for nearly a year now, taking deliveries of selected pieces from Father Massimo and securing them below Romano's home. Safe from greedy hands.

The network had adjusted well to Siena's plan, adapting to use Romano's grand home as a cover for Italy's precious art. It was a good thing, too. For only two days ago, Germany had invaded Poland. And this morning, the radio had announced that England and France had declared war on Germany. It was a tense time in Rome.

Germany's occupation of Poland had all of Europe on a precipice. Would they plunge into war as they had only twenty-five years before?

And what would the ever-increasing restrictions and distrust of foreigners in Italy mean for citizens like Romano and

Dario? She knew they talked about it with their friends at the synagogue on Saturdays, but the men never brought that discussion home.

The artwork was a valuable distraction from the threat building across the border.

"Good, good," Romano said, following behind Siena and Dario on the cellar stairs. "Now place it in the far corner and cover it with the sheet."

Siena set the painting against the wall as gently as she could and moved to collect a sheet. As she flicked out the cream cotton material her eyes caught the corner of the canvas and she froze.

Mouth falling open in wonder, she leaned forward, her fingers gently caressing the frame of the painting.

"What is it?" Romano said, coming up behind her. "Is it damaged? Oh please don't let it be damaged."

"No," Siena whispered, her breath tight. "But this," she gestured across the canvas, her fingers trembling slightly as she took in the vivid cobalt blue, the pristine whites, the passion, the rage. Her heart responded to it.

Romano squinted down at the painting, understanding filling his face.

"Di Bari," he said. "It is a famous piece. I knew him, you know. Back in the day."

"You knew the man who painted this?"

"I knew the artist, si."

Siena studied the painting, a reverie of colours playing over the swirl of the sea. Her fingers hovered over the bottom edge and a small sigh escaped her lips.

"I have never seen the sea," she whispered, lost in the power of the brush strokes.

"Never?" Dario said, incredulous. "Not even as a child? Papa took us to the seaside every summer."

"No," Siena replied. "I have never left Rome."

A soft silence fell over the room, broken by Dario's careful question. "Would you like to?"

Siena smiled, her fingers seeking the small pouch she wore about her neck and squeezing gently. "One day," she said. "But I am a woman now, and I must be practical. And we have commitments here, for the art."

Romano smiled gently. "You are a remarkable young woman. You have much to be proud of."

From her crouched position by the painting Siena looked up at the old man and she realised he meant those words.

"Grazie," she croaked.

"Now, come on," he continued. "Let's get this painting secured and enjoy a grappa on the porch."

The setting sun cast Romano's garden in a dusty orange hue. Siena leaned back in her chair, glass of grappa in her hand. Amara came to sit beside her, brushing past a rosemary bush that lined the porch as she did, releasing a waft of the herby scent into the air.

The rock of the train.
The sound of prayers.
The click of rosary beads.

Siena blinked, coming out of the grip of memory that rosemary often inspired.

"Are you all right?" Amara asked, her pale face tight with concern.

"Si, si," Siena lied. "The grappa is strong."

Amara laughed. "My papa makes his own. This reminds me of his."

"Your family," Siena asked. "They are in Turin?"

"Si, and Dario's. I believe my family are safe, but Dario's... we have seen how his people are treated here. I imagine it is the same in the north. We worry for them."

The women fell silent as Romano and Dario joined them in the gentle evening dusk.

"Father Massimo says there will be another delivery next week," Romano was saying. "The network is operating effectively. It is slow going, and we must continue to be careful. But I think we have established a good routine."

Siena smiled as the evening light danced over his face. Old and tired, but inspired, energised. Despite it all.

A bang sounded on the front door. Siena jumped. There was no reason to be tense, yet the unexpected sound had her nerves instantly on edge.

Beside her, Romano pushed himself up from his chair. "Unusual time to call," he muttered to himself as he shuffled for the door. The three of them hesitated a moment, then followed after their employer and friend. Inside, they crept, steps light, stopping by the open door to the large entrance hall of Romano's home.

"Ah, my dear Hannah!" Romano's voice carried across the polished floor. "And Ezra. It is late to call, but friends are always welcome. Come in, come in."

"We won't, grazie, Romano. It is only a brief visit," a male voice said.

Siena felt her brows furrow, leaning forward subconsciously to hear more clearly.

"Even for a brief visit, I can still be a good host. Come out the back. I have grappa—"

"Romano, we are here to say goodbye. We sail for America in the morning."

Silence fell. Siena peeked through the doorway, saw Romano standing, one hand on the door, his body obscuring the two people he had welcomed.

"America?" his voice was soft, the question hesitant. "But, Ezra, we talked about this."

"Si. Romano, I know we did. But things have changed, you must see that."

"Ezra, we cannot jump to conclusions. We must be patient."

"That time is past. Romano, please listen to reason. Come with us, we beg you."

There was a long pause. Siena glanced from Dario to Amara, but saw her own question reflected in their stares: *America? Why? Why would Romano's dearest friends from the synagogue be planning to leave for America?*

And why would they be begging Romano to go with them?

The silence stretched and Siena risked another peek around the doorway. She watched as a small dark-haired woman placed a hand on Romano's shoulder. "Please, Romano. The Race Laws have not let up as we had hoped. And now with war brewing across Europe, it is not safe. Not for our people. If another Great War starts, we will be trapped. Come with us, before it's too late."

"No," Romano's voice was soft, hushed. "No. This is my home. I won't be driven from my home."

"But, Romano—"

The man, Ezra, gently touched his wife's arm and stilled her words.

Stepping forward he offered his hand to Romano. The two men shook, their eyes meeting. From her place in the shadows, Siena could see the worry in Ezra's face. But he said nothing more.

Romano lingered at the door as his friends made their way back down his long drive, his shoulders stooping lower than usual. As he started to close the door, Siena and her two friends quickly tiptoed back outside, settling themselves on the patio as if they hadn't just been spying on the dottore.

At length the old man reappeared outside, eyes staring

across the garden. He paused, mouth twitching, then said to the night, "I am quite over-exerted. I must retire to my rooms."

"Can I bring you some supper?" Amara asked. "I have soup."

"Grazie, my dear, but no. I think I will not be long from my bed. You young ones stay up as you wish. Enjoy this beautiful night. Good night."

"Good night," they chorused back. No one pressed him on who had been at the door, or what had happened.

Not long after Romano left, Dario and Amara stood. "Romano is right, it has been a big day," Dario said.

Taking hold of each other's hands they headed for their room.

Siena only nodded. She understood. Ezra and Hannah's words did not only affect Romano. They were a warning, Jewish citizen to Jewish citizen. It mattered for Dario and his family in Turin also. It mattered for Amara as his wife. If the threat of war in Europe would bring harsher enforcement of Mussolini's Race Laws, would they be safe?

As the last rays of the sun slipped beyond the trees that lined Romano's garden, Siena wrapped her arms around herself, seeking comfort. The skin along her arms pimpled in the cooling evening, the sky now dressed in a deepening blue hue.

Romano had made his decision. He would stay in Rome. And if he stayed, so would Dario.

Siena could only pray that was the right choice, for them all.

PART 5
BARI, 1943

THIRTEEN
ALESSIA

The morning air was laced with cold, the sky bleak and streaked in grey as the first rays of sun peeked over the distant waves. The ships in the harbour, looming metallic hulks, sat squat and solid in the water. No movement yet across their decks. They were early.

Alessia turned to Niccolo and smoothed a stray lock of his hair back from his eyes. Unruly curls – nothing she did would make them behave.

He shifted from her hand, annoyance on his face. She met his defiance with a hard stare, but as his eyes shied away she regretted it. It was natural, after all. He was becoming a young man, was here to work as a man. Of course he didn't want his sister fussing him in public. It hurt her heart to see him growing up, but it also filled her soul with deep pride. If only Papa and Mamma could be here to witness it with her.

She pushed the thought aside, lest the moment of weakness show on her face. She didn't want to burden Niccolo. Today was intimidating enough without adding her emotions into the mix.

Pina and Luca walked into view, and Alessia raised her

hand in a wave. She'd discussed this opportunity with her neighbour but hadn't known what Pina would decide. They came down to the portside, Pina wearing a heavy frown.

Drawing Alessia into a welcoming hug, a kiss to each cheek, she grumbled. "A lot to expect of our boys. They'd better treat them right."

Alessia nodded her understanding, patting Pina on the shoulder in a show of support. With Marco already at war, Pina's fears for Luca would only been heightened.

"It is a good experience for the boys as they become men. We are a port town after all."

Pina sniffed loudly at that, her disapproval clear. Before his untimely death, Luca's father had been a farmer, not a fisherman. But right now, neither set of skills was a path to a job. War had seen to that, whatever Pina may say, and feel. Luca drifted to Niccolo's side. A few years his senior, he'd taken to looking out for Niccolo. Just as Marco had done before he left to fight.

"It will mean food," Alessia said softly, pitching her voice low, for Pina only. The older woman looked out over the port, remaining silent. Alessia understood. She had her reservations too. But that morning, as Niccolo's belly rumbled loudly at the breakfast table, she'd seen there was no choice. They'd broken their fast on half-rotten plums; there'd not even been stale bread to spare for the morning. It had to change. Movement further along the port caught her eye and Alessia turned. Sailors were beginning to appear on the decks of the boats, and port workers arriving from the town. Soon the silence of the port would be replaced by action, as the men prepared the boats for the day. James appeared on the dockside, striding towards them. Alessia straightened subconsciously, hand pressing her hair into place nervously as her feet shuffled. Pina eyed her sideways and sniffed again.

"Buongiorno, buongiorno," James said, hands raised to the side in greeting, smile wide. Nodding to Alessia and Pina he took Niccolo's hand, then Luca's, and shook firmly. "It is good to have such strong lads here to help."

"This is dangerous," Pina said suddenly, stepping forward in challenge. "The boats are a target in this war."

James leaned back, settling into his heels as he gave Pina his full attention. "It is true that our navy is a target. But not here in Bari. We hold the region and the local airports. There is little reason for Germany to target us here."

"I see the boats," Pina said, eyes narrowing on James. "They leave and return. They are involved in battles."

James nodded slowly. "Si, si, these vessels are all on active duty. But their targets are elsewhere. This port is for repair and planning. Not action."

Pina's frown deepened, her eyes tracking to her son. Luca was three years older than Niccolo but didn't look it. The two boys were equally underfed and lanky. Alessia saw it, the moment Pina decided. Her hand came up, reaching for Luca as her body began to turn for the port.

James saw it too and sprang forward. "Signora," he said, hand out before him to stop her. "Please, signora. I understand your fear, truly. But I would not put the boys at undue risk. You are right, we are at war and I can make no guarantees. But this." He swept an arm over the port. "This is not a target. Not now anyway." His hand came to rest over his heart. "I will promise you this. If I hear of any threat, however small, I will send the boys home. Immediately. You have my word."

Pina paused, body angled, hovering between her choices. Alessia held her breath. She had the same fears in her heart. Yet sought the same food security for Niccolo. If Pina decided no, how could Alessia decide yes? If they chose no, how could they feed their boys?

Her fingers trembled, her vision swaying slightly as her own hunger groaned deep in her belly.

Then Pina slumped, and Alessia knew that James had won.

Another sailor, younger, his face blotched with angry pimples, appeared behind James. He asked something in rough-sounding English, and James nodded.

"This is Berty," James explained. "He will take the boys down, see them to work."

"I thought you were assigning them?" Alessia said, voice tight with the sudden hit of anxiety for Niccolo's safety.

"Peace, peace," James said gently. "Berty will just get them started. I will be close by, at all times."

Beside them Pina sniffed pointedly, then turned to Luca. She fussed with the scarf at his throat, whispering hushed instructions, then, with a hard stare at James, started on her way back home.

Niccolo smiled at Alessia. "See you tonight, sister," he said, voice high and cheerful, then followed Berty and Luca down towards the hulking ships that lined the dock.

Alone now, James stepped closer. Voice lowered for her ears alone he whispered, "I will take care of him, Alessia. No harm will come to him."

"Or Luca."

"Or Luca. Alessia, you can trust me."

Alessia looked up at him and their eyes met. He was so close she could feel his breath on her face, her lips. She stepped back. A small wry smile ghosted over his mouth, then James straightened. "I will walk them home to you this evening," he said. "And give you a full report. Every detail… over supper."

Alessia frowned. "You cannot expect me to feed you," she said, incredulous. "The whole reason Niccolo is here at all is for food—"

"No, no," James said, eyes dancing with mischief. "I mean I will take you out for supper. In town. With me. As a reward for your time, I will see the boys home safe and tell you all about Niccolo's day. And I will see you well fed. What do you say?"

Alessia stared at him, her mind whirling. Of course she

should say no. It was not proper for an unmarried woman to be out with an unmarried man, alone. Especially when her papa was out of town. More, James was a foreigner and a sailor. An ally, yes, but the German's had been allies once too... Yet the thought of food: the displays of fruit and meat and bread and pastries she passed in the Piazza Mercantile. The abundance that was just there, out of reach for the likes of her and her family. Would one supper out with this man be so bad? With Niccolo fed at the port and Alessia taken care of, it would mean more for Nonna and Siena. Maybe just once?

She blinked slowly. No, it wasn't right. As much as her stomach cried out for her to agree, Alessia knew she had to refuse.

Opening her eyes she firmed her shoulders, looked straight into James's eyes and said, "Yes."

FOURTEEN
ALESSIA

Niccolo and Luca looked exhausted. Alessia stood at the door watching as her brother and Pina's son loped up the alleyway towards home, a tall figure keeping pace beside them. The image blurred, rolling back in time, Niccolo and Luca coming home from school, Marco's solid presence at their side. How many times had she waited for the boys at the end of a day, hoping that Marco would be with them? He liked to see them safely home, when his farm work permitted it. Alessia liked the stolen moments with her handsome neighbour. Her nonna and Pina watching on, knowing glances passing between them as the two friends shyly spoke.

But Marco wasn't here. He was far away, fighting for their country. A different man walked beside her brother and Luca. James. The similarity of the memory and the moment churned her stomach, and she gulped down a ball of guilt that knotted in her throat.

Shaking her head slightly to bring herself back into the present, Alessia smoothed her hand over her hair, nervously checking that the strands were neatly in place. She'd made an effort to look nice for him.

Luca waved as he passed. Niccolo paused at her side, pressing a kiss of greeting to her cheek. He smelt of grease and salt water. "Nonna has made stew," she said as he stepped through the doorway. "Wash up first."

"Si, si," he said, his fatigue clear in his words. He disappeared inside.

James stood before her. "Buonasera, Alessia. You look truly lovely this evening."

"Grazie, signore," Alessia replied, averting her eyes and hoping that the flush of embarrassment she felt at his words did not redden her face.

"Are you ready to go?"

"Si." Alessia popped her head around the curtain and called out to her nonna, "I will be home before full dark." Then dropped the curtain and moved to James's side.

He smiled at her warmly, his eyes sparkling in the soft light of dusk. "This way," he said.

He took her to a small cafe on the edge of the Piazza Mercantile. Inside was hazy with cigarette smoke, each table filled with men in Naval uniform, clearly an establishment for the soldiers. James pulled out a chair for her. Alessia sat, rigid and unsure.

They dined on pork, despite it being the nationally promoted meat-free Tuesday: proof there was meat available in Bari if you had the money or position. Alessia chewed slowly, each bite a mixture of tasty delight and shame as it slipped down her throat. So much food, and such high quality, yet in the surrounding streets the people went hungry, the children undernourished. James ordered a bottle of wine and poured them each a glass. The wine was robust and heady, and soon Alessia felt light-headed and oddly warm.

They shared a dessert of cheese and jam, and James spoke of life in England, of green rolling hills and soaking rain. "But I always wanted to travel. That's why I studied languages. Italian was by far my favourite. Beautiful." Alessia didn't think he was really talking about her language. Afterwards, they strolled through the piazza, around them other couples were taking in the gentle night. Passing the Pillar of shame, the circular statue where legend held that debtors were chained, Alessia felt the prickling sensation of judgement climb up her back, of her own growing debt that must be paid.

James led her to the harbour. There the docks were bathed in floodlights for the night shift. The large vessels of the British and US Navy floated peacefully at rest, the waters twinkling against their hulls.

James took her hand, his touch warm and comforting. She didn't pull away, but instead turned to face him. His fair hair shined in the harbour lights, his smile soft on his lips. He stepped forward, closing the space between them. Alessia's stomach flipped, her heart beating faster. He placed a hand on her cheek, thumb running over her chin. Her lips parted.

"Alessia! What a happy moment to come across you here."

Alessia jumped in surprise, hastily stepping back from James's touch. Guilt plunged through her stomach where anticipation had so recently danced.

Siena appeared from the shadows of the surrounding streets, her heels clacking loudly over the cobbles. "I was just at confession when I thought I saw you. How fortunate, we can walk home together."

"You had no right to interrupt us," Alessia whispered under her breath to Siena. "We were just out for supper."

Siena scoffed. "It looked like more than just supper to me."

Alessia rounded on her, shame heating her words. "I do not need your judgement, and I won't accept it. I have opened my home to you and shared my food. You have no right to make assumptions about my character."

"And you should not be so trusting. It was the British who bombed Rome, not the Germans."

Alessia stared at her, stunned. "That was before. James wasn't part of that."

Siena fell silent, eyes studying the cobbles beneath her feet. "I am sorry," she said at last. "I just think, without your mamma or papa here, it can be easy to make mistakes."

"You are here without your mamma or papa. Perhaps it is time you return to them."

The night seemed to stretch around them, the cold sharpening as the sky darkened. Siena stalked ahead, her face turned away.

Alessia sighed. "I didn't mean that," she said, hurrying after Siena. "I spoke in anger."

Still, Siena avoided her eyes, her arms crossed over her stomach in a gesture of hurt.

"Siena, please. I know that you are afraid for your family in Rome. It was thoughtless of me."

"I do not know what happened to my mamma and papa," she said softly.

"I know, the bombings, I am so sorry—"

"No, not the bombings. Because I never knew my parents."

Alessia stopped in her tracks, her mouth dropping in surprise. "What do you mean you never knew them? I thought you said they were lost in Rome?"

"That was my employer and friend. Romano." Siena continued walking, eyes fixed forward. But Alessia remained where she stood. "Siena, stop. Talk to me," she called.

Siena took a few more steps towards the city wall then fell still, her shoulders slumping. Alessia watched as she took a deep breath, her body heaving with the whoosh of air she expelled. Treading lightly she walked up to Siena and placed a gentle hand on her shoulder. "You can tell me," she said.

Siena eyed her in the deepening night, her hand drifting up to the pouch she wore at her throat.

"I was abandoned as a baby," she began. "Left on the steps of the church of Santa Maria in central Rome." Her hand dropped from her throat, and she faced Alessia. "I don't like to tell people. They tend to make assumptions."

Realisation rattled through Alessia. She had more in common with this woman of Rome than she'd known.

"I am sorry to learn that. I lost my mamma when I was only young. It hurts."

"Si."

"This is why you came to me," Alessia said suddenly. "Why you wanted to walk home with me, from the harbour."

Siena looked at her and Alessia could see she was right.

"I had been to church, then I saw you," Siena explained. "You and a man, alone, in the dark."

She smiled at Alessia. "My mother had to give me up. If my papa had stayed…"

"You don't know what might have happened," Alessia reasoned.

"No, I do not. But it is best to be safe in life I think."

Alessia stared and felt the understanding between them expand. Siena understood the impact of reputational damage. What had her mamma endured? To give up your baby, what an awful choice to have to make.

"James is a good man," Alessia tried. "He cares for me."

"Si, but he will leave," Siena said.

"You don't know that."

"He is not Italian. When this war is done, he will go home. It would be better if he didn't leave something behind."

She broke off, the air heavy with the unspoken warning. Shock flashed through Alessia. "I would never. Not until I am wed," she said, voice hushed.

Siena only shrugged. "I am sure most mothers of orphans thought the same."

Alessia's indignation evaporated as she read the sincerity in Siena's words. "I will not make that mistake," she said.

"People talk. Whether or not you do, they will talk."

Alessia knew it was true. She had worried about it herself in the months since James had first started to direct his attentions at her. Somehow she'd lost sight of that tonight. Her hands smoothed down her skirts as acceptance of Siena's intervention settled over her.

"Thank you for stepping in," she said simply.

"I mean only to be your friend."

"I know."

Siena nodded firmly. "All right. Now, let's get out of this cold."

FIFTEEN
SIENA

A soft knock sounded on Siena's bedroom door, then Alessia's head popped into view.

"Nonna and I are going to church. We were wondering if you would like to join us?"

A well of emotion gathered in Siena's belly. To be invited to church with the family was special. She was being included as one of them. "Si, I would like that."

Alessia stepped into her room. In her hands she held a simple cotton scarf. "Here," she said. "Stand and I will secure it for you."

Siena stood and faced Alessia. The woman's fine fingers set the scarf over Siena's hair, her touch feather-light as she tied the knot at Siena's throat. They made their way downstairs to where Bianca waited. The old woman looked at Siena, her mouth shaping into a wobbly smile.

"Nonna?" Alessia asked. "Are you all right?"

"Si, si," Bianca replied. "It is just nice that we can all go to church together."

She linked her arm with Siena's, her crooked hand patting

Siena's forearm. "It is good to have you here," she repeated, tone soft and tinged with the sound of regret.

Their eyes met. Sadness, deep and old, swam in the old woman's irises. Siena felt her brow tighten in sympathy. For what, she did not know. But she felt it: some loss or sorrow in Bianca's life, some memory resurfacing in this moment. Perhaps missing her son, far away at war.

"Grazie." It was all she could think of to say.

Out on the street, they met their other female neighbours: Pina, Lucia, Valentina and old Terese. Together they made their way through the cooling twilight, more and more women joining them on their pilgrimage.

They came to the Basilica San Nicola, the largest place of worship in Bari. Siena looked up at the shining white church, the walls shaded blue in the gathering dusk. It was even more beautiful than during the daylight hours. Beside her, Alessia smiled and gestured for her to follow.

Inside it was breathtaking. A large, vaulted ceiling covered in a bright fresco in reds and blues, trimmed in gold, gazed down on Siena. She craned her neck, her eyes soaking in the beautiful depiction of angels and saints.

The women flowed into the church, making their way to the left side and a set of stairs that led into a catacomb below. "The Vault of the Saints," Alessia whispered as they descended the stairs to a white-walled cellar room illuminated by candles. "We come here to pray for our loved ones, living and gone to God. Tonight, I will pray for my mamma; I thought you might wish to pray for yours, too."

Tears welled in Siena's eyes as she continued down the stairs into the vault. Such gentle kindness, such thoughtfulness. Alessia had a truly beautiful soul.

Inside, the women gathered at a small wood-carved altar. A single priest, robed in white and gold, stood at the altar, an ornate silver globe filled with incense swinging from a chain in his hand. He began a chant to God. One by one the women of Bari joined that chant, raising their voices to Heaven.

After, as they made their way back to the house on the edge of the city walls, the night around them silent but for the collective tap of heels on stone, Siena decided. It was time to share more about herself.

Stepping into the dim light of Alessia's home, Siena slipped the scarf from her head, handing it back to Alessia.

"Can I speak with you?" she asked.

Alessia smiled at her gently. "Si, of course. Always."

Siena, Alessia and Nonna Bianca gathered in the kitchen.

"I will make chicory. Take a seat and we will talk," Bianca announced.

Siena swallowed her nerves and took a seat. Soon a steaming serve of the bitter coffee substitute sat before her in a chipped cup. "Grazie," she said, taking a sip. It was strong and hot and bracing. Exactly what Siena needed to get her through this moment.

Her two hostesses sat opposite her, their movements calm and unrushed, despite Siena's request.

"Are you hungry?" Bianca asked.

"No, grazie."

Taking a deep breath, she slipped the necklace she always wore from around her neck and placed it on the tabletop.

"This is all that I have left of my mamma," she said.

Silence fell between them, and Siena knew they were giving her the space and time to explain what was on her mind.

"It was left with me, at the orphanage," Siena continued. "Most of the children were left with nothing. But some of us, our mothers left a token. Something they could use to identify themselves and their child if they returned."

Bianca stiffened. "You are an orphan?" She looked over at Alessia. "Did you know this?"

"Si, but only since yesterday. Siena told me in confidence."

Siena smiled, meeting Alessia's eyes, then turned to Nonna Bianca. "I should have been honest from the start. It is a habit for me to conceal the truth. People often judge."

Bianca leaned back, studying Siena's face, eyes flicking over the small pouch. "This is an old tradition, to leave a token. I thought we kept better records these days."

Siena shrugged. "Sister Agnes at the orphanage said the custom returned, after the Great War."

Bianca nodded sagely. "No doubt it will come again with this war."

"So your mamma wanted to return to you?" Alessia asked, eyes tight with pity.

"I believe so, I hope so..."

Alessia reached across the table and took Siena's hand. "I am so sorry that she never did."

The unexpected act of kindness hit Siena like a hammer to her heart. Throat closing over with emotion, she coughed awkwardly and pulled her hand away from Alessia's touch.

Bianca stood suddenly, shuffling around the table to wrap Siena into her embrace. "I am sorry too, dear child," she crooned gently. "I see the loss, I feel it. More than you know."

Siena sat stiffly in her embrace, the soft warmth of Bianca's skin so inviting. She wasn't used to affection. She'd grown up without a mother's touch. The nuns were kind, but removed. Sister Agnes had been the only one to show tenderness. Gently prompting Siena in her French lessons, an extra smile when she did well. But never an embrace, not for any of them. Together, under God's roof with her fellow orphans, they'd all been alone.

She sniffed and pulled back, breaking the contact.

"Grazie for listening," Siena said. "After tonight in the church, praying with the women and for your mamma, I wanted to share what I know of mine too."

Alessia stared at her hands, cupped together on the tabletop as if in prayer. "I am sorry," she began. "I feel I have been inconsiderate. Tonight, I took you to pray for a woman you have never known. I was thinking of the peace the Vault of the Saints gives to me, as I think of my mamma. But you never knew yours."

"No," Siena said. "I am so grateful that you took me. It was wonderful. Not knowing who my mother was is painful, but I cannot imagine what you experienced in losing yours."

Alessia rolled her shoulders and said, "I didn't say goodbye to my mamma, it haunts me."

The revelation surprised Siena who cocked her head. "What happened?"

Alessia and Bianca shared a glance across the table, years of sadness flowing between them. "Mamma was big with child. Nonna Bianca came from the big house to stay for the birth. I was so excited to see you," Alessia said to her nonna. "I didn't even hug Mamma goodbye." Tears had sprung up in her eyes.

Siena felt her head shaking, the guilt sat so heavily over Alessia, but that was not right. As an orphan, she knew the pain of a missing mother. But that love wasn't meant to come with guilt. She opened her mouth to protest, but Bianca spoke first. "My child," the old woman said. "Why have you not told me this before?"

Alessia shrugged, her eyes sliding away.

"No," Bianca continued. "You were just a child. A little girl excited to see your nonna. You did nothing wrong."

"I could have hugged her," Alessia interrupted. "I didn't even tell her I love you."

"She knew, darling," Bianca said, a sorrowful smile touching the corners of her mouth. "Chiara knew, and she loved you too. When she didn't come home, you stepped up for Nicco. I still remember finding you two together when he was just a baby. Every night before I went to bed I would check on you. You would be in your bed, the baby in his cot in your papa's room. Every morning I would find you together, snug beneath your blankets. Nicco and you, sweetly dreaming. I was so proud of you. I still am."

Siena felt the corners of her mouth wobble and breathed deeply through her nose to halt the sob that threatened to escape her lips. The peaceful image of baby Niccolo and his sister cuddled together, safe and warm, filled her mind and her heart with longing. She'd never had a sibling to sleep beside. Had never had a home or family. Not until she'd moved into Dottore Romano's home. There, with Amara and Romano, with Mila and Dario, working together to save the art of Italy, she had come to know something of that connection.

She hadn't said goodbye to Romano either.

Sorrow shot through her, piercing her heart. She'd loved him, truly loved him. Did he know? Could she give herself that comfort? She'd lost so much. But maybe, here in this kitchen in Bari, maybe she was starting to find something new.

"It is hard being a household of women," Nonna Bianca said, pulling Siena from the shadows of her emotions. "I miss my husband's steadying hand. And I miss your papa," she said, facing Alessia. "But we are making do."

"We are," Alessia said, her lips curving sadly. "And we have each other, si? All together. We will keep going."

Now it was Siena who reached out to offer comfort. "Your papa will come home. More do than do not, I am told."

Nonna Bianca spoke up. "My son will come home," she said, voice rasping.

"Nonna, can I get you some water?" Alessia said, rising to her feet.

Her nonna waved her away and pointed for her granddaughter to sit back down. "I was so angry when he chose to leave us," she said. Alessia sank back into her chair, regret breaking over her face. Siena could see the memory hurt.

"But with time I have come to understand," Bianca continued. "Your papa, he is an idealist. As a young man, he was even part of the March on Rome."

Alessia looked at her nonna, stunned. "The March on Rome? But wasn't that when Il Duce came to power?"

"It was," Bianca said. "Mussolini marched from Naples across the country. The king feared a civil war, so he made Mussolini prime minister, giving him the rule of Italy. Your papa left you and your mamma with me, and followed. He thought it was the start of a better life. We all did."

"Just before the war Il Duce paraded Hitler through the streets to celebrate his rule," Siena added. "I was there." She wrapped her hand around the pouch on the table, returning it to her neck. She had shared enough for now.

Nonna Bianca placed her hands on the table, palms up, her face raised to the ceiling. She closed her eyes and sighed. "My Auri, he feels things, deeply. He believed that Mussolini would bring about a better Italy. But that march – I don't know what happened. When he came home, he was different. Lost. He stopped painting for the longest time. Took the job here at the Pinacoteca metropolitana di Bari, moved you and your mamma here and never returned to his teaching in Florence."

"I thought that was because of me?" Alessia said. "Because I was unwell."

Bianca smiled at her gently. "That is true enough," she said. "You were always a small one. But not the whole of it. Your papa didn't know what to believe in anymore. I don't think he has since. Not until the day Marco was conscripted."

"Who is Marco?" Siena asked. She had met so many people during her time in Bari, but this was a new name.

"Marco is Pina's eldest son," Alessia said. "And a dear friend."

"Marco's papa died when he was young, so the boy gravitated to Auri. They shared a bond. When Marco received his call up from the Italian government, my son was angry. He saw all the young, poor men, boys really, being sent to fight. It wasn't right, isn't right. So Auri volunteered," Bianca said.

"They walked away together," Alessia whispered, eyes downcast.

She seemed to close up, pulling back, so Siena didn't push. Though she was sure there was more to the connection between Alessia and this Marco. It could wait. It had been a heavy day for them all.

"Well, I think it is time we retire for the evening," Bianca announced.

"Si, Nonna. I will help you up to your room."

Alessia cupped Bianca's elbow and helped her to her feet.

"Grazie, granddaughter," Bianca said, then faced Siena. "It is good to have you here with us," she began, holding Siena's gaze. "It has filled an emptiness long hollow in my heart. I am glad God brought you to our door."

Siena nodded, not trusting herself to speak, the flood of emotion that flushed through her was too strong.

"Come on, Nonna," Alessia said. "Good night, Siena. I am glad you are here too."

Siena watched as the two women made their way to their room. A new sensation had settled over her during their shared evening. Siena frowned, examining the feeling. It was brittle, its edges wavy and ill-defined. But it was there nonetheless.

Calm washed over her as she realised what she felt. For the first time since the soldiers burst into Romano's home and stole him from her life, Siena felt safe. Here, in Bari with these women and Niccolo. Here, Siena was safe.

SIXTEEN
ALESSIA

Alessia lay in her bed, eyes wide open, staring into the darkness. Beside her, Nonna Bianca's heavy breathing told Alessia she had found her rest. Rest that eluded Alessia.

She hadn't expected that a trip to the Vault of the Saints would lead to Siena sharing more of her history, and Alessia confessing hers. Perhaps she should have. Now the past would not be quieted.

Alessia remembered those nights cuddling with Niccolo. She'd wait until the house went silent, then sneak into her papa's room. There he would be, eyes open, waiting. She'd gather him to her chest and carry him to her room. Safe beneath her blankets, brother and sister would sleep. She loved the milk-sweet scent of him, the soft tufts of hair on his crown, the rolls of his arms. Niccolo always smiled then, a happy, giggling baby. He didn't smile anymore, not since their papa went to war.

The memory came without warning, surging up from her heart, in a searing bolt of panic. The day Marco told her he was going to war.

She'd been waiting for her brother's return from school, when she spied that Niccolo and Luca were once again joined by Marco. She remembered her heartbeat quickening as he made his way along the small rise to their home. But as he drew nearer, her smile had faded.

His step was heavy, his eyes downcast. Beside him, Niccolo trotted along happily, mouth moving, arms gesticulating wildly as he told some story of his day. Marco nodded, showing Niccolo he was listening, but Alessia could see his thoughts were elsewhere. Nonna Bianca noticed too.

As the group arrived at the porch Bianca said, "Luca, Pina has been asking for you. Hurry along. Nicco, inside, freshen up for dinner."

Niccolo had frowned at his nonna, opening his mouth to argue. But one stern look from Bianca silenced his protest and he headed inside. Without a word, Bianca stood and followed him within, a soft touch to Alessia's arm as she passed.

Alessia had stood alone on the street with Marco. Around them the chorus of chatter that was her neighbours gossiping and conversing as they wiled away the later afternoon hours rose and dipped in its natural rhythm. But Alessia heard none of it. Her focus, total and complete, had rested on Marco.

"A lovely evening," she said to break the silence.

"Si, si," Marco said. His eyes were still on the cobbled road, his shoulders hunched forward. Alessia would never forget that stance, cowed, sunken, so unlike the boy she'd grown up beside.

She'd cocked her head in thought, then brazenly reached out across the space between them and lay a hand on his arm. His skin was warm to the touch, soft, despite the smear of grit from farm work that covered it. He looked up in surprise, eyes sharp, then soft as they met her stare. His lips twitched in a smile as he touched her hand.

They both dropped their contact, but their eyes remained fixed on each other.

"The order came yesterday," he said, voice hoarse. "I have been conscripted to fight for our great nation."

Alessia stared at him in open shock. Another conscription from Bari? But there had been so many already. And Marco was barely eighteen.

"When?" she managed to croak.

"Next week. I told Signore Messi at the farm today. Mamma is hysterical."

Realisation slowed her heart. Her nonna had known. Pina must have said. That was why Bianca had herded the younger boys away, giving Alessia and Marco this moment.

"You cannot refuse?"

He smiled sadly. "You know I cannot."

"Where will you go?" Her mind raced through the options. Before the war in Europe, Italy had been engaged in Africa, so, so far away. Now, joined with Germany, he could be sent anywhere on the continent. Was that better than Africa? Or more dangerous?

"I do not know. I am to report to Rome for training, and I guess I will learn more then."

Silence fell between them, the hum of the neighbours' voices distant, unheard.

"I will check on your mamma."

"Thank you."

"Will you write to me?"

"I will try." Marco gave a small cough. "You know I was never strong at letters."

"Even just a page with your name, so I know you are well," Alessia said. *So I know you live*, she thought to herself. She felt a rush of sorrow flooding up from her belly that threatened to form tears in her eyes, and she straightened her shoulders. "You will come back," she said firmly. "You are strong; you work the fields. You will be all right."

Marco looked down at his feet, shuffling, and Alessia waited, giving him a moment.

"I have something for you," he said at last, eyes flicking up to her face briefly. "I wanted you to have it, to remember me by. But I am not sure..." he trailed off.

Alessia reached across and took his hand. His fingers curled around hers as he looked up. "Whatever it is, I will treasure it."

A small smile formed on his lips. Dropping her hand, he plunged his hand into his pocket, then held his fist before her.

"It is not much. I could only afford a small one."

Alessia cupped her hands and he opened his fist placing a small oval object in the centre of her palm.

Alessia gasped in surprise. There, sitting neatly on her hand was a tiny ceramic pumo. The objects were cast to look like a stylised bud of the Acanthus flower, then painted in bold colours, each signifying a hope for the future. Traditionally, couples were gifted pumos as a wedding present, to wish them well in their life together.

Marco had given her a pumo, in deep brown, the colour of grounding, symbolising protection and home.

"I know it is perhaps presumptuous—"

"It is perfect," Alessia interrupted him, and held the pumo to her heart. "I will keep it safe in my room, just for me. It will remind me that you are coming home."

And she had. When she'd moved into her nonna's room, the small gift had come with her, secreted in the dresser drawer.

Now, restless, mind racing, Alessia slipped quietly from the bed she shared with Bianca and crept across to the dresser. Sliding the drawer open cautiously, she plucked the tiny pumo from within and once again held it to her heart, taking a deep, steadying breath. Life had been so hard since her papa left, so painful, every day another struggle to provide for her family, she really hadn't had a moment to calibrate within herself.

Today, she'd almost made a terrible mistake. If Siena hadn't been walking by... But was it a mistake? She and Marco were so young when he went to war. Two years was a long time to wait and hear nothing. Had he forgotten her? Or worse? Had he gone to God?

Alessia straightened, forcing the awful thought from her mind.

She was so tired, she realised. Taking on the responsibility of the household, trying to find enough food for Niccolo, and worrying over every decision she made. She had Nonna Bianca of course, but the old woman was frail, her health fading. And with the stress of her son being away at war, Nonna Bianca needed Alessia to take charge. Alessia couldn't ask her nonna to do more, couldn't share her fears. She'd felt alone with all the decisions. The burden hers to carry.

And then she'd met James. Tall and happy, confident, with such an open-hearted smile. He'd offered her help when she needed it most: work and food for Niccolo. And for her, friendship. The feeling that someone else was looking out for her. That she was not all alone.

But it was more than that, she finally acknowledged. When she was around James her body fizzed and bubbled. Excitement ran through her veins. She was drawn to that energy, that sense of breathlessness. A contrast to the everyday grind of survival.

Alessia returned the pumo to the dressing table drawer. There it rested, silent and hidden, a symbol of Marco, of her life before.

Was that life still what she longed for? Was it still her dream? She closed the drawer.

Steps heavy and slow, Alessia returned to her bed, snuggling against the comforting weight of her sleeping nonna. Pulling the blankets right up under her chin, she watched the moonlight play over the wall for a moment, giving herself time, trying to filter through the emotions that swirled within her heart. Trying to find what she really felt. No answer came.

Releasing a heavy sigh, Alessia snuggled deeper into the blankets and closed her eyes for sleep.

PART 6

FLORENCE, 1921

SEVENTEEN
EVA

"Blast!" Eva cursed as the blob of paint dropped from her brush to the polished wooden floors of Professore Renzetti's studios. It was a warm Saturday in early spring, and Eva had brought herself to the quiet of the workroom to practise. For months now she'd been training dutifully under the professore's unforgiving tutorage. Gentle of voice and always polite, she'd felt confident when she first began under his instruction. But, while his manner never differed, his expectations of her seemed unattainably high. As she practised her brush strokes in oil and watercolour, and her sketches in charcoal, she felt her technique was only getting worse.

Others in the class received glowing praise. Alessandra from Rome was a clear favourite of their professor. The slender, elegant young woman could do no wrong. Nor could Emilia, born to parents who sculpted for the government; her talent only expanded. Every session they seemed to excel still further, drawing beaming smiles of encouragement from Renzetti, where Eva received only frowns.

But she didn't have the worst of it. At least Renzetti only gestured his disappointment in her. For Elio, he gave it voice.

"Sloppy."

"Crude."

"Pay attention."

The words were soft, diffident, yet utterly cutting. Eva had watched as Elio had quieted, drawing into himself, becoming isolated. Where at first he had joined Eva, Matteo, Oskar, Alessandra and Emilia for drinks at the small bar on the corner of their studios, as they had after their first lesson, now he declined, feigning commitments Eva knew did not exist. He ate less too: coffee only for breakfast, a few bites of pasta at lunch. She pressed him on it one evening as they dined in their lodgings, a hot meal provided by their hostess as part of their board.

"You cannot be finished already?" she'd said, as he pushed away his plate of potato and chicken.

"It is not to my taste. She does not cook like Mamma," he'd answered over loudly.

Eva had been shocked. Eating so little when a woman had gone to the effort of cooking was rude in itself, but to vocally criticise? Elio knew better than that, their papa had seen to it.

Whatever had got into him?

That wasn't a real question, because Eva knew what. Not because of their deep sibling bond, but because she felt it too. In the crushing sense of shame each time she disappointed their professore, when his eyes shied away from her work, lines deepening across his forehead. How she longed to please him. To step up to the potential he had seen in her that first day in his office in the Accademia di Belle Arti. For him to smile at her in that secret way that made her light up inside. That hope kept her going, tethering her ambitions to the anchor of Renzetti's approval.

Elio seemed to have given up.

Eva would not.

She had worked too hard to get here and waited too long as the world tore itself apart in war, her youth paused by bombs and blood. This time in Florence was her last chance to live her dream.

After, she would settle down. Whether she married or remained a spinster – there were few enough young men available after the heavy casualties of the trenches – was irrelevant. Either way, the time for her art, for her passion, was swiftly ticking away. Eva would not let that time pass without trying her best.

So, while the other students savoured an easy Saturday in the piazzas of Florence, or took day trips through the lush green of the surrounding hills, Eva toiled, hands spotted with paint, eyes dry from staring, shoulder aching from producing the same imperfect strokes, time and time again.

Dropping paint on the floor was just another sign of her deep fatigue and her fear of failure.

Taking the end of her smock into her hand she knelt on the floor and scooped up the offending blob of white. It smeared greasy streaks across the polished wood. "Double blast," she cursed, before trying again.

"Do not curse the paint, for like God, the paint is always right."

Eva's head shot up, seeking the source of the voice, though she knew his timbre instantly.

"Professore Renzetti, I am so sorry. I fumbled and—"

"Peace, Eva, peace. It is just a little white. This is a studio of art." He stretched out his arms expansively. "Paint will get on the floor. Don't fear, the maid will get it off. So, what are you working on this fine Saturday?"

He lowered his arms, linking his hands behind his back as he paced slowly towards her. Eva straightened, wiping her palms down her smock, paint streaks forgotten. A flutter started in her stomach, nerves over his assessment, and something more. As Renzetti approached, his step relaxed and confident, Eva felt her breath quicken, suddenly acutely aware that they were alone together. He stood before her canvas, close enough to her that his arm brushed hers. Eva clasped her hands together, willing her nerves to still. From the corner of her eye, she observed his face. He was so close she could see the grey stubble on his cheek, could smell the soap on his skin.

Depicted on the canvas was a bowl of fruit, an apple and a chopped pear. *Damn fruit*, she cursed to herself. Eva had been defeated by this exercise for the best part of a month. She just couldn't get the shine right. It frustrated her; the wildflowers of home and the coastal waves seemed to emerge from her brush effortlessly. But fruit...

"Enough for today," Renzetti announced. "It is glorious outside, time for a break."

"Oh, but I must keep going," Eva stammered. "I haven't got the light coming from the correct angle and —"

"And you won't get it right today." Renzetti turned to face her, expression soft as he gripped her shoulders, staring into her face.

"You work too hard. You focus on perfection. Art is not perfection. Art is living, breathing. You need to be in the world to paint it, Eva."

"But the techniques..."

"Will come another day. Today, the paint has spoken," he glanced down at the white-streaked wood, amusement in his smile. "Today, we go out."

He strode for the door, effectively shutting off any further argument.

Eva stared, stunned. She had paints to pack up, brushes to wash, her smock...

"Quickly now," he said, rounding the door.

Releasing a squeak of nerves, Eva dropped her brush into a jar of water and pulled the dirty smock over her head. Draping the smock over her canvas and grabbing her satchel she hurried after her professor.

Outside, the midday sun shone bright from a cerulean sky. Renzetti led her to a small delicatessen on the Piazza where he bought cheese and crostini, raisins and olives and a small bottle of chianti. The parcel of food wrapped in brown paper and secured under his arm, he walked her over the Arno river, the water misting a stale, brown odour in the rising heat.

On they walked, through the Piazza de' Pitti before hopping a low grey stone wall that edged the hillside. Renzetti paused to offer Eva a hand to help her balance as she stepped across onto the soft green grasses. He offered her his arm then, and Eva linked hers, a tingling sensation flushing her skin where their bodies touched. They trailed along a dirt track under chestnut trees covered in white and pink blossoms. Before her the rolling green of the Tuscan hills expanded, patches of bright green next to dusty shades, trees in bloom dotted between terracotta-roofed farmhouses and clusters of grey-green brush. The view shimmered in the heat of the sun, the sky seeming oily in its glittering brightness. White fluffy clouds puffed across the skies as gentle wheat-scented breezes rose up from the valley below.

Soon Renzetti stopped. "Perfect," he announced before dropping to sit on the soft grass at their feet. Eva joined him, curling her legs to the side and tucking her skirts neatly around her knees.

He opened the paper wrapping and spread it out like a picnic rug, arranging the cheese and fruit and crostini. Then he popped the bottle of chianti and took a deep swing. "We will have to share," he said, offering her the bottle.

Eva paused, eyeing the bottleneck. She reached across and took the bottle, tipping back her head to drink.

"More!" Renzetti cried. "Take a good sip."

Eva complied, glugging down a mouthful of the sweet and tannin-rich liquid.

"Better," he said as she passed the bottle back, wiping her

mouth. A small laugh escaped her lips as the warmth of the wine seeped through her middle.

"This cheese is the best in the region," Renzetti was saying, breaking off a chunk for her. They ate slowing, using their hands, sucking their fingers clean like children, washing down the dry crostini with more chianti until the bottle was empty. As they ate they chatted – about life, about the farm where Eva grew up, about Eva.

"The farm is small. It is hard to draw a living from the fields. Mamma struggled to feed us. It's why we both got work so young. Left school."

"Your Italian is remarkable, for such a challenging beginning."

The compliment flattered, as it should. School Italian versus dialect could be a divider of class in the Kingdom of Italy. "Thank you," Eva said. "Mamma made us study hard. She always valued that, even if it wasn't afforded to her."

"And no one was an artist? Not even in labour, like a house painter, or the like?"

"No, Elio wasn't lying about that. He brought art into our homes. Mamma didn't encourage it, nor did she discourage it. I am not sure why. Perhaps she had dreams for her son. Dreams he is working towards now. A life in a city, not bent under the sun."

Eva stopped suddenly, shocked at revealing such a personal opinion. But Renzetti took it in stride.

"It is noble work," he said. "I have land near Puglia myself, I know the region well. But if I had a son, it would not be my wish for him to work it."

"You pray for a child?"

"I pray. God can be hard of hearing."

Eva chuckled. This was a different side of Renzetti, more open and raw, skirting dangerous topics. She liked it.

Then Renzetti lay back in the grass, hands behind his

head. Once again Eva copied him. The grass was cool against her stockinged legs and her bare forearms. Above her the small green leaves of the chestnut trees flickered in the breeze, the dappled light playing across her face, warm fingers touching.

"This is art," Renzetti said. "Life is art."

Eva felt flushed with wine and sleepy with food. She placed a hand on her belly, breathing deeply as she observed the world around her, savouring the moment, being in the world.

Calm came over her, the first she'd felt since arriving in Florence, and her eyes drifted closed – peaceful, safe.

When Renzetti helped her to her feet he didn't drop her hand, keeping the contact as they walked back to the Piazza de' Pitti, the touch soft and easy and just as it should be.

At the Arno, Renzetti stopped.

"Until Monday," he whispered, eyes holding hers. "But let's keep this outing just between us, for now. I don't wish to alarm the other students and cause you to become a focus for negative attention."

"Of course," Eva agreed, readily, naively.

A small smile rose on his lips. "Just for now."

Her eyes trailed him cross the Ponte Santa Trinita, the shift of his lean limbs beneath his loose white shirt, the floating grace of his walk.

And she realised. She was in love.

The moment he was out of sight, Eva sped up. Spinning around she raced for the rooms she shared with her brother. Excitement, nervousness and no small amount of confusion flushed her senses. She had to talk to Elio, she had to tell him.

Bursting into their rooms, Renzetti's name on her tongue, she stopped dead.

"Elio? What are you doing?"

Her brother sat in their shared drawing room, his suitcase set neatly by his side.

As she closed the door behind her he stood, picking up the case.

"I am taking some leave, heading to Rome."

"Rome? But, Elio, it is the middle of the semester. You can't just leave."

"Professor Renzetti has already granted the leave. He agreed some time away from the pressure of the school would do me good."

"Agreed your leave..." Eva's mind spun. She didn't know what upset her more: that Elio had applied for leave without discussing it with her, or that Renzetti had granted it and not mentioned it today as they lunched on the hillside.

Something so magical had just begun between her and Renzetti, she could feel it. The pull she'd felt towards him from that first day in the Accademia, Eva understood it now, what the fluttering in her belly was trying to tell her... she didn't want to leave Florence. But if her brother needed some space.

"All right, but can we depart tomorrow? I have a few things to settle first."

"*We* aren't going anywhere, Eva. You are staying here to study. I am going to Rome."

Confusion knitted her brow. "But, Elio, this is our dream. Together. We do everything together."

"We did, before the war. Not now," he paused, shaking his head. "I hated leaving to fight. Hated every moment in France. I missed you every day." He looked up at her, eyes sad, dousing the last of Eva's excitement over Renzetti and bringing her fully into the moment. "It took coming here to Florence to realise that is wrong."

"Wrong? What can you mean?"

"You are my sister. It is my job to protect you. But I must also seek my own life. As a man."

"Elio, you have your own life, as a man. You are home, in Italy, and you are studying."

Elio turned away, shoulders shrugging in a noncommittal manner.

"Elio?" Eva said, coming to his side and placing a hand on his arm. "Has something happened between you and Emilia?"

She knew the two of them had been meeting in secret, sharing evenings, growing close. She didn't know the nature of the relationship, only that she liked Emilia, a lot. She'd thought they might be moving towards courtship. Had Emilia broken things off?

"No," Elio said, shaking her off with a rough shove. "No, this is nothing to do with Emilia, or you. This is about me. The professore is right, I need some time away from the paint. To rediscover my passion. And you need the freedom to blossom outside of my shadow."

Eva shook her head in bewilderment. "Your shadow? Elio, what are you saying? This is not true."

He looked at her then, full in the face, mouth twisted awkwardly. "Goodbye for a while, Eva. I am going to Rome. This is something I have to do."

Without another word, he picked up his suitcase and made for the door. Hesitating briefly beside her, he planted a swift kiss on her cheek and left.

Eva stood stunned in the middle of the room, listening as his footsteps faded down the stairs outside.

What on earth had got into Elio? She knew he was under stress. She was too.

Then Renzetti's words to her that day floated into her mind. "Art is life."

He had shown her this path too. Had taken her out to watch the clouds and smell the countryside. And it was true that she felt refreshed from the excursion.

Renzetti was a brilliant artist and an exceptional tutor. Had he seen the same need in Elio? Realised that his young student needed more to pull him from his lethargy than Eva had done?

It was possible, even probable.

Discomfort grew within Eva as she thought of the long dark nights alone, here on the outskirts of Florence. How she would miss her brother. A dark reminder of the years of the Great War and the silence of their home.

But if this separation would aid Elio, then Eva would support it.

This wasn't what she had been expecting as she raced home from the Arno, the warmth of Renzetti's touch still on her skin. But, perhaps, it was for the best. She could focus just on her dreams. She could find her art.

EIGHTEEN

EVA

The months after Elio departed for Rome passed in a slow drawl of solitude and tension. No word came from her brother, and Eva's letters to the address he'd supplied went unanswered. Alone with her studies, Eva toiled. The feeling of possibility – that she had broken through her creative block and was now perched, ready to soar – floated away on the hot dust of July. When the school closed for summer, and the other students went home or escaped to the cooler coasts and countryside, Eva remained. Her focus was unwavering, but her skill would not come.

Worse still than the loneliness, missing her brother and her friends Emilia, Alessandra, Oskar and Matteo, was Professore Renzetti's indifference. She'd truly believed something had shifted between them that Saturday before Elio left. But that wonderful afternoon on the Tuscan hillside remained a one-off. Every Saturday and Sunday she returned to practise in Renzetti's studios by the Uffizi, a hope that he would whisk her away to the grasses once again nestled unacknowledged in her chest. But he never came.

And so the thought took root. The desire, need even, to

return home. To climb on a train and run away, back to her mother's kitchen. To the smell of the dusty fields. To her nonna's pasta sauce, rich with herbs. To her nonno's tales of pirates and princesses. To return to her childhood. To wrap herself in her past and stay there.

Who was she to imagine a different life for herself? Who was she to dream of art galleries and exhibitions? Of fame and praise? How arrogant. How delusional.

Elio was right to leave. To head to Rome and seek something new. How she longed for him to return, and how she dreaded it. To see the light of passion reignited in his eyes as she was sure she would. And to have to give voice to her own truth. That she had failed.

She had wasted her youth waiting out the Great War. Now she squandered the last vestiges of her chance to marry on the foolish dream that she could be a painter.

That Saturday as she stared at yet another fruit bowl and realised she had forgotten, again, to think of the direction of the light, another blob of paint fell from her brush, then tears from her eyes.

Dropping to her feet she scooped up the offending dollop with the corner of her smock. Around her the halls of the studio were silent, still. The streets were the same. Like most of the residents of Florence, Professore Renzetti had decamped for home or the coast to escape the searing summer temperatures. He would not be coming to rescue her from her malaise. Not this time.

But his words echoed through her memory. "The paint is never wrong." She looked down at the white blob that now marred her smock and snorted derisively. Hauling the smock over her head she gathered up her satchel and strode from the room. The streets outside were cloaked in heat, shimmering hot air dancing in a fog above the overheated cobbles. The air was stuffy and difficult to breathe. Eva paced from the studio to the little delicatessen the professore had taken her to. Inside she bought cheese and crostini and chianti. Then she crossed the Arno, head low, eyes squinting in the bright light of the midday sun.

Up the hill she walked, lungs burning, calves tight. Around her the grass grew patchy, dried to brown unless under the sheltering shade of a chestnut tree. The rolling hills of Tuscany shimmered before her. On she walked, on and on, and on until the sweat streaked down her face and neck, her hair sticking against her skin, her dress wet through at the armpits. Finally, under the shade of a large oak, she collapsed to the soft grass of the hillside. She slumped back against the rough trunk of the tree, her breath coming in heavy puffs, her limbs trembling from the exertion.

Her throat was dry, and she wished she'd brought water, not the bottle of red wine.

Sitting there, back against the bark of the tree, she began to relax. Her breathing slowed, and her heart settled into its usual rhythm. Her eyes rested on the beauty of Tuscany, and she let her mind go. No thoughts or worries, no stresses or plans. No decisions. Eva simply sat in the grass and existed. Her fingers started to twitch, energy pulsing along the digits. She reached into her satchel and drew out her sketchbook, a gift from her brother. Tying her curls back from her face with a red ribbon, Eva gripped a piece of charcoal and she began to sketch. Wildflowers from the fields at home flowed from her hand, blending with the dainty posies that grew across the Tuscan grasses as Eva lost herself to the drawing.

She rose as the sun set and ambled back the way she had come, cheese uneaten, wine still stoppered. Peace had come over her as her charcoal had scratched across the pages of her book, and with it a desire to paint. Not the fruit of her tutorage, but something from her imagination. She returned to the studio by the Uffizi and by the light of a lamp, took up her brush and began.

"There she is!"

Eva jumped, the paintbrush swishing dangerously close to her canvas, almost ruining the painting she had been working on. Turning around she blinked in surprise as Professore Renzetti came into view. It was the next Saturday, she'd been in the studio each day since her impromptu afternoon on the hillside, working on this canvas. Not fruit, but the hills of this beautiful region, the flowers. Tuscany.

It was inspiring. She had felt gripped by the force of passion and had needed to put paint on canvas. The work she had produced filled her soul with joy, even if the brush strokes remained imperfect.

She hadn't expected the professor to be back from his holidays yet. Hadn't planned on letting anyone see her holiday work. Except maybe Elio, if he ever came back from Rome...

Renzetti looked refreshed. His skin sun-kissed, his hair longer, framing his face in pale waves. He wore a white shirt, open at the collar. Hands in the pockets of his trousers, he loped casually towards her. But it was not Eva that his sharp eyes were assessing. It was her painting.

Swallowing the lump that had formed a hard knot in her throat, Eva groped for an explanation. "I know it isn't on the syllabus. I've just been struggling. I needed a moment of freedom."

Renzetti lifted a finger to his lips. "Shhh." He moved past her, coming to stand directly before the canvas. Moments passed, excruciatingly slow. Eva felt the weight of his judgement on her painting as if it were her very soul he was staring into – analysing, judging. She wanted to run away, she wanted the floor to open up and swallow her whole.

She wanted him to love it.

Renzetti stared on, eyes tracking across the painting. The silence stretched. Eva's mouth opened and closed as she tried to think of something to say to break the tension and fill the silence. Do something, anything other than standing there, staring.

"You found her," Renzetti said, turning to face Eva. His eyes were dark, lids lowered.

Eva frowned. "Found who?" she asked, confused.

"Yourself. The artist I first saw in your self-portrait by the sea. She's here, in the blades of grass of Tuscany."

Eva's mouth parted in shock. "You... like it?" She met his stare timidly, so afraid of what his answer might be. A small smile curved his thin lips, and he reached across the space between them, tapping her chest with a finger, right above her heart.

"It came from here," he said. "You listened to the paint, and it showed you the way. I knew you could do it. It was always there. You just needed to find it."

He lifted his hand from her heart and feathered his fingers over her cheek.

Stepping closer, he took hold of her chin between his thumb and forefinger, his eyes never leaving hers, boring into her soul. "You are beautiful."

Eva's heart began to drum, her breath coming in sharp bursts. The moment stretched, tense like wire. Then Eva snapped. Surging forward she took Renzetti's head between her hands and pressed herself to his body, her mouth finding his. He met her movement easily, moulding their bodies together as he parted her mouth with his tongue. His hands ran down her back, gripping her legs, and he lifted her smoothly from the ground and walked them to his desk. There he put her down. Pulling back, a question now filled his eyes.

Eva, chest heaving, body vibrating with desire, met his eyes confidently. "Yes," she breathed.

That was all he needed.

Lunging forward he pulled her to him, clothes stripping from their bodies, the cool air of the high-ceilinged room tickling her flesh as he pressed her down on the tabletop.

"You are sure?" he asked.

"Yes," was all Eva replied. It was the only word in her mind. Repeating over and over and over. Yes, yes, yes.

PART 7
BARI, 1943

NINETEEN

ALESSIA

Niccolo wasn't meant to be there that day. His shift had finished. He'd come home for dinner. Tired from lifting boxes of munitions from ship to dock, ship to dock. Hands calloused and torn, bleeding. But as the last of his vegetable stew slipped down his throat, Niccolo had got up.

"Extra shift today, double pay."

Alessia had been surprised. But she hadn't argued.

How she wished she'd argued.

She stood on the raised edge of her city and watched as he loped down the stairs that led away to the port on the far side of the bay. Behind her in the setting sunlight, yellow rays dappled the winter-grey waters of the Adriatic in sparkles of white. She turned away from Niccolo and the docks he headed to, her mind seeking the peace of the waves that cupped her city. Breathing deeply of the salt and air, Alessia sighed. At least it was calm today, no scent of storm on the winds. A good day to work late, to earn extra money.

Something caught her eye. In the darkening skies above, a metallic glint sparkled from the dying rays of the sun. Tucking her hands beneath her arms to ward off the rising chill of night,

Alessia squinted curiously. A plane came into focus, too far off the coast to properly make out. Planes passed by Bari often. And this one was out to sea. Nothing to cause concern.

She'd gone inside, joined her nonna at the sink, and tidied the kitchen.

She was darning socks, Niccolo's of course – his shoes were too small, and he worked daily now, his feet pushing out and rubbing the wool against his heels – when she heard a cry of alarm. Her neighbour, Pina, her voice pitched in a wail of terror. Glancing at Nonna Bianca in shared surprise, Alessia rose, discarding Niccolo's socks, to go and investigate.

She thought it would be a fall, that old Terese had tripped, or Giuseppe down the lane. The streets of Bari were cobbled long ago, the surface uneven, and in the dark, treacherous. What was an old lady like Terese doing out after dusk anyway?

Alessia stepped outside into the biting cold. Shadows fell across the terraced homes of her nestled street, the last rays of the day had disappeared beyond the horizon. She glanced to the side. There Pina stood, head turned back towards the seas behind them, her hand raised, pointing. Alessia looked up and froze in horror. The sky before her was filled with shining planes. They flew in tight formation, crossing from the seas at her back towards the port beyond. Coming.

The sound of the plane engines made it to her ears, rising, louder and louder as they lumbered forward. It wasn't conscious. She didn't shout back to Nonna Bianca, didn't scream to Pina to take shelter. Her feet just moved. Alessia was running, her feet pounding down the stairs from the city wall, down to towards the Porto di Bari. To Niccolo. Around her the tight streets of Bari crowded in, the narrow alleyways so familiar, filling with curious faces and questioning eyes. Alessia didn't stop to warn them, she just kept running. Breaking free from the winding streets of the city, the port came into view. The sailors stood on the docks, eyes turned up, hands tented against the harsh glare of the port lights that lit their night-time work. Alessia drew in a breath and opened her mouth to scream. A plane above dived low, the roaring of the engine filling Alessia's ears, its silver belly so close she felt she could reach up and touch it. She ducked down instinctively.

The port erupted into motion. Sailors waving their hands frantically, deckhands running.

The first plane crested the port, something silver falling from its sides.

Alessia's mind barely had time to register what she'd seen before the explosion.

So loud it deafened her ears, so powerful it cracked the very walls of Bari. A plume of smoke and fire rose up from the port. One of the ships was ablaze. Men were running, mouths open screaming. Another plane swept over the city, lower, its grey nose menacing. Another silver glint, another bang, another black plume. Then another plane and another. The city shook, the port scrambled, and rubble from the surrounding buildings flew across the city. Suddenly, a flash of brutal red and flames burst across the docks. A ball of heat doused the whole harbour in fire.

Alessia surged forward. No thought in her mind but her brother's name. No plan. No idea of what to do. Only that Niccolo was at the port, and the port was on fire. She had to find him.

More planes were still arriving, more bombs falling from their bowels. And Alessia ran – as the walls around her cracked and pinged, as the earth rocked with explosions. Down the cobbles now strewn with rubble, white stone buildings turned to powder and splintered wood. Down towards the water. Down to Niccolo.

A lull of sound as the planes overhead began to disperse. A moment to hear the screams of agony from the waterside. Then a fizz and a pop and an almighty boom.

Alessia's head shot up. Before her, the centre of one of the large American vessels exploded outward in a spray of thick black oil that spread out over the water. Men on the decks were screaming, their shirts on fire from the explosion, hands to their eyes. They jumped, one after the other, right into that slick of tar that coated the seas. A blast of sulphur-laden wind hit Alessia's face, the stench choking her lungs. She did not stop. Her feet hit the wood of the dock; at her side another local woman ran, her eyes wild with fear. Together they raced towards the water and the men who swam for the shore. Above them the sound of planes had ceased completely, but Alessia didn't look up, her focus solely on the men who lined the docks, bloody wounds across their limbs. At the dock's edge, Alessia plunged her hands into the tarry black water and caught the arm of a flailing sailor, hauling him up from the sea's grip. The black remained suckered to her flesh. He fell across her, the weight of his sodden body pressing the air from her lungs. With an effort beyond her strength, Alessia managed to heave him from her, freeing herself. Her eyes scanned. "Niccolo!" she screamed, her throat raw from smoke and heat.

Above, a final plane dove down from the dark, its engines roaring. The bomb hit the surrounding buildings, releasing a cascade of stone and brick. It shattered out across the port. Alessia hunched, hands coming up over her head. But she was too slow. A piece of brick struck her temple and she collapsed to her knees. She looked up. The port was covered in ash and fire, obscuring her view.

Her head swam, her eyes blurred.

"Nicco," she whispered, and she blacked out.

TWENTY
SIENA

Siena dived.

Crouching against the edge of the Chiesa San Giovanni she stared in horror, hands cupping her ears against the violent booms that rocked the city as whole buildings exploded into clouds of dust, scattering like sand thrown on the beach by a child. She'd been to confession before the chaos erupted.

Not again. Not again.

Eyes turned outward, she saw great plumes of black bellowing up from the harbour as debris flew skyward. Another boom and the large US ship went up in an enormous ball of fire. Sailors appeared on her decks, flames leaping from their backs as they dived for the waters below.

Another plane appeared, flying low and menacing. Siena crumpled in on herself as the glinting silver bomb fell from its middle, missing the docks and smashing into the neighbouring residential district. People surged from the rubble, faces coated in powdered stone and ash, bright red wounds streaked across their flesh.

A young woman lay prone on the street. Arms outstretched

she pulled herself forward, mouth open in a desperate scream. Children, too young to be parted from their mothers, ran in panic, tears streaming from their eyes. A man appeared at the fallen woman's side, gathered her up in his arms and ran from the harbour. More parentless children appeared, eyes wild with fear and disorientation. Another flank of silver planes crested the horizon. Siena had to move. She had to get back to Alessia's home and the cellar she knew would offer some protection. She had to go.

But her limbs would not obey. Terror had her by the throat, the memory of Rome in ruins, of the fear. She could not make her body shift. A little boy came into view, hands rubbing a mix of ash and tears from his terrified eyes. Blood caked the knobbly knees that poked out from his childhood shorts. He looked left and right, dazed and confused. Terrified. A rivulet of blood ran down his face as he knelt down, covering his face with his hands, and cried out in fear.

Siena's heart cleaved.

She could not leave him so exposed. She had to act.

Panting from her own dread, she braced her arms against the stone at her back and forced herself forward. Before her the planes were advancing fast, behind her, the relative safety of the narrow paths of the old town. All she saw was the small boy. His hands were over his ears now as the growl of the approaching plane engines filled the air. The glint of a bomb. Siena was on him, scooping him into her arms as the bomb exploded over the harbour. The power of the explosion gushed from the harbour, spraying her with dust and seawater. Siena hit the ground and rolled, the small boy clutched to her chest, then curled herself around him as a rush of exploding sand fragments pelted her back. Blinking the dust from her eyes she stumbled to her feet, the child still in her arms. Eyes wild she scanned around her, searching for any sign of the child's mother. It was no use; the streets were a riot of screaming and panic. She would find his family later. What mattered now was shelter. She ran. Up the narrow pathways, winding away from the harbour, the horror of the aerial attack at her back. On she pressed, not stopping until Alessia's little home came into view. Nonna Bianca stood at the front door, eyes wide with terror.

"Have you seen Alessia? Niccolo?"

Siena shook her head.

The old woman remained rooted to the spot, not knowing what to do.

"Get inside," Siena ordered. "They will come. We have to get inside. He needs to be safe."

She opened her arms to show Bianca the shaking child in her embrace. The sight broke through Bianca's shock and the old woman stepped inside.

"The cellar," Siena said. And Bianca complied, pulling back the rug and exposing the hatch door. Down the stairs they rushed, Bianca slamming the door closed as another bomb rocked the city of Bari, plunging them into darkness to wait.

It wasn't long before the rocking blasts of the bombing raid stilled, but Siena made no attempt to leave the safety of the cellar. Her body shut down as her fear of the bombs that landed across Rome came alive once again. Bianca had lit a lamp, casting them in the warm glow of candlelight. The small boy remained in Siena's arms, his little face buried against her heart. Subconsciously Siena hummed a gentle tune of comfort to him and herself. She hoped his family were somewhere safe, prayed he had not been made an orphan this night. Bianca sat on an old chair, a waft of dust rising into the room around her as her weight pushed into the cushion.

Siena smiled at her in the soft light.

"It is surprisingly warm here," she said, trying to distract her distraught mind.

"Si, si. My son saw to that, before he moved the art here," Bianca said.

Siena blinked in surprise at the honest admission. "Here? Not at the Galleria?"

"He didn't trust the staff. Especially after the war was declared. He moved his pieces here, filled the space with his paintings... and some from others. Though I believe you already knew that."

So Alessia had told her that Siena had been sneaking around down here.

"My employer hid his art also."

"A smart man. Like my son." Bianca chuckled, voice warm with the memory of a man Siena had never met, yet whose home had offered her sanctuary, all because of a connection in Florence long ago. She hoped he would make it back from the front so she could thank him.

"Are you hurt?" Bianca asked.

Siena considered a moment, allowing her body to still, to feel the impact of the debris that had blasted her from the port.

"Some bruising. I will be all right."

"The boy?"

He stirred, whimpering in his sleep, and Siena scanned his face in the half light.

"Just afraid."

"We must find his mamma."

"Si."

First they had to survive the night.

They surfaced to a city in ruin. After a night in the close darkness of the cellar, Siena pushed up the cellar door and guided Bianca and the small boy into the dawn. They picked their way down through the city towards the port.

"Mio Dio," Bianca whispered, her gnarled old hand shaking as it covered her mouth.

The port was destroyed, the docks a smouldering ruin of charcoal, the boats half sunk in the seas. And the neighbourhood that bordered the port... it had been blown apart, reduced to ash. The sandstone that had made up most of the homes of Bari had been blasted into powder to sit in piles strewn across the city. The harbour beyond lay collapsed, the docks in splinters, the vessel hulls pockmarked with holes, the wooden sheds black from scorching fire. Around them, the residents of Bari were slowly emerging into the reality of the disaster that had befallen their homes. Nonnas stood by front doors, hands raised in wailing prayer to their God. Women walked the streets, calling for missing children, desperation in their eyes. Soldiers in groups spread out through the streets, assessing damage and offering help to the injured.

"I don't know where they are," Bianca croaked. Siena looked over at the old woman, pity slicing through her. She didn't need to ask who Bianca meant.

Deep lines of worry and fatigue dug into the flesh around her eyes and mouth, her jowls shaking from the terror that lay across her heart.

"Not again. Not again," she whispered to herself, chant-like, her horror turned inward.

"I will find them," Siena said, taking Bianca's hand and squeezing firmly. "You return home, so you are there to greet them. I will find them."

Bianca met her eyes and Siena read the gratitude there, beneath the fear. The old woman nodded once then turned back for their home.

Siena reached down and took the small boy's hand in hers. "Come now, mio piccolo, let's find your mamma."

She didn't really have a plan to reunite the child and his family, nor to find Bianca's missing grandchildren, but she had to try. She made for the Polyclinic located just beyond the port, mercifully untouched by the raid, logic suggesting that as a dock worker the hospital would be the most likely place Niccolo would have been taken. She hoped Alessia would have thought the same and would be there too. As she approached the hospital a teenage boy crossed her path. He glanced their way then broke into a sprinting run. The child beside her dropped her hand, pulling away and racing forward. The two boys met in a flurry of cries. The older boy hefted the smaller one into his arms, tears of relief streaking down his cheeks.

"Grazie, grazie," the older boy said to Siena.

"Of course," she managed to say, though her words were rough in her mouth. Her own relief and worry were accentuated by the beautiful scene of their reunion. Her eyes lingered after the boys as they headed off for the other side of town. Brothers back together. She hoped the rest of their family were safe.

One task achieved, Siena came to the front of the hospital.

Outside was in disarray. The site had been requisitioned by the soldiers the night before. Taken over for military use, but done so at speed. They had not yet had time to establish order in the face of the panic of the civilians. People of the city milled outside, calling out questions over missing loved ones, beseeching the soldiers for supplies and help. An old man cradled a small bundle in his arms, red seeping through the blanket. A girl supported her limping mother. Siena took a deep breath and pressed through the crowd. At the front, she forced herself into the hearing of one of the soldiers who stood guard at the entrance. "Niccolo di Bari, he worked on the docks."

"You will have to wait, signorina," the soldier said, looking away.

But Siena would not be swayed.

"I am a nurse," she lied. "I can help."

The soldier regarded her properly then. She watched as he assessed her claim, pupils narrowing on her, and kept her expression calm. She was a practised liar. Finally, he nodded. "All right, go through. We could use the extra hands."

She pushed past the last few begging civilians and mounted the stairs by the soldier, then stepped through the door.

TWENTY-ONE
SIENA

The smell of garlic hit her with force, overwhelming her senses and wrinkling her nose. Blinking she waited for her eyes to adjust to the dim light. Before her, the hospital was transformed. Gone were the orderly beds sectioned by rooms. Here, even the hallways were being used to accommodate the wounded. Nurses, some in uniform, some in street clothes, rushed from patient to patient, assessing quickly before moving on. A doctor, distinguishable by his white medical coat, appeared in a far doorway. Siena rushed forward.

"Medico, I am here to help. The soldiers sent me to support the dock workers."

The doctor barely looked at her. "They are the worse off..." he said, already moving away from her. "Soccorso ward."

"Grazie." Siena didn't stand still wondering where the "Soccorso ward" was; to pause in this environment where every hand was needed was to invite suspicion. She had to find the Soccorso ward, and there within, hopefully, Niccolo and Alessia. It was her best chance of finding them.

If he wasn't within...

If she wasn't...

Siena pushed the thought away. It was too early to know, and guessing didn't help. She had to trust in God and keep moving, just as the brother of the small boy she'd rescued had done.

In the end, it wasn't hard to find the dockworkers. Caught up in the flow of nurses and doctors, Siena came to a large, open room. The ward was stuffed full of injured sailors and dockworkers. The smell of garlic was even more pervasive here, mixing oddly with the sharp tang of sea salt and the iron rust of blood. The men lay in rows – some on beds, most just wrapped in blankets on the floor. Even with the extra naval supplies, there simply weren't the provisions at this small city hospital for the number of injured. The men were arranged into two basic groups: those with bloody wounds that had been tended and wrapped and those that were still awaiting treatment, a full twelve hours after the bombing raid. Siena scanned the rows of the men wrapped tight in thick woollen blankets, their faces twisted almost featureless by pain until she spotted him.

Niccolo.

A sob of relief caught in her throat and she rushed to his side. Kneeling, she seized his shoulders. "Nicco? Nicco? It's me, it's Siena."

Niccolo's eyes opened briefly at her voice, a smile ghosting across his lips. Then his eyes rolled back in his head as he lost consciousness again. Siena brushed the hair from his brow. It was wet. She frowned. He should be dry by now. He was seized by a violent shiver but did not rouse. Siena looked across the row of men, similarly wrapped up tight.

They shivered too.

Her face must have worn the question, for a nearby nurse leaned over. "Exposure," she said. "The water is cold in December."

"But it's been hours. Surely they have warmed up by now?"

The nurse shrugged. "Winter seas, and shock I suspect," she said before bustling off.

Niccolo coughed, drawing Siena's attention back to the boy. "Hurt, hurt," he croaked.

"Shh, shh," she crooned, moving to wrap him in her arms, to add more warmth to his shaking limbs. But heat radiated from his body, and when she shifted she saw a wet patch on her blouse where his body had rested. He was sweating. Sweating through the blanket.

She was about to question another nurse when a commotion across the ward drew her attention.

A man had raced into the room, boots slapping on the polished stone floor.

He was neatly dressed in naval uniform, his service hat gripped in his hand. Worried eyes took in the room, a deep frown forming across his brow. Startled, Siena realised she knew this man. It was James. Alessia's British friend.

She moved to stand and wave him over, but something in his expression made her pause.

She watched as James spied a doctor and paced to the man's side. A flurry of words and agitated hand gestures. Then the doctor looked over at the men in blankets that lay beside Siena.

His face was ashen.

Siena pushed herself to her feet, her movement jolting Niccolo who let out a great whine of pain. The cry drew James's notice, and their eyes met across the room.

He looked down at her feet, seeing Niccolo, and shock dropped his features. He hurried over. At the same time, the doctor pivoted on his heel, gesturing frantically to the nurses.

Siena frowned as James approached.

"Get the blanket off him," he ordered.

"What? No, no... the nurse told me they have exposure. From falling in the cold sea—"

"It's not exposure!" James hissed, eyes wild. He shook his

head in frustration "It's been hours. How could anyone still think it's exposure?" he continued angrily, more to himself than anyone else.

Over his shoulder, Siena saw the doctor had gathered the nurses into a huddle. One looked up, a hand going over her mouth in shock.

"James, what is going on?"

"Here, help me with this blanket," he said, moving towards Niccolo.

"James! What is going on?" she repeated.

He paused, hovering in place as if stuck between choices. The strain was clear as he faced her. Leaning against her ear he whispered.

"They need to be decontaminated."

Siena's mouth fell open in horror as his words came together in her mind, understanding like a punch in the gut.

"What happened?"

"It doesn't matter what happened. What matters is that we fix this." He gestured at the room around them, and Siena realised he was right. They had to act.

A nurse appeared beside them. "Together?" she said to Siena, who nodded in reply.

Siena knelt on one side of Niccolo, the nurse on the other. The nurse gripped the edge of the blanket and paused, eyes flicking up to Siena. "You know him, si?"

"Si."

"You might want to look away."

"Never."

The nurse held her stare a moment, then with a short nod, turned to her task.

Carefully she began to pull the blanket away.

A rich scent of garlic plumed from beneath the covers. And the smell of blood.

"Why didn't they tend to his wounds!" Siena cried before

understanding hit. The blood wasn't from a wound from the bombing. It was from being wrapped up.

As the nurse peeled the blanket back from Niccolo's skin the true horror of the medical misunderstanding was revealed. Flecks of white marred the dark wool of the blanket. Siena sucked in a sharp breath as she realised what the white was: skin. Niccolo's skin. She reached over to help with the other side of the blanket, peeling it off as gently as she could. But it was no use. No matter how slowly she pulled, a layer of flesh came away with the blanket, stuck to its fibres. Underneath was a ruin of blood. Large wet blisters, swollen to the point of splitting, had raised across Niccolo's exposed chest and arms and up his neck.

Horror closed her throat and Niccolo started to shiver again.

"He is cold!" she exclaimed.

"No," the nurse said. "It is not from cold, for any of them. It is a seizure."

Siena looked at Niccolo. He gave a weak cry, a protest of pain, and she saw his eyes open and roll back into his head once more. Siena leapt to her feet. As she did the man behind her also started convulsing, the whites of his eyes showing.

"Mio Dio," she whispered, face paling. Another nurse appeared with a gurney, and the two women hauled Niccolo up onto its top.

"Where are you taking him?" Siena demanded.

"He needs to be washed clean." She eyed Siena. "You will too."

"Me?"

The nurse pointed to the wet patch on Siena's blouse: black oil now stained the cotton. "Take it off, now! And follow."

Her movements slow from shock, Siena complied, removing her blouse, confusion and fear blunting any embarrassment from undressing in public. One foot followed the other as she trailed the gurney and Niccolo's prone body from the room, leaving James behind.

Out in the bathroom, a host of nurses, doctors and uninjured sailors stood ready and waiting with buckets of water at their feet. As Niccolo was wheeled in they stepped forward. Fast hands stripped him of his remaining clothes, his socks and boots. His body was red raw from the top of his neck to the soles of his feet. More trolleys arrived, and the men similarly stripped. They all looked the same. Tears coursed down Siena's face. Another man started convulsing, the trolley rattling impossibly loudly in the echoing room. Niccolo was gathered up by two soldiers and placed gently on the tiled floor. Buckets of water appeared, and a nurse, soaked to her skin, sponged the length of Niccolo's body.

Siena couldn't breathe. What had happened? What had happened to beautiful Niccolo?

"Come." A voice at her side made her jump. It was the nurse from the ward. "I will get you washed, then you must go. We can't have civilians here."

"I... I can help," Siena managed, though her eyes kept drifting back to Niccolo – to his poor, poor body...

A gentle hand on her bare arm. "Go home and prepare a room," the nurse said. "That will be the most important thing."

Siena met her eyes and understood.

The road to recovery for Niccolo would not be swift.

Purpose flooded through Siena as her horror was replaced by pure white-hot rage. These men had been treated at the hospital for exposure, the nurses and doctors believing their symptoms to be from the shock and the cold of the port waters. But it was not the cold that they had needed treatment for. They had been exposed to something else. Something that burned the skin from their bodies. The medical staff didn't know. So their care had been mishandled, and their welfare and lives had been placed in drastic danger. Because they all *did not know*.

Had James known?

Alessia's navy friend, who'd so kindly offered work at the Porto to Niccolo. Work on the very docks that housed this secret substance.

Had James had done this to Niccolo? To them all.

Siena stepped into the cool morning light that washed over the ruined city, hands shaking from fury, mouth set in a determined line.

She would find out.

TWENTY-TWO
SIENA

The streets around the hospital had been destroyed. Looking up the hill towards the white walls that encased the old town, Siena could see whole neighbourhoods reduced to rubble. High above them all, shining down benevolently, the bell tower of the Basilica San Nicola, its entire left side destroyed. Beyond, the harbour was in ruins. Fires still smoked along the dockside, and soldiers scurried around the blasted hulls, repairing or salvaging, perhaps both.

Siena gaped at the destruction, her heart seizing in her chest.

What had been done to this beautiful city? This place that had been her refuge, her safety. Her home. Anger flared again in her gut, reminding her of her purpose.

James.

How much had he known? How big were his lies?

In truth, the answer didn't matter to her. The hurt of seeing the destruction of this city, seeing the men lying wounded and bleeding on the overcrowded hospital floor, Niccolo's seizures, his pain – it was too much for Siena to bear. Someone had to pay. James would pay.

But where to find him?

In the end, it wasn't difficult. The destruction of the harbour and the adjacent buildings taken for military use had condensed the British Navy's operations to the centre of town. The Town Hall.

Siena mounted the stairs, a woman on a mission. A soldier eyed her, holding up a hand to stop her. She didn't break her stride. Pushing past the shocked man she shoved her way inside.

"Hey! Stop right there," he called behind her. But Siena did not slow, did not even look back to acknowledge his words. Inside she strode across the polished floor, her sand-covered soles squeaking against the tiles. A woman behind the reception desk stood swiftly.

"James Prior," Siena said. "Where can I find James Prior?"

The woman frowned in confusion, her eyes flicking up to the soldier following behind Siena.

They exchanged words in rapid English that Siena did not understand.

Irritated she pivoted away, heading for a side hallway of doors.

"James Prior!" she bellowed down the hall.

The soldier behind her shouted, his hand clamping onto her forearm.

She shook her body violently, but his grip only tightened.

"James Prior! You come here right now!" she screamed. The soldier gripped her other arm, lifting her bodily and hauling her towards the entrance. The woman behind the desk paled, backing against the wall.

"Right now, James! Or I will tell Alessia it was you!"

The soldier had her almost to the front door. Siena bellowed a last time. "I'll blame you!"

A door down the hallway cracked open, and James appeared.

He called something in English and the soldier paused,

though his grip on Siena did not slacken. James stalked forward. Siena braced herself for his anger, fuelling herself with her own. But the face he wore was not one of rage as she expected, but rather purest grief.

He spoke a few words to the soldier, and Siena felt the pressure on her arms release.

She met James's eyes, and the sorrow she saw there stifled her fury.

"Will you come with me?" he asked softly. "We can talk."

She nodded and followed him to a room down the hall.

The room was full of desks and chairs with piles of paper on various tables. An administration office on a normal day. Today was not a normal day.

"Please, sit."

Siena scanned the room. "No, I will stand," she decided.

James nodded, distracted, and ran a hand through his fair hair.

"Look," he began. "I know you are angry..."

And with just those words her temper fired again. "Angry? Angry? Do you think anger is a strong enough word? The city is destroyed, and people are dead! Niccolo..."

He took a deep watery breath. "It wasn't supposed to happen."

Siena stared at him. "What wasn't supposed to happen? What did happen? The men were covered in something. You said they needed to be decontaminated. Why?"

James looked at her, eyes beseeching.

But Siena would not be moved by his sorrow, not again. "Tell me the truth, or you will regret it," she hissed through clenched teeth.

She saw his resolve break. He slumped in on himself, becoming smaller, weaker. Then he spoke. "Mustard gas, stored in barrels. On the US Liberty Ship *John Harvey*. It was only temporary storage, it wasn't going to stay in Bari."

Siena's mouth fell open in disbelief. Mustard gas. A chemical weapon stored in Bari.

"Why didn't the doctors know? The navy could have told them." She stopped as the pieces of what she'd witnessed fell into place.

"The navy, the sailors... they didn't know, did they? No one knew. It was a secret. That's why no one realised. Why no one connected the shivers, and the scent of garlic..." she trailed off.

James was watching her, his expression tight.

"You knew," she whispered, hands beginning to shake. "About the mustard gas – how?"

She'd thought blaming him was an empty threat to make him talk. She'd never believed this...

James was shaking his head. "We didn't think Bari was a target. We're too far north for the Luftwaffe to fly. Naples is such a big port. Bari was deemed safe."

"Safe? James, are you saying you knew they had chemical weapons on that boat and you decided it was all right, because Bari was 'safe'?"

"There was no reason to believe they would attack—"

"They have bombed here before! Why would you doubt they would do it again? Why would you keep this secret?" Siena cut off as a wave of purest horror shook through to her core. "You knew before the bombs..." she said, realisation dawning. "Niccolo was wrapped up for exposure, all those men... all night. For hours. And you KNEW!"

James paled, his hands opening in a gesture of pleading. "I didn't have the authority to say."

"Don't you dare!" Siena raged. "Don't you dare! Men were dying, will continue to die, because the doctors didn't know! How many more people were exposed? And Niccolo. How could you?"

"Siena, please, try and understand."

"Oh I understand perfectly," she snapped. "You are the big

navy; you know best. We are nothing. Just the people of this nation. Unimportant. You are no better than the Germans!"

"Siena—"

"Where is Alessia?"

James stopped short, mouth working.

"You know, I am sure of it," Siena pressed, her fury igniting fire through her blood. "She would have been the first civilian you searched for. Which hospital is she in?"

"Siena, please—"

"Which hospital?"

"I had her transferred to our military hospital. It has better facilities."

"Is she," Siena swallowed. "Is she all right?"

"She was injured, a blow to the head, some... exposure. But she is stable. She will recover fully."

"And Niccolo? You saw how sick he is. Have you an update on his condition?"

"I don't know. It is too early to tell."

Siena opened her mouth to roar her rage at James but the fight went out of her. It didn't matter. It was done. He knew, she realised. He knew his choice was unforgivable.

"You aren't worth my time," she hissed, turning for the door.

"Siena... wait."

She paused, hand on the doorknob.

"Let me tell Alessia the truth. Please, allow me that."

Siena held his eyes, considering.

"The day she is well enough for visitors. Or I tell her myself."

"Grazie," James said.

"Don't thank me. My silence is not a gift for you," Siena sneered. "It is for her. She deserves honesty from you at least once in her life."

She threw the door open and strode out into the broken city.

. . .

That afternoon, she took Bianca to visit Alessia. They were not allowed to be with Niccolo, not yet. Bianca did well. As they approached Alessia's bedside, she merely stumbled, a moment of bodily shock, before bracing herself and walking steadily to her granddaughter.

The young woman lay sleeping, bandages wound around her head where the rubble had struck and around her arms where the mustard gas had burned. A large bruise was purpling on her cheek.

Bianca eased herself to sit on the bed and took Alessia's hand in her own. Siena stood back, allowing the old woman a moment.

"She will wake," Siena whispered. "James said so."

Bianca's head shook. "My beautiful, beautiful grandchild," she said. "What have they done to you?"

Her pain was crushing to watch, but Siena stood firm. These people had helped her, sheltered her, fed her. Bearing witness beside them now was the least she could do.

Bianca was old, her life too full of pain and fear. Her husband and daughter-in-law were already dead, her son's status unknown and now her grandchildren lay in hospital, victims of a brutal attack on their city. It was not how it should be; they should all be here, outliving her, supporting her in this life.

War had taken so much already from this woman. Too much.

Siena had planned to return to Rome as soon as she could, to continue her work for Romano. To Amara, and Mila. But for now those plans could wait. For now she would stand beside Bianca. Beside Alessia and Niccolo. No matter what.

She stepped closer and lay a hand on Bianca's shoulder in gentle solidarity.

"I am here," she said. There was nothing else to say.

Bianca patted her hand. "Si, grazie, grazie," she said.

Siena would stay, here with Bianca, until Alessia's eyes opened, until Niccolo's fate was revealed. Siena would stay and help this shattered family rebuild. Whatever it took, however long. Her own mission here – the book hidden in the cellar, Romano's mission – it didn't matter, not now. Now, this city, this family – they were what mattered.

Siena would be here with them.

TWENTY-THREE
ALESSIA

Alessia woke to a room in chaos. Blinking rapidly, she worked to orientate herself in the crowded, bustling space. Her lungs burned, and her mind swam. Looking around her a scene of horror came into focus. Beds, lined up in a tight row, each with a person lying on the crisp, white sheets. Some men sat propped up with pillows, mouths gasping to breathe; some had bandages around their heads, arms and torsos, blood leaking through the white material. Also women, young and old, similarly bandaged. Nurses in uniform racing between them. Two men entered the far door, a limp sailor dangling between them. A young woman, eyes desperate, a small child in her arms.

Hospital. Alessia was in hospital.

A nurse bustled up to her, movement frantic, hair awry. She pressed her fingers to Alessia's throat and glanced at the large clock that hung above the door. Nodding once at Alessia she hurried away to another patient. Alessia opened her mouth to call after her, to ask where she was, what had happened? But her voice would not come. Her throat felt ripped apart, shredded all the way down into her stomach. A wash of exhaustion weighed her down, her eyelids drooping as she fought against the pull of unconsciousness. There was something she had to check. Something she had to know. Something important. Someone... black spots swam in her vision, the room around her blurring and disappearing into oblivion.

When next her eyes opened the room was completely different. Lit by the warm orange glow of small lamps along the floor, the occupants slept, silent but for the wheeze of breathing or a gurgling cough. A nurse sat at the far end of the room, eyes sweeping across her charges. The sky outside the large windows that lined the wall was black, no moon or stars deigning to shine down on the injured people of Bari. Alessia shuffled, straining as she pushed herself into a sitting position. Her movement caught the nurse's eye and she walked quickly across to Alessia's bedside.

"Calma, calma," the nurse said, placing her cool hand over Alessia's brow.

"Where am I? What has happened?"

The nurse looked down at her with eyes full of sorrow. "The port," she said. "The Germans bombed the port."

Snippets of memory burst through Alessia's mind. The silver flames, the burning fire, the choking sulphur.

"The sailors," she said, her voice no more than a panicked scraping from her raw throat. "The boys who worked at the port. Did they get out?"

"We are working to recover all the survivors and those with God," the nurse said. Her calm tone told Alessia she was not the first fretful relative to ask these questions.

"How bad?" she panted. Breathing was difficult. Her lungs felt heavy and painful.

The nurse turned away, releasing a long breath through her nose. Eyeing Alessia she said, "War has truly come to our city."

Her nonna arrived with the morning visitors. Clad head to toe in black she made her way slowly to Alessia, Siena at her elbow, supporting her weight as she stumbled. Alessia's heart sank. Black: the colour of mourning.

Tears began to stream down her face as Bianca took her hand and held it to her chest. Siena stood back, head lowered.

"Lucia and Terese are gone," Bianca said, her voice quavering with sorrow. "I cannot find a record of Luca, but Giuseppe and Pina are in hospital in a special ward. I cannot visit them. They won't allow me in. They only just let me come to you..."

"Nonna," Alessia croaked, interrupting. "Where is Nicco?"

Bianca drew in a shuddering breath. "In the Polyclinic. They won't let me see him either."

"Will he be all right?"

Fresh tears spilled from Bianca's eyes, her head shaking from side to side. "I do not know," she whispered.

Alessia looked past her nonna to Siena, seeking answers. Siena shook her head gently. She had no more information to share.

"Oh, Nonna." Alessia reached up and drew Bianca into her embrace. The old lady leaned down, resting her head on Alessia's shoulder. The two women held each other, firm and tight against the unimaginable possibility. Niccolo.

"I thought I had lost you both," Bianca sobbed. "I thought all my babies were gone."

Alessia smoothed her dry grey curls, whispering, "Shh," as they rocked gently together, Siena watching over them with sad eyes. But inwardly her heart was cracking open. Lucia and Terese – gone. The port so devastated by the attack that they were still searching for survivors. No word of Luca. And Niccolo, her baby brother Niccolo... She would not abandon herself to despair. Not yet. But hopelessness, heavy and smothering, pressed down over her body.

She learned the full story the next day. James, his face smeared with dirt and hair grey from ash, strode into the hospital room. Alessia struggled up, lifting her head high and bracing herself. He raced across the room towards her, mouth set in a thin, firm line. Coming to her bedside he knelt on the floor, bringing himself to her eyeline.

"He will live," he said. The air left Alessia's body. Caving forward over her knees, her body began to shudder with relief.

James placed a warm hand on her back, rubbing in gentle circles as she fought for composure amid the rush of relief. Wiping the errant tears from her eyes she faced her friend. "He is well? He has healed?"

James's eyes flicked down, his throat bobbing before he spoke. "He remains badly injured. Severe burns all over his body. But he is receiving the very best medical care from our own doctors. He will live, Alessia. I swear to you, Niccolo will live."

Another wave of relief, mixed with the deepest shame, threatened to overwhelm her. What right did she have to this joy when Pina lay in hospital, her son's fate still unknown? When her city burned?

She shook her head to clear the thoughts away. "James, what happened?"

He glanced behind him, quick and furtive, then whispered in a soft voice, "Mustard gas."

Alessia frowned. She didn't know what he meant. He leaned forward, voice lowered for her ears alone. "It wasn't meant to be there," he said. "The sailors didn't know it was there. But one of the US ships was carrying mustard gas. When it exploded..."

The memory rushed back to Alessia. Of the large grey cargo vessel as it took a direct hit and exploded from its centre. The blast of thick black smoke that belched from the fires, the intensity of the flames. The smell of sulphur.

"The gas was in oil form; it coated the water. Anyone who fell into the sea, or who helped to pull survivors onto the docks," he stopped, swallowing nervously. "They were exposed to the chemical. The explosion vaporised it also. It spread like mist through the neighbouring streets. To civilians. So, so many..." He fell silent, head bowed.

Alessia gulped. "That was what burned my arms? And why my lungs hurt to breathe?"

"Si, but you are healing well. The nurses assured me you will recover fully."

Alessia closed her eyes. She'd been exposed to such a small amount. And she was in hospital as a result. Niccolo had been right there, submerged in the oil-slicked waters.

"Will Nicco recover fully?" she asked.

James turned away. "I don't know."

She clenched her teeth hard against those words. Oh Nicco. It wasn't right. She was the older one. Since Niccolo's birth, it had been her job to protect him. To protect her baby brother. It should be her in that other hospital. It should be her.

"Alessia," James prompted gently. "There is more."

Alessia met his eyes and saw the pain and guilt that shone from his soul. She raised a bandaged hand and lay it across his cheek. "It is not your fault, James. You couldn't have known."

His lips parted in a tiny sob as his composure shattered. "I am so sorry." Tears streaked down his cheeks as his features crumpled. "I knew."

The words were released on a rasping groan. At first Alessia didn't really hear them, their sound more like a breaking sob of sorrow. Then her mind connected and the slow creep of understanding twined its way through her body. She drew back from him.

"You knew?"

James remained silent, his eyes turned down, studying the woollen blanket that covered her healing body. His shoulders quaked with sobs. But Alessia felt nothing for him – no pity, no sympathy for his emotion. Her head emptied, the world going blank and numb. James knew. Her friend who offered help, knew. The man she'd begun to care for, knew.

"You may leave," she said tightly.

James looked up at her quickly, his face full of pain. "Alessia—"

"I said, you may leave," she repeated, turning away from him. She couldn't stand to see him, couldn't bear his closeness. Not now. Not ever again.

Standing stiffly, he paused before her. "I am sorry."

"It doesn't matter."

"Alessia..."

She did not turn to his words but kept her eyes firmly fastened on the far side of the ward, arms wrapping around her waist as if to protect herself from further betrayal. Her lungs burning through the strain of controlling her tears, she listened to the ring of his retreating footsteps as they echoed away through the ward and then fell silent.

Then the tears flowed. Body trembling, Alessia pressed a bandaged hand to her mouth, trying to hold in the wail of hurt that gushed from her very soul.

What had she done? What had she brought to her home?

She had trusted James. Had believed his assurances over Niccolo's safety. Not only had the port been bombed, but a deadly chemical agent had been released over her city. It had brought her to the hospital and killed Lucia and Terese. Nearly taken Niccolo. He would live. Praise God, Niccolo would live. But would he be the same?

A low keening escaped her mouth, and Alessia bent over herself, folding over in shame. She had allowed James's warmth and kindness to sway her. Worse, if she was honest with herself, it had also been his grace, his handsome manner, his eyes. The attraction she'd felt between them, her desire to be around him, to feel that bubble of energy in her stomach that excited her senses when he looked at her with those eyes.

He had turned her head. Had been wooing her. And she had let him. A dangerous, dangerous game. For what could come of it? A brief liaison. A mistake in the dark of night. And a ruined reputation when he sailed back to England. Siena had been right. Nothing good was ever there, only pain.

And Marco. The boy she loved, the man she waited for. Who'd given her a pumo, a symbol of grounding and safety. Marco, who loved her. Who she loved too. What had she done?

Alessia had been a fool. She had allowed a pretty Englishman to capture her heart and now her brother was paying the price. She could only pray to God for mercy. That He would forgive her. That His price would not be too high to bear.

Her hands came together in prayer, and her lips, wobbly from sobs, began to move in quiet lamentation as she raised her voice to God.

"Forgive me," she prayed. "Forgive me."

Time would tell if God would listen.

PART 8
ROME, 1943

TWENTY-FOUR
SIENA

It had been five years since Siena, Amara and Dario moved into Romano's home. Five years of working with the network to hide and track the great artworks of Italy. Five years of laughter, joy and companionship. For Siena, who'd known life only within the cold walls of the orphanage of Santa Maria, it was her first experience of family life. And it meant the world to her.

She had grown to love her daily trips to the market to purchase fresh supplies, the walk strengthening her body, the food nourishing her soul and filling her out. She liked her time in the kitchen cooking with Amara, the shared supper with Dario and her evenings in the library reading with Romano and talking about the history of the artworks they were striving to save. Despite the tension that continued to build on the streets of Rome, the rumours of factions rising against Mussolini and the reports of faltering battle lines across Europe, in Romano's home, Siena existed in a bubble of happiness and safety. Even the unease, brought to the door by Romano's friends Ezra and Hannah, had faded with the years as Rome and Italy settled into a new normal while war blazed across Europe.

But it could not last.

Siena had just returned from the morning markets, the mild spring winds blowing the blossoms of the trees down the drive. *Dario will have a job to do in the garden today*, she thought to herself as she stepped inside.

She heard them immediately, an unfamiliar hum of voices drifting from the drawing room. Flicking a glance towards the door she retreated into the kitchen. There she found Amara laying out a tray of chicory.

"Romano has visitors?"

"Si, they are just getting settled, two men and a woman," Amara replied.

"Do we know them?"

"I have never seen them before."

Siena put down her bag of vegetables and began to sort through her purchase.

"Romano asked me to send you in when you returned. He wants to speak with you," Amara said, wringing her hands from nerves. Rome was tense, it was natural to be nervous about anything out of the ordinary. After the last group of unexpected visitors who had dropped in, and the worries they had brought, the whole house knew to be wary.

Siena placed a gentle hand over her friend's fidgeting ones. "I will be all right, Amara. Romano will be with me."

She helped Amara arrange a selection of cakes on the tray and then made her way into the drawing room.

As she stepped through the doorway, the hum of Romano's voice halted instantly.

"Ah, Siena, my young protégé, come in, come in," Romano said, waving her over, face split in a welcoming grin.

Keeping her head low, Siena entered, eyes surreptitiously surveying the attendees. There was a man in an ill-fitting suit, the elbows patched over and the knees worn thin. A larger man with soft hands in the all-black attire and white collar of a priest. Taken aback, Siena realised she knew him; he was the truck driver from the Galleria di Roma all those years ago. Beside him sat a middle-aged woman. Her stockinged legs were crossed at the ankle, her hands were covered in dainty lace-trimmed gloves and her lips painted bright red. Her attention was fully focused on the priest, their heads pressed close in tense conversation.

The woman captured Siena's attention. There was something in the softness of her jaw, in the way she cocked her head, that drew Siena to her. Coming to the coffee table, Siena set down the tray.

"Shall I pour?" she asked Romano.

"Si. Mila?" he said to the woman. "How do you like your chicory?"

The woman looked up, finally noticing Siena, and visibly flinched.

Siena blinked in confusion but pressed on politely. "Signora, some cream? Sugar?"

But the woman continued to stare at Siena, her large eyes, rimmed with the first wrinkles of time, were wide with curiosity. She leant forward, mouth slightly parted as if in awe.

"Child," she said, her voice like music. "Where do you hail from?"

"Rome," Siena answered, confusion at the question puckering her brow.

"Si, now you are here in Rome. But where did you grow up?"

Siena smiled tightly, uncomfortable under the woman's intense stare. "Rome, I know no other city. Rome has always been home."

"Siena is the girl I was telling you about. She is very proud of our capital," Signore Romano interjected. "And a fine student of art. She has an eye for quality."

"I have had a wonderful tutor," Siena said, nodding to Romano, who positively brimmed with pride.

"But, to our purpose, she reads and writes French most beautifully. And most importantly, believes in our nation."

"Then she is perfect," the woman said, still studying Siena's face. She shook her head slightly and gestured to the empty chair by the window. "Come, join us."

"Yes, take a seat, Siena," Romano instructed, before proceeding to introduce the gathered group. "It is time that you met the people we have been working with. Father Massimo you have met before," he indicated to the priest. "He runs the deliveries for our network. This is Aldo," he said gesturing to the man in the worn suit. "He and his wife help with communication. And finally, this is Mila Pettiti, our contact in Tuscany. There was also the curator of the Pinacoteca metropolitana di Bari, in Puglia, Auri di Bari, but he has gone to fight."

The woman sniffed. "Is that what he calls himself these days?"

"Pleased to meet you," Siena said politely, though her mind swirled. Why had these people all met together in Romano's home? Wasn't the idea of the network to stay separate? To be safe.

"I see you have questions," Romano said.

Siena nodded, back stiff, limbs tense.

"Mila is here with a proposal."

"Are you an art dealer?" Siena asked.

"No," Mila replied curtly. "I grow flowers. I am not here about the art smuggling. I have a different proposal."

"Mila's husband Alfredo and I read letters together at the University in Florence. He is a very dear friend," Romano explained to Siena. "And Mila was one of my students, once upon a time. Alfredo and Mila have been helping with the distribution of works of national significance, along with Aldo and Father Massimo. But things are advancing at pace. The war is not going well, and Italy is stretched. Our work to protect the history of our nation is more important than ever. It is time we do more."

"More?"

Mila took over. "How fluent is your French?" she asked.

"I am competent," Siena said. "I was always good at languages."

The woman nodded, her mouth working quietly.

"What do you know about the anti-fascist movement?" she asked.

Siena's eyes flicked to Romano, her mind blank. "I—"

"Good," Mila said. "It is good that you have not heard of us. Secrecy is an essential."

Mila paused and took a deep breath before continuing. "There have long been groups working against Mussolini's rule. Political parties, church groups. My husband, Alfredo, is the leader of one such group."

Siena took in a sharp breath through her nose, shocked at such a brazen disclosure. Mila was watching her closely. "You have seen how we have struggled and starved under his rule. He chose to align us with Hitler and embroiled us in a foreign war. He holds us under his heel." Her eyes met Romano's and Siena saw genuine passion in her expression.

"The art was a good start, to secure our country's history. I was proud to be part of it. But my husband is right. Now we need to do more."

"We are helping the resistance," Father Massimo continued for her. "Passing messages between cells, arranging transport."

"Events are escalating," Mila said. "My husband needs Romano's help. To use his contacts, our network. And we need your help too, if you are willing?"

Romano reached over, placing a gentle hand over Siena's. "I will not lie to you," he said. "There will be dangers. More than we have faced so far in our work. But Mila has assured me that your role will be limited and discreet."

Siena rolled her shoulders, sitting straighter. "And this is for all of Italy? The poor too, not just the rich?"

"Si," Mila said. "We work for everyone."

"Then I will help you," Siena said. "What do you need me to do?"

"I need you to translate coded messages."

"I don't know how."

"That is no problem. I will teach you."

"Perfect, perfect," Mila said. The elegant woman was sitting at Siena's side, the delicate scent of her perfume filling Siena's nose. "You have picked this up so quickly."

"Grazie," Siena said, replacing the dip pen in the pot.

After their meeting in Romano's drawing room, Mila had moved into Romano's home to better train Siena to translate for the anti-fascist groups that were working in concert across Italy and beyond.

Siena had a strong command of French from school, so under Mila's instruction, she had been working to learn how to translate the coded messages they received, and pass them on. Siena had been pleased by how quickly she'd picked up Mila's teachings, and how quickly she had come to trust her. Like Romano, Mila was gentle in her demeanour, and calm in her instruction, with an open warmth that invited Siena's confidence. Furthermore, Mila was part of Romano's life and the art network. Siena had been connected to the woman for years without knowing it. That brought an unspoken sense of familiarity.

After long hours of training, the women often found themselves together in the drawing room, passing the darkening hours in easy companionship. Mila had told Siena of her life in Tuscany where she grew flowers for market.

"I once wanted to paint, but life had other plans," she explained one night as Siena sipped her chicory.

"Romano says everyone should have access to art. I have always loved it. But I never learned to paint. I wouldn't have the skill anyway. It must have been hard to give it up."

Mila had eyed her sagely. "Give it up? I never did. Creativity still fills my veins. I just express it through posies, not on canvas. There are many ways to create, even if the paintbrush does not flow for you."

The translation work was tiring, but they all felt the weight of its importance. To help the resistance, to work for the freedom of Italy and the safety of those who dared stand up to Il Duce.

"Now," Mila said, taking up the dip pen. "Watch closely."

She swiped the dip pen over the page in three broad, confident strokes.

"You are so good at this," Siena breathed. "Your hand is so steady."

"And yours is coming along. Now, your turn."

Siena took the pen from Mila and dipped it into the ink. Pen's head poised above the page, she took a moment, bracing herself before mimicking the movement. It was different from the record-keeping she had been doing at the Galleria. The ink runnier, the paper thinner, the sentences longer. It took practice not to smudge the page and to work with the new materials. And to translate clearly as she went. A lot to think about all at once.

"You are a very talented young lady, you know that, don't you?" Romano said, leaning over Siena's shoulder to observe her work. "You will be ready for invisible ink soon."

The invisible ink had been his idea: an extra layer of protection against discovery. The messages they sent could be deadly.

Siena puffed a breath of pride at Romano's words. It felt

good to be valued. She smiled up at him and saw a glow in his gaze. It warmed her soul.

"Grazie." She leaned forward, dipping the pen into the inkpot once more. The movement dislodged the pouch she wore around her neck, the pocket falling from her blouse.

"What is this?" Mila said.

Siena turned, seeing the surprise on Mila's face.

"Oh," she said. "It is my token. Left with me when my mother gave me up to the orphanage."

Mila blinked, eyes fixing on the necklace, and then she reached forward, her long fingers cupping the pouch.

"I have heard of this practice," she said, almost to herself. "You were a war orphan?"

"Si, or so Sister Agnes said."

"What is inside? If you don't mind me asking."

The old lie came swiftly to her tongue. "Nothing," Siena said. "It's just a ball of cotton."

She felt Romano step closer to her side, his warmth emanating through the air between them, enfolding her in safety. Her hand closed over the pouch, her breathing suddenly slowing as calm settled over her and she realised it was time.

For so long she had held this secret, tight and close. The clue to her past, the reason for her work with art. The hope that held her in the dark, lonely nights in the Orphanage de Santa Maria. Her impossible hope.

Romano had sensed she had a secret on the very first day they'd met. She'd spoken of her love of art, but he'd seen there was more behind her arrival at his Galleria. He'd known, all these years he'd known, but he'd never pressed her for the truth. He'd offered her only his friendship, and they'd grown close over the years, working together on their secret mission.

She'd nearly told him so many times: when they shared their first pasta in this home, when she spoke of her longing for the sea. As their years together bound them even closer, she'd wanted to open up this last part of herself, to share her secret with someone.

Now, as she sat in his home, learning to transcribe messages for an underground network, Siena realised, it was time.

It was time for her to tell him the whole truth. To share her secret hope. Her search.

Reaching up, Siena untied the knot that held the string around her neck. Placing the pouch on the table she carefully opened it, exposing the image concealed within.

Beside her, Mila went very still. Siena explained. "It used to be brighter. But over the years the paint has lifted up off the canvas. I have had it so long, looked at it so much… You can still see the colour though, the sweeping paint. I think it's water. Waves and foam. Maybe, I have never been to the sea."

"You were left with this? At your orphanage?"

"Si, I believe my mamma wanted to return for me. But for some reason she could not." Siena paused, looking up and meeting Mila's eyes. She saw genuine sorrow there. Perhaps that kindness was what loosened her tongue to continue. "It's why I wanted to work at the Galleria, with you, Romano." She glanced up at him, saw the realisation in his eyes, his lips slackened with wonder. "I thought… I thought…"

"That you might find the painting? The artist?"

Siena felt herself blush in embarrassment. "Foolish, I know."

"You must not think that," Romano said, surprising Siena with his passion. "There is always hope." A gentle hand rested on her shoulder, squeezing in a display of care.

"Grazie for sharing this with me," he said, his voice thick with emotion.

"I agree with Romano," Mila said, tone soft and reverent. She drew a chain from around her neck and held it out to Siena. Siena took the offered ornament, a simple golden cross, dented on one side.

"It was given to me by someone very special," Mila said. "It is dented, imperfect, like your token. But I will never part with it. Maybe it will lead me back to her one day."

Siena looked at Mila. "Who was she?"

A distant smile flashed over the woman's lips. She took back the cross and quickly slipped it back around her neck. "She is long gone. Only God can reunite us."

"Oh," Siena said. "I am sorry."

Mila smiled and patted Siena's arm. "There is nothing to be sorry about," she said as her eyes bored into Siena's.

"When this is done, you must come to my farm outside of Lucca in Tuscany. You too, Romano," she said, breaking the eye contact. "Come and visit. Take a break from the heat of Rome. Meet my husband. I think you would like him, Siena."

An unexpected flash of yearning shot through Siena. She had often dreamed of leaving Rome to visit the sea, but she knew she would always come back. Rome was the only city she had ever known, her home, right down to the marrow of her bones. Yet after the last few years, with the pressures that food rationing and war had brought, with the tension that rode the streets, and the gaunt faces of the children who begged for bread, Siena longed for something more. When Mila spoke of her flower farm, of the little stone cottage she called home, Siena felt the unveiling of longed-for change.

"I'd like that," she said.

"You must never give up hope," Romano said. Patting her shoulder once more, he shuffled over to his desk and retrieved his book of art from the false drawer he had fashioned to hide it, just like the one in his old office in the Galleria.

Placing the book open on Siena's tabletop, he took up her pen and dipped the end into the inkpot, before holding it above the next blank line on the page.

"What are you doing?" Siena asked.

"Ensuring that you always hold on to hope," Romano said, then pressed the dip pen to the page.

Replacing the pen he turned the book around for Siena to see.

There, written in Romano's neat, tight hand was a new entry in the book of lost art.

"Siena's Secret," Siena read. She looked up at Romano. "It is a good title."

"One day, Siena, we are going to recover every piece of art in this book, including yours, together."

"I'd like that," Siena replied. "I'd like that a lot."

TWENTY-FIVE
SIENA

Siena dipped her pen into the small pot. Dragging the tip gently over the rim, she displaced the excess ink. Fingers loose, hand poised, she made the first stroke. The clear fluid flowed over the page, visible in the reflection of the lamplight at her elbow, then disappearing as it dried. Invisible.

There had been a steady stream of messages since they had begun their work. Enough to keep them constantly occupied. This message had arrived that morning, delivered via Aldo and his wife to Mila and then to Siena. It was in French, to be rewritten in Italian. Last week's had been in Italian dialect from Sicily. All in code. Siena didn't understand what message she was passing on. She knew they were working for the anti-fascist movement, and for the Allies in France who fought against Hitler, but what exactly her messages were conveying, she could not begin to guess. It wasn't her job to understand. It was her job to translate and post.

Romano knew what the code meant, she suspected. He always asked her to read the translations to him when she was done, his eyes closing as the words washed over him. Sometimes tears would mist his eyelashes, sometimes his skin would flush red. Mostly he just nodded and sent her on her way.

The invisible ink was crucial. In the event she was stopped by the Carabinieri or one of Mussolini's goons, the blank pages would offer a buffer to discovery. They could only pray that it would work. Siena preferred not to test the theory...

Finishing her translation Siena cleaned the dip pen tip and secured the lid back on the inkpot before placing them in a box in the desk drawer. The seemingly blank page went into an envelope, addressed to somewhere on the outskirts of the city. She handed the original French message to Romano. He would burn it in the fireplace, she knew. Reducing the words to ash, hiding their activity.

The final step was to deliver the letter. That was up to Siena alone.

"Hurry back," Romano said, a muscle under his eye ticking. Something in that message had him spooked, she could tell. She knew better than to ask; he wouldn't tell her anyway.

"I will," she promised.

"God Speed," Mila said.

The street was wet with summer rain. The heat of the day misted up from the overheated cobbles in a choking cloud of steam. Siena walked swiftly, her purse, the envelope sitting within, clutched tight to her side. Around her the streets were quiet; the intense summer heat and the sticky rain sent people indoors. Her breathing came in heavy puffs, partly from the humidity, mostly from anxiety. Ahead she spied a group of German soldiers. More and more of them had been stationed in the city over the past few months, and their presence was ominous. Mila said it was because Hitler knew Mussolini's hold on Italy was weakening. Dario shouted that a revolution was coming. Romano would not be drawn on the subject. The soldiers leaned against a rough brick wall, cigarettes dangling from their mouths, the smoke curling in the thick air around them. She crossed the street, rushing behind a delivery van that churned up the road, its exhaust adding to the heat and the miasma of the city. Eyes downcast, she dropped into a narrow laneway that led away from the chatting soldiers, steps urgent as she rushed along the cobbled road. Bracing herself, she chanced a backward glance. The air whooshed from her lungs in a rush of relief at the sight of the empty lane behind her. Pausing, her hand resting against the rough stone of the terraced homes to her side, Siena closed her eyes and tried to calm her breathing. But her heart refused to slow. Taking a deep breath, she continued on.

At the post office, she purchased a single stamp. The lady behind the desk barely looked at her. In normal times Siena would have considered her disinterest rude. Today, it was a welcome blessing. Attaching the stamp to the envelope she slipped it into the postbox. Job done.

Back on the street, Siena rolled her shoulders, working to calm her nerves.

It was always this way. The rush of adrenaline when a new message arrived, the excitement of the translation task, and then the fear of discovery. And finally, overwhelming relief. Retracing her steps back to Romano's house she once again passed the relaxing soldiers. One man looked up, eyes meeting hers. A nod of acknowledgement, the dip of his head and he turned away.

Siena continued on, the middle of her back burning as though eyes were boring into her flesh. She did not look back, no matter how much she wished to.

She turned onto the piazza. Almost home now, her heartbeat finally began to slow.

Then the brutal wail of an air raid siren ripped through the streets.

Overhead aeroplanes streaked into view, silver and glistening in the sun. Siena ran. She rounded the piazza, heels slipping on the mud-coated cobbles. Her lungs were screaming, but she didn't stop. She couldn't.

The first explosion sounded. Impossibly loud, bursting from a few streets over, in the San Lorenzo quarter proper. The ground shook, the reverberation rattling up her body, her ears piercing from the sound. Then another, and another. The scent of burning wood, thick, curling smoke and death filled her nose. Then he was before her. Dario, one hand clutching Romano's upper arm, the other raised, waving to her frantically. They stood at the end of Romano's long drive, shouting to her in panic. She increased her speed, and Dario turned, grabbing her hand as she drew near and urging Romano into a jog. The old man stumbled, but Dario held him firm, pushing him forward into the wide door to his home. The trio dashed inside, racing for the cellar door. Down, down, down beneath the tiled floor into the dim, musty space they climbed. There, already crouching, eyes wide with fear, were Mila and Amara. Romano lit a lamp, and Dario sealed the door above them.

Siena crouched on the floor as Dario moved to Romano's side, helping the older man to sit on the cool floor. The five of them huddled together, Amara burying her face in her husband's chest, Mila wrapping a protective arm around Siena's shoulders, holding her tight. Above, the boom of the falling bombs continued, muffled, but there. Siena placed her hands over her ears, burying her head in her lap and praying to God for their safety and for the safety of the people of Rome.

Hours later, as the first rays of day shone in a muted orange, they climbed up to the streets of the capital. Devastation. Flames raged red on the edge of the city, and smoke coiled into the brightening sky. Entire rows of homes were reduced to rubble. People were screaming and crying. Lining the streets were men working in teams to clear stone and brick in a search for the missing.

"Stay with him," Dario said, pressing Romano to her side.

Siena nodded, and her friend jogged off, rolling up his sleeves, to join the makeshift rescue crews.

"It is over," Romano whispered beside her. Siena looked down on the old man. His cheeks were streaked with tears. Sliding an arm around him she drew him close, offering the comfort of an embrace. It was all she could give. There were no words to soothe this pain, or the ruin of Rome. Razed to the ground by British bombs.

How had it come to this? Italy, fighting alongside Germany, had seemed invincible. Now her capital burned.

"He will fall now," Romano said. Siena didn't need to ask who he meant. The tide of favour had been turning against Mussolini. As Italy's expansionist policies had led to more and more difficulties for everyday people – food shortages, poverty and fear – resistance to his brutal rule had grown. His friendship with Hitler, at first something strong and hopeful, had now brought devastation to Rome.

It would be the turning point. There would be a revolution.

"Come," Siena said, drawing the old man away from the burning visage of his city and leading him back inside to Amara and Mila and the comfort of the home they had created between them.

Mussolini was arrested the next month, and his government was overthrown. But Rome's troubles did not end there. The interim rulers tried to court Britain while dissembling to Germany. It didn't work.

While the Allied forces of Britain and France invaded Sicily in the south, Germany mobilised in the north, pressing down through Turin and Florence at speed. By September they marched on Rome.

Things changed swiftly then.

Rescued from prison and whisked away to Germany, Mussolini was reinstated as a puppet leader for Germany's occupation of the north. The people of Rome withdrew inside as soldiers patrolled, enforcing a strict curfew and threatening anyone who stepped out of line.

A life on the edge of poverty now extended to one of constant fear. Worse, the threat to Romano and the Jewish citizens of the city became solid and real. Italy had already played at rounding up those deemed "impure" but there had been little appetite for it amongst the Carabinieri. The arrival of Nazi Germany changed that.

An order was declared. For their lives, the Jewish citizens of Rome had to pay in gold, 50kgs of gold to be exact. Driven by fear, the synagogues opened their doors to anyone willing to donate towards the obscene demand. Jewish citizens lined up in droves, arms laden with jewellery, candle sticks and picture frames. Non-Jewish citizens joined too. Siena accompanied Romano as he went to contribute his wealth. She watched as a woman, fair-haired and pale, walked nervously through the synagogue doors, eyes lowered, movements tight and fearful. Romano stepped up to her, taking her hand in his.

"I... I wanted to help. I wasn't sure if I would be welcome," the woman said.

"Thank you," Romano said, eyes soft.

Together Romano and the woman crossed the synagogue to pay their contribution.

Despite the collection effort and a sizable donation from the Vatican, the Jewish citizens of Rome fell short. Or so the Nazis said. The disappointment of their occupiers was made clear in a proclamation of the "Jewish failure" across Rome.

What came next would burn the soul of Rome, and the world for decades to come.

TWENTY-SIX
SIENA

The knock on the door was loud and terrifying. Even without answering, they all knew it was not a welcome visit. The streets outside were in chaos. Looters had taken to the blasted streets, taking what they could. The soldiers of Germany had enacted a crackdown, but against the fear and anger of the citizens of Rome, their power was questionable. That wouldn't stop their brutality, however.

Romano stood slowly from the chair where he had been resting. His eyes tracked to Siena. "Check the false drawer is secured." And to Dario. "Come with me."

Siena bustled from the room heading for the library at the end of the hall. She didn't know what would be worse: the discovery the invisible ink and unfinished translations? Or the collection of art secured beneath their feet?

In the library, she ensured the box of translation tools was in its rightful place within the false drawer, a set of notebooks nestled on top to distract prying eyes. Hopefully the soldiers wouldn't search too thoroughly.

She needn't have worried, for it was not the army at the door.

"Siena! Come quickly!" Dario's cry echoed through the house. Siena turned sharply, hurrying towards the entranceway, her footsteps echoing before her on the polished tiled floor. She rounded the corner into the doorway and stopped in her tracks.

There Dario stood, a man in a ragged suit collapsed against him. Siena rushed forward to help as Romano shuffled towards the kitchen, calling for Amara. A hiss of surprise escaped her as she took in the man's face and realised it was Aldo, one of the men from Romano's network. Since their meeting in Romano's drawing room, the network had returned to their plan to never be in the same room. Communicating only through notes and coded messages. Distance, deniability. What was Aldo doing here?

Between them Dario and Siena half dragged, half carried Aldo into the drawing room and arranged him on a chair.

Amara soon appeared with a bowl of water and a washcloth in hand. Siena took them from her and knelt before Aldo. His forehead was bleeding, his face covered with dirt, and his lips trembled, spittle congealing in clumps of white in the corners of his mouth.

"Shh, shh," she whispered as she ran the wet cloth over his cheeks. It came away smeared in black and red. Aldo's eyes flickered, and he pushed himself up into a sitting position. "Enough," he said, waving Siena and her cloth away. His face was still filthy, but she relented. Something in his eyes told her now was not the time to push.

Romano and Mila came up behind her. "Aldo, what has happened? Were you caught in a raid?" Mila asked.

Aldo looked up at Romano and Mila and shook his head. Tears sprang into his eyes. Romano lowered himself onto the chair beside Aldo and took his hand. "Aldo, tell me. What has happened?"

Silence stretched as Aldo's mouth opened and closed, his chest heaving. Finally, he said, "They arrested her."

Romano went still, the colour draining from his face. "When?"

"Two days ago. She was on her way back from delivering her latest message, but she didn't come straight home. She visited her mamma. They were following her..."

"Christ!" Romano swore, hand thumping the arm of the chair. Siena jumped at the violence of the movement. "Foolish! That implicates us all."

"I told her to avoid those who might remember her—"

"Has she spoken?"

Aldo's head was shaking side to side. "I waited, hoping, thinking she would not tell them about me, that I was safe," he said. "Then they came, soldiers in grey. But I got away, I got away."

"You came straight here?"

"I waited, but she didn't come, I waited..."

Romano relented. It was obvious that Aldo was too overwrought to answer his questions. Instead, he patted Aldo's hand absent-mindedly, eyes flicking back and forth in his face.

"When did you last eat?" Mila asked, stepping forward.

Aldo's face fell, a shadow creeping across his eyes. "I waited," he whispered. "I didn't leave the apartment. I waited."

Romano pushed himself to his feet. "Amara, please make chicory, extra sugar. Do we have any of those sponge cakes left? Si? All right, plate them up for Aldo. Then make up the spare room, he will be staying the night. Siena, will you help Amara? Dario, I think a grappa is in order."

Orders handed out, Amara, Dario and Siena dispersed through the house to complete their tasks.

Later, after Aldo was fed, watered and put to bed with a belly full of liquor, they all gathered together in the drawing room. Romano sat slumped in his chair, a hand rubbing his temple, the other clenched in a tight fist at his side. Dario poured grappa for them all. Siena stood by the window, Amara remained hovering by the door.

"Grazie," Siena managed as she accepted her glass of grappa from Dario, who took a seat beside Romano. Mila also stood by the window, eyes turned out to scan the streets beyond.

Siena sipped, the harsh liquid sloshing down her throat with a bracing bite. She sniffed, blinked and gulped some more. She needed the settling warmth that spread through her limbs as the drink went to work.

"Romano, what has happened?" Dario began. "I understand someone is in trouble, but—"

"Aldo's wife, Alessandra, is dead, or soon will be," Romano said. The words landed fat and heavy, punching Siena right in the centre of her stomach.

"Dead?" she gasped. "But why?"

Romano pierced her with a stare. "For doing the work we do," he answered simply.

"But, signore, surely she is just imprisoned? Italy wouldn't put a woman to death…"

"Father Massimo rang. She was taken to confession."

"Confession? No…" Mila said, rounding on Romano.

"Si," Romano replied.

"Just a formality? They wouldn't execute a woman. Would they, Romano?"

"I don't understand," Siena said.

Romano released a long sigh. He sipped his grappa, wincing at the bitterness, then looked straight at Siena.

"Alessandra is a spy. For that is what we all are in the eyes of the Nazis. Her work with Aldo for the art, and her work now for the resistance movement…" He paused, lost in his own thoughts for a moment. Taking a breath, he continued. "The Nazis will make an example of her. They cannot show mercy to the resistance. I only pray she had no messages on her when she was taken."

"Why were they following her?" Dario asked. "How did they know she was involved?"

"Her mamma," Romano answered. "Francesca is a known antagonist. They were likely watching her house when Alessandra visited."

"Are we exposed?" Mila asked.

Siena steeled herself against her fear.

Romano shrugged. "They came for Aldo, but have not come for us. I think we might have had a lucky escape. But..." He looked directly at Mila. "This was too close. We have to stop. To lay low. Be above suspicion. Aldo will leave in the morning, and after that, no more translations. No art smuggling. No contact, at all. Understood?"

Mila nodded slowly, arms crossed over her stomach. Her fingers trembled against her blouse.

"I was wrong to involve you in this," he continued, looking to Siena and Dario in turn. "I promised that I would keep you safe..."

"I was proud to help, Romano," Siena interrupted firmly. "Our country is on its knees. I wanted to do my part."

Romano sighed heavily. "And you have. But it is enough now. The Germans are here, on our streets. The time has come to retreat, to stay alive."

And just like that everything changed. The bustling, exciting city she loved was closed away behind the heavy doors of Romano's home. Her work for the network ended. Her world was reduced to the walls of the mansion.

Outside, German soldiers patrolled the streets, stopping people at random. Food remained scarce, and stories of arrests and executions filtered through the gossip channels of the city: husband to wife to neighbour to friend to shopkeeper to customer.

The magic of Rome was gone, replaced by occupation and fear.

Dario and Amara discussed returning to Turin, concern for their families bearing down on them. Mila prepared to depart for her home and her husband too.

But Siena never thought of leaving. No matter what, Siena would remain, keeping Romano fed and his home clean. She would never abandon her employer, the old man whom she had grown to trust. Together they would endure. They just had to be patient. This time would pass; she truly believed that.

In the end no one had time to leave before the soldiers came for Dottore Romano himself.

TWENTY-SEVEN
SIENA

The banging on the door rattled through the mansion, ringing along the marble-lined halls and skittering across the tiled kitchen.

Siena and Amara looked up from their food preparation, root vegetables for stew. She felt her pulse flutter in her neck as nerves fired through her body.

"I'll go," Amara said, picking up a tea towel and wiping the carrot juice and peel from her hands.

Siena nodded. "Be careful," she said.

She watched Amara make her way out of the kitchen towards the entrance hall and returned to her peeling. Her hands were shaking. Huffing nervously, she put down the potato; she couldn't leave Amara to answer the door alone. Running her hands down her apron, she headed after Amara.

She came to the entrance hall as Amara opened the door and the world exploded.

A German soldier, tall and broad, shoved through the door, knocking Amara physically back against the wall. Amara stumbled, and a cry choked from her shocked lips. The soldier pinned her to the wall and five more men streamed into the house. Siena froze.

One soldier, clearly their leader, strode into the centre of the entrance hall and pulled the rifle from his back.

"Dottore Racah! Come out! Now!"

His voice thundered through the quiet evening. What were they doing here? Had someone from the network talked? Did they know about the art? Or worse, the messages?

Siena needed to act. Needed to slip into the darkness, find Romano and run. But her limbs were locked, her legs stiff and unyielding. She tried to shuffle back, but the movement caught one of the soldier's eyes. He whipped the gun from his back in a flash, the shining metal butt levelled at Siena's chest.

"Halt!" he shouted. Striding forward he grabbed Siena by the upper arm and manhandled her into the entrance hall before forcing her to her knees. Amara was shoved down beside her.

"Hands behind your heads. Now, where is Dottore Racah?"

Beside her Amara sniffled, tears streaming down her terrified face.

"Where?"

Siena felt the hot breath of their interrogator on her neck, the stale smell of cigarettes on his breath. She had to answer. She had to speak. Working moisture back into her dry mouth she croaked, "Out. The dottore is out."

Cold metal pressed against the bottom of her chin, forcing her head up. His eyes were bright with menace, his expression stern. "You would not lie to me, would you, signorina?"

Siena swallowed, willing her nerves to calm. "No," she managed to whisper.

The leader forced her head back further until she faced the glittering chandelier that hung from the ceiling above, the barrel of the gun digging into the soft flesh of her jaw. He held her there a moment, then shouted, "Find him." Spinning on his heel he moved away, dropping Siena's head back down.

The momentum was unexpected and she nearly toppled face-first onto the floor.

Eyes lowered, she listened to the click of boots as the soldiers dispersed through the house.

It wasn't long before two returned, dragging a bleeding Dario between them, blood dripping from his forehead onto the freshly polished floor. A sob of terror escaped Amara's lips, her body quaking as she watched her husband bleed. Then came Mila, her head held high, the echo of her heels ringing through the entranceway. And finally, Romano.

They threw him down, his slender limbs splaying out as he hit the hard floor.

Siena gasped, instinctively moving towards him. But the leader blocked her path with his rifle.

"Stay, little pup," he ordered.

Somehow Romano managed to push himself up, his arms trembling from the effort.

His eyes met Siena's. She expected to see terror and panic but was met with resolve. A smile drifted over his lips, peaceful, loving.

Then the leader stepped between them, cutting the moment. Voice heavy and rough, he spoke down to Romano. "You are Dottore Romano Racah? The Jew?"

Horror sluiced through Siena. This was not about the hidden art or the messages. This was worse.

They'd remained silent for years as the Romani people were forced from their homes, their shops taken from them, their sons and fathers imprisoned. And they'd done nothing. Now the Nazis had come for the Jewish citizens.

They'd heard the rumours, passed nonna to nonna from the northern borders of France to the heart of Rome. Of the death camps, the experiments, the extermination. But who could believe such tales?

Romano's friends had been right. When they came all those years ago and begged Romano to flee for America. Ezra and Hannah had been right.

Dear God.

Siena shuffled to the side, trying to catch Romano's eye. Deny it, she willed him. Deny it.

But he did not look towards her. Slowly he raised his head, meeting their tormentor's stare.

"Si." That was all he said.

The soldier's reaction was swift and brutal. He raised his gun and brought the butt down on Romano's temple. Romano gave a cry and rocked backwards.

Amara screamed.

Siena went to move, but Mila's hand gripped her shoulder like a vice, holding her back.

Dario surged forward only to be met by the boot of another soldier, the kick sending him sprawling.

What came next was a flurry of hands and boots and orders. Two soldiers reached down, seizing Romano's arms and dragging him to the door. Dario tried to get up again, his voice raised in a battle cry until a soldier smashed his nose. Blood spurted across the floor, and Dario crumpled. Then the soldier seized a fistful of his hair and hauled him out into the night. Both men disappeared through the front door, the remaining soldiers flowing after them. Siena looked up. Their leader stared down on her, his face impassive.

"Good evening, signorinas," he said, then saluted, his hand raised to the ceiling, and marched from the room.

Siena and Amara sat on the floor, shocked to the core, physically shaking.

More shouts resonated from outside, then the bang of truck doors, the fire of the engine.

Outside the streets rang with the sounds of trucks and gunfire, shouts and heavy, stomping boots. Screams of fear and protest, silenced by the butt of a gun.

Forcing herself to her feet, Siena scrambled for the door, plunging herself out into the October night.

But she was too late.

The soldiers and the truck were gone. Dario and Romano were gone.

Only the still silence of gathering dusk greeted her, a gentle breeze rustling the oak leaves that framed the drive as the last orange blaze of sun disappeared beyond the horizon.

The next morning Siena went searching. It didn't take long to learn what had happened. Frustrated at the challenges of occupying Rome, the soldiers of Germany had performed a raid across the capital. In one night they spread out, forcing entry into the homes of rich Jewish citizens and imprisoning them at a makeshift prison in the Palazzo Salviati.

Siena visited the Palazzo daily, watching the soldiers milling outside, hoping for a glimpse of Romano, of Dario. On the fifth day, the palace stood silent, abandoned.

"Where have they gone?" she asked a local store owner. The woman looked at Siena with pity.

"I do not know," she answered sadly. "This morning, they were simply not there."

Two days later another knock sounded on the door, and a different set of soldiers stampeded into Romano's home. They went through every room in the house, every cupboard, every drawer and down deep into the cellar, to the art they'd worked so hard to hide. Loading their arms with paintings, vases, ornaments and gold, they carted away Romano's home piece by piece to a waiting truck, filling it to the brim.

Amara, Mila and Siena stood to the side and watched.

There was nothing they could do.

Dario was gone, and Amara did not know what had become of her husband.

And now Romano, his home and his legacy had been destroyed.

It was all gone.

Only an empty shell remained. And a flickering light of hope that reason would prevail, that their men would come home.

TWENTY-EIGHT
SIENA

Mila burst into the library. "Where is it?"

Startled, Siena sat up straight.

She'd spent the night on the couch, again, the silence of her room echoing too loudly against the knowledge that Dario was gone. Romano was gone.

Mila stared down at her, her eyes red-rimmed and puffy.

"Mila," Siena said. "What has happened?"

"They have him," she croaked, fresh tears lining her eyes. She dashed them away with a furious hand. "I have just had word. The Nazis in Florence have arrested my husband."

Time seemed to stop. Somehow Siena managed to come to her feet, her legs shaking violently beneath her skirts.

Alfredo Pettiti, a leader of the Anti-Fascist movement, had been arrested. Alessandra, Aldo's beloved wife, had been executed. Dario and Romano had been imprisoned.

It had fallen apart. It had all fallen apart.

"Where is the book?" Mila said.

The bite in her words spurred Siena into action.

"Si, si." She crossed the room to Romano's desk and the

secret drawer within. Slipping the false bottom aside she revealed the large black book. Romano's book of lost art.

"Bueno," Mila said, striding over and pulling the book from the drawer. She held it before herself for a moment, her chest heaving, then pressed it to Siena's chest.

"You must take this, and leave Rome. Now."

"What is happening?" Amara appeared in the doorway, face tight with fear. "Have you news of Dario? Of Romano?"

"No," Mila said. "Siena is leaving."

Frustration flared through Siena. "No, I am not leaving." She turned to Amara. "You know I won't leave you."

Amara nodded, a wobbly smile of relief on her face.

"It is not a choice," Mila said. "With my husband in custody, we are exposed. They will question him." Her voice broke, her eyes wild with fear. They all knew what "questioning" meant under Nazi occupation. Straightening her shoulders, Mila continued. "This must get out. Our work, it can't be for nothing."

She placed a suitcase on the desk that Siena hadn't noticed she was carrying. She opened it, revealing some folded clothes. Siena's clothes. Taking the book from Siena, Mila nestled it within the suitcase. Then her hands reached into her skirts, producing an envelope. "And this – one last message for the movement."

Siena stared at her in disbelief. "But, Mila, we stopped the messages, Romano told us to stop."

"I know, I know," Mila said, eyes tracking towards the doorway. "But it is important. One last message."

She slipped the envelope into the suitcase and clicked it shut, thrusting it at Siena.

Siena took hold of the suitcase automatically, glancing down. She frowned. "I don't understand," she said.

Mila gripped her by the shoulders. "This book is all our

work, all the art that has been taken from Italy. All that has been secreted away. It is the path back."

"Signora, if I am caught with this—"

"And I swore I would never involve you again. But—" Mila cut off, head jerking up, she went still as if listening.

Siena fell silent, her ears pricking up. The low rumble of a truck engine sounded from the street outside, then stopped.

"No time," Mila said. "We have to get you to safety."

"Mila, I cannot leave," Siena pleaded.

"This," Mila interrupted, "is all that matters. You must hide it. Finish your work for Romano. Get this book out of Rome. Get it safe. Send the letter. Then forget all about Romano. Forget all about me."

Siena blinked in shock. "Forget you?"

It was all happening too fast. Romano, the first stable figure of her life, was captured just days ago and sent away with Dario. This house, which had become a home for Siena, a sanctuary of love and learning, had been raided and violated. And now Mila, a woman who had become so important to Siena, a woman she'd trusted enough to share her secret, was telling her she had to go. Alone. Siena had found connection here, the first of her life. But the world was tearing it apart. She didn't want to go. She didn't want to be alone again.

A booming knock sounded on the front door. Amara glanced towards the door, eyes wide with fear.

Mila closed her eyes, taking a deep breath. "Santa Maria..." She shook her head, then gripped Siena's arm. "You must go. Now."

"Come with me," Siena said, frantic. "Both of you."

"No, we will only slow you down. Amara and I will stay. Buy you time."

"Even if I agreed to leave you, I have nowhere to go."

"You will flee south to Bari," she said, eyes fierce. "Go to the home of Auri di Bari, the curator of the Galleria in Bari and part of our network. You heard Romano speak of him, si?"

Siena nodded, mind reeling.

"Tell him I sent you. He will keep you safe."

Siena shook her head, panic seizing her chest. "How do you know that?"

The knock on the door boomed again, followed by loud orders shouted in angry German-accented Italian, leaving no doubt as to who waited beyond.

"I knew him, long ago, in Florence," Mila said, as she forced Siena towards the back door. "He will know you from this." She shoved a folded page into Siena's free hand. "It is a sketch of his."

"A sketch?"

Another bang sounded from the front door.

"There's no time. Go. Do as I say. Get to Bari. Hide the book. Disappear. After the war…"

She fell silent, unwilling, or unable, to make a promise no one knew could be kept.

Siena's body complied, though her mind fought against reason, seeking a way out for them all.

Perhaps the soldiers were only here to raid again and would soon leave? Surely they had not been discovered for their translations? Yet as her mind churned, realisation settled over her, and she knew Mila was right.

The Nazi's had come for the spy network.

Mila had to disappear.

And so did she.

Parts of the south were in Allied hands. She didn't know what that meant, not really. Germany had been their allies first and now they conquered and killed. Now Britain was Italy's friend. But what would that friendship look like on the village streets? At least the British weren't rounding up civilians and putting them in camps.

She grabbed Mila's hand, squeezing tight, and tried again. "We can run together – all of us."

Her eyes sought Amara's. The timid young woman shook her head sadly. "No, Mila is right. You have to do this. For Romano. For my Dario. It has to mean something."

Siena's head was shaking.

"It is too late," Mila said. "You must do this last task alone. And to do that you must go. Now."

"But I need you," she said quietly to Mila.

She felt Mila's hand cup her cheek, her skin soft and plump.

Their eyes met in the dim lamplight. "You are a light in the dark, child. Hold on to that gift. I have so much to tell you—"

The sharp crack of splintering wood shattered the moment as Mila pressed some coins into her hand for a train ticket. "But not tonight. Tonight, you must run."

She left with the last rays of the sun, as the shouts and screams from outside faded with the dark. Siena waited until mid-morning. The tram rattled down the strada as she made her way to the central train station. Outside, soldiers in German field grey stood, eyes scanning all who approached. She showed her papers, her breath tight in her chest as the young soldier ran his eyes over her. Then he flicked his head, ushering her through. Relief sluiced through her, and she walked forward, knees so unstable it was a wonder she didn't collapse to the floor.

They hadn't searched her bag.

She'd got it out.

The train journey across Italy was long and slow. Far before her destination, she was forced to abandon the train, the railways blasted apart throughout the contested territory. She continued on foot. About two hours from the coast she managed to hitch a ride on the back of a farmer's truck right to the edge of Bari. She paid the man a few coins and entered the gleaming white of the port city, the cultural capital of Puglia. Beautiful, rugged and hopefully safe.

No soldiers approached her, though she saw plenty of them strolling about the centre of the town, their uniforms blue and loose fitting, different from the Germans' in Rome, but no less intimidating. The port was practically overrun with sailors, the blue, red and white flag of Britain waving in the breezes that lifted off the Adriatic. Tall white stone buildings rose around her, cutting off the sun well before the dark of sunset, cooling the cobbles. The air on her arms stood up – from the drop in temperature or her mounting nerves, she didn't know.

At length, she came to the street she sought, the home of Auri di Bari. Pausing, she straightened her hat and brushed down her skirts. She was filthy and could smell herself. But it could not be helped; it had been a long and challenging journey to reach this city. Bracing herself before the door she placed her suitcase at her feet, sent a prayer to God for help and knocked.

PART 9
BARI, 1944

TWENTY-NINE
ALESSIA

"They'll cover it up."

Alessia looked up from the clothes she was sorting and watched as Siena crossed from the doorway, bucket of water hanging from her hands.

She had been home from the hospital for weeks now, but her arms still hurt. The healing skin pulled as she went about her daily tasks, and her damaged lungs burned. There had been no New Year celebrations that year, not for anyone in Bari.

Siena had stepped up, changing Alessia's bandages, applying the creams to her burns and shouldering the bulk of the housework. Going to collect the daily rations of bread and meagre flour.

Now the water.

The air raid had destroyed the main pipelines into the city, the water supply to the fountains in the Piazza Mercantile and the sewerage severed, leaving the citizens of all of Bari, old town and beyond, without sanitation and water. The British and US navies had swung into action, driving trucks of water into the central piazzas daily and rationing out buckets to the people of the city.

But it wasn't enough. Coupled with the razed buildings, the cold of winter and the food shortages, poor sanitation had led to an explosion of sickness. Fevers had ripped through the tightly packed city, the overcrowded homes, filled to bursting with relatives from the farmlands and towns destroyed by war or requisitioned by the military for airstrips and barracks, providing the perfect breeding ground for disease.

Life went on. What else was there to do but keep going?

Siena placed the bucket of water on the kitchen bench.

"You know I am right," Siena continued as she gathered up her knitting needles and the old black cardigan of Nonna's she'd been working to mend. Bianca was still dressed in mourning. She settled herself at the kitchen table as if it were something she'd done every day of her life.

The knitting needles started their rhythmic clacking, and Alessia marvelled at how seamlessly this stranger had become a part of their lives. Arriving from Rome in the dark of evening with nothing to vouch for her but a sketch by Alessia's papa and a story of a connection from Florence. But Alessia had seen something in the woman, something that made it impossible to turn her away. So she'd opened their home to Siena. It had been a risk, Alessia supposed. But it was not one she regretted.

After a tense start, Alessia and Siena had connected, beginning that day she brought extra flour home to share. Flour that reminded the street of their traditions. Now, as Alessia watched her friend knitting, she realised a deep bond had grown between them, a bond that would never sever. It was a beautiful wonder. Perhaps that was just how things were in times of war.

Alessia turned to the bucket of water. There was barely enough to wet a dishcloth. She dipped her hands in, cleaning away the dirt of the day, ready to start preparing supper. She didn't answer Siena's angry words. She didn't have the energy to argue.

"Not much today."

A wry smile formed on Alessia's face. "We will make do," she said, an echo of her nonna's words when it was Alessia returning with meagre supplies. How life could change.

Shaking her hands dry, Alessia picked up a knife and started chopping the withered carrots Siena had sourced that morning. A simplified version of pancotto stew, was about all she could scrape together today. Once her nonna had teased her about the dish. A classic of Pina's kitchen with dried fennel seeds and fresh cavolo nero, it was Marco's favourite – one her nonna had said, eyes twinkling, that Alessia would need to master. Today, all Alessia had available was carrot, onion ends and wilted greens. She didn't even have stale bread to thicken it. It would be thin.

"You know I'm right," Siena continued from her place at the table. She'd almost finished patching a hole in the cardigan.

Alessia sighed. It seemed Siena was not going to allow her to avoid this conversation.

"What do you mean?" she asked, though she knew.

Siena paused her knitting, eyes focused on the black wool. "They won't admit the gas. That should not have happened. It would be an international incident. The armies, our government. They will hide the truth."

The clack of her needles started up again and Alessia paused, knife hovering over the carrot as she considered Siena's words. A cover-up? But how?

So many people had been affected. The sailors and dockworkers, the people who lived along the coast. The townsfolk who ran to help, not knowing that the very air they breathed was poison.

So many injuries and deaths could have been avoided if they'd only known. What a betrayal of trust for the people of her city.

Men and women blinded by the toxin, their lungs ravaged. Others, burns and scars. And worst of all for those most affected, death. They still didn't know the full impact on the people of Bari. Many of the victims had been whisked into the countryside by worried families, hoping and praying that they would recover. Alessia had seen old Leonardo pushing a wheelbarrow, his brother Don curled up inside, prayers on his lips as he headed for the farmlands beyond the walls. She didn't think Don would ever be coming home.

How could the Allied officials cover up all of that pain and sickness and loss?

James had been genuinely sorry, and deeply ashamed of the gas explosion. Her knife carved forcefully through the carrot, connecting with the wooden board with an audible thud. She stopped, eyes closing as the flare of shame raced through her, hands falling still on the chopping board. James.

He had lied to her, made her promises in the dark and sworn to keep Niccolo and Luca safe. For two whole days they hadn't known Luca's fate. Thankfully he had been secured in a hospital, healing. He'd come home to Pina's sobbed prayers to God around the same time as Alessia. Niccolo still lay suffering in a hospital bed. Alone, night after night, when he should be safely tucked in bed upstairs.

James had done that. Part of Alessia still couldn't accept that truth.

Because she had done it too. She had opened the path for it all to happen.

"The fact we were bombed at all is more relevant," she said, trying to turn her mind away from the searing guilt that had embedded itself in her soul from the moment of James's confession.

"I knew..."

"You may leave."

Siena's clacking slowed, but she kept her rhythm as she regarded Alessia. "The port was always a target, no? Given the stream of supplies."

"Yet only days before the General was saying it could never be a target. Pina heard it on the radio. He said that the Luftwaffe were stretched too thin, that they could not possibly come to Bari."

Siena snorted. "Anyone who believed that after Rome is a fool." Her needles fell silent. "I am sorry," she said.

Alessia met her eyes and read the apology there. Shaking her head, she gathered up her chopped vegetables and paced to the stove by the window, plopping them into the pot of water that bubbled on the hob. Outside, the street was quiet and dark, the moonlight silver on the black waters of the Adriatic beyond. "It's all right," she said. "I know you weren't aiming that at me."

"You aren't a soldier," Siena pressed. "James should have known better."

Alessia rubbed her arms in a gesture intending to self-soothe. The friction against her healing skin hurt.

"I should never have let Niccolo work at the port," she said, releasing the shame that stabbed at her belly, giving it voice.

"No." She heard the rustle of Siena's knitting, the tread of her shoe as she crossed the room and gathered Alessia into an embrace.

Exhausted, pushed to the brink of her ability to cope by starvation, war, fear and injury, Alessia allowed herself to be held.

After a time she moved back from Siena's embrace. Her friend gifted her a sympathetic smile. "You made that choice on the information you had. Niccolo was starving. You all were. James assured you. You cannot look back on yesterday's choices with today's knowledge."

Despite the pain in her heart, her fear for Niccolo, her shame over James, the words rang true.

"Thank you," she whispered. She stepped back, wiping her cheeks dry with her sleeve. Inelegant and rude, but she didn't care. She knew Siena didn't either.

"You never trusted him though," Alessia said. Pausing, chewing on her lower lip, she cast her mind back to that first morning as Siena watched her talking to James from across the street, the look of suspicion in her eyes. Then her intervention nights later as she walked home from the chiesa. "How did you know not to trust him?"

Siena cocked her pretty head in thought, her voluminous curls falling over her shoulder, then shrugged.

"I think it comes from growing up without my parents," she said, leaning against the bench top. "Don't get me wrong; the nuns were gentle, kind even. We were safe. Guided by God." She stopped, her hand waving vaguely in the air before coming to rest at her side. "But when we come of age, life is up to us. As girls, we can join the congregation of nuns and pledge our lives to God. Or we can leave and make our own way.

"I left. And discovered the real world."

Alessia saw her face harden, her focus going distant as if looking far away.

"It is hard on your own, without a family name behind you. People treat you differently when they discover you are an orphan."

Alessia watched as her throat bobbed before she continued. "I always tried to hide it, when I was in Rome. But a name like Siena Innocente makes that hard."

"Innocente. It is a given surname, from the church, correct?"

"Si. Normally an orphan surname, but not always. I played on the fact that people couldn't be sure. I hid where I came from. Not much of a lie really, I truly don't know where I come from."

"You are a child of Italy," Alessia said.

Siena grinned. "You are kind. Perhaps that's why I told you the truth so soon."

"You were trying to warn me, about James."

"Even for that, I would not usually be so honest." Siena grinned, taking up the wooden spoon to stir the stew. "Go and sit. I can finish dinner."

"Are you sure?"

"Si, si. You need to take it slow. You are still healing."

"Grazie."

Alessia lowered herself stiffly onto a chair at the table, contemplating as Siena tore the greens with her hands and dropped them into the stew, steam rising around her head.

"You have meant more to me in these past weeks than I can express. I don't know what I would have done without you," Alessia said, the words flowing from her heart.

"Prego, but you have your neighbours, Pina, Valentina, even old Giuseppe. You would have been all right," Siena replied, deflecting.

"No," Alessia said. She wasn't going to let Siena reject the words. "I mean it, Siena. You have looked after me. I am grateful."

Siena turned from the stove and faced Alessia. Alessia felt her scrutiny as if she were searching for a lie or trick. Finally, Siena nodded. "Grazie," she whispered softly, returning to the stew.

The floorboards above them creaked as Nonna Bianca made her way from her room to join them for dinner.

"It feels so quiet without him," Alessia said. Without Nicco, the house was hollow and empty. So was Alessia.

"He will come home."

"Si," Alessia agreed, and crossed her heart, sending a fervent prayer to God.

"He will."

THIRTY
ALESSIA

The pail of water sloshed at her side. Alessia glanced down at the bucket. The liquid inside barely reached halfway. It wasn't enough, but it was all she could get. At least it wasn't too heavy for her to carry. This was her first morning returning to the piazza; she would be grateful for small mercies. She passed the bakery. The line-up for daily bread stretched around the corner, but the door was already closed. No bread today then. A breeze drifted up from the docks. Crisp off the cold coast, it stirred the pools of stench that festered across the city, mixing the fresh salt of the sea with the acrid tang of human waste. The sewerage pipelines, destroyed in the bombing raid months ago, had still not been replaced, leaving pools of excrement to rot in the open air.

A rat scurried across her path, its bulbous body fat, its skin flaky. There had been an explosion in the rodent population, well ahead of the usual summer increase. As the air turned warmer it would only get worse. And then the mosquitos would come.

They always came.

Alessia shook her head, banishing her worries as she passed

the Basilica. The repairs on the grand tower had been completed swiftly, prioritised by the Navy. Some of the citizens of Bari were angered by that choice; what did a building matter when their children went hungry? But it gave Alessia peace. The Basilica stood as it had for hundreds of years, a symbol of God and hope. She paused, watching the sunlight as it danced across the white walls, and took a deep and steadying breath.

Times were hard, but God was still with them.

Today was proof of that. For today, Niccolo was coming home.

He had been hospitalised for more than four months, the burns from the chemicals having ravaged his flesh. His nervous system was affected, causing him to spasm. But the British doctors had not turned him out. He'd remained under their care, just like the sailors and other dockworkers impacted during the blast.

Siena said it was the least they could do after such a horrific event. She placed the blame squarely on their shoulders. Alessia could only feel relief that her brother had remained under their experienced treatment.

It had worked. Today he was coming home.

Others had not been so lucky. It was a good fortune that Alessia would not forget.

Back home she secured the bucket of water in the kitchen. Nonna joined her, a small "tsk" sounded from her throat as she took in the half-full pail.

"We will make do," Alessia asserted, trying to reassure her. Nonna Bianca only shrugged.

Alessia regarded the old woman. Her grey hair hung limp around her gaunt face. She'd lost the plump softness of age in the months of worry over Niccolo. Alessia suspected her own face mirrored that trial.

"At least Niccolo's new sleeping space is arranged," Siena said as she came in from the front room.

A series of cheers rose up from the street outside, and Alessia met Siena's eyes, seeking strength from her friend. Running her hands down her dress in an attempt to straighten the poorly laundered cloth – there was simply not enough water for washing day – she moved to the door. Luca, Pina and Giuseppe stood in the street, hands raised to the sky clapping as two men made their way up from the town below. James's uniform was pristine, the buttons of his jacket glinting in the sunshine. At his side, stooped, slow, Niccolo shuffled.

Alessia longed to rush down the road to her brother. To wrap her arm around his waist and help him to their home. But she would not take his pride. His face was set in lines of determination. He wanted to walk unaided. At his side, James kept a watchful eye, ready to step in should Niccolo falter. Again, Alessia felt gratitude. To God for answering her prayers and bringing Niccolo home, and to James for seeing her brother safely here.

As they reached the small laneway that made up their neighbourhood, Giuseppe stepped forward, clasping Niccolo's hand. He took the opportunity to also grip the boy's elbow, steadying him. Alessia breathed a sigh of relief, seeing Niccolo lean into Giuseppe's strength. He looked up at her, eyes strained from the effort of the walk, a sheen of sweat covering his face.

"Welcome home," Giuseppe said, subtly taking Niccolo's weight and guiding him into their door.

"My boy!" Nonna Bianca cried, wrapping Niccolo into her arms and ushering him inside, Siena on their heels.

"I will follow shortly," Alessia said to Niccolo as he passed. His face was flushed but happy as he allowed his nonna to sweep him to safety.

Now alone at the front of the house, James stepped up to her.

"He did well," he said, not meeting her eyes.

Alessia regarded him, arms crossing instinctively over her belly.

The ice she felt towards the British translator had thawed since the bombing raid, but it had not vanished completely. The hurt was too deep.

James saw her reluctance and a sad smile flitted across his face. "I know you will see him to health." He stepped back from her, nodding, then turned and began the trek back down to the ruined harbour and his duties below. Alessia regarded him a moment, saw the slump of his shoulders, the heaviness in his tread. A part of her heart went out to him, longing to comfort him and to ease the guilt she knew he felt over his role in the destruction of Bari and the chemical impact on her city. But the other part, the larger part, withdrew, still too stung by the lie, by the fear.

Shaking off her confused emotions, Alessia retired inside, waving her thanks to her gathered neighbours. Pina came forward, halting her with a gentle hand. "We've water if you need it," she said.

Alessia took her hand and squeezed. "There is so little to go around. I would not take your ration."

"We can spare some," Pina insisted. "If you need it. For Nicco."

"Grazie, grazie." Alessia blinked rapidly to stop the well of tears that sprung to her eyes from gushing down her cheeks. She turned sharply away, in an attempt to disguise her emotions, and headed inside. She knew Pina would understand.

Nonna Bianca already had Niccolo settled in the bed Siena had set up for him in the downstairs space. They doubted he would be strong enough to take the stairs each day. He lay on the bed, buried in blankets, as Nonna Bianca fussed with the pillows. Siena hovered in the kitchen doorway.

Alessia crossed the room and drew the curtains closed. Darkness would help her brother to rest. The movement released the faint, stale scent of her papa's cigar, puckering her nose, and she paused, glancing at his chair in the corner, long empty. At least her brother was home.

Niccolo's eyes flew open and he reached out a hand towards her.

"Leave one open," he said. "It is nice to watch the sky."

Alessia smiled at her brother, pity cracking her heart. How many days had he spent inside, unable to feel the sun on his skin? Her brother, who loved to run free through the streets with his friends. Her Niccolo. "Si, si." Her hand dropped from the final curtain.

"Would you like something to eat? I have some biscotti..."

Niccolo shook his head, eyes drooping. The effort of walking through the winding streets of Bari from the hospital had clearly taken its toll. "I think I will just rest a bit."

"You need to eat for your strength," Nonna Bianca began, but Alessia silenced her with a touch.

"Sleep, fratellino, sleep little brother," she said to Niccolo; she hadn't used the affectionate moniker in years. "We will be nearby if you need us."

She drew Nonna Bianca with her into the adjacent kitchen, then wrapped her in a tight embrace.

At first her nonna stiffened, then her old joints relaxed, melting into Alessia's strength. Soon Bianca's body began to shake as sobs wracked her body.

"It is all right," Alessia crooned, holding her nonna tight. "He is all right. He is home."

She held her nonna until the old woman's tears ran dry. Then Nonna Bianca gently stepped back. Drying her eyes she said, "I think I might take a rest myself."

"Si, Nonna, si. Rest. Everything is settled."

"Come, I'll help you up the stairs," Siena said, taking Bianca's elbow.

Alessia smiled at her, thankful for the support of her friend.

She watched the women make their way slowly up the stairs before pulling out a chair at the kitchen table and settling herself down. Fatigue, sudden and crushing, weighed down on her body, and she longed to follow her nonna upstairs to rest. But there was work to do. A meal to prepare from the ration scraps she had managed to collect. Dusting to complete. Rat traps to set. Yet her head felt so heavy, her limbs so tired. Perhaps it would be all right to rest a moment, just a moment.

She folded her arms on the tabletop and lowered her face to her forearms. Eyes closing, she gave in to her weariness and drifted to sleep.

THIRTY-ONE
ALESSIA

Rome was liberated on 4 June 1944. Mussolini captured. The capital of Italy was free. The men of Puglia read the news in the papers. The women heard by word of mouth. Knowledge of the victory spread from house to house, and before the sun had fully risen, all of Bari Vecchia was buzzing with the news.

"Does this mean the war is over?"

"When will our sons come home?"

"Our rations will improve!"

The Allied sailors stationed in Porto di Bari walked with more spring in their step and spent their pay more lavishly. At least for a little while.

It wasn't long before the sense of hope evaporated. The conquest of one city, so far from the shores of Bari, meant little for the everyday lives of the Barese people. The ration lines were still long, the bread supply inconsistent, the flour allocation minimal. The days of summer were heating up, but the rains of spring had been poor. The population of the region, so tied to the seasons that ruled the crops of Puglia, braced for a difficult harvest to come.

Alessia was in the kitchen, pulling together a thin broth and yesterday's bread, when Pina's voice rang through from the open front door.

"Come in!" she called over her shoulder, knowing Pina would let herself through the curtained doorway.

"Luca!" Niccolo's joyful voice sang from his bed in the front room, and Alessia's heart swelled. Pina had brought her younger son to visit. Luca had been on the docks that fateful day last December but had avoided the chemical burns that had ravaged Niccolo's body. This was the first time the boys had seen each other since.

The scrape of Pina's heel on the stone floor told Alessia her neighbour had made her way through. Alessia went to her, a broad smile on her lips as she kissed Pina on each cheek.

"It is good to see you," she said, honestly.

The stairs overhead creaked as Nonna Bianca made her way down to greet their visitors.

"Ah, Pina, how good you have come," the old woman said, mimicking Alessia's greeting. Pina closed her eyes, a frown on her face. "I know I should have come sooner. But it has been a difficult time."

"There is no need to explain," Nonna Bianca said.

The horror of the bombing had rattled everyone in Bari. At least their two houses had been spared death. The same could not be said for far too many of their friends. But despite that good fortune, the war still clutched their hearts. Like Alessia's papa, Pina's eldest son, Marco, had been at war now for almost three years. Not one letter had made it back from either man. The weight of the silence weighed heavily on Pina. And on Alessia, too. She missed her papa and her friend deeply.

"Grazie," Pina said. She reached down into the bag that hung over her shoulder and produced two large loaves of bread. "I thought we could share supper."

"Oh, Pina, you and Luca are always welcome here for food.

But keep your bread. We know how tight the rations are," Alessia said.

"But stay for stew," Nonna Bianca enthused. "Alessia, fetch some basil from the front pot."

"Si, Nonna."

Small knife in hand, Alessia passed Niccolo and Luca in the front room, the two young men chatting excitedly. It was good of Luca to be so friendly with Niccolo. At almost seventeen, Luca was nearly a grown man. Niccolo gravitated to his maturity, as he once had to his brother Marco. She stepped through the soft-curtained doorway and onto the street. A cooling sea breeze laced with sea salt caressed her skin. Pausing a moment, she relished the relief from the heat of the day. It was already stifling, and summer had barely begun. Scanning Nonna's pots of herbs she identified the basil plant that looked the healthiest and bent to cut some stalks full of fat leaves. The scent of the herb and the earth it grew from conjured a memory: of walking through wildflowers, holding her mamma's hand, of the feeling of safety and love. Alessia paused, allowing the feeling to wash over her, savouring it. "I miss you, Mamma," she whispered to the skies.

Movement down the street caught her eye and she turned to see Siena approaching at speed, and raised a hand to wave to her.

At the sight of Siena's flushed face, Alessia withdrew her hand. She took a steadying breath as her friend drew close, her face as dark as a gathering storm and definitely promising similar violence.

As Siena joined her at the front of her house, Alessia put on her calmest expression. She didn't need to ask what had caused Siena's mood, she knew Siena would explain immediately.

"They didn't hire me."

The air whooshed from Alessia's lungs; it was as if the words had struck her in the middle of her belly.

"I am sorry, Siena. It is difficult to find work in Bari at the moment. There are so many people looking."

Siena slumped against the sandstone wall of the house, crossing her arms angrily across her chest. "Someone more experienced has come along," she said, then snorted. "Someone used their connections, or their fluttering eyelids."

"Siena!" Alessia hissed. "You shouldn't say such things."

Siena regarded her with eyes of fire. "And why not? If it's the truth."

"You can't know it is the truth," Alessia reasoned.

"I know it is something unfair," Siena retorted. "I have experience working in the archives of the Galleria di Roma. I should have no trouble getting work at a grocery stall."

"Lower your voice. We have visitors." *And neighbours*, Alessia thought to herself. It did no good to brag about your own accomplishments. Nor to suggest others had gained their employment unjustly. Siena may be experienced, but she was also an outsider. Alessia would never say it, but she doubted Siena would have luck over anyone local.

Siena paused, visibly calming. Alessia didn't know how she did that. A whirlwind one second, then still. "Pina and Luca?" she asked.

"Si," Alessia said.

Siena nodded. "That will be good for Nicco."

A flash of deep gratitude flooded from Alessia's heart. Siena could be brash and loud. But she had a caring soul. She felt her lips quirk in amusement and busied herself with the basil to hide it from Siena.

"It is good timing," Siena said to her bent back. "I came across these on my way home."

She held out a bag and Alessia peered inside. The brown paper was stuffed full of early harvest tomatoes.

Alessia eyed her friend. Tomatoes were plentiful in the season, but not in the city. Siena was not being entirely honest with her. The grumble of her stomach and the thought of filling an extra belly at supper silenced her questions.

Sometimes it was best not to know.

"Nonna will be thankful," she said instead and led Siena inside.

The meal of tomato and basil stew and soaked bread was hearty and satisfying, and Alessia sent a prayer to God for her family and friends. Between them they always seemed to find a way to fill their bellies.

As they ate, Niccolo talked, his words a stream of joy and excitement as he traded stories with Luca. In his words, the bombing raid became an adventure, the rationing a community challenge, the lack of water a welcome break from washing.

He did not mention his shaking limbs or the long, dark hours of the night when he woke, slick with sweat and fear. Scanning Luca's face, Alessia guessed he didn't need to explain that part. Luca already knew.

"And, Luca?" Niccolo prompted. "How is the repair work advancing on the port?"

"It is tough going," Luca began, though his weight shifted on his chair uncomfortably.

"At least you have work," Siena interrupted, bluntly turning the conversation from Luca.

"Siena!" Bianca said, eyes popping from her head. "Don't be rude."

Alessia shot her friend a warning glance and was rewarded with a reluctant shrug from Siena. "Someone more experienced always comes along," she said grudgingly.

"I'm out of work too," Luca said, eyes cast down. Alessia looked at him in surprise.

Now it was Pina's turn to exclaim in surprise. "Mio figlio, why? What did you do? The port is good work for you."

"It's nearly done," Luca replied, shoulders hunching forward defensively. "I asked about the railway repairs, but the

British haven't scheduled anything until the new year. I need work now. I was thinking of the farms. Harvest season is fast approaching, and with the men still away at the front..."

"The rains have been poor," Pina cautioned. "The fields have not ripened as we hoped."

Puglia could be plentiful and generous or could leave her people to starve. If the rains didn't come, the wheat wouldn't grow, leaving less flour for bread and pasta. Coupled with the large export of durum wheat out of Puglia into the wealthier regions of the nation, little was left for the people who made it grow. The food bowl of Italy left to starve.

Luca shrugged off her concern. "You could try with me," he said, eyes flicking up to Siena.

"That's men's work," Bianca cut in.

"Si, Nonna Bianca, si," Luca said politely. "In normal times. But I hear the farmers are desperate. There are... less of us."

Silence fell over the table, each alone with their thoughts of loved ones so far away at war: papa and Marco. Where were they? What were they going through? Why had they received no letters in so long? Niccolo shuffled nervously. Alessia blinked slowly, willing herself to remain composed as she searched for something to say to lift the mood, but her mind had gone blank at Luca's words. Thankfully Siena was there to move the conversation forward.

"It is a good idea," Siena piped up before shoving a large spoon of stew into her mouth and chewing loudly. "I will come with you tomorrow. Let's see if we can get some work in the fields."

"I will collect you at dawn," Luca said.

Out on the street, as they said their farewells, Luca plucked the two loaves of bread from his mother's bag. "Here, take these."

Siena frowned at the bread.

"Luca," Alessia began. "I already told your mamma, we've enough. Keep it for yourself."

"Trust me, for a day in the fields, you will need the extra food."

"One each," Siena announced, reaching across and securing one loaf, the larger one Alessia noted, from Luca's hands.

"Fair," Luca said, a small smile hovering on his lips.

Siena slipped the roll into her skirts and turned for the house. "At dawn?" she said over her shoulder.

"At dawn."

THIRTY-TWO
SIENA

The flies harried her eyes, landing on the beads of sweat that pooled in the creases of her cheeks. Insects buzzed, their wings vibrating incessantly as they flew around her ears. Plumes of mosquitos rose up over the farmland. A smattering of rain overnight, already long sucked away by the earth, had prompted their hatching. The bugs ascended from the earth, seeking the cool morning air that blew in from the coast and the blood of animals. One landed on her arm.

Siena slapped her sweaty palm down on her bare arm but missed the irritating insect. Pausing a moment, she placed her spare hand on the small of her back and massaged, easing the sore muscles that bunched tight there. Around her rows of almond trees stood, cast in the soft blue light of rising dawn.

"Lavoro – work!" a man shouted across a neighbouring field. Siena crouched down swiftly, hiding behind the dry, green leaves of the almond grove.

She was not here legally.

Pina had been right. Puglia was officially in drought. The failure of the rains meant low crop yields across the region. Even with the number of men at war, there were too few farms seeking workers to support the desperate population of Puglia, leading to increased unemployment and hunger.

But Luca and his friends were enterprising.

Leaving the sleeping streets of Bari Vecchia before the first rays of the sun, Luca, Paolo, Enzo and Siena made the trek out into the almond fields that bordered their city. Vast tracts of groves spread in neat rows across the flat, dry earth. The group spread out through the trees, each with a bucket and determined purpose: to steal the furry nut casings and sell them on the black market.

Stretch, pick, drop. Stretch, pick, drop.

Siena had known about the black market. She had profited from it herself, securing extra flour rations and some local tomatoes. But the idea of stealing from the surrounding farms to sell had never occurred to her.

She knew Alessia would not approve. Likely she would not have approved herself, before. But life in Rome under the strains of war and the reality of everyday living under occupation had taught Siena an important lesson: nothing mattered, except survival.

The small furry nut casings sat dry and wrinkled along the thin branches. They should still be plump, the nut within growing large and fat, but even this hardy crop had been affected by the empty clouds. The groves formed an oasis of green against the white walls of Bari, encircled themselves by fields of yellow wheat: white, green, yellow. The wheat fields stretched for miles around, spreading from the coast as far as Siena could see. Men worked in those fields, harvesting the durum for processing into flour. To Siena the golden husks of wheat looked rich and plentiful; the promise of the flour that could be ground from those grains made her stomach grumble in longing. Yet in truth, they were stunted and scrappy. The further the field grew from the coast, the drier and thinner the harvest.

The farmers blamed the lack of workers, saying vast tracts of the harvest went uncollected in the labour shortage. As Siena tented a hand over her eyes and surveyed the workforce of the field before her, backs bent, sweat shining across their browning brows, she doubted that highly. It was easier for the farmers to blame others rather than accept the fickle nature of the seasons.

But it wasn't the workers' fault. The anger – the blame that circled the streets of the cities and the rows of the fields – was borne of desperation and hunger. Of resentment and hopelessness.

For years the people had gone hungry. Those of Puglia hit harder than most. War in Europe, the fall of Mussolini, the conquests of Germany and Britain – these events had brought moments of hope, soon dashed by empty flour sacks and growling bellies.

There had been protests in nearby Taranto, a city even more ravaged by bombings than Bari had been the winter before. She didn't have to be a fortune teller to know that anger was coming to the city she now called home.

She reached up again, plucking a small, shrivelled almond from its nest in the tree and dropping it into her bucket. A hand landed on her back. Siena froze in fear, her fingers wrapped around her next almond.

"Don't move," Luca's voice hissed in her ear.

Siena stood motionless, her hand raised in the tree, but her eyes scanned. Through the sparse branches of the trees, she spied him. An older man, sleeves of his shirt rolled up to expose his muscled forearms and deep tan: the farmer.

The pressure of Luca's hand shifted on her shoulder, pushing her down towards the dry dirt that covered the roots of the tree. Siena allowed herself to be guided into a crouch. Risking the movement, she glanced behind her and saw Paolo and Enzo had done the same.

Finger pressed to his lips to order silence, Luca started

forward at a slow shuffle. Siena and the others followed. Bucket cupped to her stomach, legs burning from the unfamiliar motion, Siena crept behind Luca in a low squat. To their side the farmer leaned forward, eyes squinting as he inspected the curling leaves of his trees, close enough that Siena could hear him sigh in disappointment.

He wasn't wrong, she'd seen it too; the leaves were starting to dry, inside out, and it was only July. There was a long way to go for the summer season yet.

Sweat trickled down her spine, from the heat of the sun and the nerves of possible discovery. Working hard to control her breathing Siena kept moving, keeping pace with Luca's escape. They came to the end of the row of trees, the edge of their cover. From here, they would have to make a run for it. Luca looked back at Siena, nodding to her, then Paolo and Enzo in turn. Siena braced herself, sucking in a deep breath, ready to explode into action.

Holding up a hand, Luca mimed, "Three, two, one."

The four of them burst from the cover of the grove, feet pounding onto the hardened soil, puffs of dust flying up to coat their sweat-laced ankles in grime. A loud shout rose from behind their flight.

"Hey! Thieves! Stop!"

Siena didn't look back. Eyes forward, legs straining she raced on, plunging herself through the low-lying shrubs and scratchy bushes that lined the roadside. The road lay ahead of her, long and winding, the sandstone façades of Bari city in the distance. Luca was pulling away, his longer legs moving him forward faster than Siena could match. Enzo came up on her shoulder, glanced at her in apology and overtook her, then Paolo. Lungs burning as her body fought to draw in enough air to run, Siena tried for an extra burst of speed, hoping to catch up with the men that streaked away. She risked a glance back and saw the farmer, hard on her heels. Though older than

Siena, his labour-hardened body understood exertion and was strong. He pounded along the road behind her, getting closer and closer. Siena turned back, knowing she had to push. She couldn't get caught by the farmer. The penalties for stealing were steep. But for her, the real concern was how Alessia would react. Siena didn't have another place to go. She strained every muscle in her body, feet rising and falling. She fancied she could feel the farmer's breath on her neck, feel the tips of his fingers brushing against the bellow of her blouse. Then her foot caught a root. Siena tried to catch herself, but her momentum was too strong and she plunged head-first to sprawl across the dirt track. Her bucket of almonds flew out of her hands to crash to the ground ahead of her, the nut clusters spilling out onto the dust.

Knees screaming in pain, her arm torn and burning from the impact of hitting the ground, Siena managed to push herself up into a sitting position.

A shadow fell across her.

Chest heaving as she struggled to breathe, she looked up. The farmer stood over her, face contorted in anger and exertion.

"I am sorry," she said, then looked away.

She could feel his eyes boring into her. Shoulders slumping in on herself she waited for his rough hands to grab hold of her and haul her off to the police.

Feet crunched across the path. Siena looked up and watched as the farmer loped over to her now empty bucket. He squatted down, plucking the dusty almonds from the road and returning them to the bucket before walking back to her side.

"I'll take these," he said. "Be gone, don't let me see you out here again."

Siena looked up at him in shock. "You are letting me go?" she asked in surprise.

The man shrugged. "I have my stock," he said, holding up the bucket. "No crime."

Tears of gratitude sprung into her eyes and Siena managed to climb to her feet.

"Grazie," she said, voice sincere.

"Prego," the farmer said and turned away.

She stood alone in the middle of the road, watching as the old man made his way back towards his grove. Blood pooled along her forearm and across her knees where she had taken the bulk of the impact from her fall. Slowly, relief crept through her, replacing the disbelief at his kindness. She turned back towards the city of Bari, walking gingerly on her battered limbs. It had been a lucky escape. She could return home innocent of any crime. She was unlikely to receive such understanding and kindness again.

It wouldn't stop her from trying again tomorrow.

THIRTY-THREE
ALESSIA

The sultry air was heavy and cloying. Alessia wiped a hand over her forehead in an attempt to clear the sweat that gathered there in beads that threatened to drip into her eyes. The nape of her neck was wet with perspiration. She lifted her face to the sky, hoping to catch a gust off the Adriatic, but today the winds were still, the air around her stale with the scent of bodies and dirt. She ran a hand down her dress, self-conscious of her own smell; the material was stiff with dirt. The women lined up with her were the same. The intensity of summer, the water rationing and the still-broken pipes of the city meant washing was not a priority for water usage. It had been months since the streets blew the soft soap of drying laundry through the streets of Bari. The line before her moved, and Alessia stepped into the store. It was even hotter inside, somehow. Old Maria poured a measure of flour on her scales and then tipped it into Alessia's proffered dishcloth.

"Siena is working the farms," the old woman said, regarding Alessia greedily.

Alessia knew what she was hinting. Those who worked may

have spare coin to purchase more rations, and eat better than the rest.

But despite Siena's daily toil, her pay was patchy and poor. Alessia had no coin to spare.

"Not today," was all she replied.

Maria shrugged, her attention instantly turning to the next woman in line.

Alessia walked out and stopped. Something was different.

She paused on the step, opening her senses, working to understand what had caused her heart to suddenly flutter in premonition.

Down the line of waiting women, a similar sense of urgency flowed, heads turning back towards the old town walls. Alessia's eyes followed the direction of their attention, and her breath caught in her throat. The men came first, rounding the corner, arms raised high above their heads, hands clutching tools or boards of wood. They shook their hands at the sky, voices shouting an angry chant.

"Work for men. Work for men. Women at home. Women at home."

Instinctively Alessia pressed back against the store wall, keeping to the shadows of the eves as the enraged men surged onto the street, heading for the Town Hall. As the group of protestors continued past, women appeared in their ranks. Young, old, even little girls and boys still in their ribbons and shorts. Alessia sucked in a harsh breath as Pina came into view.

Shock rattled along her limbs. How could she? With no husband to support her, her eldest son at war, and her home full of guests to feed, Pina knew better than anyone the difficulties of life in Puglia this season. She knew Siena had gone with Luca to find work in the farms that surrounded them. How could she protest against that?

Pina raised a hand, her fingers gripping a wooden spoon, her face contorted in fury. As she passed her head turned, and the two women's eyes met. Shame flashed across Pina's face, swiftly replaced with defiance as she turned away, lifting her voice to join the chant. "Women at home, work for men."

It wasn't the first such protest that Bari had seen. As the bloody war continued and the control of Puglia by the Allied forces stretched on longer and longer, the tensions on the streets expanded. Traditions ran deep in Italy. The importance of family and home, the role of women and men. And in Puglia, that expectation was especially held.

War had changed that. Twice in twenty years.

Change rarely stuck in Puglia.

Understanding that didn't assuage the disappointment that weighed on Alessia's heart at seeing the protest – at seeing Pina. Saddened, she headed home.

He was waiting for her on the street outside her home, standing tall and pristine. Clean.

Alessia shuffled uncomfortably in her dress as she drew near.

He wasn't welcome, not at the best of times. But now, as she walked home, a sheen of sweat covering all of her body, her dress stiff from grime, he was wanted even less.

She didn't wish to feel below him. She didn't want him to smell her.

"Signorina," James said, a pensive smile on his face.

"What are you doing here?"

His face fell slightly, and guilt sliced into Alessia's chest. She didn't want to hurt him, at least not anymore. But he had hurt her, and Niccolo, so deeply.

James's feet shuffled as he glanced down, shamefaced.

Alessia took a stabilising breath, fighting the confusion of emotions that battled within her – anger and worry, pain and pity – and relented.

"Are you all right?" she began, genuine care in her voice. "I know there have been riots. I believe a new protest is happening right now. Is that why you are here? To check on us? On me?"

James looked up sharply, eyes tracking over her head. "A protest? Now?"

Alessia nodded. "Jobs for men," she quoted.

He cursed under his breath and met her stare. She saw the indecision there. Caught as he was between his duty as a sailor and his duty to his heart.

"Here," he said suddenly, shoving his hand forward. In his grip was a small bottle of shining pills.

Alessia gasped, recognising what he held before her. "For Niccolo," James said, rushing now. "It is quinine, coated with chocolate. To help it go down."

"I know," Alessia breathed, stunned. The British had been handing out the chocolate-flavoured anti-malarial drug to the children of the street all summer, youngest first, in an attempt to keep the seasonal sickness at bay. But there wasn't enough. Like everything else in Italy, there was never enough. And Niccolo, being nearly fifteen, didn't make the list, even in his debilitated state.

Alessia had covered his bed with netting and prayed that the diseased mosquitos would keep away from her vulnerable brother.

"How?" she asked, hand reaching forward to take the medicine.

"It is the least I could do," James said. His fingers gripped hers as she took the bottle, holding her hand for a moment, face open and honest.

"Grazie," Alessia breathed, heart pounding in her chest.

He paused a moment longer, then dropped her hand.

She saw the regret on his face, and the longing.

"Go," she said. "We can talk later."

"Can we?" he asked, soft, hopeful.

"Si."

The strain on his face softened momentarily. Then he straightened. Nodding once, he turned for town and the protest unfolding on the streets of the Piazza Mercantile.

She watched him as he strode away towards the Town Hall and prayed the mob she'd seen advancing in protest had calmed. James had betrayed her trust and risked Niccolo's life and health.

But Alessia couldn't bring herself to hate him, or to wish him ill.

She stepped inside and went straight to Niccolo.

"Here, take these."

He took the bottle, rattled the tiny pills within and eyed her dubiously.

"It's quinine, for malaria."

"How did you get that?"

"Take one now, and then every morning," she said heading for the kitchen. Bianca stood in the doorway, sharp eyes narrowed on Alessia as she passed.

"Where indeed?" her nonna said.

"It will keep him well," was all Alessia replied.

After dinner, Siena, Nonna Bianca and Alessia settled on the front porch. A refreshing breeze had finally begun to kiss across the steamy summer streets, bringing much-needed relief. Bianca sat, resting against the rough stone wall of their home, long skirts turned up above her knees to allow her legs to feel the cool. Alessia sat beside her, one of Niccolo's two pairs of trousers across her knees, her fingers working a needle to patch some fraying material. He needed to get another season out of the worn trousers.

Along the street their neighbours slowly appeared, drawn as they were by the promise of release from the stifling heat. As the sun sat fat and orange on the horizon, Pina returned. Her dress was sweat-stained and dusty, a small trickle of blood glowed on her temple, and her hand still clutched her wooden spoon.

Bianca sniffed loudly and stood. "I think it's time to retire," she announced over-loudly. "There's a stench in the air."

"Goodnight, Nonna," Alessia said, keeping her eyes down. Siena remained sitting, but a fire had lit in her eyes.

As Bianca removed herself, a ripple of whispers flowed down the street. Pina approached.

Keeping her eyes on her mending, Alessia willed the woman to pass without stopping. She had no wish to speak with Pina, nor to antagonise her. But soon her neighbour's shadow fell over her work, and she was forced to look up.

Pina looked at her, a challenge in her eyes, but sadness twisted her lips.

"My son needs work when he returns," she said simply. "We need the money."

Pity flooded Alessia's heart. Pina's choice to protest, to stand with the men of Puglia against the women, had hurt Alessia. But in that moment, she understood.

Everyone was strained to breaking. Everyone needed more, but there was no more to go around.

Pina was simply fighting for her family, for her child. For Marco, who was so dear to Alessia too.

Who was Alessia to judge her for that?

In this time of little, in this fight for survival, who was anyone to judge their neighbour?

She stood slowly and gestured to Pina's bloody temple.

"It was violent? You are hurt?"

Tension released from Pina's shoulders, and the older woman shrugged. "Some windows were broken, and a few were aggressive. I slipped. I am all right."

"I have water to clean it," Alessia offered.

Pina smiled, understanding what Alessia was really offering. As friends, Pina had once offered Alessia water. Now, as a truce and way forward, Alessia offered the same.

"No, grazie, I will be all right."

"Si?"

"Si."

"Goodnight then."

"Goodnight." Pina paused. "You will make a wonderful wife," she said, then limped away, head held high, before the line of watching neighbours, their whispers falling silent as she passed. Alessia returned to her mending. They might not agree, but then, who did in Italy?

Tradition versus change. Men versus women. Rich versus poor. It had long been the way. It likely always would.

She felt Siena's incredulous stare boring into her side but chose to ignore her fuming friend.

Alessia could not speak for others, but she could choose for herself. And she had chosen, she realised. She had chosen her people, her community. No matter what – the people of her nation, of Puglia – Alessia would always stand beside them.

To whatever end.

PART 10

FLORENCE, 1921

THIRTY-FOUR
EVA

As the last weeks of summer beat down on the over-heated streets of Florence, Eva existed in a world of only Amadeo Renzetti. From the soft sheets of his roof-top apartment chambers on the north side of the city, they watched the sun rise and fall, limbs entwined. Slowly the bright orange of dusk began to mellow, and the currents of the wind crisping, signalling the coming new semester and a return to her studies. A return to the role of student.

Eva had not picked up a brush since that magical day in the studio when Amadeo had swept her into his arms. She hadn't thought of her work since that day either, coaxed gently from her artistic drive by Amadeo's touch.

Now, as she lay in spent ecstasy, a bolt of sunlight warming her naked body, Eva felt her mind sharpen.

She was Renzetti's woman, of that she felt sure. But she was also his student. What would that look like as her fellow pupils returned from their summer break to continue their studies?

What would it look like to Elio?

The soft scuff of footfall drew her from her thoughts, and she rolled onto her side to watch Amadeo cross to her, a tray of breakfast coffee held before him. Sitting up, she took the tray and waited as he settled beside her. The warm steam from the rich drink found her nose, and she breathed deeply, the scent bringing her senses alive. Amadeo pressed a kiss to her forehead and took his cup and sipped.

"Have you heard from Elio?" he asked, voice casual, almost distracted.

Eva felt the corners of her mouth twitch into a smile. How connected they were already; she had just been thinking of her brother.

"Not since he first left for Rome. Have you?"

Amadeo shook his head and sipped again. "I hope he will return for the new semester," he said.

A flush of worry shot through Eva and she turned to Amadeo. "I am sure he will," she said, concern for her brother and his artistic dreams beating in her heart. She knew how Elio had struggled here at the Accademia; it was a challenge she too had faced. When he left for Rome she had despaired. But over the hot summer weeks, Eva had rediscovered her passion. Surely Elio had too?

Amadeo merely shrugged. "We will know soon enough."

Crestfallen by his seeming indifference, Eva slumped. To study here in the Accademia was Elio's dream. It couldn't come to an end so soon.

"Peace amore," Amadeo said. Reaching between them, he gripped her chin gently in his fingers, turning her to face him. "Elio will make his own choices. As you must too. As we all must." Soft eyes scanned her face, his lips curving in a reassuring smile. Calm settled over Eva. He was right, she knew. He was always right. She could trust in his wisdom. He had guided her progression on the canvas, and their love. If Amadeo said it would be all right, it would be.

But still... she hoped, for her brother and their shared dream.

"All the students will be returning soon," Amadeo continued, pivoting the subject.

Eva felt her shoulders tense, sensing the direction this conversation must be going.

"You will return to your lodgings across the Arno?" It was phrased as a question, but Eva knew it was not, even as she was blinded by love.

"Si," she said quietly.

She felt the mattress wobble as Amadeo shifted his weight, collecting up the tray and depositing it on the bedside table. "Amore," he crooned, wrapping his arms around her and drawing her close. She allowed herself to be gathered up in his embrace, the musty scent of him filling her nose, igniting her senses, and her desires.

"You know I love you, don't you?" he said, mouth against her temple.

Eva nodded, her throat suddenly too tight with emotion for her to speak.

"Our time will come. Soon the world will know of my love for you," he said. "But I would not have my affections stand between you and your talent. You have a career before you, my love. I will not allow the jealousies of others to hold you back. I will not hold you back."

Eva pulled back, staring at him in shock. "You would not hold me back. You are the reason that I will succeed!"

He smoothed her hair back from her brow. "You know how people talk. You are the greatest talent that has walked into my classroom in decades. I want to see you discover all of your ability, to reach for the stars and the moon! But if people think I am giving you preferential treatment…"

He glanced away, and Eva found her hand shooting out to cup his cheek, his morning stubble rough against her palm. "That will not be. I will not allow such talk," she promised fervently.

"I know, amore," he replied, pressing his forehead to hers. "So we must be private, just for a little while. Until you are through your studies. Then we can be together, openly."

"I wish we could be honest." Eva pouted, feeling suddenly very vulnerable and alone.

"It is the best way," Amadeo said. "And you will see. In a lifetime, it is not so very long."

So logical. So confident. He always knew just what to say to reassure her. In the turmoil of coming to Florence, Amadeo had become her place of stability, her foundation.

"I love you," Eva whispered.

He replied with a kiss, soft then hard and demanding, and they gave their morning up to each other's bodies.

She returned to her rooms over the Arno that evening. Signora Pesci greeted her warmly. "It was a nice visit with your family, I trust?" Eva nodded, hating the lie, but knowing that the truth would see her turned out on the streets. It was not the done thing for young unmarried women to stay overnight with men. Scandalous. And in that moment, as she mounted the stairs to her room on the second floor, Eva realised the full truth of Amadeo's words. Their love was real and pure. But their choice to act on it before marriage would not be accepted. And it would affect how her study at the Accademia was viewed. As much as it hurt, she would have to accept this time apart, even if it felt like purgatory.

That night her room felt cold and empty. Despite Signora Pesci's immaculate cleaning, Eva fancied she spied dust motes twirling in the cool beam of moonlight that chanced a glimpse through her window. How cold this space seemed, how disconnected. After weeks in Amadeo's arms, the change grated. Lying there alone she wondered if she really cared about her studies at all. She could give them up, be with Amadeo now. Perhaps that would be the better way?

Emilia arrived back from Milan the next morning. The

shining eyes of her dear friend helped to assuage some of Eva's melancholy. As the two friends embraced Eva felt her heart lift, grateful to no longer be alone in this boarding house on the wrong side of the Arno.

"Ah, Emilia, darling, how is your family?"

"Well, well," Emilia beamed. "And how are you? Was it awful being here alone all summer?"

"The signorina ended up travelling home," Signora Pesci supplied, and Eva felt her gut plummet.

"Oh? How wonderful," Emilia said, eyeing Eva. She had said no such thing in the letters the friends had exchanged over the summer break. Eva turned from her friend's questioning eyes. "Come, let's get you settled."

Once in their rooms, Eva braced herself for the barrage of questions she knew Emilia had building behind her teeth. But Emilia simply walked to the window to gaze out over the grey streets of the quarter. "How I have missed this place. And you," she said, turning to smile at Eva. "It is good to be back, si?"

"Si," Eva agreed, feeling relief at this unexpected reprieve. Perhaps the secret of Amadeo would not be so difficult to keep after all.

The rest of her classmates returned over the next few days, and the Sunday before classes recommenced found them together at their regular cafe, reminiscing on their holiday weeks, and anxious for their studies ahead. Alessandra was in love. She'd met a family friend when visiting her parents in Rome, and swept up by that passion she was unsure if she would continue her studies. Oskar was refreshed, his summer spent travelling having inspired his purpose. "I think I want to start cartography," he announced.

Matteo was as brash and confident as always, but Eva had

known him long enough now to see the tick in his eyebrow, the giveaway that revealed his true nerves.

"And where is Elio?" Eva looked up, meeting Matteo's piercing stare. She'd known the question was coming. But just as when Amadeo had asked her days before, Eva still had no answer.

He had not written, not even in reply to her own correspondence. Their mother had not heard from him either. Lessons began at 9 am sharp the next morning, and he still had not walked through the doors into Signora Pesci's boarding home.

A warm hand on her forearm drew her attention as Emilia leaned forward. "He will be here. We all know Elio would not have given up. Whatever some of us may hope..." She skewered Matteo with her eyes, and he turned away, frowning. He was ambitious, they all knew. If someone left their studies, that was one less person Matteo had to best. Matteo stood up, grumbling something about going to confession.

"Grazie," Eva whispered to her friend.

Later that night as the two women made their way across the warm, dusty cobbles of the piazza, Eva asked Emilia, "Do you really believe what you said to Matteo? That Elio will be here tomorrow?"

Emilia walked a few steps in silence, a muscle in her jaw twitching in the pale lamplight. "You really have not heard from him?" she asked.

Eva shook her head.

Emilia sighed. "Then I do not know. Of all of us, he always seemed the most... passionate. At least at the beginning. He was like a fire, blazing. But he took the criticisms the most harshly too..."

"He did," Eva agreed, heart squeezing at the memory of her brother's desolate face the last time she'd seen him. When he chose to leave...

"Amadeo encouraged him to go to Rome," she found herself saying.

"Amadeo? You mean Professor Renzetti, surely, Eva!" Emilia admonished. Eva frowned, feeling the heat of embarrassment flush her cheeks. "Si, Professor Renzetti. Elio and he had grown close. It is merely how my brother referred to our tutor."

She felt Emilia's suspicion in the tightness of her friend's body, but she said nothing as they continued on through the gathering dark.

"It was awful when he left so suddenly," Emilia said. "We were all so surprised. I was surprised."

Eva braced herself. This was the closest either her brother or Emilia had come to admitting that an affection had grown between them. An affection Elio's silence had surely stifled.

"We all must follow our own paths," she said, squeezing Emilia's arm in comfort.

"I guess that is true," Emilia agreed, but her voice remained soft, sad. Eva stopped, turning her friend to face her. "Emilia, you have a true talent. Your father and mother are artists at the height of their skill. You will find your way to the sun with them."

"Grazie for your belief." But her head shook and her stance stiffened. "It has been a long summer, that is all. And how I have missed you!"

The shift in focus was liberating.

"I have missed you too," Eva said as the flood of joy for the friendship blossomed through her.

And as the two friends embraced beneath the looming red dome of the Cattedrale di Santa Maria del Fiore, Eva realised it was true. Whatever her brother had decided for himself, Emilia was her true friend.

THIRTY-FIVE
EVA

The room was hot with tension. The air stale with the sweat of suspense. Emilia crossed the room and forced the window open with a grunt, the wood of the frame swollen with heat.

A breath of wind drifted in off the Arno, tickling the sheen of perspiration that rested on Eva's upper lip. She licked off the salty evidence of her nerves and straightened her posture.

Professor Renzetti was late. Their lesson should have begun half an hour ago.

Scanning the collection of her fellow students – dressed in their best, easels set ready, hands fidgeting in laps – Eva realised it was intentional. Their professore was making them wait on purpose.

The realisation made her blink in surprise. Had he done this at the start of their studies too? Making them sit in expectation, allowing their inner tensions over the study to come to boil inside them? She couldn't be sure. She'd been so worked up that day, so nervous about the lesson to come, that she barely remembered any of it. But she suspected he had made them wait, had made a grand sweeping entrance to capture them all in his spell. But why?

To make them uneasy?

To force them to face their fears?

Or something else...

The echo of leather soles slapped from the hall beyond the door, drawing Eva from her thoughts. The room around her fell silent, still. A collective air of anticipation was breathed in. And the door swung open. Amadeo Renzetti strode in. But he was not alone.

Beside him strode Elio. The two men walked in time, heads turned towards one another, lips moving in fervent conversation.

Eva's mouth fell open in shock. Elio had returned from Rome? But when? As she'd said her bedtime prayer the night before, she'd accepted he would not be back in time for the new semester – had sent a prayer to God to watch over him and give him peace.

Yet here he was, strolling into the lecture room with Amadeo, chatting casually.

Elio glanced up, smiling across the room at her. She shoved down her surprise and smiled back, though she suspected it didn't reach her eyes. He had been gone for months and had not sent word to her even once. How she'd worried. How she'd prayed.

And now here he was. Returned. But it wasn't to her that he came first.

It was Renzetti.

The two men paused on the edge of the circle of students, sharing a companionable laugh before shaking hands. Then Elio turned to take up the one spare easel in the room. The one beside Eva, that she'd prepared for him, hoping against hope. He took his seat, rolling up his sleeves as if everything was exactly as expected, and turned his attention to their professor at the front of the room.

"Students," Renzetti cried, lifting his arms high above his

head. "Welcome. I hope you are refreshed after your summer sun and that you practised our lessons from last semester..."

A pause. "Si, Professore," they chorused in answer.

"Bravo, bravo," he said. Then, looking directly at Eva, eyes twinkling, he said, "Because we are about to throw it all out, and learn how to be truly great!"

By the end of the day's lessons, Eva felt lost and confused. While she'd toiled at her canvas, doing her utmost to "follow the paint", her efforts afforded her little more than a cursory glance from Renzetti. Elio, however, was heaped with praise and honours.

Watching from the corner of her eye, Eva saw how her brother's brush attacked his canvas, his movements stabbing and intense. Again and again, Renzetti was drawn to Elio's side, his body twitching, his expression elated. At the session's end, their professore took Elio's canvas in his hands and held it up for all to see. At first all Eva saw was a spray of colour, but as she studied her brother's work the shape of a man in silhouette came into focus. Around his head a whirl of colours, violent in their movement across the canvas. She didn't know why, but it made her uncomfortable.

"The beginnings of greatness," Renzetti announced, before returning the canvas to the easel and shaking Elio's hand.

"Think on today," he said to the class. "Until tomorrow, you are dismissed."

Eva began to clean her brushes, her limbs moving automatically as her mind whirled. All the confidence she had gained over the summer, and in Amadeo's bed, had vanished in one lesson.

Was he simply keeping his distance for show?

Or had she really slipped back to her poor performance?

She was so deep in her thoughts she didn't notice that Elio had come to her side.

"Gelato?" he said, and Eva jumped. Turning, she faced her brother, a deep frown creasing her forehead. "You didn't write. Not even once." The words were sharp, hurt and honest, and Eva didn't back down from her tone.

Elio smiled softly, nodding. "I missed you too," he said. And just like that, Eva forgave him. A flood of relief replaced her consternation and she hugged Elio close.

"I'd love a gelato," she said, pulling away. "But you're paying."

They walked arm in arm through the streets to the piazza. There, Elio purchased two small paper cups of gelato, lemon flavoured, the last of the seasonal fruit from the coasts of Tuscany. Handing one to Eva he led her to the steps of the Galleria. There they made themselves comfortable, savouring their sweet treats in the warm afternoon sun.

"You've improved," Elio said between licks of his icy delight.

"I am not sure professore thinks so."

"He does," Elio assured her. "His eyes were lighter as he watched you work. You know he isn't one to give much praise."

"He could not praise you enough!" Eva countered incredulously.

Elio nodded, eyes tracking over the square as he finished his treat. "I think," he said at last, "that Rome was good for me."

Eva cocked her head at him in silence, allowing him the time to find his words and continue.

"It is a big city, Eva. Bigger than I imagined. Full of people, and so... filthy. But, under that layer of grime, there is a beautiful soul. And that is where I found it."

"Found what?"

"My reason. The core of my love for painting. It is in the people of the streets. In the too-thin child begging for bread, in the torn shirt of the labourer, the tired eyes of the desperate mother.

"Poverty, Eva. It is everywhere."

Eva frowned. "We know of poverty, Elio," she said gently. "We saw it in Papa's fields. It has been kept from our doors only by Papa's clever dealings on the land..."

"A responsibility that will one day be mine," Elio said, clenching his jaw. "And one I increasingly doubt I can perform."

"What do you mean?"

He turned to her, taking her hands in his, his fingers slightly sticky from the melted gelato. "Eva, Italy is not what she once was. Before the war, things were different. Now... now, there is growing restlessness. There are no jobs for the men I fought beside. Children go hungry. And the government sits back and feasts off us all."

"Things are not so different—"

"They are! We were once an empire! A rich land of trade, art and science. What are we now? A holiday stop for wealthy foreigners? We used to be more. And we can be again."

"Elio," Eva said, squeezing his hand. "I don't understand."

"In my travels, I read a newspaper article by a man named Mussolini. It led me to a group of political thinkers. They are part of a new movement, looking to elevate our country. They call it Fascism. It's based on traditions, returning us to the Italy we once were."

"Politics? Elio, you've never given time to such things."

"And that has been my mistake. Don't you see, Eva? All our lives we have seen the men toil on Papa's land and seen their children going hungry on market day. You used to sneak lollies for the maid's daughter..."

Eva smiled at the memory: chubby fingers reaching for her candy; bright, joyful giggles as the candy was popped into a grinning mouth.

"But the wolf has never been far from our door," Elio continued. "You saw how those with more land lived. In their grand homes, with their fields. And how they threatened Papa, constantly working to sneak his land from under him. To claim everything for themselves.

"It doesn't have to be that way. Italy can be different."

"Through politics?"

"Through each of us. These men, they talk of a new path. One that will make us all equal, and safe and fed. A return to our true roles—"

"True roles? What do you mean?"

"Family, Eva. Family must come first."

That she understood. She would do anything for those she loved. "And this realisation, this has opened your art?"

"Amadeo told me that I had to find my reason, my passion. In here," he reached over and tapped Eva's chest just above her heart, exactly as Amadeo had done that day in the studio. "My reason is Italy."

"Amadeo," Eva whispered in surprise. Her brother had called their professor by his given name, as she had once done before Emilia.

Elio huffed a rueful smile. "Disrespectful of me. I should not refer to our professore so casually. You are right to call me on it. I only meant it in affection. He has shown me what I needed to see. Allowed me to find my calling. I feel close to him because of that."

His eyes shone bright with love, and happiness flooded through Eva. Gratitude for the wonderful man that was her Amadeo. He had taken the time to understand her brother and had shown him a path through his self-doubt.

So overcome by emotion was she that her lips parted, ready to tell Elio everything about her summer with Amadeo. How he had helped her to find her passion too. And her first taste of love. True and forever love.

But Amadeo's wish for secrecy silenced her. Though it pained her to keep something so vivid and exciting, so important, from her brother, she knew she would not betray her lover's confidence. The time to tell Elio would come.

Instead, she simply agreed. "He has shown you the right path. And you have walked it. I am truly happy for you, Elio."

"He has. And so have the fascists I met. I always loved our country, Eva. War... it took that from me, at least for a time. But in Rome, I found that love again. It is in me. Finally, I see what we were fighting for. And what I must keep fighting for."

"Through your art."

"And my voice. If we stand together, Eva, we can all be safe and fed."

"And live our dreams."

"Live as we should."

Eva liked the sound of that.

THIRTY-SIX
EVA

The semester wore on as the afternoon air cooled, and Eva felt bereft. Renzetti made little time for her, outside of sweaty clutches in the storeroom, or down narrow alleyways on the way between the studio and his apartments. The excuse of protecting their secret always on his lips.

In the studio she toiled, but that moment of brilliant inspiration from months before continued to elude her. Amadeo offered her nothing more than disappointed frowns, or small noncommittal nods.

At the easel beside her, Elio flourished, his work increasingly bold in colour and design.

Within the first weeks of the new semester, he stopped coming to the cafe with Eva and the others, feigning fatigue, or "other commitments". Eva wasn't the only one who wondered where he was really going. She didn't miss the growing disappointment in Emilia's eyes, the question in her face as she glanced at Eva: what was Elio doing?

Eva honestly didn't know, and she was just so tired...

Fatigue had settled over her as the autumn browned the trees of Florence. Bone-deep weariness, the like of which she'd not experienced since the malaise of malaria she'd suffered as a child, pressed her down. Each morning when Elio parted the curtains to the pale new day, Eva woke stiff and sore, her limbs heavy, her head pounding. The sensations did not lift with breakfast, nor did the walk to the studio through the calm streets of the city buoy her spirits as it used to. It was like she'd drunk too much wine the night before when all she'd sipped was lemonade or orange.

No one seemed to notice her malaise, and Eva didn't wish to admit to it. She'd worked too hard for too long to admit the fresh doubts that seized her in a vice-like grip in the quiet hours of the night.

Eventually, she admitted her fears to Elio, in a stolen moment the siblings shared between classes with their professore.

"I just feel so lost," she confessed, desperate for reassurance and support. Elio had been the same only a few months before. He'd gone to Rome and found inspiration, and now he flourished. So she spoke of her challenge, seeking his encouragement, his understanding and guidance.

She got nothing.

Shrugging distractedly and turning away, Elio said, "Perhaps this life is not for you."

Eva's step faltered. "Elio? Why would you say that? This has been our dream for as long as I remember. We talked of this as children..."

"We were young. We didn't know how the world truly worked. We do now."

"What have you seen that changes my path so directly?"

"You are a woman."

Shock blasted through Eva. "That is not new information."

Elio breathed a laugh. "No, it's not. But realising what that means... The patriots in Rome—"

"Oh, Rome, Rome, Rome! That is all you talk about. Come

on then, what did the all-wise boys of Rome say?" Eva cut in, vicious. A swell of hot anger was bubbling up within her, driven by a sickening feeling that she knew where this was going.

"The *men* in Rome," Elio continued calmly, voice as patronising as though he was speaking to a wilful child, "explained the importance of our roles. Male and female. We are different, after all. Society functions best when we honour that. Men provide, and women are mothers. It is what you are born for. Perhaps this direction is taking you from your true desires."

Eva stared at her brother, flabbergasted. "You know I harbour no desire to be pushed aside by men. You have seen Mamma's life, at the whim of Papa. Poor because of his choices. You would wish that for me? The whole point of coming to Florence, of taking control of our lives, was to elevate ourselves above our station. To find more for ourselves."

"Eva, I know," Elio said. Placing his hands on her shoulders he faced her directly. "And in that we were partly right. But it is not your job to do that. It is mine. I am the man of the house – or will be when Papa finally accepts my help. The care of you and Mamma, and my future wife and children: that is my responsibility. Hopefully you marry well, and your husband will care for you. But if not, Eva, you know I will always ensure you are safe."

Eva jerked away from Elio's grip. "How can you say this?" she hissed, tears of hot frustration welling in her eyes. "When you went to war I had to stand tall. I worked alongside mamma under the hot sun of harvest. I did as much – more – than any man to keep our family fed."

"I know, and I will always be grateful. But don't you see? This is where the problem started. We went to war, and women were forced from their true purpose, into men's work. Then the men came home, but there was no work for them, and women had forgotten their place. And now, the country is trying to rebuild, to return to its power. I've been meeting with others here in Florence. They agree; it is time to return to our traditions."

Eva stared at Elio. "That's where you have been going? To meetings about traditions? You should be studying your art. You should be supporting me."

"Eva, you are unhappy, tired, drawn. Can you not see that I might be right?"

Eva eyed her brother in the deepening twilight. Her mouth opened to refute his words, to argue that art was her calling, her passion, her purpose. That she wanted more than a life in a home, at the whim of a man. That she wanted, no, *deserved* more.

But the words died on her tongue. Self-doubt, deeply rooted since she'd first arrived here in Florence, surged up through her. She thought of the bliss of waking in Amadeo's arms, the safety and joy of each moment with him. What a contrast that feeling was to the negative fear of toiling in the studio, her paintbrush failing with every sweep over the canvas.

Was her body trying to tell her something through the deep fatigue and crippling anxiety that punished her daily? Would it perhaps be easier to give up?

Could Elio and the men in Rome be right? Were Italy's woes founded on drifting away from traditions? Was she part of that loss of soul?

The doubt cut through her core, shaking the very foundations of her purpose. The fire went out of her anger as she plunged into a deep well of fatigue.

"Eva? Are you all right?" Elio asked, concern lacing his words.

"Si, Elio, si. I am just tired," she replied.

"Then let's get you home."

"Si, grazie," Eva said, and allowed herself to be escorted to her room.

PART 11

BARI, 1945

THIRTY-SEVEN
SIENA

As winter stretched its cold reach over Puglia, the war in Europe was closing in on Hitler. The men of Bari sat on street corners, puffing cigarettes and talking of the victory to come.

Indoors, the women tightened their skirts with twine and added herbs and stale bread to thicken stews as best they could to fill their families' bellies.

With the advance of the Allied forces across Europe, the supply lines of the navy had been stretched thin. Coupled with the drought the summer before and the logistics of moving food back into the country, little was left for the civilians of Italy.

Siena had had enough.

She'd tried it Alessia's way, respecting the rule of the house that had welcomed her beneath its roof. She'd looked for work. When that failed, she'd joined Luca and his friends to raid the surrounding farms, selling shrivelled almonds and olives on the black market. But the takings were meagre, the reward paltry.

Around her people protested, argued and rioted. Citizens of Puglia rose up and demanded that the Navy do something to lessen the burden on their families. It had started in Taranto, when housewives, driven by the concave bellies of their babies, had taken to the streets and demanded change. Soon the unrest had found its way to Bari.

Siena had turned away, choosing compliance.

Pina had not.

Taking up her wooden kitchen spoon she'd marched with the men of Bari and demanded a return to traditional values. A return that would see Siena permanently sidelined from carving out a life for herself, and would see Alessia's table bare.

Yet Alessia had shown compassion and forgiveness to her neighbour. The history between their families was a bond that held.

As the rising warmth of spring blew across the land, the fields remained barren, and Siena knew something more had to be done. Learning through the gossip of the streets that Mussolini had been executed while trying to escape his punishment was the final straw.

She was hungry. Alessia was hungry. Even Niccolo, who got the lion's share of their rations, was little more than skin and bone.

Enough was enough.

No one was going to help them. They had to take what was theirs.

She waited until Alessia had left the house, out on her daily run to collect their rations. Then she sprang into action.

Coming into the front room, she stood before Niccolo, legs wide, arms crossed over her chest.

"We need more food," she announced.

Nonna Bianca, sitting in the far corner mending a scarf, looked up sharply.

Niccolo pushed himself up from the comfort of his pillows and regarded Siena with bright eyes.

"Si, that is true," he said. "But what can we do?"

"What can *you* do?" she asked, eyeing the boy.

"I can't work..." he began.

"No, you can't. And maybe never again." Harsh words. True words. "But you can come with me."

"What is this?" Nonna Bianca interrupted. "Come with you where?"

"To the bakery."

Bianca frowned, not following. But Niccolo's eyes lit up. "You are going to... like Pina?"

Siena nodded. "Si, like Pina. But I am not coming back empty-handed. We will gather the others, and we will take our bread. Today. You can come too," she said, facing Bianca.

The old woman stared at her in shock.

Siena pushed on. "The delivery truck comes today. It will arrive at noon. And so will we. We will stop the delivery and we will take our bread. Bread for us and for every person who comes with us. Not the meagre ration, but as much as we can carry. Will you join me?"

Niccolo paused a moment, uncertainty filling his face. Then he straightened, pulling himself up on his unsteady legs. "I will," he said.

"Nicco—" Bianca began, but Siena silenced her with a glare.

"It is his choice. We have followed the rules, and we have starved. You have cared for Niccolo, and we have starved. It is time to act. To join the rest of Bari in revolt. It is time to fight for our stomachs to be filled." She held her hand out to Bianca. "Come with us."

Bianca stared at her offered hand. The room fell silent and tense as she considered.

"No," she said finally.

Siena frowned. Bianca's refusal hurt more than she'd expected. But she would not be deterred. Rallying her confidence she faced Niccolo. "Are you ready?"

"Si."

"Then we go."

She turned to leave, Niccolo on her heels.

"Wait." Bianca's voice stilled her step. She regarded the old woman with curiosity. "Let me get my scarf," Bianca said and shuffled from the room. Siena smiled.

They gathered the neighbours: Pina, Luca, old Giuseppe and his visiting friend Nonno Francisco. Grim-faced they moved as one down into the town centre. As they walked people took notice. Looking up from their gardens, their porches, their storefronts. Some turned away. Many joined.

By the time they reached the centre of Bari Vecchia, they numbered in the thirties. Old men and women, some children. All too thin, too gaunt of face. Filthy. Starved.

They were right on time. Rounding the corner onto the cobbled street of the bakery, the delivery truck came into view. The truck was parked, two men busy carrying bread from the tray.

Breaking into a run, Siena led the charge. The others followed. Arms high, empty baskets whirling in the sky above their heads, they ran at the truck. The world went silent. The distant slap of the sea, the cries of the seagulls, the hum of the docks, disappeared. Siena heard only the breath in her mouth, the rap of her soles on the stone, the rush of blood in her veins.

To her right, Niccolo hobbled, faster than she'd have expected, eyes fixed forward with singular purpose. To her left, Pina sprinted, her wooden spoon held aloft. A few paces behind, Bianca opened her mouth in a roar of anger as she raced forward with the mob.

One of the delivery men looked up. He froze, his face draining of colour. He dropped the tray of bread in his hands. A lusty cry rose from the back of the charging crowd, cutting through the city, the desperate call of a dying beast erupting from the fray. The bread delivery man suddenly sprang into action. Grabbing his fellow worker, he made for the truck, jumping in and swinging the door closed…

...Too late. Siena was there, hands gripping the truck door and holding it open.

The crowd at her back advanced. Hands, arms, legs and a fury of limbs and screams, and the man was dragged out of the truck and discarded on the street.

Like waves over the sand, the hungry people of Bari crested over the truck, pulling, pushing. Unable to pry the truck tray open they kept smashing against it, gripping the high rim of the tray and rocking. Push, pull, push, pull, until the truck toppled onto its side, one driver still inside, screaming. The contents of the truck rolled out over the street, and like water the protesters of Bari flowed over it, grabbing, tearing, shoving, each for his own.

Niccolo went down, skidding on his knees. Bianca fell backwards, her head cracking on a loose cobblestone. Bread flew through the air and grasping hands fought to tear each loaf from their neighbour and claim it for themselves.

What started as a march of unity descended into disarray in the blink of an eye.

Caught up in the motion of the raid, Siena fought. Her hands flashed forward seizing loaf after loaf after loaf, her teeth bared in a vicious hiss of warning. Elbows cracked against her ribs, fingers ripped at her hair and one of her loaves was snatched. A snarl erupted from her core as she whirled around to see who had taken her bread. As she spun another hand clamped over her remaining loaf. Siena struck out, the palm of her hand smacking into the forehead of an old man, knocking him off his feet. She didn't know him, and in that moment, she didn't care. Pivoting back to the truck, she surged forward again, groping blindly for more bread. A knee connected with her jaw and she grunted at the pain of the blow, dropping to her knees with the shock that rattled through the bones of her face. Her eyesight blurred. Shaking her head to clear her vision, she pushed up, hand striking forward.

A high-pitched whistle pierced the air. Everyone froze, staring at each other in a collective moment of realisation before bursting into action once more. A final dash for food before the police arrived to arrest them.

It was chaos. Screams filled the air as they struggled for the final scraps of bread. The whine of the whistle grew louder, closer, and the rioters pivoted in panic, rushing from the truck and dispersing through the streets. Siena spun, following. Arms laden with loaves, a grin of victory on her lips.

Then something connected with the back of her head.

Dazed, she pitched forward. Unwilling to release her grip on the bread she careened into the cobblestones, elbows first. The pain fired through her joints as her bones took her weight. Her head tipped forward, smacking onto the stone with a sharp crack.

She lay like that, sprawled over her baked goods, breathing hard as pain pulsed through her. The whistle sounded again, right beside her. It cut through her senses, and she stumbled to her feet.

She swayed a moment as her senses returned, groggy, slow. Blinking the sweat and street dust from her eyes, she looked around her.

People lay on the street, blood on their knees and heads. Pieces of torn bread littered the cobbles.

And to the side, Niccolo.

He sat near a streetlamp, arms wrapped around his knees.

No, not around his knees. Around Bianca.

Siena dropped her loaves, her fight for every piece forgotten as she stumbled forward.

Niccolo looked up at her, eyes full of tears.

"She won't wake up," he said. "Help me, Siena. She won't wake up."

. . .

Nonna Bianca lay on Niccolo's bed in the front room. Siena stood watching the slow rise and fall of her chest as Alessia wrung out a wet cloth, placing it over her nonna's head.

She still didn't know how they'd managed to get the old woman home. But they had. Somehow, Niccolo, limping heavily on his weakened and over-exerted legs and Siena, her head still throbbing from whatever had hit her, had managed to carry Bianca's prone body up the hill to the wall of their home.

Alessia had arrived home soon after.

She'd seen Niccolo's strained and dirty face and rushed to his side. Then she'd see Bianca. Unconscious, pale, breath rasping.

She'd looked at Siena, a question in her eyes.

Then shocked realisation and fury.

She'd got straight to work, cleaning the wound on Bianca's head, settling her to comfort on Niccolo's bed. Gently, tenderly.

She'd not said a word. To Siena, or to Niccolo.

But the silence wasn't a nice one. And Siena knew it was merely a reprieve. Nothing more.

Guilt churned in her belly as she looked down on the injured Bianca.

What if she didn't wake?

Restless from worry, she paced outside. The street lay silent. Their neighbours, raucous that morning as they'd joined Siena's march for sustenance, had now withdrawn indoors. Astonished at their behaviour. Ashamed.

She took a seat on the porch and rested her head in her hands. Her skull throbbed, the pain forming red blotches in her vision. Sliding her fingers through her hair, she felt something crusty. Her fingers came away dusted in red. She had been bleeding. She didn't care. Dropping her head in her hands once again, she sat alone, despondent.

"Can I clean it?"

Siena looked up, knocked from her silent vigil by Alessia's soft voice.

Her friend stood next to her, a wet cloth in hand.

"Save the water," Siena said.

"Just a wipe. To prevent it from getting worse."

Siena sighed and nodded, and Alessia sat beside her. Gentle hands turned her head to the side, as Alessia surveyed the wound on the back of her skull. Then the cool relief of a damp cloth pressed against the red-hot pain.

Siena clenched her teeth as a part of a scab was brushed off. Tears leaked from her eyes. She didn't deserve this kindness.

"I'm sorry—" she began, but Alessia sniffed loudly.

"Not yet," she said. "I know you are, and I will accept your apology. But not yet. I am not ready."

Siena fell silent. In awe of this woman and the quiet strength she conveyed, where Siena felt only rage.

When Alessia finished cleaning the wound, Siena felt her stand and silently retreat, leaving Siena alone with her guilt and shame.

Siena closed her eyes, and for the first time in a long time, sent a prayer to God. The church mattered to her, but life had been so busy trying to help Alessia. This place, this city and this family had hooked into her heart – into her soul.

She'd come for safety. Sent running from Rome by the threat of Nazi discovery, Romano's book of art in her possession. Her only goal to keep that book of records safe.

And she'd found she could not leave. Did not want to leave.

She loved them. Bianca, Niccolo, Alessia. She loved them all.

Today she'd risen, thinking to take what they needed. What they deserved. And all she'd done was hurt them.

She opened her eyes and looked out over the harbour of Bari. The waters twinkled brightly in the failing daylight, shining crisp and clear. So many months of living here now, yet the glowing beauty of the coast still captured her heart.

Rome had been liberated. Safe in the hands of the Allied forces. Siena could return. Her purpose, the whole reason she was here, Romano's book. She could complete her work. Return to Rome, find Mila and Amara and begin the next task.

Perhaps it was time to leave. Perhaps...

"Alessia! Siena! Come quick, come quick. Nonna is awake!" Niccolo's cry hit her heart, and a sob broke from her throat. Standing swiftly, she rushed inside.

True to his word, Bianca lay on his bed, milky eyes open, an embarrassed grin straining the corners of her mouth.

"Nonna," Alessia said, coming into the room and helping Bianca to sit up.

Bianca allowed the help, to a point, then shooed Alessia away. "Stop fussing, stop fussing," she said.

Siena watched her friend step back, her expression tight with concern.

"I am all right. Really. I am."

No one said anything. Bianca sniffed in irritation. "How much did we get?"

She eyed Siena, and Siena felt her mouth drop open in surprise. This was not the reaction she'd expected from Nonna Bianca. "I... we... you..."

A huff of disapproval. "All that and you came away with nothing. Foolish. We will do better tomorrow."

"Nonna," Alessia cut in. "This was not a good thing. You can't just steal bread."

"And why not?" the old woman challenged. "They keep the best for themselves."

"Who does?"

Bianca pierced her granddaughter with a glare. "The sailors, the butchers, the bakers. They keep the best, the bulk, and they take coin to give it to others who can afford to pay more. You know this is true."

"Attacking a delivery truck isn't going to stop that."

"Maybe not, but it sends a message. The message that we are watching."

Something shifted inside Siena with those words. A fresh determination building within her.

"Like the protests," she said. It wasn't necessarily about the reason for the protest. It was about the noise. About standing up and saying it wasn't right. It wasn't enough. They had to fight. They had to keep fighting.

Bianca met her eyes. "Exactly."

Alessia turned to Siena. "Please don't do this again," she pleaded.

But Siena's mind was far away, connecting dots, realising pathways and options.

"Siena?" The urgency in Alessia's voice drew her back to the moment, and Siena reached forward, taking her friend's hands in hers.

"I will not riot or raid again, I swear."

"Grazie," Alessia breathed.

"But I will not stop either," Siena continued.

Alessia met her eyes, and the two friends stared at each other, seeking understanding, and acceptance.

"I am sorry," Siena said at last.

Alessia gave a breathless laugh and looked away. "I forgive you," she said.

Relief flooded through Siena as a smile drifted over her lips.

It was all right, she realised. She was all right.

But things would change.

She would change them.

Starting tomorrow. She had to return. It was obvious, she now saw. The need had been building for so long.

She needed answers, for herself and for her country. For what she'd worked for. The time had come.

Siena needed to return to Rome.

THIRTY-EIGHT
SIENA

She'd been watching him for months. As the seasons shifted and the farms around Bari fell dormant for winter, robbing her little group of thieves of produce to pilfer, Luca never seemed to go without, even though his home was full of mouths to feed. As the buds of spring sprang to life across the trees, Siena had worked out why. And it was her route to Rome.

The large proportion of local produce that was sent to Rome gave rise to schemes for profit. Wiley locals found ways to conceal extra food and supplies and sell them to smugglers for money.

Alessia had been right when she warned Siena her extra money would do little good. The amount of food making its way out of Puglia not just for the requirements of Rome, but for the profit of the very same people whose neighbours starved on the streets of Bari, was appalling.

Tonight, Siena would profit too.

Siena waited in the shadows. The night sky darkened around her, the sound of the waves off the coast growing louder as the temperature plummeted with the light. Most of the streetlamps stood dark and unlit, the cost to fuel them long too high to maintain. Two men appeared before her, Paolo and Luca, just as Luca had said. In the grey dusk, they slipped into the butcher's shop. A truck pulled up at the front, headlights dimmed. She pulled back, lest she reveal herself too soon. A door banged, followed by a loud stream of curses. Heavy footsteps, the thud of weighty objects being dropped into the truck tray. Meat, Siena knew, large cuts, syphoned off without a hint of fear. The authorities didn't care, so long as the soldiers got their ration.

Another bang, this time the truck doors, and the headlights blazed into the night.

For a group of smugglers they had a lot to learn about subtlety.

Warily, Siena peered around the corner of the brick building at her back and watched Enzo, who'd brought the truck, disappear into the night. The engine fired, and Siena pounced. Rushing from the shadows, she advanced on the vehicle, throwing open the side door and jumping in beside Luca. She'd overcompensated her leap, her momentum flinging her against Luca and smooshing him against Paolo in the driver's seat.

"What the hell?" Paolo's face flashed around from the driving wheel to pierce her with an icy stare.

Calmly Siena pushed herself up into a sitting position, arranging her skirts and smoothing her blouse. Expression impassive, she returned Paolo's stare.

Beside her Luca had righted himself, but his hands were twisting nervously in his lap. Paolo's eyes flicked down to the anxious movement, and his lids narrowed. "She's with you?"

"She just needs a lift to Rome," Luca said, voice tight.

"And back," Siena interjected.

Paolo ignored her, his attention now all on Luca. "Why?"

Luca glanced down at his feet, shoulders bunching in. So Siena answered. "Because you are stupid."

That got Paolo's attention.

"Excuse me?"

"You are smuggling meat to Rome, no? In the truck tray. But the roads are slow, and this shipment is late. And underweight..." Paolo blinked in surprise. Siena knew that even the smuggling trade was low on supply. She continued. "You need to get to Rome and try to trade up for more weight, less value. So you don't disappoint your contacts. I can help."

"Why should I trust you?"

Siena offered him a withering stare. "Because I will arrive in Rome with you and the black market meat. I have just as much to lose as you do."

"Then why would you take the risk?"

"I have to know..." she answered, her voice breaking. She turned away, suddenly unable to maintain her mask of strength and confidence. The worry in her heart was too deep and sharp, it took the breath from her lungs.

"Know what?"

Siena faced him again, her anger flaring, a buffer she'd always carried with her. "Will you take me to Rome or not? Because if you are leaving you had better do so, and quickly. It is a long way, and the roads are slow. You don't have time for this."

Paolo held her stare a moment, two, then, with a breath of violent irritation, he jerked around in the truck and pressed down the accelerator, the vehicle lurching forward.

Siena exchanged a glance with Luca, his eyes solemn, lips pale. He offered her a small, nervous smile, but she turned away. She didn't have the time for his concerns.

Only her own.

. . .

The journey to Rome was long and uncomfortable. The suspension on the old truck had seen better days, and the road had fallen into disrepair. Extensive efforts had been made to improve and reseal the more direct route to Rome, but that had been deemed for "military use only". Civilians were not permitted to use it. That left the old road to Rome. Windy, unkempt, covered in potholes from weather and overuse, sections blasted away by Allied or Axis bombs; it made for a challenging journey in the bright light of day. At night it was downright dangerous.

Siena settled herself as best she could on the worn leather seat of the truck. Bouncing along, she stared out at the trees that lined the roadside, highlighted by the pale moon as they whizzed past, eerie white skeletons reaching for the sky. At some point she must have dozed off, head resting against the cold, hard surface of the truck window, because the jolt from a particularly large pothole caused her limp body to bang against the truck frame, shocking her awake.

Outside, the trees had thinned, their branches now illuminated in bronze and red as the first rays of the sun began to blaze on the horizon. As they drove, more houses appeared, stone and brick, clustered together between the trees. Soon the groups of houses became continuous, the height of the buildings growing taller and taller, the homes themselves narrower, and, as they entered the city proper, dirtier, shabby. As the bright yellow of proper dawn lit the dusty streets of Rome, they passed a neighbourhood reduced to rubble. Large, cracked stones, blasted bricks, splintered wood, collapsed apartment blocks. No one had come to repair this quarter; perhaps they never would.

Siena sat up, poking her finger into Paolo's side to get his attention.

"Turn right. We aren't far now."

He said nothing, but she could feel his irritation. Nonetheless, he followed her instruction and turned the truck. It wasn't long before the streets became achingly familiar and heart-crushingly different. There was the old oak she passed daily on her route to the markets to buy food for Romano, and there were the ruins of the old synagogue where he'd worshipped. The house beside it was destroyed; the whole roof had collapsed under the weight of a Nazi explosion... or an Allied one. The closer they drew to her destination the harder her heart pounded. What would she find at Romano's beautiful home? The old man in residence, returned from his wrongful imprisonment, curled on the couch, and quiet? A home razed to the ground by war? Or worse – nothing, and no answers? Would she find Romano?

Her stomach spasmed in a burst of anxious pain, and Siena took a deep, centring breath. Luca heard, turning his head sharply in question.

She forced a smile to her face. No matter how deep the fear she felt went, she would not show it. Not yet. Nothing would make her threaten this chance to know... to have at least one mystery answered. However, it may break her heart.

They turned onto the boulevard: wide, once lined with trees, now a chaos of rubble and splintered wood, the leaves long dead and blown away, leaving branches like pointy skeletons. Homeless, lost. Siena gripped her hands in her lap and worked to control her rising fear. One breath in, one out, repeat. It is done. It is done.

The old manor came into view. It seemed untouched. The cream stone, the brick bracings, the flowering vine, bright pink buds just blooming, reaching for the wrought-iron railings of the balcony. At first.

As they drew nearer the truth slowly revealed itself. The front garden had been obliterated. The once-grand drive lined with trees had been reduced to dust. Of the perfect green grasses, nothing remained. Then she saw the house itself. The front had not survived, nor had the right side. Gone was the sweeping entrance; the whole second-floor balcony had collapsed over the marble stairs that led within.

"Which one?" Luca asked, though Siena could see he knew; he had been watching her since they'd turned onto this drive.

"That one," she confirmed, pointing.

Paolo slowed the truck, crawling to a stop before the destroyed drive.

He killed the engine, and a familiar tense silence fell over the vehicle. It was the quiet of mutual understanding. No matter how little Paolo trusted her, or how annoyed he was by her presence, they'd all been touched by the devastation of bombing raids. There was no joy to take from this scene. Paolo may not like her, may be mad that she'd forced him to drive her to Rome, but no one wished this hell on anyone, especially their own people.

"We will wait," he said. And Siena knew he meant it.

She opened the truck door and stepped gingerly onto the street. A flurry of air whipped along the dirt-strewn road, blowing up a cloud of powdered cement and dust, the grit catching in her eyelashes. She blinked rapidly, to clear the grounds from her eyes and to hold back the tears of pain that threatened to overcome her, and took her first step.

The sound of a door shutting behind her shattered her composure, and she whipped her head around. Luca stood by the truck, eyes lifted to the broken home beyond.

"What are you doing?" she asked, genuinely confused.

"Who knows what is in there?" he said, then stepped up beside her. He said nothing else. He didn't need to. Siena understood he was coming with her, but it was her move. She walked forward.

The house echoed, the steps gone. Carefully they picked their way through the rubble that had once been Romano's beautiful home. What had become of this place of refuge? What was left?

At the bulk of stone from the fallen roof, she felt Luca pause, but Siena pushed on. Beyond the fallen façade, it seemed rooms still stood. Making her way forward she pulled her cardigan tighter, closer. She dared not raise her voice in call; she did not know who dwelt within.

Her feet scuffed through grime and dirt. To her left a golden shard of light caught her eye, the smashed remains of a small painting by Masaccio, overlooked by the raiding soldiers.

The old man would never have left it out so.

Tears sprang to her eyes at the understanding that one abandoned painting foreshadowed. Romano had not returned home. Her knees wobbled as the sobs began to work their way up her throat. Romano wasn't here. Which meant...

A skitter of stones rattled to the right. Siena spun around, noting Luca as he mirrored her movement.

A figure stepped from the shadows of destruction and Siena could not hold in her sob any longer. Crying out in a mix of joy and sorrow, she rushed forward and wrapped her arms around Amara. The young woman went stiff and then clutched Siena to her, the nails of her fingers biting into Siena's back as she clung on as if she would never let go.

After a moment Siena pulled back, assessing the girl. Part of her answer was in Amara's sorrowful eyes.

"Where?" she asked.

"Come inside."

Siena sat at the familiar kitchen bench, Luca and Paolo beside her as Amara prepared chicory coffee. Gentle sunlight lit the scene, peeking in through a large, cracked window pane that faced the ruined front garden. Siena watched as a scrawny sparrow picked through the cement fragments and dirt in search of worms. Perhaps worms still lived here, if nothing else.

The bitter and sweet scent of chicory curled up from her

cup as Siena wrapped her hands around the delicately painted mug, warming her body, and her memories. Amara sat opposite her, mirroring her stance as she savoured the hot liquid that slipped down her throat.

"He would have hated you seeing the house like this," she said. And Siena was surprised at the rueful laugh that erupted from her soul. Luca eyed her, and she looked away from his wary face.

"What happened?"

Now it was Amara's turn to look away. Swallowing a large gulp of chicory, she gripped the table in her free hand and allowed a tear to slip down her cheek.

"They broke through the door just after you left. I knew they wanted Mila. I told her to go, but..." She paused, eyes seeking Siena's, begging for understanding, for forgiveness.

Siena reached forward, taking Amara's hand in hers. "I do," she said simply. "I do."

An uncertain smile dressed Amara's lips for a moment, then was gone. She continued. "They rushed in, guns in hand. And they took her. She didn't resist. She just went limp."

Siena breathed in a violent breath, clutching Amara's hand as the young woman gave in to a flood of tears. "One of them hit Mila in the head. He didn't need to, she wasn't resisting. She went down and didn't move.

"They gathered her up then dragged her, bleeding and unconscious, from this house. They took her..."

Siena clenched her teeth at the pause, and forced herself to be patient, even as her body screamed for details.

Her need for truth overcame her. "Where did they take her? To the prison?"

"She was arrested, held for a week or two, then released. She returned to Tuscany."

Mila lived. The relief seized Siena; it was more than she'd dared to hope for.

"What about Romano and Dario? I know they were sent away. Have you heard anything?"

Amara met Siena's eyes, purest grief flowing from her wide pupils. The look stilled something in Siena's soul. "What happened to the Jewish citizens?" she managed to whisper. Amara looked away, as if what she was about to say was too painful to face.

"You know they were taken out of Italy. I have heard nothing more. No one will tell me of my husband." She closed her eyes, body twitching, then continued. "We have all heard the rumours of the camps for the Jewish..."

Siena slumped back as shock curled through her soul.

She had. Prisons. Persecution. Death.

Was there hope left in this story? For Romano? Old and weak.

For Dario? Young and vulnerable.

"What did you do?" she asked.

Amara looked up sharply, and Siena rubbed her hand in reassurance. "I mean for you," she clarified. "There was nothing you could do for them."

Face now a wreck of pain and tears, mucus streaming from her nose, Amara cried, "I hid, here. I didn't know what else to do. I couldn't help them. I couldn't save anyone. So I hid. And then more bombs came. They even blasted the Vatican. What was left for me? More soldiers came, and I hid and I hid and I hid, and then you arrived. And I don't know, I don't know..."

Siena shot to her feet, rounding the table in two strides to gather Amara up in her arms. "It is all right," she said, her voice comforting. "You did the right thing hiding. We've all heard the stories of what those soldiers do to women. You had to hide. There was no other choice. I am just glad they didn't return."

Amara sniffed. "They did return," she whispered, a hand coming to rest over her stomach. "More than once."

Siena went still, eyes on the small round of the young

woman's stomach. A heavy breath issued from her as she took in the woman's meaning.

She met Amara's eyes. Glistening tears gathered together as she pressed her forehead to Amara's. "It will be all right," she promised. "I will take care of you. The orphanage of Santa Maria, here in Rome. Go there, ask for Sister Agnes. She was good to me. She will help you."

"But what do I tell her? How do I explain?"

"We are at war," Siena said. "To be a woman alone in your condition is not unusual. Say that your husband is away. Say that you have nowhere else to go. It is the truth. Or the truth that matters at least."

"I prayed that you would return," Amara said, voice soft. "For once God has listened."

The women broke apart, and Amara wiped her tears.

"It mattered," Amara said suddenly.

Siena cocked her head at her young friend. "What mattered?"

Amara smiled. "The last translation. A group of resistance fighters made it to the Allied border, because of you."

Siena stared at Amara. "How can you know that?"

"Mila told me before she left the city. What was in that last message. About what you did."

Amara's eyes filled with pride as she gazed at Siena. It was too much. Siena didn't deserve that praise. After all that Amara had been through in service to their network: the loss of her husband, the attack of angry soldiers, the destruction of Rome around her. The fear, the unknown, all faced alone so Siena could run.

The praise was for her, not for Siena.

"She gave me her address in Tuscany – for you." Amara stood and paced from the room, returning with a slip of paper. "When the war is over..." She pressed the paper into Siena's hand, an address written in Mila's fluid script. How many places would Mila send Siena to, she wondered. When would this all end?

Siena felt a tremor rattle through her body, and Amara's words settled over her soul. Resistance fighters saved.

Was it worth it? In sacrifice for Dario, for Amara? For Romano? She didn't know. Doubt gripped her mind and twisted. Romano stayed for the art, Dario stayed for Romano. Siena had made that sequence happen. What had she chosen for them all?

"It was the right thing to do," Amara said, answering her unspoken thoughts. "For Italy."

"What about Dario? And Romano? What about you?"

"That is not your fault, Siena."

Siena could not meet her stare. This woman who'd given so much. Her future uncertain. "I will visit you, at the orphanage. Give my name to Sister Agnes. You will be cared for."

The women embraced one final time. Siena pulled away first, turning for the truck without another word.

THIRTY-NINE
SIENA

The road back to Bari was long and slow, but Siena barely noticed, lost as she was in her sorrow and pain. Dario, gone. Amara, brutalised. Romano... She clutched the pouch she wore on her chest through the cotton of her blouse and sent her prayers to God.

Paolo dropped her in the Piazza Mercantile. Siena climbed from the truck without a word. Listless and heavy, she turned for home.

"Siena, wait!" Luca ran up behind her, grabbing her elbow to halt her step.

Siena stopped and waited.

Their eyes met in the dawn light. Siena turned from the pity that radiated from his face.

"Siena..." he began, but his words dried up. His hand dropped from her arm.

"Take this at least." He thrust a leg of pork wrapped in butcher's paper towards her, and she took it. The smuggling run had gone well, trading the meat of Puglia for oil and sugar and other luxuries. This leg, scrawny and tough, was all that was left over from their successful endeavour.

"If you need to talk..."

She walked away, pork dangling from her hand, leaving Luca standing alone in the piazza, his offer unacknowledged.

For Siena had nothing to say to him. He wouldn't understand. No one would.

She trudged up the small rise that led to the wall-nestled neighbourhood of Alessia's city home.

There she sat in silent vigil, this young woman Siena now called a friend, family even. Or so she had thought. Now, everything felt numb, distant.

Alessia looked up and saw her approaching. Her hand flew to her mouth, and she rushed down the cobbled street, closing the small space between them.

"Where have you been? I have been worried to death! Nonna hasn't stopped praying. What has happened?"

Still, Siena said nothing. Instead she simply pushed the wrapped leg of pork into Alessia's hands.

Alessia took it, blinking once in surprise before darkness fell over her features.

"Where did you get this? A few tomatoes, some flour, that's one thing. But pork!" Her words were ice, clipped with rage, but Siena felt no flush of emotion in response. No need to defend her choices. What did Alessia's anger matter now? What did anything matter now?

"Rome. Smuggling run," Siena answered flatly.

She regarded Alessia's red, flushed face and saw the moment her ire broke, the swift return of concern.

"You went to Rome? You went home? What happened? Siena, talk to me."

But Siena wasn't ready for Alessia's understanding. She didn't deserve it. Not yet. Perhaps never.

Siena pushed through the curtain that veiled the door and paced across the cool tiles of the entrance to the stairs. Bianca looked up from the kitchen alcove.

"Mio Dio! You are home. How I prayed."

Siena ignored her and mounted the stairs. Behind her she heard Alessia's soft whisper to her nonna. "Leave her, something has happened."

"What has happened?"

"I do not know. I think she needs time."

Siena barely registered the words. She headed for her room and buried herself beneath her blankets.

An imperceptible amount of time later – hours, days, moments – a light tap on her door drew Siena from her malaise. Poking her head out from her blanket cocoon, she watched as Alessia stepped softly into the chamber. Gone was the look of concern, replaced with a calm openness.

Siena pushed herself up in her bed and gestured for Alessia to come sit beside her. The springs of the bed squeaked as Alessia took a seat. Without a word, the two women clasped hands.

"I am here," Alessia said. "I will listen."

"I am sorry," Siena began, the sorrow already sealing her throat.

"Shh," Alessia crooned, pulling her forward into a strengthening embrace. Siena rested her head against Alessia's shoulder and told her everything: how she used Luca's smuggling run to get to the capital and why she had to go to Rome; about Mila's arrest; about Amara and her baby. And finally, about Romano and Dario and their unknown future. Everything, except the book of art that had started this all. The book that had shaped all their choices, that had led her here.

"I think... I think," she stuttered between sobs. "This is all my fault. Romano might have left for America with his friends if not for me. But he stayed, and they came for him, and Dario, and took them away. We've heard of those camps, of what happens to the prisoners. And despite all that, I left. I ran here to safety, leaving Mila and Amara. I should have stayed. I should have stood with Amara and protected her. It's my fault. It's all my fault!"

"Nonsense," Alessia retorted. "None of this is your doing."

"It is!" Siena wailed, pulling away from Alessia's kindness. "I should have stayed. I should have helped."

"You are not the reason Hitler invaded. And you are not the reason Romano chose to stay in Rome."

Siena gulped down a sob, blinking tears from her eyes.

"Amara said something similar," she whispered.

Alessia held her shoulders, squeezing gently. "Then I think this Amara is a sensible young woman."

Siena half laughed, half sobbed at those words, and something released in her stomach. She still felt numb, but perhaps now a little lighter. Subconsciously her hands went to the pouch that nestled against her chest, seeking the comfort of the object's presence.

Noting the movement, Alessia said, "It is beautiful that you have that piece of your mamma. It connects you." Siena smiled sadly.

"It makes you wonder, doesn't it?" Siena replied. "This little piece of my mother. Who was she? Why did she leave me behind?"

"Perhaps she was unwed?"

"A common story at the orphanage."

"Yet she hoped to be reunited with you."

"Si. If she'd come back, this would have identified me. Babies do change a lot."

"I think I would have known Niccolo at any age. That boy has always looked devilishly cheeky," Alessia said, an indulgent grin spreading on her face.

Siena felt her lips match that grin, Niccolo's impish face

swimming in her mind. Despite everything the lad had been through, he was still kind, like his sister. Quiet but strong.

Alessia patted her hand affectionately. "Will you come down for supper? We have made lentil and pork bone stew. The neighbours are gathering outside to share in it."

"I am not hungry—"

"Come down," Alessia said, voice gently insistent. "We will all have meat today because of you."

"I thought you disapproved of the smuggling."

"I most certainly do. And the stealing. But..." Alessia paused, lifting her head up high and imperious. "I will not waste what comes into my kitchen," she said, in a beautiful mimicry of Nonna Bianca.

Siena laughed out loud and wiped the last tears from her eyes.

"We must not waste Bianca's cooking," she agreed, still grinning.

"Come then," Alessia said, standing up. "Come and share with us all."

"Si," Siena said, rising and taking Alessia's offered hand. "I will."

FORTY
SIENA

Supper had been wonderful. Everyone had joined: Valentina, Pina and her parents, Luca and Giuseppe, even Paolo the butcher's son had swung by, all adding their bread ration to the feast. And feast it had been. Not for the quantity of food, but for the feeling of community. For togetherness. An echo of the orecchiette evening she'd shared here when she'd first arrived in Bari almost eighteen months before. The missing people left an emptiness – Terese and Lucia – but still there was warmth.

A warmth shared too rarely of late.

Yet, despite the night of uplifting spirits and her lack of sleep due to her secret journey to Rome, Siena could not settle. She lay in her bed, tossing and turning, the pale light of the moon an irritation, the scratch of the blanket, usually ignored, chaffing anew. Her stomach growled its hunger; even the portion of meat in her stew had still been too meagre to counter the months of undernourishment. In spite of her fatigue, her heart beat loud and insistent, her limbs burning to move. She let out a snort of irritation. What use was this unwelcome energy now? It was the dead of night; the house slept. She could do nothing useful for the risk of waking the others.

Frustrated, she flopped over onto her back, eyes wide, staring up at the wooden beams of the ceiling. The familiar weight of her pouch rested against her chest. It felt heavier somehow, cold despite the warmth of her body, vibrating though it didn't move, a pulse reaching down into her very soul. She plucked the pouch up in her fingers and held it before her eyes. Beautiful and worn; hope and hopelessness. Suddenly it seemed to represent everything that Italy was in this very moment. Everything her life was.

Despondent, she dropped the pouch and lay her hands over her stomach, willing herself to sleep.

It would not come. No matter how she tried to still her body and mind, her eyes simply would not close. She released a heavy sigh and allowed her mind to admit her troubles. It was time.

Rome and Florence had been liberated the summer before. But Siena had stayed on. Her excuse had been that Bianca and Alessia needed her help with Niccolo, and to survive the cold of winter. Then as the beginnings of spring had begun to stir she'd found her way to Rome. To Amara, and the horrible truth. But also to Mila's message: her address in Tuscany and her final instruction to Siena.

She'd been putting it off, she knew, but now it was time to finish what she'd started. The reason she was here in the first place: Romano's book of lost art. His life's work.

Nestled safely in the cellar of Auri di Bari's home, the book was the key to recovering the art of Italy that had been hidden, protecting it from foreign hands, and some that had been stolen, tracked by Romano's meticulous network.

The dear old man would not be coming back from the camps of Germany, Siena knew that deep her in heart. She couldn't let his sacrifice be in vain.

It was time to see the book safely to Tuscany and Mila

Pettiti. So she could save the art of Italy. For the nation's future and for Romano.

It was time for Siena to leave Bari.

She rose on soft feet and padded across the room and out into the hall. The night was warm enough that she didn't need a coat. Quietly she made her way down the hall, her step light, keeping away from the boards she knew would creak. She passed Nonna Bianca and Alessia's room, then Niccolo's, so recently reinhabited. It had been good to see him regaining his strength and stride. Gliding down the stairs she made for the front room and the cellar door obscured beneath the rug.

A memory flashed through her mind of a different night in the room. When she was new to this city, to this house. When the fate of Dario and Romano remained unknown; when her only goal in Bari was to hide Romano's book and wait. A memory of a night when Alessia discovered her, sneaking, disrespecting this home and this family who had welcomed her.

And forgiven her.

No, not forgiven, it was more than that. Alessia had understood her.

Siena had thought she would be thrown out on the street. She'd even packed her suitcase in preparation. She had waited and waited, and... nothing.

Siena bought extra flour and a community meal was shared. She learned to make orecchiette.

Siena had doubted the family's kindness at first and had thought it a trick. She went through the next weeks walking on eggshells, always expecting the hammer to drop and the boot to come.

It had not.

Still had not.

She'd come to know it never would.

For these were good, good people. They had harboured her, sheltered her, protected her, fed her.

And helped her.

Then the war had taken over. Blowing up their world and turning all of Siena's plans on their head. And Siena had been happy to be distracted. With Romano gone, the mission in hiding and Italy falling apart around her – Axis forces to the north, Allies to the south, civilians caught between the opposing sides that battled for Europe – having a place to call home was special.

The picture fragment that hung around her neck, the clue her mamma had left, the puzzle piece she'd longed to return to its whole, the answer of her past – did it really matter? Did the mother who had left it with her really matter? She had abandoned Siena after all. She'd left a token but... But the hard truth was that she'd never returned.

All her life Siena had dreamed of her mamma. Proudly boasting to the other orphans of the day her mother would come back for her: "She will be tall", "She will be rich", "She will be beautiful", "She will look like me".

She always believed her mamma would return.

But she never came.

As Siena eased the large cupboard door open, coughing as the movement freed a pile of dust into the air to assault her lungs, a new sensation settled over her heart: acceptance.

She did not know who her mother was. The woman who'd left the painting fragment – had she been an artist? Maybe. Or a collector? A maid who'd torn the edge of her employer's artwork?

Siena had no answer and likely never would.

But the people here, in Bari, in this house: Alessia, Niccolo and Nonna Bianca. The neighbours Pina, Luca, even Enzo and Paolo. And somewhere out there, and here within her heart always, Dario, Amara, Romano...

Sister Agnes.

How had she not understood it before?

Motherless, she was. But not without love. Not without family.

She had a family. Not of blood, but of love.

She would honour that. How she wished she could tell Romano in person: that she understood, finally. She had a home and a family. That she had known them for years, in her heart. Her mind just needed to catch up.

She opened the cupboard she had secreted the book of art within. It had been rocked by the blasts of the air raid that fateful December when Bari burned, and its contents shaken, but the boards had held strong. Bracing herself she lifted a pile of objects aside, searching for Romano's book. There it sat, still in the blanket she'd wrapped it in so long ago. She pressed a hand against the back of the cupboard to steady herself and reached down. But the back of the cupboard gave, her hand plunging through the thin wooden panel. She fell, sprawling over the cupboard, her legs akimbo on the rough stone floor. A muffled thud sounded from behind the cupboard. Frowning, she pushed herself to her feet and eyed the back of the cupboard. There was a large crack through the wood where her hand had rested, but it was not the back of the cupboard.

Another panel of thicker wood showed through the crack.

Siena stared in astonishment. It was a false back. Like the false drawer that Romano had fashioned for their secret work in his office and home in Rome.

Leaning forward, Siena reached her hand through the crack, fingers grasping. Paper, soft and crackling, connected with her fingers. She pulled, and the papers came free.

The momentum sat her on her bottom on the dusty cellar floor, but Siena didn't notice. For in her hands, she held a sketchbook. Large and heavy, leather-bound.

A hidden sketchbook.

The hairs along her arms stood to attention, and a sudden chill seemed to envelop the room. Puffing a breath to steady her nerves, Siena pinched the corner of the cover between two fingers and turned.

A charcoal image was revealed, what seemed like an outline of Bari harbour. She turned the page again – another sketch, this time a detail of the bottom of a fishing boat at low tide. Again, and a scene of the city streets, the washing wafting in the breeze off the bay, so well shaded Siena could almost feel the caress of the sun-kissed cotton against her skin. Again and again, she turned the pages as scenes of Bari revealed themselves. It must belong to Auri, she decided. But it simply didn't feel right. These sketches, these were... different. More honest, more real.

She turned the page again and saw a place she did not know. A sweeping hill, lined with wildflowers. On another page a chunk of cheese on a rug, a detailed depiction of a man's polished boot resting against blades of grass. It was in black and white, but Siena could see the green lushness of the grass in her mind's eye.

She flicked on. More and more scenes of hills and a river, a beautiful bridge arching across it.

Where was this? She wondered. It wasn't Rome.

The edge of a page slipped out from the sketchbook, a tattered-looking corner. Carefully Siena drew the page from the book and gasped.

The book slipped from her fingers as she stared at the folded lump she'd extracted.

The page was folded in the middle, the material thick to the touch. Only it wasn't a page at all. The folded bulk was made of cotton. It was a canvas. The frame had been removed and the material folded, but it was a canvas nonetheless.

She unfolded the image. Flecks of paint, broken from the creasing of the canvas, fell like dust from the image, sprinkling over her lap, along with something larger. Siena glanced down at a beautiful, bright red ribbon but dismissed it, for all her attention was on the image painted on the canvas. A sweeping scene of Bari harbour before the boats of the British and US Navies had arrived. Bright blues, crisp whites, dramatic and passionate, stretched across the cotton. Siena barely noticed for the focal point of the painting had caught her eyes. On the side of the canvas a young woman was depicted – a beautiful profile, obscured by a mass of brilliant curls, a bright red ribbon in her hair. Around her neck, golden and shining, hung a cross. Siena's fingers traced the outline of that cross. Her breath caught. She knew that cross. She'd seen it around Mila's neck. This one was new, undamaged; all the points of the cross were square, the gems in place. But there was no doubt in Siena's mind that it was the same cross. The cross Mila had said would lead her to her lost loved one.

Her eyes caught something more, something lower, and her body began to tremble.

The edge of the material was torn, a jagged tear that cut through the base of the canvas. A missing sweep of blues and whites.

Siena knew that tear. Heart pounding, Siena's hand gripped the pouch that nestled around her neck. She opened the pouch, pulling it free. Fingers trembling, Siena aligned the images and gasped.

It was a perfect fit.

Siena's hand shot to her mouth, covering the grunt of shock that ripped from her throat.

She went still, the pieces of her life fixing together like a child's puzzle, everything falling into place.

Because she didn't need to ask Alessia who this woman was. No, she doubted Alessia would have an answer. But she knew who did.

She needed to go Tuscany.

PART 12

FLORENCE, 1921

FORTY-ONE
EVA

"I have your results," Doctor Grecco said, as he settled at his desk. Eva sat in the cool space of his office, Emilia beside her, clutching her hand.

Her friend had worked wonders finding a doctor who was willing to see her, alone, without a husband at her side, especially given her probable condition.

"It is as you expected; you are with child."

The air left the room, replaced by a hollow pressure that bore down on Eva's ears and smothered her mouth. She couldn't breathe. Her mind seized up, her thoughts frozen in place. "With child". She understood the words, but could not comprehend them.

She felt Emilia squeeze her hand, then heard her voice as she spoke to the doctor. Her words seemed muffled, far away. Eva blinked, then realised they were looking at her.

"I'm sorry, could you repeat that?"

"I said, I believe you are around three months along. Would that sound right to you?"

"I... I suppose so."

"You are in good condition, healthy, strong. I see no reason to suspect the pregnancy would fail naturally. Though one can never be sure, especially in the early stages. But if you take good care of yourself and rest you will do fine."

The doctor fell silent. Eva felt his stare, hot like searing coals. "You will tell the father of course... He should come and see me too, so he knows what to expect."

Her eyes snapped up, meeting the doctor's knowing look. "Indeed, I... I will," she managed.

"Grazie, medico," Emilia cut in, coming to her feet. She helped Eva to stand. Eva's knees felt insubstantial, loose. "We will be in touch."

Unable to hold on to her thoughts, Eva allowed Emilia to take the lead, and her friend whisked her from the doctor's office and back to the privacy of the small chambers Eva shared with Elio, above Signora Pesci's home.

Emilia sat her on the bed and wrapped her in a blanket. "I will be back momentarily," she said before disappearing downstairs.

True to her word, she soon returned, a cup of steaming milky coffee in her hands. "Here," she pressed the cup into Eva's grip. Eva watched through the veil of steam as Emilia shut the door, setting the lock. She then gathered up a blanket and rolled it into a sausage shape and pressed it against the gap between the door and the floor.

"We don't want any unwelcome ears," she explained as she came to sit beside Eva. "Take a sip, it will help."

Unable to argue, Eva followed her friend's instruction and sipped the coffee, bitter and hot. Bracing. She felt the warmth spread through her limbs and realised she was cold. A great shiver rattled up through her body as tears, hot and furious, sprang into her eyes.

"Oh, Emilia," she cried, turning to her friend. "What have I done?"

"Shh, shh," Emilia crooned as she plucked the cup from

Eva's shaking hands and settled it on the floor, before pulling her into a tight embrace. Eva slumped against her friend, giving in to the fear and shock that had been building within her since the doctor had said those terrifying words. "You are with child."

Pregnant. How could it be true? She'd been so careful with Amadeo. Followed all his advice to prevent this exact event. "We will have a family one day, amore," he'd said. "When you are famous."

But one day had come sooner. And they weren't even officially a couple yet.

The scandal!

"It will be all right," Emilia was saying, her hand smoothing the hair from Eva's face.

Breathing deeply, Eva worked to gain control of her emotions. Sitting up, she wiped the tears from her face and straightened her skirts.

"That's it," Emilia said. "Good girl. Now, you don't have to tell me who the father is, but… do you and he have an understanding?"

"An understanding?"

"Has he made a promise to you?"

"Oh!" Eva understood. "Well yes of course. He loves me, he tells me all the time."

Emilia frowned, her eyes flicking to the side before she smiled. "Well, that is good. I assume he is here, in Florence?"

"Yes."

"All right. Your father isn't here to speak for you, as he would normally. So, you will have to tell Elio."

Eva looked at her friend in horror. "Elio? But why?"

"You need a male family member… to make sure. To speak for you and ensure that this man does the right thing."

"You think he wouldn't?" Eva asked, breathless.

"I do not know. But he was happy to risk your reputation by taking you to his bed without a formal engagement." She paused, taking a deep breath. "It would be best to be cautious and tell Elio everything. It is his duty as your brother to protect you, after all."

The words stung. Protect her. Just as Elio had so recently espoused. The role of men and women.

And suddenly Eva realised just how foolish she had been.

Amadeo's passions, her love for him, had overwhelmed every instinct, every warning her mamma had given her. She'd allowed him to take her to bed. Had believed his promises and had never asked for anything official. His reasons had seemed so sensible, so caring.

But now she was vulnerable. What if he didn't wish to marry her? What if he denied her? Would people even believe that the child was his?

No. She stopped her swirling thoughts. This was the panic talking. Amadeo loved her; she knew that was true. He would marry her. He wanted to marry her. She was being silly. It was just the shock, that was all. If Emilia knew the father was Amadeo she wouldn't be so worried.

Peace settled over Eva. It was going to be all right. It was unexpected, sooner than planned, but part of their future. It would all be well. With Amadeo, everything always worked out.

And they could stop pretending.

She turned to Emilia. "Thank you, my dear, dear friend, for all you have done."

Finally, the joy of what she had just learnt surged through her. She was pregnant! She was having Amadeo's baby. She was going to be a wife and a mother.

Elio had been right, this was what she really wanted, deep in her heart. Her mind had not realised it, all these months fighting with the canvas, believing she wanted and needed something more. But her body had known and God had guided her path.

Eva was going to be a mother. Eva was going to marry Amadeo Renzetti.

For the first time since she'd arrived in Florence, she knew everything was going to be all right.

"Elio, can we speak in private?" Eva stood at the door to her brother's room. Elio frowned. "Now isn't a good time, Eva."

"Elio, please."

She saw his face twitch. Something in her voice had cut through his dismissal. He stepped back from the door and moved to allow her in.

"Can I offer you coffee?" he said.

"I'm pregnant."

Elio froze. Slowly he turned to her, face white with shock. "What?"

"It's all right," she said quickly, holding her hands up to placate. "He loves me, and we plan to be wed. We just got the timing a bit wrong..."

"Eva!" Elio raged, spittle flying from his mouth. "How could you be so stupid?"

Eva jerked back in surprise. Elio's face had turned crimson red. "Elio, it is all right. The father is Amadeo. He is wealthy and successful. It is a very prosperous match. We will be very happy..."

"Renzetti? Our professore? Eva... please tell me you mean a different Amadeo?"

Eva shook her head, a bemused smile on her lips as she took in her brother's horrified expression. He, of all people, should know how honourable Amadeo was.

"The one and same, our professore, Amadeo Renzetti. We started courting over the summer. He wanted to keep it quiet so it would not affect my studies. But I see now that you were right... I don't want to paint. I want to be a mother—"

"Eva," Elio interrupted. His voice was soft, rasping. She stopped and looked at him. He'd gone ashen. "Eva, Professor Renzetti is already married."

The floor disappeared beneath her feet. Eva stumbled forward a step. Elio caught her before she tumbled. Blinking rapidly she looked up at her brother. "Married? But he said..."

"He is married, Eva," Elio said gently, eyes softening in pity. "Her name is Gabriella. She is the source of his money, his success. They live on her country estate in Molise, just north of Puglia. It is where he was for most of the summer."

"There must be some mistake," she said, head shaking side to side.

"There is no mistake," Elio said. "I met her, in Rome. Renzetti introduced us when he visited me over the break. She is a little older than the professor. They've never managed to have children..."

He kept talking, but Eva didn't hear his words, the rush of blood in her ears suddenly drowning out all else. Amadeo visited Elio in Rome? Amadeo had a wife?

Bile rose in her throat. Realising she was going to be sick she lunged for the window but didn't make it. Vomit splashed to the floor, her knees gave way and she fell, a howl ripping from her soul.

"Mio Dio."

Elio came to his knees with her. "No! No! No!" she screamed, fingers bunching into her hair, latching onto fistfuls of her curls and ripping viciously. "You lie, you lie!"

"Eva, please. Stop." Elio gripped her wrists and forced her arms down, before wrapping her in his strong arms and holding her firm.

"Let go. Let go," she wailed, her throat raw from her cries and the acid burn of losing her stomach.

"Be still, be still," Elio repeated, over and over, restraining her with his crushing embrace, forcing her to stop her thrashing.

Soon her screams quieted, replaced by violent, flooding tears that coursed down her face in rivers. "How could he? How could he?" she moaned.

Elio didn't reply, just held her tight against his chest.

Eventually, her tears dried up. Her strength gone, she allowed Elio to gather her up in his arms and carry her to his bed.

"Rest," he whispered as he pulled a blanket up over her. "Stay here with me tonight. It will be all right, Eva. I promise."

She looked up at him in the dim evening light that peeked through the window.

"How?" she croaked, throat raw and aching.

"I meant what I said, Eva. I will always look after you. Professor Renzetti has wronged you most appallingly. He has lied and cheated you of your honour. He has lied to me too, I fear." He fell silent. Gazing down on Eva, her brother smoothed a lock of her curls from her face. "I will not allow him to get away with it, Eva. I will not."

"But wait, Elio. He does love me. I know he does. Please, don't hurt him."

Elio's eyes shone with wrath in the soft light. "I will fix this, Eva. Trust me. Sleep now. Sleep now."

He snugged the blanket to her chin, planting a kiss on her sweaty forehead, and Eva found her eyes were heavy. So, so heavy. Unable to struggle on she gave in to her weariness and collapsed into a deep sleep.

FORTY-TWO
EVA

The wind rattled through near-bare branches, tossing auburn leaves across the cobbles at her feet. One leaf caught on top of her foot, its dry body dragging gently over her stocking. Eva looked down and shook the leaf free. The wind caught it in a sudden rush of power, whisking it up towards the greying evening sky.

"Eva, come," Elio said. "We don't want to be late."

She bit back her retort. If they were late, it wouldn't be on her account.

She'd been ready for this meeting for weeks now. She had heeded Elio's instructions and kept mostly to her rooms. The lie of a seasonal chill the excuse to keep her from the studio. And from Amadeo Renzetti.

As Emilia had advised, Elio had insisted that he be the one to negotiate the situation with their professore: what was to be done about Eva and the baby growing inside her.

It had taken longer than she'd expected. Her girlish heart had believed Amadeo would choose her, his true love. That he would find a way to end his loveless marriage to Gabriella and make their love, and their child, official before God in a beautiful ceremony in the Cattedrale di Santa Maria.

It could never be more than a dream, however. Amadeo was already married, there was no place at his side for Eva as his wife. They could run away together, pretend to be wed and live a lie. Did such a deception really matter if their union was true in their hearts? Could she live with that secret sin? Could it be forgiven?

Over the long cooling days in her chambers, Eva fell further and further into her fears. To have a child out of wedlock would be the end of her future, her hopes and dreams. She would be cast out of her communities. She would never find a husband. She would be at the mercy of her father's kindness, and he was not a forgiving man. What if he disowned her?

The alternative was unthinkable. To end the pregnancy, by choice. A sin, pure and simple. And one God definitely would not forgive. It would allow Eva a future. The doctor had hinted at the option, she knew where to go for such a service.

But what would she tell Elio? And Emilia? That the pregnancy had ended naturally? Would they believe such good fortune?

Would it be good fortune?

For the pregnancy to end would be an answer to her problems. She could return to being Eva the art student and put this whole mess behind her. She would remain soiled, and impure, but without the proof of a child her ruined reputation was something she could conceal.

Yet, however appealing such an outcome might seem on the surface, it was not one she could hope for. Because already, in the few weeks that she had known of the baby in her womb, purest love had blossomed in her heart.

She did not know this child of her and Amadeo's bodies, this unborn baby, who signified so much turmoil in Eva's life. But she didn't need to. Despite the uncertainty and fear, the possibility of ruin, Eva loved the child growing within her body. This infant had her whole heart.

She didn't know what Elio had managed to arrange with Amadeo, but one thing was sure in her mind. She would be a mother to this baby, and she would love it with all her soul.

As they came to the narrow alleyway that led to Renzetti's rooms, Eva felt her pace slow. An old thrill of excitement lit in her breast. How many times had she snuck here, body alive with the anticipation of Amadeo's touch? How many nights had they passed entwined in ecstasy, skin streaked in the sweat of passion?

It had all been a grievous lie.

Back on those summer nights, she'd known exactly what awaited her beyond that wooden door. Renzetti's arms, his lips, his firm hands, his lust.

What awaited her today?

The answer she dreamed of? Or a future in ruins?

What would Elio expect her to choose?

What had Renzetti chosen?

Elio paused at the door, looking back at her. His expression softened, his eyes full of pity in the warm glow of the streetlamp.

"Ready?" he asked.

Taking a deep breath that settled to the bottom of her lungs, Eva lifted her chin and nodded once.

Elio knocked.

And the door opened.

A shadow fell over Elio, the light blocking Eva's view.

"Signore, it is good to see you," an unfamiliar voice said.

"And you, signora," Elio replied. He glanced at Eva, waving her forward. She stepped up. An older woman came into view: tall and slender, her neck bedecked in gemstone-encrusted jewellery, her head held high and regal.

"This is her?" the woman said.

"It is," Elio said. "Signora Renzetti, this is my sister, Eva."

Eva felt her mouth go slack as understanding dawned. Signora Gabriella Renzetti. This was Amadeo's wife.

The woman cast her eyes over Eva before giving an unimpressed sniff. "Come in then," she said, and turned for the stairs.

Eva looked at Elio in shock, seeking answers, but her brother would not meet her eyes. He faced forward and mounted the stairs, determination in his step, leaving Eva no choice but to follow. She closed the door behind her.

Signora Renzetti led them to Amadeo's drawing room. Eva watched her cross the threshold, her movements regal, as if she floated across the carpeted floor. Following behind her Eva felt stunted, inelegant, clumsy. The room was lit by a dim lamp, a fire crackling in the hearth, despite the mild night, warming the room beyond comfort. Eva felt a sheen of sweat break out over her skin even before she saw Amadeo. He stood at the far end of the room, one arm resting on the shelf of a bookcase, eyes downcast, cigar in hand. The smoke of the cigar mixed with that of the fire, creating an unwelcoming musky aroma. Eva gave an involuntary cough.

Signora Renzetti looked sharply at her, then, clicking her fingers in an audible snap, addressed Amadeo. "Put that out now. It is not good for the baby."

Amadeo obeyed, his movements furtive, sheepish, as he tossed the cigar into the fire before returning to the shelf. He still had not met Eva's eyes.

"Sit." The signora pointed at a chair by the window. Eva and Elio complied. "Not you," she said, eyes skewering Eva. "You stand here."

Eva stepped into the middle of the room. She could feel a trickle of sweat run down her spine and hoped it wouldn't pool in the small of her back and show through her dress. Signora Renzetti began to circle her, eyes flicking up and down her body, expression unreadable. Eva tried to keep her breathing steady, but the older woman's unexpected presence and her piercing assessment had thrown her completely. Of all the scenarios she had imagined, the presence of Amadeo's jilted wife had not been one of them.

At length, the older woman gave a curt nod, then walked calmly to an elaborately decorated chair and sat down. The room was silent as she adjusted her skirts around her, smoothing the cool purple silk into neat lines that draped over her feet.

Suitably settled, she looked up at Eva. Something flashed in her eyes, and Eva frowned. It wasn't the hot anger or resentment she'd expected; it was more like sorrow. For what? Herself? Was she realising that she had lost her husband? Had this been some bizarre meeting to allow her closure?

The urge to apologise rushed up from Eva's soul. To tell this woman she hadn't known, that she was truly sorry. But what would that do to help? It didn't change the facts. However unknowingly, Eva had wronged this woman. How brave she was to come here and face her husband's folly. Respect filled Eva's chest. Signora Renzetti was a strong woman. She would be all right. She would find a new path.

Eva understood now; Amadeo had chosen her and their love. They could not marry, but it was all right. They would still be together.

"I accept," the signora said. Relief flooded Eva's limbs so quickly that she nearly stumbled. She was about to say thank you, to praise Signora Renzetti's compassion, when the woman continued. "She can stay at the estate until it is done. Then you can collect her." Her attention had turned to Elio.

"No visits, it would prompt questions. She is just another maid, hired for the household. Maids don't have visitors. And you," her scrutiny fell on Amadeo. "Will not be welcome either. You and this girl will never again be together, alone or in company. Is that understood?"

Amadeo nodded, face long.

Eva frowned. "I am sorry," she said. "I... I don't understand—"

"It is for the best," the signora said. "You will be free to carry on with your life as if this unfortunate event never took place. And I will have the child I always prayed for. Some good can come from my husband's... indiscretion."

"Child? What child? Pardon me, signora, but I don't think—"

Signora Renzetti heaved a heavy sigh. "Are you slow?" She turned to Elio as if seeking an answer. "I won't risk a dim-witted child."

"Eva is highly educated and astute. She is simply in shock," Elio supplied.

Eva looked at him, confused. What was going on?

"I see," the signora said, her patience clearly coming to an end. "Then I will be crystal clear." She turned to Eva, leaning forward, her posture focused and determined. "Eva, you are to come with me to Molise. There you will live as one of my maids. I will have doctors attend to your every need, in secret. Once the child within you is born, you can return home to your family. The baby will stay with me and my husband, as our child.

"You can move on, find your own husband. And we will raise the child as ours. An heir to my family estate. A wonderful life. It is far better than you deserve, but the child is an innocent..."

"Raise my baby? What?" Eva interrupted, horror choking her throat. She turned to Elio. "This can't be the agreement? Elio? This is my child." Her hands seized her still flat stomach as her eyes welled with tears.

"Eva, calm yourself," Elio hissed. "This is the best possible outcome. Your child will have a family and security, love..."

"This is my child," Eva insisted.

"Oh be reasonable, girl," Signora Renzetti snapped, her voice dripping with disdain. "What alternative is there? You have the babe out of wedlock? What life would that be for the child? For you? Impossible, hateful future. A real mother could never condemn their child to such a life. So what other option is there? Find a man before you start to show? I won't allow such a deception. Besides, that child is as much my husband's as it is yours. You have no choice but to accept. I have agreed to take the child in as my own. To raise it with love, in a good and stable family." Her eyes flicked a warning glare at Amadeo. "The baby will grow in security and happiness, never knowing of this hideous secret. A proper life. For the child. And for you. That is my gift.

"Don't make me doubt you deserve it."

Eva stared at the signora, then Elio. How could her brother agree to this? How could he expect her to give up her child?

She opened her mouth to refuse. To throw herself at Amadeo's mercy. Remind him of the love they shared. Implore him to reconsider. She would beg. She was not so proud.

A heavy hand landed on her shoulder with a thud. Startled, Eva looked over. Elio stood beside her, legs braced for battle.

"She accepts," he said.

And that was that.

"I hate you!" Eva screamed at Elio. They were back in their rooms above Signora Pesci's house. The walk back through the streets of autumn in Florence had been as frosty as winter. Eva had no words. She tried and tried to find a way for Elio's plan to make sense. To see how it could ever be the right choice for her and her baby.

Objectively, the child would have a wealthy home. It would live safely, with all its needs attended to.

But it would be without its mother. Without Eva.

How could that be the right choice? To deny a baby the loving touch of the woman who birthed it?

And how could Elio think this was the right path? After all his talk of the role of women as mothers, and Eva needing to accept her true calling? Now he wanted her to ignore that passion in her soul? To turn away from the very thing he had argued she was born to be?

It didn't make sense. None of it made sense.

"Eva, be reasonable. There is no other way. Renzetti is married; we cannot change that." He stepped towards her, but Eva saw red. How could her brother, her twin, not understand? How could he expect her to give up her child?

"No," she said, turning from his reach. His hands gripped her sleeve and she jerked away. His finger caught the edge of her necklace. The force of her shove snapped the delicate chain and her ornate cross fell to the floor of their room.

"Eva, look what you've done." He knelt down to gather up the pendant, but Eva was too furious. She stepped forward and swung her leg. Her shoe caught the cross and propelled it to the other side of the room, into the wall. It landed on its edge, the right point of the cross denting, the gem popping free.

Elio stared at her flabbergasted. Then his lips firmed. "You are insane," he said, his voice a cold hiss. "I will leave you to gather your senses."

Pivoting on his heel, he stormed from their apartments and out into the dark of a Florence night.

Eva sank, down, down, down into a well of utter despair. Her feet slipped from beneath her, her body crashing to the floor. But she didn't feel the impact, didn't note the warm air that seeped up from Signora Pesci's fire through the cracks in the boards. For Eva's very soul was ice. There was no fight left within her. Rolling into a ball, she hugged her knees to her chest, eyes staring unfocused at the pale wall. And gave up.

. . .

That night, Emilia came to Eva's room. Eva watched from the floor as her friend entered, Elio on her heels. Emilia paused in the doorway, looking down at Eva, curled on the floor, and her face contorted in fury.

She'd turned to Elio, red climbing up her neck.

Words were exchanged, but Eva was too far within her own exhaustion to hear them. She saw Emilia's worried glance back at Eva, lying unmoving on the rough wooden panes of the floor. Emilia nodded as Elio explained, but the timbre of her whispered replies was angry and reproachful. In the end, Elio left, face blotched crimson, lips drawn into a thin line. And Emilia came to Eva. Gripping her arms her friend helped Eva rise from the floor and guided her to the bed against the far wall. As she did, Emilia's foot hooked the fallen pendant. Eva allowed herself to be tucked in. Emilia dipped down, collecting the pendant from her shoe before slipping into bed beside Eva.

"Here," she whispered, looping the pendant back around Eva's neck.

Eva looked down at the cross: dented now, imperfect.

Fresh tears sprang to Eva's eyes. "It's ruined," she said. "My birth cross, a gift from my nonna, ruined."

"No," Emilia said. "It has lived. As we all do, dented by life, but we continue."

Emilia drew Eva into her arms, enveloping her in a warm, comforting embrace.

It was a kindness Eva could not feel. The cold of her shock and sorrow too deeply rooted into her soul.

For what could she do? What power did she have?

None.

Not even her own brother would help her.

She lay in bed, still and numb as Emilia held her.

Her eyes were just beginning to droop when she felt her friend's whisper against her ear. "There is another way."

Eva's eyes flew open as hope flooded her heart.

"What other way?"

"We run."

PART 13
BARI, 1945

FORTY-THREE
ALESSIA

The house was unusually still as Alessia made her way into the kitchen. The pale blue of early dawn glowed through the worn cotton curtains, casting the silent room in an eerie glow. Normally Siena would already be up, preparing for the day. But after all that had transpired the night before, the smuggling and the horrible truth she'd learned about her loved ones in Rome, Siena must be exhausted. A late start was natural and necessary. It took rest to recover from loss, she knew that intimately. They'd all slept long when her mamma didn't come home.

Putting thoughts of Siena and her mamma aside, Alessia paced to the pantry to collect yesterday's bread. Placing the stale loaves in a large bowl, she covered them with water and sprinkled over a small portion of sugar. She set the mixture aside and poured some water into the kettle and set it to boil.

It wasn't long before Nonna Bianca joined her. Alessia smiled at the ageing woman as she hobbled across the tiled floor. The slowness of her step told Alessia her joints were troubling her, but she knew well enough not to comment. Bianca had her pride.

She wandered over to the mix of bread, water and sugar,

and taking up a wooden spoon, poked the harder pieces of bread, the knobs, helping them to disintegrate into the gruel that would break their fast.

Thudding steps on the stairs announced Niccolo's imminent arrival.

As his sleepy face appeared around the entranceway to the kitchen Alessia felt herself frown. Still no Siena.

Bianca must have caught the confusion on her face for she cleared her throat and said, "She was up late in the night. Cleaning in the cellar. I don't think she could find her rest, after everything..."

Alessia flicked her eyes to look up the stairs toward Siena's room, a question on her lips. But she chose silence, returning to the kitchen and her family to share the first meal of the day.

She understood; Siena needed time.

After breakfast, Alessia took Niccolo with her to the Piazza Mercantile, hoping to secure fresh bread for the day, water and maybe some fresh fruit. He was walking much better now that the damage to his legs had mostly healed. But the skin had tightened, scar tissue forming over the once raw burns. The doctors said it would loosen further with time and use. A morning walk would do him good.

As they stood at the fountain in the square filling their bucket, Luca appeared. Alessia drew herself up tall and squared her shoulders. She knew the truth of what the young man had been up to now. Always a sweet boy, good to his mamma and friendly with Niccolo, the responsibility of trying to provide for his mamma and grandparents had pushed Luca down a dangerous path. How things had changed since his brother Marco had gone to war. Would Luca have fallen to smuggling had his older brother been here to guide him? She didn't know, but the thought made her miss Marco even more deeply. Always so solid and dependable. Somehow, despite it all, she felt Marco would have protected Luca, protected them all.

Luca approached cautiously, coming to stand at her side.

"How is she?" he asked.

Alessia's heart warmed. There, in his quiet concern, was the boy she'd grown up with.

"Still in bed. Rome was a lot for her to deal with."

Luca regarded her with sad eyes. "I am sorry," he said. "I am just trying—"

Alessia placed a hand on his arm, stopping his words. "We do what we must," she replied and realised she meant it. For what else could any of them do? They had to survive.

A tentative smile touched his lips.

"Well," Alessia said to Niccolo. "Say good day to Luca." Then looking straight at the young man. "We must get on."

She didn't need to turn back to know that Luca's stare trailed her all the way down the street.

Making her way back up the small rise to her home, basket too light from her trip to the market, Alessia worked to ignore the stagnant air that sat thick and moist over her city. Even in spring the sun was hot in Bari, warming the streets, turning the sea mist into a miasma of humidity that slicked the skin and caused clothing to stick. At least there was enough water for washing now, she reminded herself. A small mercy.

"Has Siena risen?" she asked Nonna Bianca as she began the preparation of the day's pasta: mixing the dough and rolling it out to form orecchiette.

"No, I have not heard a peep out of her."

Alessia huffed. She understood her friend's sorrow, she really did. But wallowing in her room was not going to help anyone.

"Nicco, go up and knock on Siena's door. Don't enter without her permission though."

Niccolo rolled his eyes. "I am not so rude."

"Says the boy who rolls his eyes at his sister," Nonna Bianca cut in. "What do you say now?"

Niccolo's mouth twisted to the side, as his eyes lowered to the floor.

"Sorry, Alessia."

Alessia nodded through her discomfort. She knew Bianca was right to discipline the boy. And Niccolo was right to listen. But before the bombing he would not have acquiesced so easily. It had driven her crazy. His insolence, his stubbornness. She'd lamented her papa's absence as her little brother grew into a man without his father's guidance. Pushing at boundaries, becoming a man himself.

Since his return from the hospital, he had withdrawn into himself, never arguing, just agreeing.

The eye roll had brought a spark of hope to Alessia that the old Niccolo was returning, but Nonna Bianca had snuffed it.

As her brother made his way upstairs, Alessia ventured, "We should be gentler with him. He is still finding his new way."

"And we don't want that to be the wrong way, do we?" Nonna Bianca said, expression stern, eyes not lifting from her knitting.

Alessia suppressed a sigh. "Si, Nonna," she agreed.

A shout of surprise sounded upstairs, quickly followed by thudding footsteps.

"She's not there!" Niccolo announced loudly as he rushed into the kitchen.

"What do you mean?"

"I mean, I knocked and she didn't answer, so I knocked again and went in, and it's empty."

Alessia frowned. Had she done it again? Raced to Rome in the back of a smuggling truck? But no, that didn't make sense. Siena's smuggling contact was Luca, and Alessia had seen him in the piazza.

"She must have gone for a walk. She's done that before, in the mornings," Alessia reasoned.

"Not this time," Niccolo piped up.

Alessia cocked her head at her brother in question. "Why do you say that?"

"Because her belongings are gone."

"What do you mean her belongings are gone?"

"Well, like I said. When she didn't answer, I went in and the room was empty. Her bed was perfectly made. Her dresser cleared. So I opened her cupboard—"

"Niccolo!" Nonna Bianca scolded. "You know better."

"Well, it's good I did," he countered, defiance flaring in his tone. "Otherwise we wouldn't know that it was empty too."

"Empty?" Alessia pressed.

"Si, all her clothes are gone. There is nothing there."

Alessia met her nonna's eyes over Niccolo's head, concern writ over her face.

Could Siena really have left? Packed her things in the dark of night and snuck away? They'd grown so close these past months. Been through so much. Could she really simply walk out, without so much as a goodbye?

The swirl of emotions was overwhelming, Alessia felt them churn in her belly.

"She left a note."

Alessia's eyes snapped to her brother. "A note?"

"Si, on the bed."

"Niccolo, why didn't you say? Give it to me."

He looked at Alessia, forehead creased in confusion. "I didn't touch it," he said. "You said not to touch anything."

Nonna Bianca gave a snort of exasperation. "That part he obeys. Go see," she said to Alessia. "Bring it down to us."

Niccolo was right, Alessia thought as she stepped into Siena's room, it felt empty. She crossed the rough wooden floor to the cupboard and peeked inside. Nothing hung from the rail, the drawers were cleaned out.

Turning slowly, she cast her eyes over the room. There on

the bed sat a fat white envelope. Slowly she walked towards it. Running her hand over the patchwork quilt, she reached over and plucked up the envelope. It was light but lumpy. Something was nestled within.

"Open it, open it," Niccolo said as she entered the kitchen. Alessia sat down at the table beside Nonna Bianca and held the envelope before her. Her hands shook. Her mind was spinning. Flicking a glance to her nonna for encouragement, she gripped the edges of the envelope and tore.

The paper gave and the contents fell out onto the tabletop. A folded page and something soft.

Alessia reached down and gathered up the fallen necklace. Frowning, she stared at her palm. It was the cotton pouch, the ornament Siena always wore around her neck. The token from her mother.

"What is it?" Nonna Bianca said, leaning closer.

"Her necklace."

Bianca sniffed. "It is a goodbye," she said, standing stiffly. Alessia heard the note of sadness in her voice and saw the water that lined her eyes.

"There is a note."

"That would be for you," Bianca said, not looking back as she shuffled towards the front door, taking her leave. "As is the necklace."

"Would you like to hear it?"

"It is for you," Bianca repeated and disappeared outside.

Alessia watched the curtain that covered their doorway swishing slightly from Bianca's passing. She'd be tending to her herbs, Alessia knew. Getting on with the day as if nothing was out of the ordinary. But she knew Bianca had been upset by Siena's departure. She'd seen the sorrow in her gait. Her nonna wasn't ready to face those emotions yet.

Silent and gentle, Niccolo came to sit beside her. Without a word, he wrapped an arm around her shoulders and hugged her close. Alessia turned into his hug, taking comfort from her brother's closeness.

Wiping the tears from her cheeks, she pulled back from Niccolo. His hand reached down and picked up the small pouch. His mouth twisted to the side.

"She wore this?"

"Every day. It was a gift from her mamma."

He studied the small folded pouch, turning it around and around before handing it back to Alessia.

"Will you wear it?"

"Si."

His eyes fell on the folded note.

"Shall we read it together?"

"Si," Niccolo said.

FORTY-FOUR
ALESSIA

The war in Europe was declared over on 8 May 1945, but life in Bari continued much the same. The British and US forces stationed in the harbour lessened but did not fully withdraw, and the Italian government announced from Rome that their allies would stay on to help with the rebuilding effort.

For Alessia, Niccolo and Nonna Bianca little changed. Ration lines remained, food was scarce, but at least there was no longer the fog of fear that fresh bombs could fall from the skies at any time.

That nightmare was finally over.

But not the fear of the war's reach; all was not yet as it should be. Too many men remained unaccounted for, including Marco – and her papa.

Then he returned.

Alessia was in the kitchen rolling spaghetti when his loud, deep voice rumbled through the house, and the world went silent.

"My family."

Niccolo's face exploded into a smile. Nonna Bianca came to

her feet, hands over her mouth. Alessia turned, following their gaze, and there he was.

Tall and imposing as always, but thinner, leaner through the face, the material of his shirt hanging off his shoulders.

"Papa." The word cracked from her throat as her head shook in disbelief. "Is that you?"

"Si, my child, si."

Alessia was moving, her motion feeling as if she was working through dough, but her mind remaining stuck on the edge of the table, unable to keep up with the rest of the mix. Yet somehow, despite her wobbly limbs, she crossed the kitchen towards the father she had not seen or heard from in over three years. Niccolo got to him first, his too-long limbs folding around their papa, his head almost level with his father's. Alessia stumbled over just how tall little Niccolo had in fact grown, and how stooped her once proud papa had become.

There was no time to dwell on the thought though, as now it was her turn. Her papa's arms came around her, crushing her to his chest. He was thinner, painfully so, but that embrace held no less power. As her own arms wrapped around him, she felt outside her body. She relaxed, her knees giving. It was as if every muscle in her entire being suddenly let go of tensions held so deeply she'd not even realised they were there. And she knew – for the first time since her papa walked away to fight alongside Marco – she was wholly and completely safe.

That evening after a lean supper of bread and soup, the family gathered in the front room, savouring the cooling breezes from beyond the curtained doorway. Auri took his normal seat in the large padded chair, his body filling the space so long empty and cold. Niccolo curled up on the rug at his feet, his head resting on his father's knee as if he were still a boy, not the teenager the years had seen him grow into. No one chided him. In the corner, Nonna Bianca's knitting needles clicked. It was all so familiar, so normal, that Alessia's heart expanded, and her eyes watered with tears of gratitude.

"So, tell me more about this girl," Auri said.

Alessia crossed the room, taking a seat beside her papa. Adjusting her skirts, she shrugged. "Siena just appeared one day. A woman named Mila Pettiti sent her to you, asking you to give her sanctuary."

Auri frowned slowly. "I do not recognise that name."

His eyes tracked over to his mother. "Did you know her?"

"No," Nonna Bianca said, not looking up from her knitting.

"She also had a sketch, one from your days in Florence. I believe this Mila may have been a student of yours," Alessia continued.

"Do you have the sketch?"

"No, Siena took it with her when she left."

Auri leaned back in his chair, hand rubbing at the rough stubble on his chin, considering. At length he shrugged. "It is possible, I had many students," he said. "This Siena, she stayed here for more than a year?"

"Si, I was hesitant at first but... I remembered what you and Mamma always said: this is a house of God, we help those in need."

Pride shone in her papa's eyes, and Alessia felt the warmth of his approval flow through her. It was good to know she had made the right choice.

"Your mamma taught me that lesson. I am proud you have heeded her strength."

"Grazie, Papa. But in truth, all the homes of Bari have taken on extra residents. The war forced many from the farms and smaller towns. We don't have extended family to care for as they did. It was right that we helped where we could. We all had to pull together."

Auri's attention drifted, his eyes unfocused as if he was

reliving a dream. "It was much the same on the front," he said, then fell silent, his left hand tapping lightly where it rested on his knee. Alessia held in her questions. She had seen other men of Bari return from war, witnessed their dull eyes, their nervous gestures. She knew great pain lurked in their memories. She would be there to help her papa heal, when he was ready to share.

Tapping his knee a final time, Auri returned his attention to Alessia. "And you don't know where she is?"

"Siena? No. She left a note. All it said was, 'I hope your papa returns.'"

"And the necklace," Niccolo interrupted.

Her papa raised his eyebrows at Alessia. "A necklace? That's nice."

Alessia drew the rough twine from her neck and handed over the pouch.

"She always wore it," Alessia said.

The pouch lay in her papa's large worn hands, so small and fragile against his rough skin. A frown creased her papa's forehead, and he squinted at the pouch. Using the edge of one of his fingernails, he gently picked at the knot that bound the pouch to the string. The pouch unfolded across his palm, revealing what appeared to be the edge of a canvas, a depiction of the sea.

"Oh," Alessia breathed. "I didn't know it opened."

Her papa's face snapped towards her, his eyes blazing as he shot to his feet, knocking Niccolo as he did. He gripped the unfolded pouch in his fist and thrust it towards Alessia.

"What is this?" Spittle frothed over his lips, his teeth clenched.

Alessia physically baulked, involuntarily lurching away from her papa's ire. She glanced down at Niccolo, now crouching on the floor, his eyes wide with shock. "I... it was in the letter from Siena. Like Nicco said," she managed to stammer. "It was her necklace. She always wore it."

"And how did she get it?"

Alessia gaped at her papa, her mouth opening and closing like a fish on the sand. "It was left with her at the orphanage. From her mamma. A token she called it..." She trailed off, watching as the red flush of rage melted from her papa's face, his mouth going slack as the new lines of his skin deepened further still and his hands began to shake.

"Have you seen this?" he rasped over her head to Nonna Bianca.

The old woman had gone white as a sheet, her cheeks jiggling. She nodded slowly. "Si, but it was just a scrap. I didn't realise..." Her words tapered off.

Auri sank back down into his chair, staring ahead, unseeing, lips moving in silent prayer.

Time seemed to pause as he looked up and met Nonna Bianca's eyes across the room.

"It is hers," he said to Bianca.

Her nonna said nothing.

Alessia watched as they stared at each other, locked together in a realisation she could not understand.

Gulping down her confusion, Alessia whispered, "Papa? Who are you talking about?"

Auri faced her, a look of wonder now shining from his eyes, the side of his mouth lifting in a grin. A single tear streaked down his cheek.

"She called me Elio," he said softly. "Mamma called me Auri. The two nicknames for my given name, Aurelio. Nicknames from the two women I loved most in the world. They each held half my heart."

Bianca sobbed, tears streaming down her face, her body trembling. Alessia waited.

"Her name was Eva," he continued. "She was my sister."

FORTY-FIVE
ALESSIA

Alessia followed her papa down the stairs into the cellar. Behind her, Niccolo loped, his arm linked with Nonna Bianca, helping the old lady to navigate the descent. It was usually Alessia's job, but after this revelation... she could hardly face her nonna or her papa.

A sister who ran away. A daughter who was lost. A lie told every day since. Eva.

Taking a sharp breath in through her nose, Alessia worked to control her reaction, to keep her face blank, her expression neutral. She didn't understand, but she wanted to. She would give her papa a chance to explain.

Her foot scuffed over the stone floor of the cellar, layered in the dust of time and neglect, a single set of footprints tracking through the centre to a large cupboard, its doors still open. Siena. Her papa walked to the cupboard and went still, his body slumping.

Alessia approached and stood with him in silence.

Tears sparkled on the stubble of his cheeks, and sorrow tightened Alessia's throat.

He looked so weak, so vulnerable, standing there, war-thin

and worn, aged beyond his years. He'd only just made it home from battle. What horrors had he endured? Alessia knew about bombing and death as a civilian. What had he seen as a soldier? No letters had ever made it home. Was it all too terrible to share in a message? Too painful to recollect even on a page?

But he'd made it home. Where so many families wept over a coffin, the collars of their black mourning dress soaking from tears, her papa had walked right in the door. Thin and weak, but whole.

Only to have his world blown apart by some stranger he'd never met.

A secret held tight and close for all of Alessia's life, exposed in the moment of his return from death and blood.

She was confused, angry even. His revelation had rattled her to her core. But she loved her papa and she was so glad to have him back. Alessia placed a gentle hand on her papa's arm and squeezed. He glanced down at her, eyes brimming with tears, and patted her hand with his own, before stepping forward, breaking the contact between them. He reached into the old cupboard, then grumbled to himself in irritation. Standing back he scanned the room. His eyes fell on an old desk set against the wall. Something sat on its top. A sketchbook. He gave a rueful laugh, crossing to the desk. Hand twitching, he reached out to the book, his fingers grazing the cover. Nonna Bianca shambled over. Her papa placed an arm around his mother's shoulders, the two staring down at the sketchbook. The soft crackle of time sounded through the room as he flipped the pages one by one.

"I thought you destroyed it," Bianca said.

"I couldn't," her papa choked. "She was so talented."

A warm hand slipped into hers, and Alessia turned to Niccolo. He looked lost, bewildered. Just like she felt. She squeezed his hand tight, and they joined their papa and nonna together.

Auri shifted to allow them to see. "This was her sketchbook. I bought it for her before I left for the war... the first war." He fell silent, teeth grinding over some distant or recent memory. Then he started turning the pages again. Page, after page, after page, filled with charcoal depictions of Bari and of the fields of wildflowers that grew at Nonna's old home, the big house.

"They are so real," Niccolo said, and Alessia hummed her agreement.

Their papa nodded sadly. "She was always the artist," he said. "We only made it to Florence because of her."

Alessia eyed him, noting the flush of shame that crept up his neck. Then he pulled a folded canvas from the sketchbook. Laying it out over the desk, he took the pouch from Siena's necklace. With careful, almost reverent movements, he aligned the scrap from Siena's necklace along the torn edge of the canvas. A perfect fit. Alessia could barely breathe. She scanned the completed canvas, saw the woman standing by the seas of Bari, her head looking away, obscuring her face.

"This is Eva," her papa said.

Alessia stared at the painting, at this woman who was her aunty. Who had she been to Siena? Why did Alessia's friend have part of this canvas around her neck?

The questions burst from her in a rush. "Why didn't you tell us about her? Why did you hide her from us? What happened to her?"

Nonna Bianca gave a painful wail, her gnarled hands coming up to cover her face.

"We tried to find her – we tried, we tried. My daughter, my daughter." She began to sway on her feet, fist pounding her chest over her heart, crack, crack, crack. "We failed you, we failed you," she moaned. Niccolo went to her instantly, grabbing her hands to still the violent beating of her fists and enfolding her in a hug.

"Calma, Nonna. Calma," he whispered, rocking her gently.

Alessia watched as her nonna stilled, her body going limp in Niccolo's arms.

But she didn't join them. Grief pulsed from her nonna and her papa. She should have hurt for them. She should have felt a wave of sorrow and rushed to comfort them. But her mind had emptied, her senses dulled. Like walking through a blanket-thick sea mist before a storm, Alessia could not see a way out, could not understand.

"Why?" the word reverberated in the cavernous space of the cellar. No one spoke. Even Nonna Bianca silenced her cries. Everything went still.

"Eva made a mistake," her papa began. ""She had an affair with a married man, our professore at the Accademia in Florence. His name was Amadeo Renzetti. He was brilliant and passionate, and a rogue." He stopped, shaking his head. "I trusted him," he whispered, more to himself than anyone. Swallowing audibly, he continued. "When Eva told me she was pregnant, I couldn't believe it. I was so angry. What could I do? How could I fix this?"

His eyes sought Nonna Bianca, but she had turned away, burying her face in Niccolo's shoulder. Hiding from the past. From the truth.

Auri heaved a sigh. "I went to Amadeo, searching for a solution. And he gave me one.

"I thought it was brilliant. A way to save my sister... my Eva..."

"What solution?" Alessia asked.

Auri closed his eyes and pressed his fingers to his forehead. "We agreed Amadeo and his wife should take the baby. That Eva should never be named as the mother. To keep her reputation intact, to give her a future..."

Alessia blinked. Such a plan – could any mother agree to it?

"What did Eva say?"

Bianca wailed again. "My daughter. I am so sorry, my daughter."

Alessia glanced her way, saw the barely contained panic in her brother's face. She should go to him. Stop this and get him out and away. Keep him separate from this terrible secret. She should protect her fratellino.

But the need to understand overwhelmed her reason. She turned back to her papa. "What did Eva say?"

Her papa sucked a deep breath in through his nose. "She agreed. We didn't really give her a choice."

"But," Alessia said. Because there was a but; they were all here in the cellar because there was a but.

"But then... she disappeared."

Nonna Bianca groaned.

"Alessia." Niccolo's panicked hiss reached her ears but she was beyond caring.

"You looked for her?" she pressed.

"Of course..."

"But you didn't find her?" Her voice was rising, ratcheting up as her tension mounted.

"No... I—"

"And you hid her existence from us?" It came out as a screech. Tight and hoarse, from the base of her throat and her soul.

Silence fell over them, heavy with omissions.

Her papa met her eyes, sorrow and sadness glowing on his face. "Please understand."

But the boil of angry confusion had taken Alessia over. This lie – this was a big lie, a huge lie. She'd only ever faced such betrayal once before when German bombs fell from the sky.

"Why did you lie?" she screamed.

Auri crumpled then, the little remaining strength in his body vanishing as he sagged forward physically, hand on the desk to steady himself.

"Eva was gone," he said simply. "We had to keep going. We had to endure."

A memory flashed through Alessia's mind. Of this cellar, the night Siena had arrived. Of another torn canvas. The heat of fury raced from Alessia's stomach. Pivoting, she strode across the room to the gingerly balanced stacks of canvases and frames that leaned against the wall. Her fingers danced lightly over the dust-shadowed frames as she searched. Then she gripped the gilded frame and pulled. Out came a large, bright picture in oil paint, the sweeps of the brush so thick that the cellar lamp cast shadows over the canvas from their strikes. The left of the image was missing, the canvas torn away, leaving a ragged edge. The painting Siena had found that first night she stayed. It seemed so long ago.

She whirled around to face her papa, holding the picture before her. "This was her, wasn't it? In this family portrait. You threw her away."

Aurelio's face fell, his skin blanched. "When your mamma and I moved to the city, we wanted a fresh start. To leave all that behind."

"Don't you blame my mamma."

"I didn't mean—"

"She was your sister. Eva was your sister." She could not stem the rage, could not quiet her mind, her soul. It was an inferno, a boiling pan of stew, frothing over, covering everything in a sticky mess, but she could not stop.

"You destroyed her memory!"

She watched her papa struggle within himself. He looked up at her, hands rising, voice beseeching. "Please, Alessia. It was scandalous. She was unwed. And she had run away. You know how it is in our country. We are a traditional people. We would have been shunned."

"You could have said she had died. You could have kept her memory alive."

"Si, but..." He sighed, turning away.

"But what?" Alessia demanded.

"But I believed in Mussolini's Italy," Auri cried. Red now blotted across his skin.

Alessia felt the air escape her lungs as her mind rushed forward, connecting dots.

"You went to Naples, for the March on Rome. Nonna said." Her eyes darted side to side as the terrible truth came crashing down on her. "You marched on Rome with the fascists, you believed in their values. Oh!"

Her hand covered her mouth as her stomach dropped from her body. "You disowned her. Because she was the wrong woman for Italy. You decided to remove her from your life. You disowned your own sister."

"Alessia." Nonna Bianca's voice cut through, hard and raw with anger. "How could you suggest such a thing?"

Alessia glared at her papa. "Did you even look for her?"

"Alessia."

"Did you?"

Aurelio did not meet her stare. "No."

Now it was Nonna Bianca's turn to stare. "No, no, no, you searched," she croaked at her son. "You asked far and wide."

"I never searched. She made her choice. She left me. And I was angry. So, so angry," Aurelio said. He clasped his hands in front of him, pacing away. "I tore her from my paintings. I destroyed her artwork. Burnt her canvases. All of them. Everything except that sketchbook and her portrait by the sea. I erased her from my life because she left me!" he shouted, knees visibly shaking. "I continued my study in Florence, took up the offer to tutor. I forced her out of my mind, out of my thoughts. I was so angry at her. For choosing to leave me. For choosing her baby over me. I was her family. Me." He beat his chest. "Her twin. She should have chosen me."

The room was still, each person silent as they witnessed

Aurelio's confession. Alessia was reeling. He had wiped his sister from his life. Hidden her image, torn her from their family history. Alessia had had an aunty. Nonna Bianca had had a daughter. How could they make such a choice? How could they?

Warily, Alessia spoke. "Yet you kept the sketchbook." It wasn't a question. It was the reach of a hand across time, to offer her papa a chance at redemption.

He looked up at her, head loose on his shoulders. "Si, because, under the anger and the hurt, under it all, I never stopped loving her."

He was trembling, but the heat had gone out of his words.

A sob echoed through the room as Nonna Bianca clutched her heart.

"I realised my mistake too late. A hospital in Lucca contacted me. She had given birth, but she was in trouble. The whole time, she was only a few towns over..."

Alessia felt her breath quicken as the pieces of this story began to fall into place.

"I was too late," her papa continued. "By the time I made it to Lucca, Eva had passed away."

"And her child?" Alessia whispered.

Auri turned away from her question, rubbing his face with his hands, shoulders bunching in.

"It is time," Bianca said from the side of the room, moving from Niccolo's protective embrace. "It is time, my son."

Auri looked at his mother. She nodded her eyes full of sadness, a sorrowful twist on her lips. Alessia watched as her papa accepted Bianca's words, his large frame withering still further as he faced the past. And the puzzle completed in her mind. At that moment, all the confusion, all the rage, all the anger in her heart fell away. A torn canvas by Eva di Bari. A baby. An orphan. Siena.

"It is all right, Papa," she ventured, stepping forward. "I

understand." She stepped forward again. "Siena was Eva's baby. She didn't know. But when you saw that pouch... You knew it was the token Eva left with her child. Left with Siena at the orphanage. I have put it together."

Auri's eyes met hers, a world of pain swirling within them. "No," he whispered. "Siena was *one* of her babies." He paused, heaving an impossibly heavy sigh. Coming forward he took Alessia's hands in his, his skin ice cold where they touched.

"Alessia," he whispered. "My sister, Eva. She didn't have one baby. She gave birth to twins."

The world disappeared from beneath Alessia's feet.

PART 14

LUCCA, 1921–1922

FORTY-SIX
EVA

The first light of dawn reflected off the River Arno as Eva and Emilia made their way to the main train station of Florence. Their destination: anywhere else. They each carried one suitcase, packed to bursting with the few belongings they could cram inside. For Eva, her sketchbook, a few clothes and her original submission painting that had won her a place at the Accademia and had started all of this. Emilia had insisted that she not leave that behind; she would not be coming back.

At the waiting train, Eva paused, looking out over the waking city. The white walls of the buildings shone pale yellow in the early morning sun, the terracotta tiles a muted orange in the cool of winter.

"Together," Emilia said, her words an offer of possibility, a choice. It was up to Eva to follow through. She boarded the train.

They stopped in Lucca, a small town near to the coast of Italy. Not famous, or loud or busy, a simple village. Somewhere they could disappear.

Together they found lodgings in the spare room of an old nonna's home. Her husband was recently deceased, her children had moved away. Old Giovanna was glad of the company and kept the rent low.

Eva found work at a local tailor, Emilia at a florist, and for months they passed their days in quiet hiding, telling each other stories of the life they would craft together once the baby had come.

Snug together in their shared bed one night, the friends whispered, offering hope in the dark as they navigated their changed reality.

"I think we should buy some land and start a farm," Emilia said.

"And grow flowers," Eva enthused.

"That sounds perfect."

Eva shuffled, working to find a comfortable angle to rest her growing stomach.

"What is it?"

"It is nothing, I just feel... full, all the time."

Emilia laughed softly and inched over, giving Eva more room.

"It is more than that. There is something on your mind. Tell me?'

Eva huffed a breath and reached down, taking Emilia's hand. "I don't want to sound ungrateful," she began, then paused.

"Go on," Emilia encouraged. Eva eyed her in the silver moonlight that filtered through Signora Giovanna's worn curtains. "I am so glad to have you here with me," she said. "But I can't help but wonder why you are here. You gave up your studies to help me. You gave up Elio..."

"Elio was not much to give up," Emilia scoffed.

But Eva felt the tension that coursed through Emilia's body, pressed together as they were in this small bed.

"You cared for him, loved him even. I could see it when you looked at him."

Emilia released a heavy sigh. "Was I so obvious?"

Eva squeezed her hand in reply.

"Fair enough. Si, I cared for your brother very much. That first semester, when we met at the cafe and talked over coffee, I thought something was growing between us. It started with just sharing our thoughts on our lessons, our feelings and our struggles. Then it grew. He drew me a sketch of a beautiful harbour. Watching him as the pencil glazed over the page, it was beautiful to see. When he gave me the sketch, I thought... Well, it doesn't matter what I thought. You know what happened. Elio became withdrawn, then he went to Rome..."

Eva closed her eyes. She knew what Emilia was saying: she'd felt abandoned then too.

"When he returned, I had hope. He had such fire and passion back. I thought the man I loved had come back. But..." She stopped, her mouth working as she thought. "Your brother is broken. Perhaps from the Great War, or something else... I can't be the one to fix him. What he tried to do to you. To force you to give up your child." Her head shook and Eva saw a tear track down her cheek. "I could not love a man who would do that to a woman, especially his sister."

Now it was Eva with tears wetting her skin as love and thanks swelled up within her, for this friend beside her and the chance to keep her child that she had brought.

"Those men he has been spending time with. Their ideas for Italy—"

"Are no excuse for Elio's choices."

"Grazie," Eva said, grateful for Emilia's loyalty. "I don't know what I would have done without you."

"Prego. We are in this together."

It was weeks before Giovanna realised Eva's secret.

As her stomach began to swell against the waist of her skirts,

Giovanna sniffed. At first, Eva joked that her rapidly rounding belly was from the ample substance fed to her by her generous landlady. But as the frosts of the new year deepened, browning the countryside around Lucca and crisping the air, she could no longer deny Giovanna's suspicions.

"Signora," she said one evening as they were preparing for bed. "Can we talk?"

Giovanna paused at the washing basin, wet cloth pressed to her face. Eva noted the distinct rise and fall of her shoulders as she breathed deeply, readying herself to answer.

"A war death?" the old woman said. "Your husband?" She turned, pointing directly at Eva's protruding belly.

Eva released a slow breath, vying for time. The months simply did not add up. The Great War had finished over three years before. She could not possibly be a war widow.

Giovanna sensed her hesitation and explained, "Not all died on the front." She raised her eyebrows expectantly and Eva understood. The landlady was offering her a story, a way to explain her pregnancy without a husband to care for her. A tale that would be believed and accepted. That would inspire pity.

"Si," Eva whispered, eyes glancing down. Hating the lie, but understanding the need.

Giovanna finished drying her hands. "You take my bed."

"No, no," Eva began.

"You take my bed," Giovanna insisted. "I will share with Emilia. You are with child. Very big with child. You need proper rest."

"But, Giovanna, your back," Eva reasoned.

The old nonna huffed. "Your baby is what matters now. My bed. We will talk no more of it."

Eva's time came with the first buds of spring. Giovanna ran water and brought towels; the ruse about a war husband might work on the streets, but in a hospital there would be administrative expectations, records and names. A home birth, without the questions, was an easier path.

Eva strained and cried and pushed and bellowed, Emilia beside her for every moment of the agony. When she thought she could suffer no more her child was born. Giovanna wrapped the squalling babe in a blanket and lay it on Eva's chest. A pair of perfect blue eyes stared up at Eva and her heart bloomed with purest love.

"She is a strong one," Giovanna said.

"My daughter," Eva crooned. Then gasped in agony as another powerful contraction tore through her stomach.

Giovanna frowned and knelt between her legs.

"Mio Dio," she exclaimed, taking the baby from Eva and handing her quickly to Emilia. "You must push again. There is another."

"Another?" Eva's eyes almost popped from their sockets in shock. But her body gave her no time to consider further as another pulsing pain ripped through her core. A few minutes later, Giovanna held up a second child, smaller and silent.

Eva lay sprawled on the bed. Every part of her felt shredded and sore. She breathed, working to recover her senses. Then she noticed the silence. Pushing herself up on her elbows, Eva looked across at Giovanna. The old woman had her back to Eva, the second baby still in her arms, obscured from Eva's sight. "Giovanna? Why isn't the baby crying? Giovanna?"

The old woman didn't answer. In Emilia's arms, the first baby slept peacefully. She met her friend's worried face. Eva felt her breathing quicken as panic began to replace the aching fatigue.

The baby still hadn't cried.

"Oh no," she sobbed. "No, no." Somehow she managed to swing her legs over the edge of the bed. Her feet hit the floor with a thud and pain tore up the insides of her body. But it didn't stop her. She moved towards Giovanna. One foot, then the other. Still, the room was silent. No cry, no words of comfort from Giovanna. She'd almost reached the old woman, her hands reaching out to her, when the purest sound she'd ever heard strained out, filling the room. It was a small cry, more a mewling, but to Eva it was music. Giovanna turned around, her face red with exertion, sweat beading along her brow, but her mouth was split in a beatific smile.

"She is well," she said.

"She? Another girl?"

"Si, smaller, weaker. But she is here."

Eva gathered the blood-streaked baby from Giovanna's arms, holding her child to her heart. "You made it, baby," she whispered softly. "And your sister too. You made it."

"And so did you," Giovanna said, her eyelids heavy now. Seeing Giovanna's fatigue reminded Eva of her own. Fuelled by the fear for her child, she'd forgotten the hours of labour she had just endured. But the toll had to be paid. Her knees quaked, her legs suddenly unreliable.

"Bed," Giovanna ordered. She didn't have to ask twice.

The week that followed passed in a haze of pain, sleep, feeding and exhaustion like Eva had never known. But through the fog of fatigue, the broken sleep, the worry and the discomfort, Eva was buoyed by love. True, deep love. She slept with the babies cradled at her side, fed them, kissed them and breathed in their milky scent. It was a bubble of perfection that Eva was happy to stay in, for as long as possible.

But life had other plans.

She noticed Giovanna giving her long looks as she came in with trays of soup and bread to sustain her as she healed. Then one day the old woman set her hand to Eva's forehead. Sleeping, Eva barely stirred at the touch.

A "tsk" clicked from her throat as Giovanna threw back the covers, exposing Eva's body to the cool air of the room.

"Don't wake the girls," Eva mumbled, eyes opening into a narrow slit against the light of the room. She saw the frown on Giovanna's face but was too tired to ask what was wrong. Her eyes fell closed again as sleep reached up for her.

"Wake up!" Giovanna's voice cracked like a whip. Eva opened her eyes. The room was blurry and out of focus. She blinked, trying to clear the sleep from her vision, but she couldn't seem to bring the features of Giovanna's face into alignment.

"Sit up," the old woman was saying. "Up, up."

Eva pushed her hands into the mattress, but nothing happened. It was as if her fingers went right through the mattress. "How strange," she whispered.

Giovanna hissed. Reaching down she gathered up the two babies, carrying them across the room to lay on the nearby chair.

"No," Eva managed to say. "They stay with me."

"You can have them back in a moment," Giovanna said. "When did you last get out of bed? Wash yourself?"

Eva regarded Giovanna vaguely. "This morning."

"And what day is today?"

Eva's head swam, her mind slow, like feet stepping through sucking mud. "I..."

A church bell sounded outside. The loud clanging ricocheting through the streets of Lucca. "Sunday," she said.

Grumbling, Giovanna took hold of Eva's arms. "Stand up."

Eva tried to comply. Her legs felt like stone blocks as she struggled to lift them off the mattress, the weight of her thin nightgown holding her down. Somehow she managed. Standing before Giovanna she swayed on her feet. "I am just so tired," she said.

Something warm gushed down her legs, landing with a splat

on the floor. Eva looked down. The movement rocked her head, and again the room began to spin.

She was dimly aware of Giovanna's panic. "Mio Dio," she cried as her hands gripped Eva's gown, pulling it up to expose her lower body.

"There has been some bleeding," Eva managed to say.

Giovanna placed her hands on either side of Eva's face, holding her steady as she looked directly into her eyes. Eva smiled. "You have been so kind to me."

Beyond Giovanna's shoulder Eva saw Emilia step into the room.

"You too, my friend."

Giovanna's face twisted into a grave expression. "It is all right. I will pay you back."

Brow furrowed with concern, Giovanna called to Emilia. "Fetch the medico." Emilia raced from the room while Giovanna helped Eva back into bed, settling her stiff body on the mattress and laying Eva's head in her lap. The old lady soothed her palm over Eva's brow and sang a gentle lullaby, rocking Eva to sleep.

Hours, days, moments later, Eva was roused again. This time it was a man she opened her eyes to. It should have shocked her, should have had her calling for decency. But she was just too tired to care.

Giovanna hovered behind the man. "You see, doctor," she was saying. "It is the birthing sickness."

The words made no sense to Eva. And where were her baby girls? Giovanna had them...

The blanket was moved from her and Eva shivered at the cold touch of the air. Her skirts were lifted, the rough sensation of dried blood scratching over her skin, and a firm hand pressed on her belly. She cried out as a sharp pain shot through her core.

"She must be brought to the hospital," the doctor was saying.

"What of the babies?" Emilia said.

"There is no room for healthy patients."

"But they need her milk."

"There is a church..." Giovanna said.

"It is all right," Eva said. "I am just tired. It is all right."

Eva managed to hold her eyes open, watching Giovanna's face floating above her, expression full of sorrow. "I will see the babies are safe," Giovanna said.

Eva frowned. Safe? Of course, her babies were safe. They were with her.

She heard a ripping sound that roused her from her stupor. Looking over, she saw Emilia standing by her painting, the corner torn, a section of canvas in her hand. She opened her mouth to protest the destruction of her work, but the thought slipped sideways, disappearing into a fog. She collapsed back into her pillows.

She felt Giovanna's hand in her hair, felt the red ribbon being pulled gently from her curls. Eva reached up to take it, but somewhere between the movement and the moment her fingers touched the soft silk, she fell into darkness.

PART 15
CONSEQUENCE

FORTY-SEVEN
ALESSIA

Bari, 1945

"When I heard from the hospital, I left straight away. But I was too late." A hush descended over the cellar.

Alessia swallowed against the ache in her throat, the ball of pain that had formed as her father recounted this story. This horrific, dreadful story. Across the room, Nonna Bianca stood in silence, eyes red from crying. Niccolo remained by her side but, unsure of what to do, simply lingered nearby, watching anxiously.

Alessia returned her attention to her papa as he continued. "She was so small. So frail. Lying there on the mortuary table. So... insubstantial. A shell of my beloved sister. My twin."

He straightened, rubbing a hand over his face and taking a deep breath.

"The babies?" Alessia ventured.

Regret filled his face. "Signora Giovanna could not care for them, and the hospital was overstretched. She had handed them in to the local church. Each with a token: a folded piece of Eva's greatest painting, and the red ribbon from her hair." His gaze fell on the open sketchbook on the desk, the beautiful ribbon that lay across the page.

"But there was a mix-up," he said. "Like all places for orphans in Italy, the church was overwhelmed. Too many orphans of war, and too many given up by families unable to feed them... Struggling for space, they kept the weakest children only in Lucca. The strong ones were... distributed.

"Eva's firstborn was hale and hearty. She'd been sent to a wet nurse in the countryside. I tracked the woman down, but the baby was gone. Sent to an orphanage with more space." He stopped. Turning to Bianca he pleaded. "You know how I tried to find the baby. You know."

"Si, my son, si," Bianca said, voice breaking on each word. "I know. I know." There was forgiveness in her tone, love and understanding. This search – for the baby – this had been real, Alessia realised. It was his atonement.

"And the other baby?" A sense of dread had spread across Alessia's chest, a belt tightening around her lungs, squeezing, slowly, slowly, slowly. Her body was fizzing, trying to warn her, trying to prepare her. Auri looked into her eyes, hands raised in supplication, and Alessia knew.

She knew.

He didn't have to say it. And yet, he did. She needed to hear it, she realised. Needed to hear the words.

She met his stare and held it. A challenge and a show of strength. Her nonna was right, it was time to tell her the truth. All of it.

"Eva's second born was sickly from birth," he began. "The nuns kept her in Lucca. I found her easily, the red ribbon..." Walking to the desk he picked up the ribbon, running its soft length between his fingers. "I took her home to my mamma." A glance at Bianca. "Saw her fed and clothed. Watched her fill out, though she was always small for her age. She started to smile, to laugh." A light had come into his voice, happiness washing over his features, despite all that was unravelling in this terrible moment. A memory that surpassed it all. "She was so beautiful, so joyful. Always happy, giggling. I fell in love with her."

"What did you name her?" Alessia croaked, hands clenched tight at her sides.

Auri closed his eyes, taking a deep, bracing breath. "It is as I have always told you, my child," he said, opening his eyes and meeting her stare. "For my grandmother. I named you *Alessia*."

She'd known what he was going to say, but the words still hit like a punch to her heart. The air whooshed from Alessia's lungs. The walls of the room seemed to press in, suffocating, heavy. Her hands gripped the collar of her dress, the material suddenly too tight, too close. She pulled, trying to free her throat to breathe as her lungs puffed like bellows. Suddenly the cellar was too tight, too close. She had to get out. Out of this tiny cellar. Out of this space, this house, this reality.

She pivoted, racing for the stairs.

"Alessia!" her papa called. But Alessia didn't stop. She charged up the stairs, across the house and out onto the streets of Bari.

The evening air was soft and warm, the pastel light of the setting sun casting a gentle glow over her neighbours' houses. Too soft, too warm, no, no, no. Pina and Luca looked up at her, but she didn't stop. Turning away from their curious stares, she ran. Along the edge of the city walls, past the Basilica San Nicola, through the gates to the sea. She ran. Ran until her shoes hit the rocky coastline that bordered Bari, holding back the waves. And continued running, plunging her feet, shoes, stockings and skirts into the blue water of the Adriatic, splashing out through the waves. She ran and ran and ran.

Collapsing to her knees, the water came to her waist, soaking her to her skin. Hands braced on her thighs, she knelt in the currents, the waves lapping gently around her. She inhaled deeply. Drawing the scent of salt and sea and air into her lungs, down deep to become a part of her. One thing, one thing that was real and true, despite all that had just been said: the seas before her, around her, in her, were real. She closed her eyes.

Her mamma's face filled her vision. Her gentle smile, her kind eyes. Her lullaby filled her ears, a song of safety, of warmth, of love. Alessia bundled in her arms, her touch strong and unyielding.

Alessia opened her eyes. The vision faded; the woman she'd called mamma disappeared like sea mist over the waves. For the woman she remembered as mamma had never truly been hers. Never...

"She loved you as her own."

The words found her from the shore, and Alessia turned.

Her papa stood ankle-deep in the waves. The strengthening winds off the Adriatic blew his shirt behind him like a sail. "I did too. And always will. Come out of the water."

Alessia hesitated, the waves of the sea rippling around her. It was all so, so much. She didn't know what to say, what to feel.

But her papa was watching her with such open love, such longing. Alessia's legs began to move, lifting her and carrying her to his side.

He took her hand and helped her up the rocky edge of the bay, before sitting down on the flat of an outcrop, arm wrapping around her and tucking her into his chest, as he had so many times when she was small.

Alessia stayed there, leaning into his strength, felt his warmth seeping into her limbs and allowed herself to be comforted by that familiar strength and love.

"Where is she?" Alessia asked. She knew her papa understood her question.

Auri, or as Eva had called him, Elio, squeezed her shoulder. "You remember the wildflowers at the big house? Where we lived with Nonna and Nonno when you were very small? Before we moved to Bari?"

The muscles of her face relaxed as the memory of walking through the plumes of daisies and irises, her mamma's hand in hers, filled her mind.

"Si."

"I took her there. It was her favourite place as a child. I took her home."

"Did Mamma—" she paused nervously. "Did Chiara know Eva was buried there?"

"Chiara was your mamma," Aurelio said firmly. "She truly loved you. And yes, yes she did. I think that's why she took you for walks through the flowers. So you could be near both of your mammas."

Alessia watched the gentle waves before her, the hairs on her arms rising in the chill air. Two mammas, lost in childbirth. A sister and a wife. What pain her papa had been through. Such loss.

"Why didn't you tell me?" Alessia asked.

Aurelio sighed heavily. "For the same reason I pushed my sister to give you away. Because of the stigma. You would have been a bastard child, born of sin. I had learned I didn't care. That love mattered so much more than ideals; the March on Rome taught me that. But the world doesn't work that way.

"So I chose to tell a different story. The story of a man and his wife who had a baby and then moved to Bari for work. It was for your future."

"And the other child? My... sister? Siena..." Her mind stuttered on those words; that revelation was almost too much to comprehend. These last eighteen months, her own sister had been by her side. Supporting her, helping her, guiding her... and she hadn't known. Neither of them had known.

Aurelio squeezed Alessia's shoulders, pulling her closer. "There was no trace. Records were poor, the number of abandoned children... I chose to protect you. But I never stopped hoping."

Alessia nodded against his chest, the quiet strength of her papa a comfort against the turmoil of the truth.

She felt him stiffen slightly and looked up. "What is it?" she asked.

She saw the bounce of his throat as he swallowed anxiously. "I was wondering about the girl, Siena? Your sister. What is she like?"

Despite the flood of confusing emotions those words provoked, a genuine smile broke across Alessia's lips. "Siena? She is stubborn and pushy and opinionated," she began, and felt her papa chuckle. "And difficult and argumentative. And the best friend I think I have ever had."

He went still. They sat together, feet in the seas that cupped their city, eyes turned to the horizon. Alone in their thoughts and memories, together in this moment of truth.

Then Alessia stirred. "We need to find her. Tell her who she is."

Aurelio released a breath. "I suspect she might have worked it out when she saw the painting."

"So where did she go?"

She felt her papa start and looked up at him. His lips twitched into an uncertain smile. "I think I know," he whispered.

Alessia waited, watching as his features settled into a look of amazement.

"Where?" she prompted gently.

"To the first woman I asked to be your mother. My first love. The woman who never stopped looking for your sister. My Emilia."

FORTY-EIGHT
SIENA

Tuscany, 1945

Siena stared out over lush green fields framed in a blaze of colour and light. Two heads bobbed up and down between the rows of sunflowers and oleander, one topped with a neat straw hat, the other a mess of greying hair. It had taken months to grow back when Signore Alfredo Pettiti was liberated from the internment camp at Teramo. But as his face and body filled out from nourishment and safety, so too did his hair return.

His smile was still waiting.

Siena breathed in deeply, allowing the rich scent of earth and green and life to fill her from the inside out. She'd been here almost a month now. After seeing the painting in Alessia's cellar, she'd set out immediately.

And she'd been welcomed by open arms and eyes full of tears.

Siena had known it the moment she'd seen the sketch: the young woman, beautiful and serene, the Bari sea at her back, a riot of curls held back by a red ribbon. Curls just like Siena's. The sketch was perfect in its detail, right down to the gem-studded cross and the too-fine chain links. In that instant, Siena had understood: her journey to Bari for refuge was also her journey to her past.

The sound of tyres on the dirt drive drew her from her thoughts, and she glanced over her shoulder.

They were here.

The old car pulled up and Niccolo bounded from the back seat, his eyes alive with joy. She barely had time to brace herself before he wrapped her up in his arms, his embrace fierce and warm. A sound, half laugh, half sob, escaped from her lips. Alessia followed her brother, her gait more reserved, sedate. As she came upon them Siena saw her eyes were full of tears.

"My friend," Siena said, unsure.

"My sister," Alessia replied, reaching out and taking Siena's hands in hers, her grip gentle but strong.

Siena scanned Alessia's face, as if seeing it for the first time. The resemblance was there, in the lines of her mouth, the shape of her eyebrows. Siena had just never noticed it before. Similar but different. Friends. Sisters.

Behind them, Nonna Bianca made her way down the small hill on unstable legs. At her elbow, supporting her stride, was her son.

Aurelio Gabriel Bareletti. Auri di Bari in his professional life. Elio to his sister. A former student of Dottore Romano Racah, part of Romano's network of art smugglers, and Siena's uncle.

Siena felt her body stiffen as he approached, noted his tired eyes, the strain of emotion that puckered his mouth. He and Nonna Bianca stopped a few paces away. Bianca stepped forward, her face a canvas of feelings held deep in her heart.

"I knew you were family." She kissed Siena once on each cheek. "I felt it in my heart." The sagging skin of her jaw vibrated with her sobs as she flung her arms around Siena, pulling her close.

Siena allowed herself to be held, to feel the love that flowed from this woman to her. What she had endured. A mother who had lost her daughter, forced to pretend that child had never existed...

The old woman released her, but Siena felt the reluctance. "We will give you a moment." Bianca gestured for Niccolo to follow her back to wait by the car. They walked across the yard to stand in the shade of the oak tree.

Siena faced Aurelio, or as her mother had known him, Elio. Alessia watched on.

She felt unsteady, disconnected from her body, distanced from this momentous moment.

"For you." He produced a small posy of bright purple irises from his jacket pocket. "They were her favourite." She didn't need to ask who he meant. Reaching out, she took the flowers, the delicate purple petals slightly dented from travel but beautiful nonetheless.

Aurelio cleared his throat. "I loved her, Eva, your mother, very much. I thought I was doing the right thing..." He gestured his hand, out into the world, while his mouth was unable to find the right words. "If I'd known what would happen to her..."

"I know," Siena said simply. "But you didn't know what would happen. No one could have."

He wiped a stray tear from his cheek, eyes tracking over her shoulder and down the hill to where Mila and Alfredo toiled. Siena turned with him. Alfredo looked up, noticing that their guests had arrived. Siena saw him call to his wife, who turned slowly, face shaded by her large sunhat.

"Are you ready?" Aurelio stood still, staring over the flower fields, and his throat bobbed. He glanced at Alessia who nodded.

"Then come," Siena said.

The crunch of footfall sounded as they made their way down the hill. As they approached, Mila straightened and removed her sunhat, blinking against the bright sunshine. She stared at Elio.

Tears rolled freely down Aurelio's face and he plucked a handkerchief from his pocket to mop them away.

Mila, known to Aurelio as Emilia, moved to Aurelio, and Siena's breath caught in her throat.

The friends stared at each other.

A lifetime flowing between them.

The first love of youth. The shared passion to study art.

And the mistake. Elio's mistake.

Siena knew the story now. Of how Eva's brother sided with her lover Amadeo and planned to take her child from her. Eva hadn't known what to do. But Mila had.

"Emilia," Aurelio whispered.

"I prefer Mila now," Mila replied. "It is what my husband, Alfredo, calls me."

"Si, Mila," Aurelio said.

Mila's eyes looked past him to Alessia. "Oh," she cried, a sob tearing from her throat as she went to Alessia and gripped her shoulders, surveying her face.

Alessia allowed the scrutiny, though Siena could see the tension in her body as Mila held her firmly. Eventually, Mila dropped her hold on Alessia and said, "You have grown so strong. So beautiful."

Her attention returned to Aurelio. "You have done well as a father."

Aurelio's face crumpled, scrunching up as he fought an internal battle.

"I am so sorry," he stammered. "For what I did to Eva. For what I did to you."

"It was also me," Mila said, hand patting his chest in a warmly affectionate gesture. "I told her to run. When things went wrong, I waited too long to tell the hospital about you."

"I ruined so many lives."

"I have built a good life," Mila said. She gestured out over the fields of summer flowers, the blooms bright and plump with the season. Bees buzzed through the rows of flowers, their flight unsteady from their legs laden with pollen. A warm breeze drifted up through the valley, bringing with it the heady scent of the pollen, the rich earth, the green grasses, and lighter, but still there, the tang of salt from the sea that rolled in the distance.

"Yes, a good life..." Aurelio agreed as he scanned the flowers beyond. His head dropped down, lips trembling. "Eva would have loved it here." Heaving a heavy sigh, his eyes sought and found Siena, who blinked in surprise. Warmth and guilt cracked his face as he looked at her.

Siena returned his tentative smile; they had a lot of catching up to do.

"Come," Mila said, gesturing towards the house. "I have home-made lemonade, fresh. Let's take a moment out of this heat."

They paused under the oak, Aurelio introducing Mila to Nonna Bianca. The old woman placed a hand on each side of Mila's face, bringing their foreheads together. "Grazie for my granddaughter," she said simply.

"Prego," was all Mila said in reply.

Inside, Mila's husband Alfredo poured lemonade, while the rest of them took a seat around a rough-hewn wooden table. Mila reached across, taking Siena and Alessia's hands.

"Your mamma... she loved you both, so, so much," she said, voice breaking. "She didn't want to give you up. She fought so hard. Even when they took her to the hospital, she never stopped asking about you. You were her last words, her final thought. I made a vow to her, that I would find you both, protect you. She gave me this." Mila's hand went to the cross she wore. "To guide my path to you, a connection from her heart to her babies."

Nonna Bianca was crying heavily now. "That was my

mamma's cross," she sobbed, facing Alessia. "Your Nonna Alessia, your namesake. I never knew what became of it."

Mila slipped it from her neck and handed it to the old woman. "A part of your daughter, a keepsake."

"Grazie."

Mila's attention returned to Siena. "I never stopped searching for you. When I met my husband, Alfredo," she smiled warmly at him and he nodded, his kind eyes shining. "He joined my search. But then war... other priorities. I never thought the art network would be the path to you. When I saw the pouch at Romano's... I wanted to tell you everything, but it wasn't the right time."

Tears spilled down Siena's face. She knew the truth now. The orphanage in Lucca, overwhelmed by an influx of charges, had disbursed some across the country. Siena was not a child of Rome, at least not initially. Her childhood dream of a rocking train, the sense of fear, the click of beads: it was not imagined. It was her past. Swaddled in the arms of a kindly nun, nose pressed against the sprig of rosemary she wore, Siena had been whisked beyond the reach of Mila and Aurelio. If not for the fall of fate that sent her to Sister Agnes in Rome, perhaps she would have had a family sooner. Aurelio and Mila were in love and bound by guilt and grief over Eva's passing. Together they'd searched for Siena. But Aurelio had given up. Worried for the health of the babe they had, Alessia, he'd chosen to stop the search. Mila had not.

The moment Siena saw the torn painting of Eva, the cross nestled against her chest, she'd known Mila held the key to her past. The interest Mila had shown in her token, the cautious warmth in the woman's manner. God had brought Mila and Romano together in Florence when she studied art history from him, as Emilia. God had also brought Siena to Romano, so her true lineage could be revealed to her.

That moment in Romano's drawing room, Mila had realised

who Siena was. So, when the horror of war bore down on them, she had sent Siena to the safest place she knew. Siena's home. Ignorant of the truth, Siena had taken Romano's book of art and done as Mila had asked; she'd run. She'd gone home.

Aurelio cleared his throat. "I should not have given up on you," he said, eyes filled with regret.

"Mila and I searched for you. We had a beautiful plan, to find you both and be a family... But the trail went cold, and Alessia was so sickly." He looked to Alessia, talking now to his child, face full of the desperate hope to be understood. "Emilia... Mila and I parted ways. I took you with me and met your mother Chiara. We were happy. Truly." The words of love hung in the air, heavy and meaningful.

Then Aurelio faced Siena. "Please understand. Alessia was so weak, she needed me. I—"

"You chose the child you had, and you were right," Siena said firmly. Alessia frowned at her, but Siena smiled, serene understanding cascading through her.

"Alessia needed a father," she continued to Aurelio. "She needed to get strong. You gave her a future, and Niccolo too. The world turned as it turned. Our mother is not here, but I am, and Alessia and Niccolo too. I would not choose a world without them in it. Life fell as it did. I am sad that my mother is not here, but I would not trade that past for this present with Alessia or Nicco."

She met Aurelio's eyes and saw the gratitude shining there as he nodded. It was all so much for Siena to try to comprehend. That the dear friend she'd found in Bari, her Alessia, was actually her twin sister; that Nonna Bianca was truly her nonna; that her mother, Eva, died fighting to stay with her babies. With Alessia and Siena. She had never been abandoned. She had been loved beyond compare.

Now, after all of the years of questions and doubts, of

searching and sorrow, somehow, she'd found her family. Because of Romano. Because of his book of lost art.

"Our father," Alessia said, the word catching in her throat. She coughed, then continued. "The professor. What happened to him?"

Siena and Alessia both looked to Aurelio. The man frowned deeply. "Amadeo Renzetti, how I have worked to find a path to forgiveness for that man…"

Mila leaned across the table and patted Aurelio's arm. "You have to forgive yourself first," she said.

A muscle ticked in Aurelio's cheek. "Professor Renzetti was a charlatan. He pretended to be my friend, then ruined my sister. He stood for nothing but himself. After Eva's disappearance, he left the Accademia in Florence, returning to his wife's family estate. They wiped their hands of the situation. When I came to the hospital in Lucca and found you, I was glad to let him go. From the moment my eyes perceived you, you were mine, and mine only. I would never have given you up." He studied Alessia's face as he spoke.

Siena could feel the emotion of his words. She waited for the flash of envy she expected that love to illicit, but it never came. She felt only gratitude that this man had saved Alessia.

As if her thoughts had touched Alessia's, her sister looked at her and asked, "Why did you really come to Bari? I understand it was about safety. But the coincidence…" Her hand gestured vaguely in the air.

Siena could see the turmoil that swirled within Alessia's heart – understood this was a huge life-altering truth that she was navigating.

"Show her," Mila said.

Siena rose from the table and went to her room. There, nestled safely in her desk drawer, sat Romano's book. She hefted it up, the weight a lodestone, an anchor of comfort to hold on to as she found a way through the labyrinth of secrets that now lay exposed.

Siena placed the book on the table before Alessia and explained. "My employer at the Galleria di Roma." She halted. "My nonno, for that is what he meant to me. Dottore Romano Racah, was tracking Italian artworks. Every piece that was taken to Germany. And all the pieces that he worked to hide."

"The network?" Aurelio asked, looking up. "You were part of Matteo's network for the art?"

"Si," Mila said, eyebrow quirking up at Aurelio's surprise. "Our friend, Father Matteo Massimo, was our group's liaison. I never thought he would really turn to the cloth. But Matteo was only in communications. Our true director was Romano Racah. Do you remember him? He taught us art history. He sought us out because of our connection as friends in Florence."

Aurelio had gone still, mouth slack.

"We didn't know about each other until later," Mila continued. "Romano kept us separate. It was safer that way. But the war advanced, and things changed and we needed more contact. You, Aurelio, had already left for war. Those of us who remained came together in Rome: Romano Racah, Matteo Massimo, Alessandra and her husband Aldo. Not Oskar of course." She paused, eyes lowering. "Not all of us made it through the occupation." A small shake of her head then she straightened. "But we did not stop our work to secure artworks in cellars, attics and private collections. And we tracked what was taken and where. At least, we tried.

"Romano kept that record, dutifully."

Aurelio's hands moved towards the book, but he didn't touch it. A look of pure reverence had lightened his features. "I wanted it to work, but I didn't believe it could."

"That's why you were really in the cellar," Alessia said suddenly, looking at Siena in open amazement. "You weren't looking at papa's art, you were hiding the book."

Siena felt a flush of shame redden her cheeks. "Si, that is right. And I am sorry for the lie."

Alessia stared at the book. "May I?" she asked.

"Please."

Her slender fingers gently lifted the cover, flicking through pages and pages of records. The empty column designed to mark the recovered works remained a blank space throughout the tome.

"Now that the war is over, the time to complete Romano's work has come. We can use this to track down our country's heritage. To start again after our years of pain and torment," Mila said.

Siena turned to Aurelio. "What did she call it?" she asked.

"Scusi?" his brow furrowed in confusion.

"My mother, Eva, her painting. The one my pouch was made from. What did she call that artwork?"

"Oh," Aurelio said, eyes unfocusing as if he looked back through time. "*Bari Seas*. We went there once, on holiday with my papa. You remember, Mamma?" He turned to Bianca.

"Si." A wistful sorrow had come over the old woman as she remembered her daughter, buried so long inside, now freed from her heart. "She loved the water."

Siena pulled Romano's book across the table to herself. Flipping to the last few pages, she found the entry Romano had made for her: *Siena's Secret*.

"I showed Romano my token, the edge of a painting I now know was my mother's. He listed her painting here for me, Eva's painting. One of the missing paintings of Italy."

Aurelio leaned over her and took in the page. "*Siena's Secret*," he whispered. "I like his title."

Siena smiled a small, private smile, Romano's kind face forming in her mind, his easy laugh, his kind eyes. She rose, walking quickly to her room and collecting a pen and inkwell. Back at the table she took up the pen and dipped the tip in ink.

With careful precision, she pressed the tip to the page and wrote in the *Status* margin beside *Siena's Secret*: Recovered.

"The first one," she said, glancing at Aurelio, then back to the book. "Romano once promised me we would travel the world together and find each piece of lost art in this book. I dreamed of that journey with him. But he is gone, he cannot join me on this quest." She paused. Taking a deep breath, Siena faced Aurelio, the man who was her uncle, the man who represented the family of her blood that she had always searched for. The man who'd failed her mamma, but who'd loved and protected her sister Alessia, and dearest Niccolo and Bianca. An imperfect man. But an honest one.

"Aurelio?" she asked. "Will you help me to find them all? Will you help me complete Romano's work?"

Aurelio regarded her in silence, his eyes misty with tears.

"Si, my niece. Si."

FORTY-NINE
ALESSIA

Bari, 1945

He returned with the dusky colours of autumn. Alessia accompanied Pina and Luca to the train station, the older woman unsteady on her feet from nerves. Luca held her elbow, protective and alert.

It had been four years since Pina bid her eldest son farewell on his way to the battlefield. Alessia could see the hope and fear that fought within Pina's heart. Joy that she would once again be with her son, worry over who he may have become.

Marco was not the first man to return from war. After the fall of Hitler in Berlin, there had been a steady stream of soldiers returning from the front, Alessia's papa and his secrets among them. Often the return had not been the vision of joyful reunion families had dreamed of through years of separation.

Reticence where jubilation was expected, cold instead of warmth. Boys who left with a bounce in their stride returned men: unshaven, sunken-cheeked, hollow-eyed.

The unrest on the streets of Puglia continued.

Pina with her wooden spoon held high. Siena and the bread

truck. And now the returned soldiers, desperate for work. Hunger. Anger. Fear. The people of Puglia had been through so much as war ravaged Europe. They wanted safety. They wanted justice.

It wouldn't change anything, Alessia knew. Real change took time.

That was tomorrow's burden.

Today, all that mattered was that Marco was coming home and Alessia would be there to support Pina and welcome him back.

The train pulled up on the newly rebuilt railway, brakes squealing against the dust that coated the wheels, a high-pitched whine of protest as tonnes of metal were slowed to a stop.

Passengers descended, all men in uniform, clean, but stained, torn, worn. Alessia's eyes scanned the soldiers as they disembarked. Though they were of different shapes – tall, short, squat, hunched, soft, lean – all walked with the same heavy step, eyes cast down, mouths set in a straight line. Mothers, wives and girlfriends rushed forward, arms wide, cheeks wet with tears, their rejoicing cries echoing through the station walls. They met their men like colliding with a stone plinth. Soft, loving arms wrapping around a statue.

"My son!" Pina suddenly shouted, racing forward through the throng of welcomers. Alessia and Luca followed Pina's round frame into the mass of sweating bodies and tearful cries. Marco appeared before her, a stranger wearing her friend's skin. He stood rigid as a sobbing Pina enveloped him in her fleshy arms. No emotion showed on his face, not even the barest flicker of recognition. Like a puppet, guided by instinct, his arms came up to pat Pina on the back. His mouth opened and a single phrase passed his lips, hushed, deep. "Si, Mamma, calma."

Then something beautiful happened. It was as if Marco's body remembered, his muscles relaxed into Pina's embrace, the tension sluicing from his shoulders. His eyes closed, and he buried his face in Pina's neck, his hands pinching into her back, clutching onto her as he began to shake with sobs.

Pina held him, whispering softly into his ear, words just for him, Luca hovering nearby. Alessia watched on, heart in her throat. She longed to add the warmth of her embrace but knew to stay back. Right now, Marco needed his mamma.

Pina pulled back from her son, hand cupping his cheek as she studied his face. He blinked at her, eyes swollen from tears. Pina sniffed and nodded. "Home," she said, turning from the crowded station. Marco followed without a word, Luca on his heels. Alessia joined them, keeping herself slightly apart, longing filling her soul.

That night, returned to the privacy of her own room, she opened her dresser drawer. Reaching in, she took out the brown-painted pumo and set it on the dresser top and whispered to the dark. "Welcome home, Marco."

Perhaps because he was young, perhaps because of his family name, or perhaps just from luck, Marco was selected as part of the work team tasked with the ongoing repairs of the railway lines out of Bari. Alessia often passed his work crew as she made her way to the bakery to line up for the daily bread. Dirt smeared his face, his hands red raw where they gripped the handle of a shovel. Each day, she would call out a greeting. "Buongiorno, Marco, ciao!"

His head would jerk up, eyes sharp and alert. Seeing her, his expression would soften.

Each evening she sat outside their home with Nonna Bianca and the women of the street, waiting to greet their men as they returned home from a day of toil. She waved to Marco. He waved back, but he didn't come to say hello.

As she watched his bent frame, weighed down by some

force only Marco could see and feel, Alessia wondered if perhaps his silent distance was a blessing. He had burdens enough to carry. He didn't need hers to be added to his back. There was a lot she needed to tell him. Of James and the bombing of Bari, of the riots and protests on the streets, of the girl who came to stay, Alessia's sister, her twin. But it could wait.

It took a week for Marco to visit. The night was mild, the air still as Alessia pushed the doorway curtain aside. He stood on the street, hair set neatly to his scalp, dressed in a fresh shirt. In his hands, he held a loaf of bread.

The rations were still tight. Alessia opened her mouth to refuse the bread.

"Mamma will insist," Marco said, and Alessia nodded.

"Tell her we are truly grateful. Niccolo will be thrilled to see you. Come through."

She led him into the small front room where Niccolo sat reading. He had returned to school when the war ended, his choice. It made Alessia happy. As Niccolo turned to see who had arrived, his face split into an honest grin of purest joy. "Marco! My brother!" he cried, pushing himself up onto his unsteady legs.

"Little Nicco," Marco cried, his face lighting up in the truest smile Alessia had seen him give since his return. "Not so little now." Her heart squeezed in her chest as her brother and dearest friend embraced, and Marco settled himself on the chair beside Niccolo. The two fell into the easy chatter of familiarity, and Alessia excused herself to the kitchen. There, Nonna Bianca waited, hands already busy peeling the overripe carrots and half-rotted onions. She wore a blue scarf, back in colour for the first time since the bombing of the porto. "We've stale bread from yesterday, I think it's enough," she said. "He will stay to eat?"

"Si, I hope so," Alessia replied. "He brought this." She placed the fresh loaf of bread on the kitchen bench. Nonna Bianca eyed it and nodded.

"Gather some fennel from the front pots, it has not grown as I had wished, but this is a reason to use what we have."

Alessia didn't argue and went to collect the green-leafed herb. Fresh fennel was not the same as dried seeds, but the stew would be closer to Marco's favourite dish with at least some fennel flavour.

As she bent to cut the fragrant leaves from the stems her eyes caught movement down the lane. Standing, the lush scent of fennel fronds filling her nose, she watched as James approached.

He stopped a few strides from her and doffed his cap, his hands picking at the rim nervously. Alessia waited in silence.

"Signorina," he began. "I..." the words died on his tongue. It didn't matter. She knew why he had come. The British and American forces stationed in Bari had been thinning out for weeks, leaving behind only a skeleton of officials to ease the "transition" for her nation. It was time for James to return home, just as Siena had said he would. Alessia's heart had fought against that undeniable truth, had created a fantasy where James might stay. A passion, an excitement in the face of the grinding world of survival. But it had never been real. She knew that now. Only one man had ever been real. James was fire and excitement. Marco was the very earth beneath her feet.

At least James had come to say goodbye.

Alessia stepped forward and placed a gentle hand on his shoulder.

"Grazie for all you have done for my family over these past years. And for your friendship," she said. "I will remember you and smile."

Their eyes met and Alessia read the regret that swam in James's soul. It was too hot, too passionate. Once it would have swayed her, fizzed her stomach and confused her mind. Not anymore. Alessia knew what mattered to her now. She would not be distracted again.

She removed her hand and stepped back. "I wish you a safe journey home to England. Be happy."

His face fell. "Nothing more to say?" he asked.

"What else is there?"

He released a heavy sigh, eyes watching as his feet shuffled. "I wanted to ask—"

"Italy is my home," she stated clearly.

Resignation settled over his features.

"You have been a good friend," she said. "You will live a life of love."

"I wish..."

He stopped; between them, there was nothing left to wish for.

"Live well," Alessia said.

"You too," he whispered.

Alessia smiled at him, full and honest and real.

As she watched James walking away down the cobbled streets of her city, Alessia made a choice. She wouldn't tell Marco about James after all. For really, what was there to tell?

That a friend had helped her? That a man had smiled her way? No.

James wasn't the part that mattered, Alessia knew that now.

There had been a lot to process since the war ended. At first, Alessia had felt a deep and heartbreaking loss. That the woman she called *Mamma* was not truly hers. That the man she'd believed was her papa had lied. But with the healing that time allowed, she'd found peace within it. Mamma Chiara would always be her mother, just as her papa Aurelio would always be her papa. But when Alessia visited the Vault of the

Saints in the Basilica San Nicola, she now honoured Eva, her birth mother too.

And Niccolo? He was still her cheeky fratellino, her little brother. He always would be, no matter how large he grew. He would find a path, and she would help him.

Despite the revelations, a simple truth remained: the love of the family she'd grown up in was unaltered. Not by her papa's secret. Not by her nonna's lies. Not by the truth of her parentage and the whispers that surrounded her childhood. At the heart, nothing had changed. The love, the care, the family – those things were always true. Nothing could take that bond away.

Alessia had gained something precious. With the painful truth had come a new connection. A twin sister and dearest friend. Siena had said it perfectly on that bright summer day in Tuscany:

The world turned as it turned.

She was right.

The truth was that it was all right. Because every choice, every mistake, every lie, all of the messy chaos that Eva and Elio created, every piece of it, was underpinned by love.

The world turned as it turned.

Siena had said she wouldn't change any of it.

Alessia would not either.

As James's straight back disappeared around a corner, Alessia felt peace settle over her body, muscles relaxing into the salty air that gusted gently around her. Breathing her city deep into her lungs, she felt content.

She padded across the street to Pina's door and knocked. Pina looked harried and drawn. Like many citizens of Puglia, her parents had returned to the countryside to rebuild their homes. But worry for Marco as he readjusted to life in Bari still strained Pina's days.

"Marco is staying for supper. Join us," Alessia said. "We have fennel."

Pina's tight face relaxed. "Si, grazie."

Because what else do we need but each other? When life is tough, the answer is community.

"And Luca, if he is home?"

Arm in arm Pina and Luca walked through the curtain into Alessia's home.

In the kitchen, Nonna Bianca stirred the bubbling stew. Marco and Niccolo had come in to join her, chatting happily together, shrouded by the steam of her cooking. Pina and Luca entered.

"Ah, Pina, come, come," Nonna Bianca called, face flushed from the heat of the stove.

"Luca, settle this argument for us..." Niccolo chimed as Marco shuffled to make room for his brother at the table.

Alessia paused in the doorway, watching. Her thoughts soared up, travelling high into the skies above Bari, into the soft water vapour that glided across the continent of Italy, far across the land to the north where her papa and Siena continued their search for the hidden art of Italy. She'd received the letter only yesterday, Siena writing of their time in Rome visiting Amara, newly settled at the orphanage of Santa Maria as she awaited the birth of her child. Now they ventured further, uncle and niece bonding, working together to patch up their nation. To complete Romano's Book of Lost Art.

A man Alessia had never met. But a man she loved. For all he stood for. For all he did for Siena.

A man they would always remember. Always.

Here, Alessia and her family, her brother, her nonna, her neighbour and her sons. Here they had come together, people of Bari, of Puglia, rebuilding their lives after years of war. Here, in the steaming warmth of her nonna's kitchen. The community that had been beside her since the beginning, the family that together had survived the war. And at the table, beside her brother, sat Marco, the man she hoped she would one day marry.

"You got the fennel?" Nonna Bianca asked.

"Si, Nonna. We will eat well tonight," Alessia replied and went to join them.

Marco looked up at her and smiled. And in that moment, she knew; it would be all right. With Marco by her side, it would be all right.

And she understood.

One day, when the time was right, she would tell Marco everything about her family, about herself. One day, when the healing was done she would take him to a field of wildflowers, of orchids and oleander, and tell him of her two mammas: one who fought and one who accepted; of her papa who bore the weight of his lie; of her nonna who stayed silent for tradition; of her amazing twin, Siena, who was changing the world through the art of Italy; of her love for Niccolo that could never be changed. And of her love for Marco, a love that is forever.

And they would gather together, all of them: Papa, Nonna, Niccolo, Siena, Mila, Alfredo, Pina, Luca and Marco. Before them all, she would tell Marco that she would love him forever, that she wants to be his wife. And in that field, together, they would plant purple irises.

A LETTER FROM THE AUTHOR

Dear book lover, thank you for reading *The Keeper of Lost Art*. It is a novel of which I am immensely proud, and I am grateful for your support in giving it a go! If you want to join other readers in hearing all about my new releases and bonus content, you can sign up for my newsletter.

www.stormpublishing.co/lelita-baldock

And for more information about all new releases and bonus content, you can sign up here:

www.lelitabaldock.com/writing-newsletter

If you enjoyed this book and could spare a few moments to leave a review, that would be hugely appreciated. Even a short review can make all the difference in encouraging a reader to discover my books for the first time. Thank you so much!

When I first began my research for *The Keeper of Lost Art* I had no idea how much scope the story would take on. But as I read witness accounts of people of Italy and the multifaceted experiences of World War Two across the nation, I knew it was a tale that had to be told. To me, Eva, Siena and Alessia became so much more than characters on a page. I hope I was able to draw you into their stories and capture a snapshot of this pivotal time in history that must never be forgotten.

Thanks again for being part of this amazing journey with me, and I hope you'll stay in touch – I have so many more stories and ideas to entertain you with!

Sincerely,
Lelita

ACKNOWLEDGMENTS

When I first began the research for *The Keeper of Lost Art* I knew I wanted to tell a lesser-known story of Italy during World War Two. I had no idea how deep and vast that story would become.

Weaving the story of Eva, Siena and Alessia together over the pages was a magical challenge. There was no shortage of moments where I worried I had bitten off more than I could chew. But the story of Italy during fascist rule and World War Two would not let me turn away, and I am so grateful I didn't.

This narrative pushed me, and excited me, and I have loved every moment of the challenge.

The greatest thanks must go to my incredible editor, Kate Gilby-Smith from Storm Publishing, who trusted my vision for this novel from the start. Your guidance and encouragement ensured that the threads of the tale came together in the most beautiful way – thank you.

To my friends and family, thank you for understanding when I cancelled plans or went home early to edit. Your constant support and cheerleading get me through the tough times.

To my wonderful husband Ryan and our Jazzy-pud, we got through another one! How awesome are we?

And finally, to everyone who has read this novel, you have given me the greatest compliment by joining my journey. Writing novels and reaching readers is my ultimate dream.

Thank you for making that dream a reality. I hope you came to love Eva, Siena and Alessia as deeply as I did.

Printed in Great Britain
by Amazon